Saddle Up a Good Horse

The Cowboy Kids of Mirror Valley

Sam Finden

Sam Finden

ISBN:0615805337
ISBN-13:978-0615805337

DEDICATION

This book is dedicated to my parents, Stephen and Susan Finden, and to my sister, Sunny Bowman.

CONTENTS

ACKNOWLEDGMENTS

God, first and foremost. My family and friends back in Minnesota. Matt Albertson. Rebecca Benz. The Iacovetto, Tellier, and Hartley families of Steamboat Springs. Zac Hearnsberger in Bandera. And Jason "Shortcut" Williams.

1 A New Face in Town

Sitting in the dirt next to the flat trailer tire, the young man hadn't looked like much. From where sixteen year-old Kacey Loftus was working, behind the cash register at her family's general store, she could see the Lamplighter's back parking lot. In it was a truck and horse trailer that she didn't recognize, but that wasn't altogether uncommon. July in Mirror Valley was tourist season, and even though most tourists were simply dudes who came around on vacation from their hectic city lives, some were just like the locals- riding their own horses into the mountains surrounding the town. These folks were often up from some unbearable heat at home, and it wasn't uncommon to see Texas or Arizona license plates on the rigs that stopped in for bags of horse feed or various camping supplies.

Kacey couldn't see the plate on this particular trailer,

1

but she could tell that the rig had set its owner back a pretty penny. The gooseneck trailer featured shiny polished panels covering the bottom third of the trailer's exterior. In the front, curtains were visible through small sliding windows. These treatments meant that the trailer's front half contained living quarters- a modern recreational vehicle complete with running water and a refrigerator, among other creature comforts. Not many trailers in Mirror Valley were set up like this one- most were basic livestock trailers that had open stalls for either cattle or horses. While a custom-built horse camper might be nice, it was considered foolish for a rancher to own one.

The young shopkeeper was lost in thought, silently daydreaming about what kind of horse trailer *she* would design if money were no object, when the store's screen door slammed, startling her. She quickly set down the dog-eared magazine she'd been holding and looked toward the door. Into the shop stepped the young man with the flat tire and the fancy trailer, and Kacey was instantly speechless.

Tall, straight, and strong, the young cowboy's posture conveyed a brand of easy confidence, the likes of which lesser men of all ages would try to emulate but would never truly possess. The young man's entire six foot and two inch frame was in perfect proportion, as if he'd been cast from some sort of "stereotypical cowboy" mold. On his feet he wore square-toed boots that showed signs of both wear and care. Attached to the boots were a pair of plain steel roping spurs, their shanks and straps barely visible beneath the bunched lower legs of his otherwise tight blue jeans.

Kacey's eyes lingered too long, she knew, at the tall buckaroo's belt, which was adorned with a just-right sized buckle. It was a trophy buckle that proclaimed "Hill Country Shootout," then "Champion," and featured an engraved depiction of a team of mules pulling a covered wagon. Above the hard-won buckle, the young man wore a red plaid pearl-snap shirt that hung perfectly from his square shoulders. The sleeves were rolled up past his elbows, revealing muscular forearms and hands covered in sooty black brake dust.

"Hi," he said in a pleasant voice, and then flashed a smile that revealed deep dimples on either side of his mouth.

"H-h-hi," Kacey stammered, her cheeks beginning to flush.

"Have you got a wash room I could use?" he asked, raising his soiled hands in front of his chest for her to see.

"Uh…yeah, we've got one. It's down in the basement. Through that door," she pointed, "and at the bottom of the steps."

"Thanks…I'll be right back," he smiled again and looked Kacey squarely in the eyes. She felt her cheeks redden once again and was glad that he'd started for the stairs. Who was this good looking stranger, she wondered. Possibilities raced through her mind like a northern wind through a barbed wire fence. She managed to compose herself fully by the time she heard his spur rowels jingling as he came up the staircase.

3

"Find it alright?" she asked coolly when he reached the main level again, then immediately wished she hadn't. *Now he must really think I'm some dumb girl*, she thought. *Of course he found it alright, he wasn't an idiot!* Her cheeks began to redden once more, but she managed to keep herself from turning away. If he took exception, though, or noticed her gaffe at all, he didn't let on.

"Oh yeah, thanks. Felt good to wash up," he answered, his eyes perusing the various pictures and advertisements on a bulletin board behind the counter, and then looked back to Kacey. "My name's Austin, Austin Mathers," he said, extending his hand.

"Kacey…Loftus," she said, and returned his handshake. "You just up here for a pack trip?" she asked. She had figured that must be the case, as she'd never seen him before but he was obviously no dude.

"No, actually. I'm moving here for a while," he replied. "Kind of an unusual situation."

"What do you mean?" Kacey asked. She was very interested, and knew all of her girlfriends on the high school rodeo team would be jealous. It would be wise of her to get as much information as possible about Austin, who was sure to be the small town's newest heartthrob.

"It's a long story, pretty strange. That rig…" he said, pointing through the window at the Lamplighter's back lot, "belongs to some friends of my mother. The wife and daughter are into show jumping, big old warmblood horses, you know?" Kacey could tell from the way he said it that he didn't think much of show jumpers or the very

4

expensive horses they rode.

"The husband was a big-time oil man from Houston; I'm from Texas, by the way," Austin was leaning on an elbow against the free-standing metal shelving that ran from the store's side walls to the center, one leg cocked like a horse tied to a hitching post. The rows of shelves fell short of the store's center by three feet on either side, creating an aisle six feet wide that ran from the entry door to the counter. Nearly two-thirds of the building's depth was arranged in this manner, with the remaining portion divided into a large back storeroom and a small bookkeeper's office. Kacey's mother Janie spent several hours each day in this room keeping track of the store's financial affairs. Mrs. Loftus also used this space as a sewing room where she designed and made matching outfits for the girls on her daughter's rodeo team.

"Anyway, the husband got a wild hair to buy a cow-calf operation up here. Bought a spread over on the west side, river running through it- a real nice setup, hasn't been worked for a while. Unfortunately, he didn't, doesn't, know anything about cattle…" Austin's eyes rolled slightly, letting on that he was entertained by the oil man's ranching aspirations.

"You're talking about the old Kissner place, aren't you?" Kacey had grown up in the valley, and she knew each ranch by name rather than by address.

"Not sure- we just drove past it on the way in. Today's the first time the boss has seen it, too," Austin said, rolling his eyes a little harder this time. "I figured we'd pull in and get to work on the place right away, but he wanted to grab a bite first. Then we picked up a nail in the trailer tire about a mile from here, so I've been working on that."

"I'm sure it's the old Kissner place. Are there two pipe corrals next to the barn?" Kacey had been friends with the Kissner family's children when they still lived in the valley. Their father, Randy, had defaulted on the mortgage nearly ten years before. She distinctly remembered chasing calves around those stout corrals as a little girl, though.

"I couldn't say, honestly. Neither could the old man- Mr. Crandall, my boss- he just pointed it out from a map that his realtor mailed to him." Austin shook his head when he finished talking, as if the true lunacy of Crandall's situation, and his own, had just occurred to him. "We drove by and he just pointed out the window and said 'There she is!' and that was that." Austin smiled boyishly and shrugged his shoulders.

"So how do you fit in? You said that Crandall's wife is friends with your mother…?" Kacey was curious.

"Oh, yeah, sorry. I forgot that part," Austin acknowledged her question with a wave of his hand. "My parents split up a long time ago; I don't remember a time when my dad was around. Anyway, I lived with my mom's parents from the time I was thirteen on. Mom was around, but she travelled a lot for work and it didn't make sense for me to live with her," his voice conveyed sheer indifference, and Kacey could sense that not much bothered him. "Before I came up here, I lived with my grandparents at their little ranch outside Bandera, but

6

Mom and I are still close."

"Anyway, Mom, somehow, became friends with the Crandalls. She heard that Mr. Crandall was thinking about getting into cattle and she suggested that I talk to him about it. 'Guess she figured I was enough of a hand to advise him," he shrugged. "So one night I went over to Mr. and Mrs. Crandall's house for a nice dinner and he told me about his new ranch. I could tell he was really excited, like a little kid on Christmas. I started asking him about specific things regarding the ranch, the cows, all of that. Instead of answering, he just offered me a job."

"So you're working for this Mr. Crandall? I guess you're graduated then, huh? How old are you, anyway?" Kacey was afraid of the answer he'd give to her last inquiry. She desperately wanted for him to be her age- he made most of the local guys look like little boys. Austin was a man, and a handsome one at that. He seemed to be polite as well, from the way he'd removed his felt hat when he'd introduced himself to the way that he made and maintained eye contact while they were speaking.

"I'm seventeen. I've got one more year of school, but I figured I could do that and work the ranch at the same time," he answered. "How about you? What's your story?" The two chatted a short while longer, but soon Mr. Crandall emerged from the Lamplighter with a Styrofoam container in his hands. "Well," Austin said, nodding toward the window," that's my cue." He took a few steps toward the door, and then turned back again. "It sure was nice talking to you. I'm sure we'll see each other around." With that, he tipped his hat and exited the store. Kacey could hardly take her eyes off him as he jogged lightly back to the shiny pickup truck.

2 Barn With A View

"Quit!" The sharply executed order came from behind the rump of a very stout rust-colored mare name Daisy, who was working on Tate "Skinner" Sanders' last nerve. For nearly an hour the lanky seventeen year old had been attempting to remove and replace the horse's shoes, and was nearly done. He had removed the mare's worn out shoes easily enough, first using a farrier's rasp to file off the bent points of the old shoeing nails protruding from the walls of each hoof. Then he took up a pair of nippers- an old, unsharpened pair- and began to remove the shoes by closing the jaws between the shoe and the overgrown hoof, then prying the tool's long handles back and forth. He worked his way around each shoe until it came off in his grasp, nails and all.

Daisy had stood squarely for the removal of her

9

worn-out shoes. As a dude-string horse, she had been shod three times per summer, every summer, for nearly two decades, and she was well-accustomed to the routine. She lifted her feet without fuss and allowed for the necessary work to be completed more times than not. Today, however, when it came time to put her new shoes on, she decided to test her farrier's patience by pulling her feet from his grasp on several occasions. Also, she took to leaning against Tate as he worked, which wore on him both physically and mentally.

Once more the mare put her weight against the young farrier, and he could take no more. He turned his special diamond-shaped shoeing hammer sideways and rapped the horse's belly three times in rapid succession. Daisy skittered away from the discomfort and assumed her most sorrowful look, as if she were a too-eager cow dog that had just received a reprimand from its master. Tate knew better, and decided to let the mare think about things for a moment while he stretched his back.

He walked out from the open barn's alleyway, where he'd been wrestling with Daisy, toward another, smaller building across the gravel parking lot. It was a metal-sided pole building, twenty feet wide by forty feet deep, and was painted green to match all of the surrounding buildings. The High Prairie Equine Center had been home to all manner of horse and livestock shows, everything from dressage symposiums to jackpot ropings. It had also served as the home field of the Mirror Valley High School

Rodeo Team for the past 40 years.

The building Tate was approaching denoted this fact with a weathered plywood sign, its hand-painted lettering reading "Mirror Valley Rodeo," perched above the bent and battered steel garage door. Tate lifted the door cautiously so as not to make a ruckus, then stepped through onto the cracked concrete floor inside. Along both side walls, saddles hung three-high on simple wooden racks. Between the rows of saddles, coffee cans were screwed into the walls at eye level, and from these rusted cylinders hung bridles, halters, and reins.

It was plain to see that the left side of the building was used by the ladies' rodeo team members. The saddles on this side were dressed up with silver accent plates and distinctive floral tooling. Some featured bright, neon-colored seats, while others sported exotic animal-hide designs on their breast collars, saddle pads, and matching headstalls. The left side of the tack house represented flash and fancy, and everything was put up on the racks in painstaking order.

Tate headed for the right side of the building- the boys' side. Devoid of the girls' fashionable display of rhinestones and leopard print, the boys' side was very similar to what one might find at a working ranch. There existed a sort of controlled disarray, a situation where, if every person took care of themselves and didn't bother anyone else, things were just fine. Fewer riding saddles sat on the racks, a necessity because most high school rodeo boys only had one good roping saddle, and they needed it to do their ranch chores at home. High school rodeo cowboys often showed up for practice with their saddle in the bed of the ranch pickup truck and their horse in an open stock trailer behind it.

In the place of regular riding saddles, however, there were bareback riggings made of rawhide, bull ropes with their rosin-coated tails, and bronc-riding saddles with no saddle horns. Also draped over the saddle racks were sets of highly decorated leggings, or chaps. Spurs of all different types hung on their leather straps, one pair on each coffee can. A pile of old lariat ropes, their stiffness and smooth feel now gone after countless dallies on rubber or mule hide horn wraps, sat in a pile beneath one of the bronc saddles. The ropes would be cut up and used for various tasks around the rodeo grounds, or would be given away as gifts to young buckaroos in the audience at their next performance.

At the very back of the shed, amidst a collection of seemingly mismatched harness leather, Tate found what he'd come for: a set of old saddle bags. Inside he found a bottle of pain killer tablets, of which he took three, and a roll of athletic tape. It seemed like every time he came out from under a horse there was a new cut on one of Tate's hands, and today was no exception. He wrapped the tape neatly around a deep cut on one finger after rinsing the wound in clear water.

Tate put the saddle bags- the "horse shoer's

emergency kit," as he referred to it- back on a hook on the wall, then closed up the tack house and headed back to work. His summer job working as a farrier was making him plenty of money but he worried that it would wind up causing serious injury, particularly to his back. Because he was so tall and gangly, it didn't take much to make Tate sore. Also, with his seemingly effortless ability to get into accidents and hurt himself, Tate knew that it probably wouldn't be very long before he wound up getting kicked, stomped, or hurt in some other way.

It was this blatant clumsiness that had led to Tate earning his "Skinner" nickname in the first place. When Tate was four years old, his father bought him a small paint pony to ride. For as hard as he tried, though, Tate could not stay in the saddle. It was almost comical at first, and Tate's mother joked about her son's lack of coordination with her girlfriends. That all stopped rather abruptly, though, when Tate fell off onto a rock and broke his leg badly.

While he was recovering, Tate's dad brought home a pair of Shetland ponies and a cart from the local sale barn. Tate quickly learned how to harness, hitch, and drive the team, and soon earned notoriety when, as a seven-year-old, he donned his Sunday best and drove his team down the highway and into town from the family ranch. The county sheriff was waiting, hands on his hips, when Tate emerged from the Loftus family's general store with a sack of groceries in his arms. Mrs. Loftus snapped a quick photo of the exchange through her store window. A week later, on the bulletin board at the Lamplighter, a "Wanted: 'Mean' Muleskinner Sanders" poster went up with the photo on it, and that was that. Everyone in town knew Tate by his nickname, and he still, on occasion, drove teams of horses into town. The only difference was that, now, Tate stayed off the main drag to avoid any trouble with the law.

Back in the barn aisle, Daisy had apparently decided that leaning on Tate wasn't worth taking a licking, and she stood quietly while the young farrier expertly completed his job. He loaded the mare into a small two-horse trailer attached to his truck, then cleaned up his work area. He had been shoeing clients' horses at the High Prairie Equine Center for a while, bending the rules by not paying the venue any fees, and he wanted to keep it that way. After sweeping the barn aisle with a push-broom and picking out a nice hoof clipping to give to the family dog, he hopped in his truck and headed to Daisy's home ranch.

Fifteen minutes later, Tate turned off the two lane highway and passed beneath a massive log gate frame. It was built for the long haul, with two thick uprights connected by an even thicker cross-piece which extended past the sixteen-foot span by five feet on either side. The uprights had been set deeply into the ground to withstand the weight of the cross member, and the three bare-log pieces were fastened together at the joints with black iron straps. These stamped steel pieces were fastened to the posts on either side, then bent over-top of the cross piece to hold it down.

On the cross member, also in black iron, was the name of the place- Hatchet Creek Ranch- bookended by metal silhouettes of horses. The green metal gates that hung from either side were fastened back, out of the way, and the long gravel driveway beneath the framework showed signs of recent grading. All along the driveway there were flowers planted in rusted, old, otherwise unusable water troughs. There were shed deer and elk antlers in matched pairs, each set carefully placed in and around the retrofitted flower gardens. Everything on the drive in was designed to convey an authentic western feel to whoever observed it.

Tate arrived at the ranch headquarters, a series of low-slung buildings that framed a several-acre area of level ground amid the rolling sage-choked pastures that stretched out nearly as far as one could see, until they were swallowed up by the towering mountains that surrounded the valley. Carefully, so as not to put up much dust, Tate pulled his rig over to a weathered round-rail corral. Adjoining the corral was a brand new two-story barn, the only tall building on the property. Winters in Mirror Valley were often very windy, and time had proven that ranchers with second stories on their barns wound up spending more time repairing roofs than those without. Also, virtually all of the ranchers in the area fed large round hay bales to their cattle in the winter, and these were stacked in outdoor bale yards rather than in a hay loft on the second story of a barn.

Tate exited his pickup truck, and was just about to open the back door of his trailer when he heard a voice call out from behind him.

"You bringing my Daisy-girl back, Skinner?" The question was rhetorical, simply a way for Julie Dean, 18, to begin a conversation. Tate nodded to her, then climbed into the small side-by-side trailer's unoccupied stall. Reaching into the manger area in front of Daisy's head, he untied her lead rope from a stout steel hoop welded to the wall. Julie stood back and watched Tate as he expertly backed Daisy out of the trailer. He made sure, with the Hatchet Creek Ranch's pretty young stable manager watching, to coax the sorrel horse backwards carefully. With each step the mare took toward the foot-tall drop at the trailer's edge, he offered Daisy some reassuring words and a pat on the neck. This was the sort of care that earned Tate referrals and repeat customers.

"Where do you want her?" he asked after he'd backed Daisy completely out of the trailer. He knew full well that the freshly shod horse was supposed to spend one day in the corral- it was a routine that the Hatchet Creek operation stuck to in order to guard against lameness in its string. Despite this knowledge, he thought it was wise to ask the vivacious young stable boss anyway.

"Over in the corral is good," she said. "How was she today?"

"Oh, about the same as last time. Pretty good until the last foot, then she started leaning on me," Tate answered, walking backwards toward the gate so he could look at Julie while he led the horse. When he reached the corral gate he spoke again," That crack in her left front is healing up nicely." He pointed at the horse's foot, where a slight crack was barely visible just above the new steel shoe, "Doesn't seem to be bothering her at all."

"Yeah, she's fine," Julie said confidently. "We turned 'em all out for the winter on Mac's, just threw 'em in with his string, and she came back with that sand crack." As she spoke her curly auburn hair bounced from side to side, ringlets framing her pale face perfectly. Julie had never been brought up in the back-of-the-bucking-chute debates that Tate's male rodeo teammates often held comparing the beauty of the town's girls, but he had always found her quite attractive.

"Must've been some dry country, 'put a crack like that in a dark hoof like hers…," he trailed off. Tate didn't mind talking with Julie, and wanted to continue, but he was at a loss for what to say. Looking up at the steeply-pitched roofline of the new barn, with its' glassed-in cupola and rod-iron weather vane on top, he found a new topic. "So how's this 'Wisconsin' barn working out?" he asked sarcastically, referring to the building's Midwestern dairy-like lines.

"It's actually really nice," she said. "The bottom part is split up into stalls and a wash stall, which we'll never use," Julie rolled her eyes emphatically, and Tate could tell that she disagreed with the ranch's decision to include the show-barn feature. "Upstairs, though, it's really cool. Wanna see it?" she asked, already leading the way to the open barn doors. Tate followed her, anxious to see the second story. Hatchet Creek Ranch was advertised as a "beautiful, romantic getaway," and he noticed that the scenery, particularly the view of the redheaded wrangler's departing figure, definitely lived up to its billing.

3 Latigo Eyes

"Get 'er all patched up, Son?" Mr. Crandall asked cheerfully. He was a stocky man, and though not overly heavy, his garb and posture did little to disguise his pot belly. The way he stood now struck Austin as funny, with his shiny ostrich-skin boots pointed to either side and his big felt hat kicked back on his head. It made him look like a cartoon character, Austin thought. The young man had to try hard not to laugh as he answered.

"Yessir," he said, "all set to go." Austin climbed in the passenger side of the boss's new one-ton pickup truck, then quickly jumped back out. He rounded the front of the rig and walked to the side of the trailer, where he opened six flip-down windows. Behind each one of the barred-in openings stood a weary horse that would benefit from the fresh air on their short journey to the ranch.

Retaking his seat in the cab, Austin went to work on his lunch- a club sandwich on wheat bread, French fries that were now cold, and a pickle spear. His boss had started back toward the ranch, and by the time Austin finished his lunch, they were pulling in. He wiped his hands on his jeans and got out of the truck, surveying his new home for the first time.

"Well, what do you reckon we ought to do first?" Mr. Crandall asked. He was trying hard to project an air of confidence, but Austin knew better. He had seen the older man's eyes get very big as they pulled into the overgrown farm yard, and knew that his boss was suddenly feeling overwhelmed by the prospect of rehabilitating the ranch. Truthfully, Austin was unsure as well, though he'd never let on to Mr. Crandall that he was having doubts.

The old ranch had been neglected for quite some time, Austin decided. The grass had grown very high, as tall as Austin's waist, and swished loudly as he walked around the corral near where they had parked. The pen was well constructed out of discarded oil-rig drilling pipes, and the fence lines stood straight and true just as they had when first built. Many ranches and rodeo arenas in Texas had been made in a similar fashion. It gave Austin a strange sort of comfort to see the rusted pipes used in this familiar way.

After taking stock of what they had to work with, Austin came up with a plan. He and Mr. Crandall first walked around the closest corral again, checking the fence for trouble spots. Then they walked a grid-like pattern through the pen, carefully searching for anything that may be dangerous to the horses. Occasionally they found a fence post, a length of barbed wire, or some other rusty remnant of the ranch's past. These things were picked up and moved to a newly designated trash area where they would be out of the way.

They found a tubular steel gate lying in the grass nearby, and together they hung it back on its hinges. With a gas-powered weed trimmer, Austin cleared around the gate until it swung freely. He also cleared a large area inside the corral and piled the clippings up with a rake. When his boss asked about it, the young man explained himself.

"The reason we're doing that…" he said, pointing, "is, well, there are a couple of reasons." Mr. Crandall looked on expectantly and Austin continued. "Mostly it's because not many horses like to eat tall grass. They're not like cows or mules that will eat anything. I'm guessing that the horses we brought are used to short grass." Mr. Crandall nodded, soaking up the young man's words. "Also, they're gonna want to lay down tonight because of the long road trip, and they'll want short grass for that, too."

"But what about the piles of grass? Why didn't you just leave it lay?" the boss asked.

"That's for soaking up the mess we've got in the trailer after hauling those horses across the country, unless you feel like using a mop!"

Finally, after two long days on the road, they were able to unload the horses permanently. The weary equines were released into the corral, each one taking a few slow laps around the enclosure, glad to be out of the trailer. One of the young horses opted to throw his heels toward the sky, bucking in a playful expression of relief and exuberance at his newfound freedom. Most of the horses, though, just walked around and explored their new home.

Austin attached a hose to the trailer's built-in water tank and ran it into a large plastic trough in the corner of the pen. As the trough filled, each horse came in for a drink. He noticed how gaunt the boss's five warmblood horses looked, their ribs clearly showing beneath shiny coats. Also, he observed how healthy Digger, his stocky buckskin quarter horse, looked in comparison. Despite the fact that his horse wasn't worth a fraction of what Mr. Crandall's jumping-turned-ranching horses would sell for, he decided he'd still much rather own the buckskin.

With the horses safely out of the trailer and with the mid-afternoon sun starting to wane slightly, the men finally had a chance to relax. They found a good spot to park the rig and, after clearing the area with the weed trimmer, backed the trailer in and unhooked it from the truck. Austin loaded all of the tools they had brought into the truck bed, and then pulled the truck over to the ranch house. The house's low wraparound porch would serve as their tool storage shed, at least until they got the outbuildings straightened up and organized.

Mr. Crandall, who had suggested in a yawning tone that Austin take to organizing the barn next, was soon sprawled out on a dusty overstuffed sofa inside the spacious single-story house. It was late in the afternoon, Austin reasoned, and his boss seemed like the type that would nap every afternoon if he could. It made no difference to the young cowboy, though. He had plenty to get done, with or without the old man's help.

The old, low barn sat adjacent to a feedlot-like network of corrals, its timber-frame construction mirroring that of the ranch house. It was a simple design with just four windows on each side and a pair of large sliding doors on either end. Inside, box stalls divided the two long walls into sections. The concrete floor was covered in a mix of moldy straw and dust and the air inside was heavy with the stench of moldy straw.

Austin began clearing the barn aisle with a push broom and a shovel, piling the debris into a wheelbarrow and dumping it around the side of the building. Slowly he made progress, and with each load he removed the barn began to regain its formerly attractive and functional design. The ruggedly constructed stalls stood straight and would do a fine job of holding the boss's warmbloods. Mr. Crandall's horses were accustomed to being indoors, and though these stalls were a few feet smaller in both width and breadth than their Texas counterparts, they would contain the "stall babies" just as well.

It was nearly dark by the time Austin finished bringing the barn up to snuff. There were a few things that still needed attention, small items like hinges for one stall door and a new switch to operate the simple circuit of glass globe-encased lights running down the aisle. Taking a small notebook from his shirt pocket, he made a note of these things with a worn-down nub of pencil. He wracked his brain, trying to remember whether or not he'd seen these items in the general store that afternoon, but could recall nothing. Nothing, that is, except for the cute brunette behind the counter named Kacey.

If all of the girls in Mirror Valley were like her, Austin thought, this move to the mountains would prove to be a good one for him! Despite the fact that Mr. and Mrs. Crandall's 15 year-old daughter Jessie fancied him as her own, Austin was more than open to finding out as much as he could about Kacey Loftus. The way she'd caught his gaze and held it fast like a well-stretched latigo holds a cinch tight, the girl's eyes were amazing. She seemed to weigh and measure every part of him while maintaining conversation, and that sort of scrutiny would normally drive Austin crazy. This time, though, he longed to ask her what she thought.

Heading for the ranch house, Austin looked over the horses in the corral. In two days the boss was having four truckloads of cattle delivered, 25 overpriced cow-calf pairs to a truck. Between now and then the horses would need to vacate their corral to make room, but that could be dealt with tomorrow. For one night, at least, they would stay in the pen. Austin left the corral gate and swished through the overgrown gravel farm yard, then climbed the steps to the porch. He would see about taking the boss's truck back to The Lamplighter for dinner, secretly hoping that the general store, with its pretty attendant, would still be open.

4 The Right Place

"Well, here it is," Julie waved her arm toward the barn's cavernous second story. It took Tate a moment to realize that they were still in a barn- there was no sign of livestock in sight, save for the Longhorn cow skull and horns that greeted them as they topped the stairs. This barn looked like a replica of the old cattleman's clubs Tate had visited with his grandfather in both Fort Worth and Chicago. The deep brown woodwork and hair-on-hide sofas were a spot-on depiction of those smoky rooms, where fortunes had changed hands without so much as a signature when times were good and beef prices were high. It was clear that whoever had designed this loft had borrowed their inspiration from these well known but scarcely mentioned establishments.

"Wow!" Tate exclaimed, spinning rapidly where he stood and taking in the room's details. It was enough to set Julie to laughing, which caused a flush in her cheeks. He noticed that she looked pretty just then, and smiled quietly so as not to embarrass her. They walked out into the center of the open plank floor and Julie pointed out the room's features.

"Okay, so over there on the wall is the fire place. Why they put it on the second story, who knows!? Luckily it's a gas rig, so I don't have to lug firewood up those steps," she said, her hands folded across her chest. "Then, over on the end is the bar. It came out of some old whiskey joint in Calgary- in one piece! They couldn't frame in the end wall until it was installed…"

"Man, they spared no expense, huh?" Tate was amazed at the luxury of the room, as it was much fancier than any place he'd been in Mirror Valley. "I'd heard that the new owner had some dough, and I guess this proves it. Who is he again?" he asked.

"His name is Mark Rivera, and he's kind of a jerk, actually," she said matter-of-factly. "Made a ton of money on some fly-by-night internet thing, now he thinks he's a business man." She had a sour look on her face, reminding Tate of a child who had just popped a piece of lemon candy into her mouth.

"What's he doing that's so wrong?" Tate asked, then readied himself for what he knew would be a laundry-list of problems. Julie was known as an opinionated girl, and he figured she'd gladly let loose on the absentee ranch owner. Instead, though, she just shrugged.

"He just thinks that his money will make everything the best. He believes that horses, cabins, cows, everything is just a matter of how much money you can spend instead of how much time you put in." That much was plain to Tate already. The fancy gate, the barn's loft with its expensive décor, all of the new equipment on the property; it all bespoke the fact that Hatchet Creek Ranch was on a whole other level of extravagance when compared to the other local dude ranches. Still, it surprised Tate that she had chosen not to elaborate. He was about to pry further when, from the barn aisle at the bottom of the stairs, they heard someone shout.

"Hello!?" came a man's voice. "Is anybody here? The sign at the front said to check in at the barn…"

"Sure thing, c'mon up!" Julie hollered down the steps in her best western drawl, then turned to Tate and winked. She leaned in close and told him quietly, "These city people love a cowgirl with an accent!" She then grabbed his hand and dragged him over to the top of the steps for an introduction. He didn't mind her hand in his, not one bit, and wished the incoming guests hadn't mounted the steps so quickly.

Topping the staircase and spilling into the room were three of the most stereotypical dudes Tate had ever seen. The gentleman who led the way looked as if he'd fallen head-first into a pool filled with gaudy, overpriced western wear and had been forced to purchase some of it, lest he drown. Atop his head sat a highly stylized, crushable brimmed hat that was no more a cowboy hat than was the man wearing it a cowboy. Tate had seen models like this one, shiny oilskin numbers with leather "Stampede String" and a decorative hat band made of pheasant feathers, in several high-end fly fishing shops in the big city.

Below the hat was a round, red face. The man's breaths came rapidly, as was often the case with visitors unaccustomed to Mirror Valley's high altitude, and it took him a moment to speak.

"Howdy, partners!" he said in a perfectly squeaky voice. "Jim Hudgens, pleased to meet you," he extended his hand toward the pair. Julie stepped in and took the reins, shaking his hand vigorously.

"Of course, Mr. Hudgens, I've been expecting you. I'm Julie, the stable manager, and this is Tate Sanders, our horse shoer." The two men shook hands, and Tate had to stifle a laugh as Mr. Hudgens' leather fringed sleeves swayed when his arms moved. "And you must be Mrs. Hudgens," Julie continued, turning to the man's wife. "I understand that you're looking forward to photographing the Valley's wildlife?"

"Yes, very much so. And please, call me Ruth," the woman said warmly.

"Yes, ma'am. I've spoken with a neighboring ranch about taking advantage of their drainages- there's a big herd of elk summering there- and they were very accommodating."

"Oh, that's just fantastic, Julie. Thank you so

much!" Ruth said, her eyes squinting with pleasure.

"Excellent. We'll worry about the details tomorrow, but I'm certain that you'll enjoy it." Julie was on a roll, and Tate noticed that she'd gone from a laid-back country girl to a high-class western concierge in short order. "And you must be Jesse," she said, extending her hand to a short fourteen year old boy clad in sagging pants and skateboarding shoes. The youngster shook her hand limply, but beneath his oversized sweatshirt hood and sideways baseball cap, Tate could see that the kid's eyes were nearly bulging out of their sockets. The sight of Julie's womanly curves, particularly those hidden just at the boy's eye level by the strained pearl snap-buttons of her pink and blue plaid shirt, were nearly too much for him to endure. After the young dude's eyes had lingered for a moment too long, Julie took notice and squeezed his hand sharply. Jesse's eyes popped up to meet hers, and then turned away quickly. He had been caught looking and he knew it.

The Hudgens family began telling the locals all about their trip west from Cincinnati, where Mr. Hudgens was a very successful financial planner. Before too long, though, Julie interrupted pleasantly.

"Sorry to jump in, Sir. Tate, would you please go harness up Babe and Belle so we can give the Hudgens' a ride up to Cow Camp? We'll take the buckboard." With that, Tate excused himself and headed for the harness shed, near the big barn's south end. He didn't mind not having to sit around and listen to Mr. Hudgens drone on and on about the virtues of curbside check-in at the airport, and he didn't mind helping the ranch out, despite the fact that he wasn't getting paid. Tate hoped to go along to Cow Camp, which was Hatchet Creek's base camp for its guests, in order to spend some more time with Julie. Also, he knew that Hatchet Creek Ranch employed Mirror Valley's best camp cook, Rodney Watts. If he made it out to Cow Camp free of charge, Tate was certain that old Rodney would pay him well in tasty chuck.

Tate had Babe, the left-hand molly mule, nearly harnessed by the time Julie was able to excuse herself from the Hudgens family. She poked her head around the corner post of the open-air shed slowly, hoping to catch a glimpse of Tate without him knowing. She'd known Tate Sanders for years, and had always considered him a nice kid that was good to have around- a real hand. Lately, though, she'd begun to recognize him as more: a talented, handsome young man whose distinct skill with horses made her swoon.

"That kid about came unglued when he saw you, Julie," Tate said from beneath Babe's belly, where he was clipping the harness's heavy leather quarter straps into place. Julie had no idea how he'd known she was there- his back was turned, and she was sure she'd been silent on approach.

"You saw that too, huh?" she replied. "I thought maybe he was gonna start drooling on his shoes. It was like he'd never seen a girl before!" She moved across the harness shed's dirt floor and lifted Belle's collar from the hook it hung on above a stoutly built two horse feed trough. As she lifted the heavy padded leather oval, Tate reached under the right-hand mule's chin and unclipped a wall-mounted chain from its mule's halter.

"Can't say as I blame him," Tate said sheepishly. "Boys and men both are trained from birth to look for what you've got going." The tall cowboy looked at Julie as he gingerly pulled the collar over the mule's head, and winked slyly when he caught her eye between the animal's large, floppy ears. She quickly blushed and turned away, and Tate smiled broadly.

"I'm trying to say that, if you weren't paying so much attention to that kid, you'd probably be sour at me for the exact same thing." Tate looked at her squarely over the mule's rump while they both pulled the breeching taut around Belle's hind end. Instead of looking away like before, though, this time the cowgirl leveled her gaze on him.

"No, I wouldn't either, Tate!" she said emphatically.

"No? Why's that?" Tate asked.

"Well, from you I'd consider a look like that as a compliment and I'd be flattered," she said. "That Jesse kid is creepy, but you're sweet." Now it was Tate's turn to be embarassed, and he quickly ducked his head to begin connecting the cross reins from one mule's harness to the other's bridle so that Julie wouldn't see

31

his red cheeks.

Tate backed the team out of their stall expertly, then ground-drove them over to a recently purchased buckboard-type wagon. It was nearly brand new, he could tell, because all of the painted metal hardware still shone glossy and bright. A few years of sunshine and rain would dull the finish of the rig, but for now it looked like it was fresh off the showroom floor.

As he hooked their tug chains to the wooden yolks and evener on the wagon's tongue, taking care to match the length from one mule to the other, Julie hopped up into the spring-loaded seat behind the team. Glancing over his shoulder, Tate noticed that the girl was staring off into the mountains that lay north of the ranch. He also noticed that the pre-dusk light was doing a fine job of highlighting every aspect of the pretty young woman that had beguiled Jesse Hudgens.

"You ever wonder what city people do in the evening, Tate?" she asked. "Do they look hard through the smoke and the smog and try to find this…" she motioned toward a brilliant setting sun with her arm, "or do they just do city stuff like go to the movies or out to a bar?"

"I reckon they do what their friends do until they can't stand it," he replied thoughtfully," and then they come see us for a little dose of that." He motioned toward the western sky with a thrust of his chin, his hands still occupied.

"Maybe you're right," she said. "I just don't understand how anyone could want to live someplace where they couldn't see all of this!" Tate pulled himself up into the buckboard's seat, having finished hitching the mules to it. She slid to make room and handed him the long leather lines. He gathered the mules into their bridles with an even pull to make sure they were paying attention, and then spoke to the pair calmly.

"Babe, Belle, Up!" he said briskly, and the rig went rolling out toward the front parking area. As they passed Tate's rusty truck and trailer and headed toward the Hudgens family's luxury rental SUV, Julie scooted over in the seat so her leg was touching Tate's. He looked down at the shapely denim thigh, then up at its owner. She was looking right through him.

"You're all right, Tate," she said. "You wanna come with up to Cow Camp?" Her eyes dared him to say no. He nodded and she smiled wildly. "Good!" Julie said. "I was afraid I'd have to cuddle up with Cookie in the bunkhouse to keep warm!" She flared her eyes and smiled, then jumped off the stopping wagon to begin loading the Hudgens' luggage.

Tate thought that maybe he was in for more than just a good meal in exchange for his help this evening, and the possibilities excited him. After loading the guests and their considerable amount of truck (all in new, matching bull-hide cases and duffels,) he ran to his truck and retrieved a felt hat, a long duster coat, and a holstered single-action pistol on a cartridge belt. Donning these items in plain view of the new arrivals, which prompted Mrs. Hudgens to snap several pictures, Tate swung back up into the wagon's seat and headed his team for Cow Camp. In the last traces of a fiery-red day's light, Tate looked over at the copilot, with her curly auburn hair tucked beneath a woolen ranch cap, save for a few ringlets that fell gingerly about her face, and he smiled. As the mountains finally blocked out the sun's light completely, and with the waning moon still hours from rising and providing some illumination, the rig traveled toward its destination in total darkness. He took up a relaxed position in the driver's seat, and was pleasantly surprised when Julie's head came to rest on his shoulder.

Thinking back to their brief discussion about enjoying where one lived, Tate couldn't help but smile again. "Yes sir," he said lowly, so as not to disturb his sleeping passengers or the pretty girl dozing on his shoulder. "This certainly is the place for me." And with that, he turned his attention back to the clip-clopping hooves of Babe and Belle.

5 Roping Pen Girls

The dust hung in a cloud over the roping arena, a soft pillow of airborne particles churned skyward by the hooves of a small group of roping steers and the horses used for chasing them. It was the sort of dust that made a horseman long for a drink of water to wash away the cotton-mouthed feeling they got after riding a galloping horse through the haze. Each run down the arena, with a header and a heeler chasing after a short-horned yearling steer, kicked up more and more dust. It got so bad, eventually, that the person releasing each steer had to make sure the previous team of ropers was safely out of the way before opening the chute again.

All summer long, the Langston family's Seven Bar Seven Cattle Company had been putting on ropings like this one on Wednesday nights. It was a chance for the local ranchers to get together and compete with one another while keeping up with the Mirror Valley gossip. As many as ten trucks and trailers could be seen parked outside the Langston's fully-lit roping pen, and cowboys and cowgirls of all ages were welcome to throw their loops. Oftentimes mothers, daughters, fathers, and sons would all take turns backing their horses into the box on the same night.

On this particular Wednesday night, there were nearly forty people in and around the pen at the 7-7. The majority were seated on horseback, either roping or moving cattle for the ropers. Kacey Loftus fell into the second category, as did her friend Lisa Short. The two girlfriends were polar opposites in appearance-Kacey had long legs, long brown hair, and a mature look and demeanor. Lisa, on the other hand, was short and petite with a decidedly child-like appearance. Her short blonde hair was littered with colorful streaks and feathers, and her eyes featured copious amounts of mascara and eyeliner that made her look several years younger than her actual sixteen.

The pair sat at the far end of the roping arena, near the head of the cattle return alley, aboard two sleepy horses bearing the 7-7 brand. The Langston family always had plenty of cow-horses around their place, as the 7-7 offered "cattle drives" to tourists several days per week in the summer. More often than not, their dude-safe horses were retired roping prospects that could still get up and down the arena in short order. Tonight, though, the horses the girls were mounted on would simply be used for pushing cattle back down the arena at a walking pace.

"So what's your deal!?" Lisa said, absently picking at the inside seam on her blue jeans. Both girls sat with their right legs draped over their saddle horns and down the left side of their horses' necks. It was the sort of position that was only comfortable to someone who had spent countless hours in the saddle, like the two young cowgirls had.

"What do you mean 'what's my deal?'" Kacey said, unable to wipe the smile from her face.

"You know what I mean, Kacey! You've had this goofy grin on your face all night. What gives?" Lisa pried. She could tell that something had put her normally reserved friend in a silly, girlish mood. From the moment she'd hopped into Kacey's car at The Lamplighter and heard the top-40 pop playing on the stereo in place of the usual country music, to the way her friend had repeatedly checked her reflection in the rear-view mirror, Lisa knew that something was different. After a little more prodding, Kacey finally had to give in.

"Okay, fine. It's not a big deal, really," she said, trying hard to suppress a smile.

"I'll be the judge of that, missy. Tell me!" Lisa was insistent, nearly beside herself with anticipation.

"There's this guy, a new guy, who came into the store. His name is Austin Mathers, he's seventeen, he's from Texas, he's working out at Kissners' old place, and he is GORGEOUS!" Kacey blurted out, then looked away. It wasn't like her to get so worked up about a boy, and she felt rather silly talking about it. When she turned back toward Lisa and met her gaze, the small blonde let out a squeal that alerted everyone in the arena. When the crowd realized that everything was okay and went back to their roping, the teenagers continued their conversation in earnest.

"Oh my God, Kacey, tell me everything! What does he look like? Is he tall? Does he like you? Are you going to go out with him?" Lisa's questions came in rapid-fire fashion, and Kacey put up her hands to slow the bubbly girl's pace.

"I don't know, Lisa. He's super cute, really tall and slim. Not sure if he's a rodeo guy or not- he's a cow hand though. I only talked to him for a while, then his boss came out of The Lamplighter with lunch and he had to go." Kacey suddenly got quiet. "He seems like a real man, Lis'," she said in a hushed tone, then flashed her eyes widely at her friend.

"You're totally in love, aren't you? You already want to take this guy home to your mom and dad, don't ya?" Lisa said teasingly. Then, suddenly, she assumed a mischievous look and leaned as close as she could to her friend. "Or, maybe…"she said, putting her hand on Kacey's thigh, then sliding it between her friend's blue jeans and the smooth leather of her borrowed saddle, "you DON'T want to take him home to your folks." Her eyes lit up wildly. "Maybe you want him to take you somewhere, anywhere." She squeezed Kacey's thigh in a way that, if they weren't best friends, would be completely inappropriate.

"Whatever! I do not!" she said, trying unsuccessfully to keep from blushing.

"You do! You're bad, Kacey! Shame on you!" Lisa razzed. Kacey couldn't keep from laughing, so she quickly swung her leg back over the saddle and kicked her horse into a trot. As she bounced away, though, Lisa called after her loudly so that everyone could hear. "Don't worry, Kacey, I'm sure he likes you! He'll probably call you tomorrow!" Kacey shook her head and tried hard not to smile as she approached the other end of the arena. Lisa was a good friend, she knew, and was just giving her a hard time.

Reaching the business end of the arena, where the ropers were staging for their runs, Kacey was met with more than a few strange looks because of Lisa's loud comments at the other end of the pen. She quickly dismounted and tied her borrowed horse to the fence, then took a moment to loosen the saddle's cinch. Satisfied that her horse was comfortable and secure, Kacey made her way over to an old bath tub sitting on the ground in the corner of the arena.

The Langstons were nothing if not resourceful, and the bath tub was proof of that. Years ago, the enamel-coated steel tub had been one of many installed in a roadhouse motel on the edge of the big city. An electrical fire had reduced the building to ashes a few years after it was built, and the Langstons had salvaged the tub from the rubble. Now, it and several more like it were used as water troughs on the 7-7 place.

Instead of water, though, the trough in the roping pen was filled with ice and canned drinks. There were three kinds of soda and two kinds of beer available. As riders arrived in their trucks at the start of the evening, the tub filled quickly with everyone's contribution to the cause. It was an unspoken rule- if you came to rope, you brought something to contribute. If you didn't, you wouldn't be invited back.

Kacey reached into the icy water and pulled a can of diet soda off of a six-pack she and Lisa had brought from the store. As she turned to walk toward the elevated announcer's tower to get a better view, a horse and rider came loping toward her. She looked up and saw Hunter Langston, 18, atop a young grey gelding, its neck damp with sweat.

"Hey Kacey, will you grab me one?" he asked coolly from atop the prancing dappled horse. Hunter was a compact sparkplug of a man- the type who looked like he could handle himself in any sort of situation. What he lacked in height was easily made up for in wiry strength, which had served Hunter well while riding bulls on the high school rodeo circuit. Two years before, in his sophomore season, he became the youngest cowboy in history to ride every animal he faced at the national finals event, capturing the championship easily.

"Sure thing, Hun'," Kacey replied. She had known Hunter for as long as she could remember- their relationship was a long, laid back friendship and nothing more. There had been a few short-lived, well-intended attempts at romance between the pair over the last few years, but each time had simply confirmed that they were better off as friends. She reached into the cold water of the makeshift cooler with both hands and raised two plastic-ringed six packs for him to choose from. "Which one do you want?" she asked, then handed him his selection.

"So what's your girl Lisa squealing about?" Hunter asked, popping the top on his can. He leaned forward and crossed his arms, then supported himself by laying one muscular forearm on the top of his saddle's large, Wade-style horn.

"Oh, nothing…" Kacey trailed off, trying not to blush. Her eyes looked in every direction but his, and for good reason. When she did finally look Hunter in the eye, he was grinning impishly and she knew that she'd been busted.

"Okay, out with it," he said, trying to stifle a laugh. "Who is he?" There was a moment of silence between them while Kacey mulled her words over. Finally, she stepped close to Hunter's horse and told him all about the new face in town. She knew that Hunter would be skeptical of any boy she dated. He was sweetly protective of her.

As she spoke, he absently watched the goings-on of the arena. Her words were finding their mark, though, and she felt confident that her concerns were being heard by the young cowboy. His dusty brick-top

41

hat nodded at all the right times, she noticed, and he occasionally answered one of her comments with a request for a better explanation. After a long conversation, Hunter reined his gelding around and left her with a few parting words.

"Well," he said, "I think I'll have to meet this Mr. Wonderful from Texas." He was looking back over his left shoulder, his hips and arms moving in time with the prancing horse's footsteps. "Don't worry, I won't let him know that you're already naming his kids!" he said slowly, and then winked and spurred the grey into a spirited half-jog. Kacey watched her friend disappear into his own cloud of dust.

I hope he doesn't embarrass me!, she thought.

6 Cow Camp

"Well, Rodney, you've outdone yourself again," Tate said to the cook, looking back over his shoulder. In front of him was a large sink full of dirty dishes, and Tate was scrubbing feverishly. The back of Hatchet Creek Cow Camp's mess hall was everything any greasy fry cook could ever want and more: a spacious and well lit kitchen with the latest and greatest appliances.

"Thanks, Kid," the older man replied as he pulled a soiled apron over his head and deposited it into a laundry basket behind the swinging door separating the kitchen from the dining room. "I hope those city folks liked it-that youngster was kinda skeptical."

"I think they liked it well enough, Cookie. If not,

that's their problem!" Tate had gorged himself on Rodney's handiwork, eating as much as possible. This evening's fare had included a pot of beans, twice-baked potatoes, Caesar salad, homemade cornbread, and some substantial Porterhouse steaks. Rodney had added a sweet brown-sugar rub to the steaks before grilling them over a wood fire, and Tate couldn't ever remember having a more tender Porterhouse.

"You like apples, Kid?" Rodney asked absently from where he stood, half way down a flight of steps that descended into an old-fashioned root cellar. "I think I might still have some here, somewhere." The pudgy cook peered into the shaded corners of the dank room, looking for his ingredients. "Aha!" he said when he found what he was looking for- a bushel basket of crisp red apples.

"Sure, Cookie, I like apples. Why?" Tate was finished with his scrubbing and leaned back against the sink, a white dish towel draped over his shoulder.

"Oh, I think I might just whip up something real quick for dessert. Never you mind, Kid. Now get out of here, would ya? Go sit around the fire with the guests- you've done more than enough work here." Tate was so accustomed to helping out that he hadn't really thought of what he was doing as work, but he could see how Rodney would think otherwise. He'd been chopping wood and serving dinner and sweeping the floor and doing dishes since they had arrived at Cow Camp.

"Okay, Rodney, I'll go sit down. You let me know if there's anything I can do, though…" Tate said.

"I'm good, Kid. Go on, now! I'll bring you and the guests some dessert in about an hour." Rodney was insistent, and Tate took the hint. He walked through the swinging door and across the dining room floor toward the mess hall's front entrance. As he walked, he admired the stuffed elk and deer heads mounted on the walls, their antlers creating towering shadows on the ceiling.

One animal in particular caught Tate's attention- a mule deer buck whose massive antlers had grown every which way. Tate wasn't a trophy hunter by any means; usually he shot the first legal animal he could, then used every single ounce of meat on the carcass. Despite that fact, he was still envious of this buck. Most men in the area had never seen such an enormous animal outside of the pages of a hunting magazine, and Tate wondered how the animal had been taken locally without him hearing about it.

Tate pondered the animal as he pulled on his duster and walked out the front door and down a small grassy hill to the campfire. He'd have to ask Julie about the buck when he got the chance.

Approaching the fire, Tate could see the Hudgens family was beginning to settle into the laid-back way of things at Cow Camp. Mr. Hudgens was roasting a puffed-up marshmallow over the fire while Mrs. Hudgens continually looked up at the vast night sky and sighed. Even Jesse looked glad to be there- he sat, carefully whittling away a stick's bark with a Swiss Army knife. Across the fire from the guests sat Julie, and the very sight of her made Tate smile.

"Hey you! What took you so long!?" Julie shouted

when she saw his lanky shadow approaching through the pitch-dark night. This alerted the Hudgens family to his presence as well, and by the time he sat down, all eyes were on him. It was an odd moment, one that called for an odd response.

"Oh, I was just checking on the horses," Tate fibbed, his eyes opening widely. "Old Widowmaker ought to be ready to ride tomorrow, if you wanna try him, Jesse…" He tilted his head back just enough to catch the young city slicker's eye beneath his hat brim, and winked plainly. The boy, who had never been near a horse and was terrified at Tate's comment, eased slightly.

"Oh, sure thing!" Jesse joked. "I'll ride the Widowmaker. Not a problem!" He waved his hands in a display of his supposed lack of concern. "Do you have any spurs I can wear?" he asked goofily. "I wanna make sure that he'll get up and go for me…"

"I think you'll be fine, Jesse," Julie interjected. "He only bucks really hard for the first 30 seconds or so. After that, he's a peach." She smiled broadly, and the firelight danced in her eyes. Both Jesse and Tate took notice immediately. Suddenly anxious to defer their attention, Julie spoke again. "Tate, will you go in that shed and dig out Lefty's old flat-top?" she asked sweetly.

"Sure thing," Tate answered immediately. Truthfully, he realized later, that she could have asked for anything and he would have said yes. She had a hold on him- that much he knew. He walked over to an old, low shed and opened the double doors. In the fire light, he could barely make out the shape of a guitar leaning against

46

the wall just inside the door. He picked up the instrument and headed back to the fire.

"You play the guitar, too!?" Mrs. Hudgens asked in disbelief, already reaching for her camera. "What part of the cowboy lifestyle don't you fit, Tate?"

"Oh, I don't know. I can pick a little bit I guess. No promises, though- it may be awful!" he replied, sitting down next to Julie. In reality, Tate had been playing the guitar for nearly as long as he'd been driving teams of horses. It seemed that wherever Tate Sanders went, music followed. He even sat in with visiting bands at The Lamplighter on occasion, if they needed another musician. Tate knew his way around a lot of instruments, but the guitar was his favorite.

He played for nearly an hour, taking requests and making up silly songs about the group at hand. The Hudgens' were delighted, and Mrs. Hudgens laughed so hard at some of Tate's lyrics that she needed to wipe away tears from her cheeks. Mr. Hudgens and Jesse also looked to be enjoying the impromptu concert immensely, and were rolling with laughter.

Rodney came out to the fire with a tray in his hands, and on the tray were 6 servings of freshly baked apple cobbler complete with ice cream. The cook was praised over and over, and took the compliments shyly. When Mrs. Hudgens asked for his recipe, Rodney surprised her.

"I'm afraid I can't tell you, ma'am. I'm not sure how I made it, myself. There's a heap of butter, some apples, flour, cinnamon, an egg, and some sugar. But other than that, I don't have a recipe. Just kinda threw it together..." Rodney answered her.

"Well, whatever you did, Cookie, do it again. This is great!" Julie commented. Her praise was seconded by the rest through their mumbled "Mmmmmmhmmmm's" and nodded heads.

"Some of us can ride and break horses, some of us can shoe horses, and some of us can throw a bunch of stuff in a pot, add fire, and have it come out okay," Rodney said thoughtfully, then paused for a moment before continuing. "I knew a feller in Old Mexico who couldn't see to shoot or lift a saddle, but he could make a pot of frijoles that would bring a tear to your eye. I've never met anyone who was meant to do just one thing, 'ceptin' him. Good old Pedro- we called him Petey- He could cook up a boot and make it taste like a twenty-dollar steak."

"Isn't it odd how, sometimes, you'll find someone who just does what they're best at?" Mr. Hudgens furthered the discussion. "For example, my uncle Marty used to make decorative bird houses for people. Every day after work he'd come home and go into his little shop and make really intricate bird houses, then he'd sell them for a tiny profit at a flea market. He could have been building custom cabinets or doing other things with his talent that would have made him more money, but he chose to do what he was best at- building bird houses."

 The group sat and thought for a moment about his story, but soon the silence was broken by a coyote yipping in the distance. It was joined by another, and another, until there was an entire pack of predators yapping at the stars.

"Oh, what's that?" Mrs. Hudgens asked, frightened. She looked around uneasily, and it occurred to Tate that he was witnessing something very interesting. This was a woman who had never been away from the city, never been in a situation like she was now. To her, the harmless coyotes were a terrifying pack of wild animals that would try to hurt her like the proverbial Big Bad Wolf.

"Don't worry about that, Ma'am," Rodney said calmly. "That's just the Coyote Choir singing you a song. No need to worry, unless you're a rabbit." The cook's words soothed Mrs. Hudgens' concerns, and soon she was fully engaged in the fireside goings-on once more.

7 Gap in the Fence

Back at the newly renamed Crandall Ranch, Austin Mathers was enjoying his first day ahorseback in nearly two weeks. Between the long drive from Texas and all of the work he'd been doing at ranch headquarters, where 100 cow-calf pairs had arrived and were quickly running out of grass in the corrals, Austin had hardly looked at his horse. Today, though, he was in the saddle and loving it.

His five-year-old buckskin gelding, Digger, was clearly enjoying his respite from the company of the warmbloods. The stock horse pranced and tossed his head with every step, and Austin had to keep a tight rein. It was early in the morning, and the sun's rays were slowly working their way down the western slopes that lay ahead of him.

Today's work was riding fence, a task that never seemed to end for ranchers in this part of the country. Between the heavy winter snow load and the numerous elk and deer herds in the area, fences needed mending every spring. Some forward-thinking ranchers had devised a "lay-down fence" system, where wire and posts were laid down each winter, then erected as an entire unit the following year. The system required metal posts to be pounded in place permanently. Wooden posts attached to the fence wires would be held to the metal posts with loops of wire, and the entire length of fence would be pulled taut at the ends with a ratcheting fence stretcher.

Unfortunately, there was no "lay-down fence" on the Crandall Ranch. Austin wasn't sure what was in store for him today, as this was the first ride anyone had taken out to inspect the old fences surrounding the ranch's pastures. Nearly four thousand acres were said to be fenced and cross-fenced, but the realtor hadn't been able to furnish a reliable map of the land to Mr. Crandall. Austin carried a compass and a large notebook in his saddle bags, and he occasionally stopped to make a note or to draw a picture. His would be the only map of the ranch, at least until Mr. Crandall could have an aerial survey conducted.

The young cowboy was at home in the saddle and relished every moment he got to spend atop Digger. There was a sharp chill in the air this morning, and Austin was glad for the insulated canvas vest and silk wild rag he'd pulled from his war bag and donned before saddling up. When the sun rose completely and cleared the mountain peaks on the east side of the valley, he'd be plenty warm. For the time being, though, he was pleased to have warm gear on.

Austin had been riding for nearly an hour when he came to the break in the fence. He tied Digger to a small Aspen tree nearby and went to work. Using a pair of specially designed pliers, he cut off the lowest of the four strands of barbed wire at the posts on either side of the gap. Using these odd lengths of wire, he spliced the top two strands and tightened them by winding short logs in between the parallel wires of the splice. As he spun these tightening "handles," the wires rose on both sides of the repair, singing as they slid through the rusted fence staples pounded into the old wooden fence posts.

Satisfied that his three-strand repair would hold cattle, Austin moved on. Whenever he came to a corner, he carefully checked the H-braces for rotten wood pieces. If he found one in bad shape, he fixed it with a length of Aspen trunk, cut from the nearest stand of trees with a collapsible saw he had in his saddlebags. Also, Austin kept meticulous notes on his hand-drawn map. He took his time in calculating distances and felt that he had a good handle on how big this pasture was. As he made his last left turn and headed north toward the ranch headquarters at the end of the day, he did some calculations in his head. With Digger on an instinctive course for home at a worn out pace, Austin took out his notebook and double-checked his figures.

When he rode into the ranch yard and toward the barn, Mr. Crandall emerged from the house and came to meet him at the hitching post. Mr. Crandall had expressed his interest in riding fence to Austin the night before, but thought better of it after his big warmblood mare named Olga pitched a fit as he tried to saddle her this morning. Austin had a sneaking suspicion that Mr. Crandall didn't have much confidence in his own ability with horses.

"Well, how did your ride go?" Mr. Crandall asked anxiously. He grasped the buckskin's reins and rubbed the horse's sweaty neck vigorously as Austin dismounted. The young cowboy swung down without grace, his left foot getting caught in the stirrup, making him bounce on his right foot and nearly causing him to take a spill. Digger was suddenly alert and skittered sideways to distance himself from his rider's clumsy hopping. Mr. Crandall's eyes got wide with fear, and Austin's suspicion was confirmed.

"Sure is a beautiful chunk of ground, Mr. Crandall," he said honestly. "I only got through this front pasture here," Austin pointed to the west, "But, man alive, it's a beauty. Goes about three hundred acres, I figure, with a decent fence all around. We can turn the cattle out in there as soon as you please." He grinned at the older man, glad to project an air of confidence. "I'd say there's enough grass and water in that pasture to run these cows and calves for most of the summer. We'd better think about bringing on some more stock once we get it all fenced properly."

Mr. Crandall nodded thoughtfully. "I'm pleased to hear you say that, Austin," he said. "We might make a go of it after all!" The older man was beaming, and it was good for both of them to enjoy a truly optimistic moment. Happy occasions like this had been rare since their arrival, and the day's exploration of their ranch was a welcome change of pace. Just hearing about it made Mr. Crandall happy, and he wanted to celebrate. "Get your pony put up, Son, we're gonna head to The Lamplighter for the night. Sound good to you?" he asked.

"Sounds great!" Austin exclaimed. "Give me twenty minutes, Mr. Crandall, and I'll get Digger taken care of and I'll grab a quick shower."

"You got it, friend. I'll feed and water the other horses while you're washing up," Mr. Crandall said, starting for the barn. Austin quickly removed his saddle and hung it on a rack in the barn, then took a moment to rub Digger's sweaty back with a few handfuls of long grass. The gelding leaned into Austin's body in a playful exhibition of strength, and the young cowboy finished his post-ride routine by backing his horse into the stall, using kind words and a gentle touch to maneuver the animal.

Austin ran for the house and made short work of rinsing away a day's worth of dust and sweat. He quickly put on a clean pair of jeans and passed a wet rag over his boots to remove the dust. He burst through the front door and down the porch steps. Mr. Crandall had the truck warmed up, and when Austin climbed in, the pair took off toward town.

8 High Country Honky Tonk

"Jim, stop it!" Mrs. Hudgens squealed with delight as her husband spun her around and around on the dance floor. Her voice faded into the din of electrified country music as they passed the table, where Julie Dean and young Jesse Hudgens sat. It was Friday night and The Lamplighter was packed with people. A live band and cheap drinks made for a big crowd on summer nights in Mirror Valley.

The Hudgens family had transformed before Julie's eyes in the past week. When they arrived, she and Tate had joked about the dudes from Ohio. They were entirely out of their element. Soon, though, Mr. Hudgens proved game for every opportunity the Hatchet Creek operation could offer. He rode horses and worked cows, camped under the stars, bathed in an icy creek, and smiled the entire time. His wife was slightly less adventurous, but she had still managed to try a lot of new things.

Most surprising to Julie was the progress that fourteen year-old Jesse Hudgens had made. That first evening in the barn's loft, she would have sworn that Jesse would be nothing more than a nagging pain all week. Instead, though, the young skateboard punk had turned into a respectful and upstanding buckaroo. On this night, his family's last night at Hatchet Creek, Jesse looked picture perfect sitting on a barstool in the smoky neon haze of The Lamplighter.

Jesse's new image and demeanor was due, in no small part, to his nearly constant tutelage by Tate in all things cowboy. Realizing that girls like Julie went for guys like Tate, which was quite obvious to everyone at this point, Jesse spent his week shadowing and learning from the farrier. He made a point of talking less and saying more, like Tate did. When he came inside for a meal, he removed his hat like Tate. And when he spoke to others, he now looked them squarely in the eyes like Tate did.

Mr. and Mrs. Hudgens had picked up on Jesse's shadowing right away, and they brought it up to Tate and Julie in short order.

"Tate, it looks like you've got a buddy. Are you okay with that?" Mrs. Hudgens had said across the fire, careful to keep her voice low so as not to embarrass her son, who was splitting wood with an axe only twenty feet away. The guests didn't want to inconvenience Tate whatsoever- he wasn't even an employee of Hatchet Creek, they knew. They certainly didn't want to make him feel like a glorified babysitter.

"Oh, I don't mind, Mrs. Hudgens. Jesse's welcome to hang out with me if he wants. Heck, maybe I can teach him about cowboyin'," Tate had replied. The lanky youngster pushed his felt hat back on his head, his arms crossed over top of the acoustic guitar in his lap. "I'm happy to keep an eye on him. It'll be fun," he had remarked.

And indeed, it had been fun for everyone involved. Mr. and Mrs. Hudgens got a chance to worry about one another for a while, rather than concerning themselves with Jesse's whereabouts. Each morning they emerged from their cabin refreshed and wearing telling grins. With Jesse spending his nights wherever Tate told him to sack out, Mr. and Mrs.Hudgens had plenty of time to reacquaint themselves romantically.

Julie was thinking about the past week, absently stirring her drink with a straw. Suddenly she snapped out of her trance when she heard her name being called. Looking around, she saw Kacey Loftus standing next to the table. The younger cowgirl was dressed to kill, with a rhinestone-laden shirt and belt glimmering brightly in the bar's neon lights.

"Hey! What's up, Lady!?" she shouted, rising from her chair. Jesse rose as well- another example of the etiquette he'd picked up from Tate. The girls, who had been teammates on the high school rodeo team the previous year, embraced tightly. After exchanging pleasantries, Julie introduced Jesse.

"Kacey Loftus, meet Jesse Hudgens," she said matter-of-factly. The two teens shook hands, with Jesse trying hard to keep his eyes on those of the beautiful girl. "Jesse and his folks are staying with us this week," she elaborated, pointing out the youngster's parents as they danced past the table once again. "He, well, *we*, have been hanging out with Tate Sanders a lot," Julie said, which drew a mischievous look from Kacey. "We've been having a good time together, haven't we Jesse?" she proclaimed, punching the youngster's arm across the table.

"Oh, for sure- I love it here!" Jesse exclaimed, his eyes moving from Julie to Kacey, then back again. "I wanna stay here with you guys!" Jesse wasn't kidding-his whole outlook on things had changed since he'd arrived. He had learned about horses and nature and people and girls and guns, and he absolutely loved Mirror Valley. Tate had taught him more in the last few days than he'd learned in ten years of schooling.

The band, which had been playing for over an hour without a break, decided to take five. The dance floor cleared out and thirsty two-steppers made their way back to the bar for a fresh drink. Mr. and Mrs. Hudgens appeared back at the table out of breath, smiles on their faces. Julie made introductions and pulled up a barstool for her friend to sit on. Kacey graciously answered the guests' questions about life in the Valley, high school rodeo, school, the family store, and her future plans.

Tate could be seen across the dance floor, making

his way toward their table. He'd been sitting in and playing lead guitar with the five-piece band. The musicians had come into town for the weekend without their regular guitarist, whose wife was having a baby back in the big city. Rather than cancelling the gig, though, the band had asked the owner of The Lamplighter if he knew of anyone who could help out. He called Tate immediately.

It took Tate a while to get to their table- he was sidetracked by a pair of twenty-something coeds who were hanging all over him, trying to get him to dance to the hip-hop house music that was blaring over the P.A. system. They were dressed in short denim skirts, designer bull-hide boots, and tight tank tops- the typical getup for college girl tourists on vacation. It was easy to see that they didn't know Tate's true age; in the neon glow of the bar, he looked several years older. He politely declined their requests, promising to dance with them later.

Finally, he reached the table, where the entire group applauded his performance. His cheeks reddened slightly as he thanked them for their kindness.

"My, Tate, that was some fantastic playing!" Mrs. Hudgens exclaimed. "I haven't seen a lot of rock and roll country music like this, but I sure like it!"

"Aww, thanks ma'am," Tate said genuinely. "I thought you'd like that honky-tonk sound. You two were sure dancin' up a storm!" He turned around to look at the dance floor, leaning his elbows on the tall pub table behind him. Out on the hardwood, Kacey and Julie were dancing with each other in a provocative manner that was far from a western two-step. He looked over at Jesse, whose eyes were locked on the two young cowgirls.

"Jesse, what are you lookin' at?" Tate asked sarcastically. The boy's eyes were as wide as saucers, and he turned to Tate slowly, not wanting to look away.

"Oh, nothing," Jesse said, sheepish for the first time in a week.

"Are you sure?" Tate continued, turning away. "'Cause it kinda looked like you were starin' at those girls out there..." he said, pointing out to the dance floor. "Look, they're askin' for you." Jesse turned his chair quickly toward the dance floor and was surprised to see Julie and Kacey pointing directly at him. They were swaying to a heavy beat, their bodies pressed tightly together. Their sly smiles told Tate what was going on: the girls intended to make Jesse Hudgens' last night in Mirror Valley a memorable one.

"I don't know, Tate. I'm not a dancer," Jesse said with hesitation. "I'd look like an idiot out there."

"First of all, you're gonna have to dance eventually," Tate said. "Women always want to dance, no matter what. If you don't do it, some other guy will." Jesse was drinking in the advice. "And, secondly, if you go dance with *those* girls, ain't nobody gonna be looking at you!" Tate winked at the younger boy. "I tell you what- let's both go dance with those girls. You take the brunette, ok?"

"Sure," Jesse said, already on his way to the dance floor. The two cowboys met the girls and began to spin them around the floor rapidly. Jesse was nervous, but

Kacey was doing a wonderful job of helping him feel confident. She pressed her body tightly to his as they twirled around the floor, smiling and guiding him without taking the lead.

When the song ended, Kacey hugged him and whispered, "Thanks for the dance, cowboy." Then she kissed him on the cheek and turned away, leaving him standing in the middle of the dance floor, dumbstruck. Suddenly, he realized what had just happened and an enormous smile came across his face. Jesse stepped over to the bar and ordered a fresh drink, then went back to the table.

Kacey was sweating from her dance floor exploits, and headed toward the door to get some fresh air. She stopped for a moment to say hello to an old family friend seated at the end of the bar, then continued through the front hallway. Passing the door to The Lamplighter's dining room, where hungry cowboys and tourists could grab a bite to eat until midnight on the weekends, Kacey could have sworn that she saw a familiar face seated at one of the tables.

9 Cow Dogs for Sale

The ride into town had been peaceful for Mr. Crandall and Austin. They had been putting in long days all week, trying hard to get their ranch up and running. Mr. Crandall, who hadn't spent much time doing manual labor in the last decade, now wore a bright red sunburn on his neck. His hands were calloused and his shiny ostrich boots were now scuffed and caked with manure.

When they got to The Lamplighter, the parking lot was filled with pickup trucks, a row of motorcycles, and an occasional SUV. Mr. Crandall parked in an open space and the two walked toward the door. An overhead light cast a circular glow on the ground around the battered steel door, and the shadows of several people could be seen leaning against the outside wall, their cigarettes glowing brightly in the dark.

Inside, the men were led by a waitress to a stout table and chairs in the middle of the dining room. She was a shapely thirty year old named Wendy with dishwater blonde hair and a perky demeanor. After a brief conversation about the day's weather, Wendy took their drink order and left them with plastic-clad menus. There was one other party eating in the spacious dining area, an elderly couple who were dressed up for a night on the town.

"Well, what do you think about the valley so far, Son?" Mr. Crandall asked, leaning back on his chair. Since the drive up from Texas, the two men had been so busy that they had rarely said more than a few words at a time to one another. There simply hadn't been time for small talk. With no deadlines or restrictions now, they felt comfortable "chewing the fat," as Mr. Crandall called it.

"I like it, Sir. It's pretty, it's not a hundred degrees all the time, and it's genuine cow country. The only thing I'm not sure about yet are the folks up here- I've only met one person my age so far." Austin had spent more time talking to horses and cows than to other people in the past week, and hadn't learned anything about the local kids. He hoped that he'd get a chance to meet some of his future classmates soon.

Wendy reappeared and took their order- they both wanted the daily special, prime rib, with a baked potato and a cup of soup. The pair talked over their progress on the ranch and Austin made notes in his small notebook. Things were coming together at the ranch nicely, they agreed, but it was still a long way from complete. Within the next week Austin wanted to check fence in another one of the pastures, clean and organize the Quonset hut and the machine shed, order and receive hay in the bale yard, and get the horses shod.

There was one other thing on Austin's agenda, something that he'd been considering for a while. After their food arrived, he brought it up to Mr. Crandall.

"I've been thinking," he said, taking a sizeable bite of his dinner roll. "I think we ought to get a cow dog. With only two of us around, and me going back to high school this fall, it'd be good to have some extra help."

" A dog? Really? People use dogs for cows? I thought they were just for sheep," Mr. Crandall replied. "I don't see why not, though. Go ahead- get two of 'em if you like. Make sure they're friendly, though! If you think they'll help, I'll pay for 'em."

Austin was pleased with his boss and excited for the new opportunity. Selecting and training a working dog would be his foray into one of the oldest and most rewarding of buckaroo traditions, second only to the relationship between a cowboy and his horse. A well-trained cow dog could move cattle faster and more efficiently than most horsemen could, but a poorly-trained dog could make things very difficult. As usual, though, Austin was unafraid of the challenge.

They finished their meals and, when Wendy suggested the apple pie, they had dessert. Mr. Crandall was just settling the bill when the band began its second set loudly in the bar area.

"Let's go get us a drink, Son. I think there's probably some pretty young girls out there for you to dance with!" Mr. Crandall winked across the table at his young friend. Wendy approached, bringing Mr. Crandall his change. The older man spoke playfully to her as she got closer. "Wendy, will you come have a drink with us when you get off?"

"Oh, I suppose I could have one. It is a Friday night, after all," Wendy responded with a sly smile. "You're my last table. Plus, I think there might be a few gals in there who'll wanna take this cowboy for a spin." She squeezed Austin's shoulder as she said it, and he smiled boyishly at the older woman in reply.

As the pair walked down the hallway to the bar, they passed a large bulletin board with announcements, advertisements, and other public notices pinned to it. Austin paused for a moment in front of a hand-lettered sign that read: "Cow Dogs for Sale: Blue Heeler Puppies." There were pre-cut strips with the seller's phone number on the bottom of the page, and Austin tore one free and tucked it into his shirt pocket. Further down the bulletin board there were a number of business cards tacked to the wall.

There were cards for everything from fencing supplies to house painting, and it took Austin a while to find the one he was looking for. Finally, he removed the thumb tack from an index card reading: "Skinner Sanders' Shoeing Service; Tate Sanders-Farrier." Tucking it into his shirt pocket as well, he hurried to catch up to Mr. Crandall, who was already pulling out a stool at one of the tall pub tables.

Austin was about to sit down next to his boss when, suddenly, a pair of hands came from behind him and covered his eyes.

"Guess who?" came a girl's sultry voice, barely louder than a whisper. Austin felt her breath on the back of his neck, and he could smell her perfume through the lingering aromas of cigarette smoke and spilled beer. *Whoever this girl is,* he thought, *she sure smells nice!*

"Oh, I don't know," Austin said playfully over his shoulder. "Can I get a hint?"

"Nope, no hints," the girl's voice said. "Just guess." He felt her body press against him lightly but intentionally, and it made him look around quickly to see if anyone else had noticed.

"Well, I've only met one girl in this town so far, so I guess you must be…Kacey?" Austin really hoped the girl turned out to be Kacey Loftus- she'd been on his mind an awful lot lately.

"Bingo!" Kacey said, stepping around in front of the tall young cowboy as she replied. She looked up and smiled when she saw the look on his face. He was clearly taken aback by the transformation she'd made, from mid-week store clerk to dolled-up honky-tonk girl.

"W-w-wow!" Austin said, unable to help himself. His eyes rose to meet hers, and he noticed her faint eye shadow and bright lipstick. "You look, just, wow!" he told her. "How are you?" She hugged him appreciatively and motioned toward the open table.

The pair sat down at the table, where Austin introduced Kacey to his boss. She jumped right into a lively conversation with the older man, which gave Austin a chance to admire her more thoroughly. Kacey was dressed to impress and it was working- he spotted several men around the bar room whose attention was turned to the leggy brunette, her tight jeans and fancy shirt doing a fine job of showing off her figure. In the neon glow of the bar lights she could easily pass for a college-age co-ed instead of a sixteen year old girl.

When the band eased its way into a slow song, Austin decided to interrupt his boss's conversation and ask Kacey to dance. The two teenagers worked their way into the middle of the floor and settled into a comfortable rhythm. It was a popular song, and Kacey sang along as they danced. Austin could hardly avert his eyes from hers long enough to steer around the other dancing couples as they circled the crowded floor- she was one of the prettiest girls he had ever seen. He hoped that her personality matched her external beauty; she really seemed like a nice young woman, someone Austin wanted desperately to know better.

The song ended and they separated from one another, applauding the band.

"These guys are pretty good, huh?" Austin said, leaning in close to be heard. He noticed that even her hair smelled good.

"Yeah, they've been up here a few times- always a really good show," Kacey said, nodding. She pulled him against her with one arm, pointing at the band with the other, and spoke again. "That tall guy playing the guitar is a friend of mine, Skinner," she said. "He's just filling in for their normal guitar player."

Austin nodded, absorbing what she had said. Suddenly something clicked in his head, and he turned to her. "Wait, did you say Skinner? As in 'Skinner Sanders' Shoeing Service'?"

Kacey smiled and nodded. "Yep," she said, "that's him. Tate is his real name. He's pretty good- does a lot of the dude ranches' horses around here. Not the fastest farrier around, but he does good work."

"I just grabbed his card off the board," Austin told her, smiling without knowing why. "We've got six head that need shoes in the next couple of weeks. Can you introduce me?"

"Sure thing, I'd be happy to. We'll wait 'til he's done pickin', though," the slender brunette replied. She was going to say more, but was cut off by a tap on her shoulder. Wendy was standing there when she turned around, smiling.

"Hi, Kace'," she said. "Mind if I take this youngster for a spin?" She and Kacey had known each other for years, and the younger girl knew that she'd soon be visited at work by Wendy to gossip about the handsome young man.

"No problem, Wendy," Kacey replied. She leaned into Austin, her arm still around him, and whispered in his ear. "Don't let her tell you any stories about me, okay cowboy?" With that, she turned toward the table and left the dance floor. Austin noticed several of the men on the dance floor, as well as two members of the band, watching her intently as she departed. It made him smile to know that he'd just been dancing with the prettiest girl in the place.

Wendy proved that she knew her way around a dance floor, with moves that made Austin look like a trained swing dancer instead of the clumsy novice he normally resembled. They danced to a pair of fast songs, then one slow one. It was during this last dance that Wendy made sure to tell Austin as much as she could remember about Kacey, her family, and her past boyfriends. It was the sort of information that Austin had to take with a grain of salt, but that could still prove useful eventually.

As they finished dancing and returned to the table for a fresh drink, Austin noticed that Mr. Crandall hadn't moved from his seat. Fearing that his boss might not be enjoying himself, the young cowhand whispered to Kacey, asking her to take Mr. Crandall out onto the floor while he got the old man a fresh beer from the bar. She agreed and asked Mr. Crandall to dance. He was surprised, but quickly accepted her invitation with a smile.

The band played for another hour before the house lights came back up, signaling that it was closing time. Kacey grabbed Austin by the hand and pulled him through the crowd toward the stage. She introduced Austin to Tate and then to Julie, who was close by Tate's side. The men spoke briefly and shook hands while the girls made small talk and giggled. It made Austin feel good to be a part of something so typical- teenagers flirting and hanging out on a Saturday night. He liked the valley already, but this evening cemented the fact that this was a place he would be happy to call home.

10 Training Days

The silky grass swished softly against the stocky buckskin horse's legs and belly as Austin rode slowly through one of the newly fenced pastures. Since arriving at the ranch he'd done a lot of different tasks, but fixing fence was the most time-consuming. Whenever he got a chance, he saddled Digger and worked on the dilapidated barbed wire borders. Austin didn't mind, because the solitude gave him ample time to think.

Today, though, he wasn't stretching wire or rebuilding corner braces. Instead, he was simply tending to the ranch's cattle, which had finally been moved from the pens at headquarters out into the pasture. It was a monumental occasion for both Austin and Mr. Crandall- they had worked hard to bring the old ranch back to life, and moving their first herd out onto lush grass was a sign that the worst was behind them. *Whatever happened now,* Austin thought, *at least their cows and calves were putting on weight.*

It was a bright, sunny day in the valley with temperatures in the middle sixties, and skies were clear for miles in every direction. A slight breeze made its way through light-barked Aspen trees, fluttering their green teardrop leaves loudly. The tall pasture grass rose and fell like a windblown lake's surface, with the sun glaring off each blade of green. Austin smiled to himself- he couldn't find anything to complain about today!

Last night, with the cows out on good grass and the fences fixed, Austin finally had a chance to check out the boss's horses. Unfortunately, he didn't like what he saw- while the Crandall family's warmbloods may have been excellent jumping prospects, they knew very little about being cow horses. That part didn't surprise Austin. *They simply haven't been taught to work,* he reasoned. The thing that did bother him, though, was the horses' apparent lack of respect for humans.

Austin had summoned Tate Sanders to trim and shoe the ranch's small remuda earlier this morning. When he arrived, the pair walked around the ranch headquarters and compared notes about Austin's progress in resurrecting the old homestead. There were several items that Tate suggested, things like replacing a gate latch and adding an automatic horse waterer. It was just the sort of help Austin had been missing, and he was glad for the farrier's recommendations. After their once-over, they walked to the barn and pulled the first jumping horse out of its box stall and into the barn aisle.

The first horse they went to work on was a young sorrel gelding named Wiley. He was a beautiful animal, nearly 17 hands high and well proportioned. Wiley possessed a very different sort of conformation when compared to the typical cow horse breed, the American Quarter Horse. Where Austin's buckskin was short and stocky, the boss's young steed was long and lean. And, as they soon found out, his attitude was a tribute to the Argentine Thoroughbreds represented on his pedigree- Wiley was hot-blooded and obnoxious.

When Tate went into the stall with the fancy leather halter in his hands, Wiley turned his tail toward him and cocked one leg, ready to kick. Tate sweet-talked his way around the horse's back end without incident and spent a moment letting Wiley smell his hands. After haltering the horse and leading him up and down the barn aisle a few times, Tate put Wiley in the cross ties and began to remove his old shoes.

Wiley leaned on Tate and pawed at him, bit him on the back, and smacked him repeatedly with his long tail. He danced from one side of the aisle to the other, taking up all of the slack in the chains that bound him. He whinnied and squealed constantly, which riled up the other horses in their stalls. It took Tate nearly an hour to get Wiley's shoes off and his hooves trimmed. Neither of the young men wanted to risk injury by climbing back underneath the powerful gelding to try nailing on a new set of shoes. The cowboys took a moment to consider their next step.

"Tate, I'm real sorry for these nags! I just assumed that they must be good to shoe, for how much they cost," Austin apologized profusely. "I'd have never guessed that they'd act like this…"

"Oh, hey, it's okay," Tate said, leaning his back against a stall door. "I've been kicked at before, I'll be kicked at again. Comes with the territory…" Tate's hat was tipped back on his head and beads of sweat marked his brow. It was hard work wrestling with a 1200 pound animal.

"I'm pretty well disappointed in these guys," Austin said. "I suppose I should have worked with them a little bit before you got here, run 'em around the pen or something."

"Yeah, sometimes lunging a spunky horse will help them stand still," Tate replied. "But, if I had to guess, I'd say these horses never got shoes without a tranquilizer shot first. Pretty common for spendy ponies like this…," he motioned with his rasp toward Wiley, who was standing quietly in the cross ties, looking as innocent as ever.

"You think so? I suppose… the trainer's barn where we picked them up was a real fancy place, but it wasn't a real friendly outfit," Austin remarked. "The trainer lady was out coaching when we showed up, screaming her head off at a riding class full of 8 year old kids. I could see her being the type…" Austin despised horse trainers and owners with more money than sense.

The rest of the morning had gone similarly for the farrier and the ranch hand- each one of the warmbloods behaved as if they'd never been shod. Tate and Austin discussed their options and decided that, for the time being, the jumping horses could stand to go barefoot. There were very few rocks on the Crandall Ranch, and the horses weren't being used every day, so it seemed to be a good solution. Austin's horse Digger, however, stood quietly and received a new set of shoes because the buckskin got a saddle every day.

After Tate left, Austin came up with a plan to teach the boss's horses some manners. Mainly, it involved handling them as much as possible. The more human interaction they got, the better, so Austin decided to take Wiley with him when he went to check on the cows that afternoon.

Days ago, while Austin was cleaning out the old tack room in the barn, he had found a weathered sawbuck pack saddle tucked away in a corner. It was a simple, ingenious design, the sort of saddle that had been used since the west was first settled. A wooden framework, or tree, combined with thick leather straps and a pair of woven cinches made any horse into a portable supply closet.

The straps and cinches on this particular saddle were in fine shape, so Austin decided to use the rig on Wiley. The tall gelding put up a little fuss when Austin tightened the mohair snugly and tucked the breeching under his tail, but he quickly realized that the saddle was there to stay. Austin left the sorrel in the barn aisle to consider things while he saddled Digger, and when he came back, Wiley had a look of resignation on his face.

An old-time cowboy had once told Austin that a pack horse should always be loaded to its' limit, so he looked for a way to do just that. In the tack room he found a set of heavy canvas panniers, large bags that hang on either side of the horse, and he filled these with thirty-pound blocks of salt and minerals for the cattle. With three square blocks on each side of Wiley, combined with an axe and a saw, Austin knew that the jumping horse would definitely work hard enough to earn his feed this afternoon.

He balanced the panniers so that they each weighed exactly the same amount, making up the scant difference with several lengths of rope, a few bottles of water, and a small sack of grain for the horses. It was very important that the load be perfectly balanced, as many trail wrecks had been caused by unbalanced loads shifting off to one side of a horse. Since Austin didn't have anyone helping him this afternoon, he certainly didn't want to repack a tall horse like Wiley on the trail. When he was satisfied that the panniers were even in weight, he hung them on the saddle's wooden cross bucks and let them flop against Wiley's sides.

Thirty minutes later, both horses and the lone

rider were sweating profusely. Since departing from the ranch headquarters, Wiley had pulled against Austin's every move. No matter which direction the young cowboy attempted to lead the jumper, he balked. Austin wound up dallying the horse's lead rope around his saddle horn, forcing the sorrel to follow his buckskin saddle horse every step of the way. A half hour of this tug-of-war left the horses in a sweaty lather.

Arriving at the pasture gate, Austin dismounted and opened the loose barbed-wire passage. He led his horses through and tied them to the corner brace, where they stood quietly while he replaced the gate. After pulling the wires taut and slipping a wire loop over top of the gate post, holding it upright next to the corner brace, he removed Wiley's panniers and placed them on the ground.

Austin decided to leave Wiley tied while he made his rounds. *Maybe he'll learn some proper manners while I'm gone,* he thought. The young cowboy quickly unsaddled the pack animal and rubbed him down with thick handfuls of lush pasture grass. Wiley nickered appreciatively, the first sign of affection Austin had seen out of the big red horse.

Austin retied Wiley high and tight to a stout Aspen tree nearby, making sure the horse was unable to eat or drink while he was hot. It was a commonsense practice, an attempt to ward off a digestive condition known as colic, when a horse's intestines tied themselves into a knot. Many horses had colicked and died over the years, and it was a cheap way to lose a good horse. Mr. Crandall would be very disappointed if one of his wife's prized horses died because of such an easily avoidable condition, and Austin planned to keep the horses healthy at all costs.

Back on the fence line, Austin took a moment to set each salt block on top of a fence post where he could reach it while ahorseback. Now, he could ride up to a post and grab a block, then take it to a spot in the pasture and deposit it for the cattle to use without ever getting off of Digger. It took him less than an hour to drop off the six blocks, and another thirty minutes to inspect the herd, which was smartly settled into a shady stand of Aspen trees alongside a small stream.

Satisfied that none of his cows or calves were sick or hurt, Austin headed back to the gate where he'd left Wiley. The tall red gelding whinnied loudly as they approached, and Austin had no trouble getting him to stand quietly for re-saddling. It seemed as if Wiley knew that they were headed home, and he wanted to behave. The pair of horses and lone rider made their way back toward ranch headquarters at an easy pace, and when they reached the barn Austin concluded that Wiley wasn't such a bad horse after all- he just needed more days like this one.

11 Open Invitation

The phone on the wall of the Loftus family store rang loudly, startling Kacey off her perch behind the front counter. She had always disliked the store's phone- it had a loud, abrasive ring that demanded immediate attention, which she understood was the point. Still, it made her cringe whenever the phone rang. The main reason she disliked it, though is that there was rarely anyone exciting on the other end of the line. *Oh great,* Kacey thought as she approached the phone, *it's probably another telemarketer trying to sell me vinyl siding!*

She picked up the receiver and gave her customary salutation. "Hello, Loftus General Store, Kacey speaking..." she trailed off, unenthused. It was the sort of thing she did out of habit, having worked the counter since the age of twelve. On the other end she heard a lot of noise, then a man's voice.

"Yeah, yeah, that'll be good, Tommy. We'll just put the panels up against that shed for now," the familiar-sounding caller said to someone in the background. It was clear that, whoever was calling, they were trying to do two things at once. Suddenly the voice came through, intended for her. "Hello? Kace'? Are you there?" the voice asked loudly.

Kacey knew exactly who the caller was. "Hi, Hun'!" she exclaimed through the phone. She hadn't seen Hunter Langston since the night at the 7-7 roping pen way back in July. It was coming on September now, and she was glad to hear from one of her oldest friends.

"Kace', how's life? You're still holding down the counter, huh?" the bull rider ribbed her. They had always poked fun at one another, and she expected nothing less than sarcasm from Hunter.

"Yep, still working my tail off like usual," she replied in a light, sing-song tone. It had always been so easy, so comfortable, talking to Hunter. They could go months without exchanging a single word, but the next time they spoke it was like they never missed a beat. Kacey knew that friends like that were few and far between, and she valued Hunter as one of her closest confidants.

"That's not what I heard, sweetheart," Hunter said sarcastically. "Old Cookie Watts from the Hatchet Creek outfit said he saw you out on the front deck, laying on a lawn chair with a bikini on! That's not work, if you ask me- that's flirting with the whole wide world!"

"Call it what you want, Hunter. I work really hard down here!" Kacey said defiantly. She did sunbathe occasionally, but there hadn't been any complaints, especially from the visiting cowboys eating their lunches on the patio at The Lamplighter. Kacey knew that Hunter was just doing his best to ruffle her feathers.

"I know you do, Kace', I know you do. Hey, listen," the young man said through the phone. "We've got a herd up on Mac's place that needs to come down before long. 'Bout three hundred head of cows and about as many calves."

"Yeah, Julie told me that you guys were leasing Mac's pasture this summer. Seems like a lot of good grass up there. But what's that got to do with me?" Kacey inquired, her mind racing. She wondered just what Hunter was thinking.

"Well, I figured that it might be a good end to the summer if we invited everyone, and I do mean everyone, to push the herd back down to our low pastures. It'll take a couple days, then we'll have a big party to cap it all off," Hunter said assuredly. "I called you because I need to order a bunch of supplies, first of all, and because I want you to spread the word…"

"Okay, I guess I can do that," Kacey said. Plenty of people came through the doors at the general store during the week, and she would be sure to fill them in. It was the sort of thing she came by naturally-shooting the breeze was her specialty. "Do you want me to invite anyone in particular?" she asked, trailing off.

"Nope, nobody in particular- just invite everyone you know and everyone you don't. We aim to have a big time. Heck, you can tell all the outfits to bring their dudes with if they want- we just need to find enough horses," the young cowboy said quickly. "Look, Kace', I've gotta go. We're shipping some yearlings out today and the works are a mess- sorry. I'll call you later with a supply list, okay?"

"Sure thing, Hun'," Kacey replied. She knew her friend had quite a few things going on at once, and she wanted to help. "I'll put the word out right away!"

"Oh, and Kace'?" Hunter asked just before hanging up.

"Yeah, Hunter?" the pretty cowgirl replied, anticipating some last-minute detail that couldn't be ignored. She focused hard on what he was going to say, closing her eyes and listening.

"Call your Texican cowboy friend and ask him to come out, too. I wanna meet him," Hunter said, surprising Kacey. She smiled and replied that she would, gladly, extend an invitation to Austin. Truthfully, she had been thinking an awful lot about the tall Texan- and she hoped the same was true in reverse.

12 The Boss's Education

A swift wind blew around the corner of the barn, nearly dislodging Mr. Crandall's expensive felt hat from his head. The oil man was leaning on the barn's double door frame, his shoulder resting against the roughly sawn boards. Just inside the barn, Austin was brushing Wiley's coat with a stiff-bristled curry comb, making sure to remove any caked-on mud or debris. Something as simple as a small twig, unnoticed between the horse's back and a saddle pad, could cause the horse to develop a saddle sore that would take weeks to heal.

Satisfied that Wiley's back was fit for work, the Crandall Ranch's young foreman went to the tack room and came back down the aisle with a beautiful, brand new saddle in his arms. It was a fine example of high quality leather work, with intricate floral tooling covering the entire skirt. The fleece on its underside was deep and white as snow, and every edge and seam fit together as if the whole saddle was one piece of leather.

Austin realized that this saddle was worth far more than his own- *It's worth more than my saddle AND my horse combined,* he thought. It certainly was a nice rig, one that he would gladly ride in. Truthfully, he'd thought about riding in it several times, and had nearly put the fancy saddle on Digger once. The only reason he had refrained was because of the way Mr. Crandall had talked about it on the drive up to Mirror Valley. He said that he had ordered it custom-made down in Houston, and that he couldn't wait to ride the range in it. To take that first ride away from Mr. Crandall seemed impolite to Austin.

Wiley stood quietly as Austin tightened the new latigo, pulling the cinch tight around the sorrel's barrel just behind the forelegs. As little as a month ago, Wiley would have cow-kicked at Austin when he tightened the strap, but now he stood respectfully. For the last six weeks Wiley had been in training and it looked like it was paying dividends. The horse's manners had improved tremendously.

The former jumping horse got a matching headstall with long split reins. Austin expertly made the horse open his mouth for the snaffle bit by sticking his thumb inside its mouth, thumbing the gelding's gums between the front teeth and the rear molars. This bridle was not unfamiliar to the horse; over the last three weeks Austin had been putting rides on Wiley each day, retraining him to be a ranch horse. Today had been the goal: he wanted Wiley to be safe enough for Mr. Crandall to ride without fear.

That would be a tall order, though, because Mr. Crandall turned out to be terrified of horses. The older man had spoken several times in a joking manner about "getting bucked off a rank cow horse," talking about it like he was an old-time trail drover assigned the task of breaking an entire herd of colts, rather than a middle-aged ranch owner riding a bunch of spoiled jumping horses. Austin knew that Mr. Crandall had some trepidation concerning horseback work, and attempted to reassure his boss.

"Yes sir, Wiley here has been as sweet as apple pie lately," the young cowboy said, tying on a set of saddle bags as he spoke. "He started out a little bit hot, wouldn't respect people. Now, though, you can see that he's a pretty good boy." The older man nodded consciously and stood tight to the wall, looking to Austin like a timid youngster at a junior high dance. "He just needed to learn how to work a little bit, that's all," Austin shrugged and raised his eyebrows at his boss.

"Well, we'll see what happens I guess," Mr. Crandall said, sighing. "It's been a long time since I rode a horse, though. I hope I remember how."

"Aww, don't worry about it Mr. Crandall. I'm sure you'll be fine once we wear the rust off of ya'," Austin remarked. "If you have any questions, just ask me. And, if it's alright with you, I'll give you a few tips along the way…"he trailed off.

"Absolutely, Son, please do. I've watched you ride every day and I can tell that you know what you're doing, so please tell me whenever you see anything." The boss's comment made Austin feel good, and he humbly thanked the older man for his kindness.

The pair made their way out of the barn and into the nearby corral, where Digger was tied to the fence. Austin had decided on this spot for Mr. Crandall to ride Wiley at first because it was a small, confined area that would instill confidence in the rider. Also, it would keep the lanky young horse from attempting to take off with a novice on his back. With the grass and weeds now trimmed to the ground by cows and calves, the corral was much like the arenas Mr. Crandall had been watching his daughter circulate at horse shows over the last few years.

Austin led Wiley out into the middle of the corral and held the horse's head while Mr. Crandall got on. It was comical watching the older man try to get his short, stocky body onto the long and lean jumping horse. Finally, after plenty of grunting and a few failed attempts, the boss's old jeans were planted in his new saddle. He looked around from high atop the sorrel, smiled, and picked up the reins.

With his boss safely aboard, it was time for a little refresher course. Austin strode over to the fence and tightened Digger's cinch, then placed a square boot toe in the stirrup and swung into the worn leather seat. He moved his gelding toward Mr. Crandall at a walk, and when he got to the older man, they both reined their horses toward the rail to begin the lesson. For half an hour, Austin and Mr. Crandall walked, trotted, loped, and backed their horses around the pipe enclosure. When Mr. Crandall looked comfortable enough, Austin rode over to the gate and opened it from atop his horse.

The pair rode across the farm yard and through the pasture gate, and then headed up to higher ground where the cattle would undoubtedly be. It was getting to be a warm day, and Austin knew the mother cows would be dozing in the shady Aspen groves at the far end of the pasture. Their calves would likely be chasing one another around in the nearby meadows, playing as only baby animals could. It was often the sight of a dark Angus calf darting in and out of the trees that alerted Digger to the herd's whereabouts, and his ears would perk up accordingly. Good cowboys knew to pay attention to their horse's body language, and Austin used this tactic to find his cows in short order on most days.

Looking over, Austin saw Mr. Crandall scanning the countryside, taking it all in. It occurred to him that this was the first time his boss had explored the ranch. Without a safe horse, he'd been confined to ranch headquarters since their arrival. *What a relief this must be*, Austin thought, *to finally see what he's been pouring his time and money into.*

They rode at a brisk trot up a grassy knoll, and were nearing the top. Austin made sure to ride up close to his boss because he knew that the view from atop the ridge was spectacular and he wanted to see Mr. Crandall's reaction- it was bound to be a good one. With rugged spruce-laden mountains seemingly rising out of the tops of the dense stands of Aspen trees that covered the rolling pasture hills, like skyscrapers projecting their tops away from the urban struggle down below, the Crandall Ranch was the most beautiful place Austin had ever been.

"My Lord!" Mr. Crandall exclaimed, awestruck. "I

can't believe this is on our place, Austin!" The older man's voice quavered a bit, and Austin knew the older man was having an emotional moment. It was a breathtaking view, and the young cowboy knew that with the stress of the last few months, combined with not seeing his family and a recent drop in oil prices, the tears his boss was shedding were long overdue.

Not wanting to embarrass Mr. Crandall, Austin made a show of dismounting and checking his cinch so that his back was turned to the older man. After a moment, he remounted and looked over the ridge with Mr. Crandall. Digger walked up beside Wiley and peered down into the valley, scanning for anything out of place in the beautiful expanse of trees and grass. Suddenly both horses' ears perked up and Austin followed their gaze across the open terrain, into a thick clump of Aspens. There, in the shadows of the canopy, was the herd.

Mr. Crandall saw the cows shortly after, and it nearly started the waterworks once again. The sight of his dream come true- a working cattle ranch in the mountains- was almost more than he could bear. He held it together, though, and spoke slowly to his young partner.

"This is the most beautiful thing I've ever seen, Son," the man said. Austin could do little but nod and smile. "I'm sure glad you got this horse shaped up so we could come up here together. You're doing a great job, Austin. I mean it..." the boss trailed off.

"Thanks Mr. Crandall, I sure appreciate the opportunity you've given me. 'Won't be long and we'll have the rest of those jumping horses broke for ranch work. It'll be nice- you can have Mrs. Crandall and Jessie come up and ride herd with us! Think of that, Mr. Crandall!" Austin was genuinely excited- the Crandall Ranch was running smoothly, and he wanted his boss to be proud of what they'd accomplished. Bringing his wife and daughter to the Mirror Valley would be a sure sign of that pride.

They rode over to the herd and inspected each animal visually. Any signs of sickness, such as lethargic behavior or a snotty nose, were documented in Austin's shirt pocket notebook with an ear-tag number and a description of the symptom. If an animal displayed signs of sickness for a few days in a row, Austin would rope, tie, and treat the animal. Nearly two months into their ranching career, they hadn't lost a single cow or calf, so Austin reasoned that their system for herd health was working just fine.

After checking out the cattle, the two men rode back toward ranch headquarters. The setting sun caused their long shadows to dance on the hills off to the east, and dew was starting to collect on the thick grass in the shade. Looking back into the pasture as he waited for Austin to open the wire gate, Mr. Crandall saw two paths from Wiley and Digger meandering through the damp green brome stems.

"I'm gonna be sore tomorrow, Son, but I'm sure glad I got to go with you today," Mr. Crandall said as they were removing the saddles from Wiley and Digger. "That, this, it's all exactly what I hoped for. We're doing it:: we're really ranching!" The excitement and contentment was obvious in the oil man's voice, and it made Austin smile.

"Yes sir, we had a good day, huh?" Austin asked rhetorically. "It's days like this one that make me really glad we moved up here."

"I'm glad too, Austin. I'm glad too," the boss said quietly. "Now why don't we get cleaned up and head into town for supper? I don't really feel like cookin' tonight." Mr. Crandall waited for a response.

"Sounds good, I'm up for that. We'd better not sit down before we leave home, though- I'm so tired, I don't think I'll get back up!" Austin said. With that, they headed for the house to get ready for dinner. The young cowboy was really looking forward to a big meal and lively conversation. As Mr. Crandall pulled the truck around, Austin thought of another thing he hoped to get in town: another chance to see Kacey Loftus.

13 Puppy Love

There was a large cloud of dust trailing Tate's battered pickup truck and horse trailer as the rig lumbered down the long driveway to Hatchet Creek Ranch. Inside the cab, an unlikely trio was thoroughly enjoying the ride. Tate was behind the wheel, Austin rode shotgun, and a squirmy blue heeler pup was between them. The dog could scarcely sit still, opting instead to climb all over the other two occupants in order to look out the truck's side windows. This brought on a slew of boyish giggles from the young men, who occasionally scolded the pup as halfheartedly as possible.

The cowboys were headed to ranch headquarters, and from there they would head on to Cow Camp for the night. The idea of sacking out in a weathered bunkhouse, eating Rodney Watts' tasty chuck, and mingling with the Hatchet Creek outfit's dudes promised to be enjoyable for Austin. When Tate had passed along Julie's invitation, though, he'd done so with a sly smile that had Austin a little concerned. *Maybe they've got something up their sleeve,* Austin thought later. Still, he had accepted the offer immediately.

Mr. Crandall had returned to Houston on business for the week, and Austin knew enough to call him for his blessing. Not surprisingly, the older man consented without hesitation, citing Austin's need to get out and about as plenty of justification for the day off from riding fences and checking cattle.

Finally, after innumerable licks from the pup and a seemingly endless series of rain ruts in the gravel driveway, they arrived. As the cowboys climbed down from the seat, Julie hailed them from her post in the open doorway of the two-story barn. Austin was about to reply when, in a flash of grey and black fur, his new pup leapt through the open truck window and made a beeline for the redheaded stable manager.

The dog came to rest at Julie's feet, sitting and whining loudly, begging to be petted. Suddenly the tough young woman melted, fawning over the pup as if it was a newborn baby. She cooed and hugged the heeler, which was, in turn, licking her face and neck.

"Austin, is this your dog?" Julie asked, clutching the pup tightly to her chest. "He's the most precious thing I've ever seen!"

"Yep, that's my new pup. He's a wild one, but seems to be pretty good…" Austin trailed off. Truthfully, he was very proud of the dog. He'd never had one growing up, and had not realized how fulfilling owning a working dog could be. Now, though, he beamed every time the pup did something right.

"I tell ya', Julie, that dog's got it. I can tell," Tate interjected from the barn entrance, where he stood chewing on a long grass stem.

"I'd say he does," she said, still looking like a child on Christmas morning. "He's got eyes like my dad's dog, Bo, kind of sharp lookin' but kind. And Bo was one of the cow-eatin'-ist dogs you'd ever holler at." Tate took this as high praise, and he almost blushed with pride.

The two cowboys unloaded their horses from the trailer and turned them loose in the first available corral. Digger and Whiskey, Tate's big bay horse, set out to explore their new confines. Quickly, though, they lowered their heads and began eating the sparse remnants of a round hay bale left over from the previous winter. Digger lifted his head suddenly and whinnied across the fence at a horse Austin hadn't seen before.

A beautiful dappled grey mare stood in a nearby pen, her nearly black mane and tail waving in the wind. She looked like she was running at breakneck pace, even while standing still. Austin's trained eye devoured the horse and found no flaws in her conformation or upkeep. She was beautiful.

On the iron fence rail behind the mare hung a saddle with a bright pink seat, a matching bridle, and a loudly colored saddle blanket that fit right in. The saddle had pink metal stirrups hanging from its fenders. It was a barrel racing saddle, Austin could tell instantly. *Whose horse is that? And why is that racing outfit hanging on the fence?* He wondered silently.

Tate led Austin through the impressive barn, pointing out the amenities. The young Texan looked around with wide eyes. This was the finest barn he had ever set foot in, and he felt bad about wearing his manure-caked boots inside. His dog, however, had no such regrets. The pup ran up and down the aisle, ducking into each and every open box stall to smell whatever needed smelling.

They reached the end of the aisle and mounted the roughly planked staircase up to what Austin thought would be a simple hay loft. To his amazement, the upper portion of the barn was a full-scale lounge. Austin's reaction was very similar to the one Julie saw Tate display on his first trip inside the barn. He seemed awestruck, completely baffled as to how all of these fine furnishings made their way into a hay loft.

This bewilderment soon took on a whole other level, though. Austin's dog had been circulating the loft, but quickly ran out of his sight behind one of the high-backed leather chairs in front of the fireplace. Concerned that the pup might be causing some trouble, Austin rushed to make sure. Rounding the chair, he saw his dog receiving a loving scratch from none other than Kacey Loftus.

"Well, hello there stranger," Kacey said in a failing voice, almost as though she'd suddenly lost her nerve. Austin could understand, and the feeling was certainly mutual. He tried hard to compose himself.

"H-h-hi," he stammered, again reduced to mush by her remarkable eyes. No matter how many times he came across Kacey, she always affected him the same way. It bothered him a little, but intrigued him far more. "What are you doing here?" he asked pointedly.

"Oh, I just got an invitation to Cow Camp for the night," she replied, her mind working. "And I suppose you got the same…?" Kacey could smell the matchmakers' work all over this setup.

"Yep, I got the whole 'come on up and sit around the fire with the dudes' line from Tate," Austin said dryly. He, too, was making the connection.

"Exactly what I heard from Julie!" Kacey said, then smiled broadly. "I guess we're set up, huh?"

"Well, I can think of a lot of things worse than this," Austin said, having regained his natural easy confidence the moment Kacey smiled. He chanced a wink at the end of his response and was pleased when she reached up and squeezed his hand. In an instant he knew that this trip to Cow Camp would be a rewarding experience.

After visiting for a while on the plush leather sofas, enjoying sodas from behind the impressive bar, the four young wranglers welcomed a group of dudes from South Florida. They were four women: a mother and her teenage daughter, a recently widowed woman of forty, and an empty-nester in her early fifties. They appeared to be in good spirits despite the long travel day, and the conversation remained lively over drinks in the loft.

Tate and Austin left the party visiting upstairs and went down to harness a team for the wagon ride up to Cow Camp. It was a treat for Austin to learn Tate's tricks in dealing with the mules- he had only driven a handful of wagons, and he'd never had occasion to harness a team. Most of his involvement with wagons had been from a distance, having served as a horseback "outrider" for a chuck wagon racing team. The young local showed Austin what to do and when to do it, then supervised as the Texan got both mules harnessed.

When they drove around the front of the barn, the girls were all out in front and were playing with Austin's dog. The mules' ears perked up warily with the pup running around, but they kept walking as instructed. Finally coming to a stop in front of the barn, Tate looped the lines around a peg on the wagon and climbed down to assist the ladies with their luggage.

The women had brought several suitcases each, and with so much truck the cowboys wondered about having enough room in the wagon for all of them to sit. As big as the wagon was, there was hardly a spare inch of floor space available for the ladies to put their feet. Deciphering the situation quickly, Austin decided they needed to unload some of the bags. He wanted to try something he'd seen done once before on a ride in the Hill Country of Texas- packing gear on a riding saddle.

The tall Texan first went to the tack shed and fetched a thirty foot length of half inch manila rope. Its original smooth surface had been roughened and frayed from years of service, but Austin didn't fret. He knew that a worn, rough rope would hold its bight much better against a load, and would do a fine job of keeping whatever he packed in place. Coming back into view with the rope over his shoulder, with his dog trailing him obediently, he looked the part of a handsome, old-time cattle drover. The women, even the older ones, were caught looking when he picked up his head.

Smiling at the thought, Austin went about the business of packing his horse. Digger was tied to the back of the wagon with a rope halter, and wore a saddle already. Austin found the midway point of the rope and tucked a loop between the saddle's pommel and Digger's withers through a hole in the front of the saddle. He pulled enough rope free to throw a few turns in it and loop it over the saddle horn. Pulling his slack backward, Austin draped the ends of the rope over either side of his horse, who stood calmly.

Next, he evaluated the cargo he had to pack. Selecting two similarly shaped cases, Austin hefted each one carefully to figure its weight. Actual numbers were not important, as there was very little chance that the burden would approach Digger's maximum payload, but any load needed to be balanced for safety. One case was slightly heavier than the other, but this was no big concern. Austin decided that, after the entire load was buttoned up, he'd tie his slicker and gun belt to the lighter side to even things out sufficiently.

He counted on what packers called a "barrel hitch" to get the cases safely to their destination, and laid the ropes out accordingly. It took a little finagling and retightening to get the load to sit squarely on Digger's sides, with the bottom of his load coming to rest just above the top of the stirrups. When he was satisfied, Austin tied his slicker and gun belt to the faint side and prepared to depart. He and Tate helped the ladies into the wagon and saw to it that they were comfortably seated on something relatively soft for the trip. They had the puppy with them, and Austin reasoned that was a good a place for a green cow dog as any.

"Austin, why don't you ride Whiskey up there an' I'll drive team?" Tate queried rhetorically. Julie had already taken up her perch in the wagon's spring seat, looking quite attractive despite her stained canvas jacket and woolen ranch cap, and Austin knew that his friend intended to accompany his girl. Truthfully, he couldn't blame him. Austin felt excited for the chance to ride drag with Kacey, hoping they'd get a chance to talk.

"Sure thing, Tate," he replied. "Anything special about him I need to know?" Austin hadn't taken a good look at the bay horse yet, and knew better than to assume anything about a mount. If the bay had any quirks, now would be the time to learn them. Tate was the one asking for someone else to ride his horse, so it was his duty to divulge anything that might make the ride uncomfortable for Austin.

"I reckon that, after ridin' those jumper nags over at your outfit, Ol' Whiskey will be a breath of fresh air. Just keep your heels down, savvy?" Tate replied plainly. He'd seen Austin buck out two of Mr. Crandall's warmbloods in recent weeks, and knew the young cowboy could ride. He felt confident in his friend's horse sense and ability, enough to trust him with his favorite mount, Whiskey. The bay had spirit, that much was true, but was not mean. If there was a rodeo to be had, it would be a short one and Austin would be the victor.

Austin retreated to the corral to saddle Whiskey. The horse came right up to him and stood quietly, occasionally looking over his shoulder at the cowboy. When he pulled the latigo tight and affixed the back cinch snugly, Whiskey lowered his head contentedly, as if he wanted to work. Austin took this as a good sign.

He led the horse out in front of the barn and checked his cinch. Sure enough, there was almost an inch of slack between the mohair and the horse's barrel. Holding its breath was a trick almost every horse learned at a young age, and had been the cause of many wrecks along the trail. Austin had fallen off a naughty runaway pony years ago when the saddle slipped, and since then he'd remembered to walk a horse off after tightening the cinch the first time. *They can't hold their breath when you walk them around*, he reminded himself.

Kacey rounded the far corner of the barn on her grey, looking every bit the cowgirl. She had changed her stripes once again, Austin thought, from casual store clerk to honky-tonk angel to now, classic ranch woman. Each new dimension of this girl intrigued him more than the last one, and he instantly decided that this was his favorite memory in the valley thus far. She was stunning. Her faded, just-right sized blue jeans were hidden by artfully crafted leather leggings, or chaps. Her high boot tops were worn outside the cuffs of her jeans, and beautiful spurs adorned the heels. Not surprisingly, the bands and shanks of her spurs were anodized a perfect pink, matching her stirrups.

Her paisley printed shirt was covered with a leather vest. She wore a rounded brown felt cowboy hat with a stampede string. Leather gloves held split harness leather reins in the left hand. The other hand came to rest on her thigh, where it absently fiddled with a lariat affixed to her saddle horn. And on her hip was a proportionately sized leather holster, out of which Austin noticed a set of ivory pistol grips protruding. Should the worst happen, she had the required tool to dispatch a suffering horse, or to dissuade a charging bear.

She looked unbelievable, like a dream. The women in the wagon hurried to snap photos of the beautifully rugged cowgirl, and she obliged them for a moment by standing still. Everyone was staring wholeheartedly at Kacey, including Austin. He couldn't get enough of her. Suddenly he sensed someone staring in his direction and looked about instinctively. Julie was sitting on the wagon seat, peering through him with a knowing grin on her face. Caught, he reddened and returned her smile.

When she'd had enough of posing, and anxious to deflect the attention she was receiving, Kacey walked her horse around the front of the wagon. She spied Austin standing next to Tate's horse and understood his delay. Whiskey wouldn't stand still for him, and the bay was quickly working itself into a frenzy. Knowingly, she rode to the horse's head and took hold of one of the reins. With another horse in the immediate vicinity and with its head held, the bay stood for Austin to mount.

"Well, cowboy, you're sittin' pretty now. Let's go," Kacey said, looking right into Austin's eyes. "The sun's getting' low, and we'd have to wait another couple hours for the moon to show, so you'll have to take me for a moonlight ride some other night!" She was only half kidding. The fading orange sunlight reflected on her face, Austin noticed, and it looked like her eyes were on fire.

Tate drove the wagon off with Digger in tow, and after a few moments the riders followed at a trot. The scene could have easily been relevant a century earlier, with nothing out of place but Kacey's wildly colored saddle and spurs. Austin reflected on all that had happened from the first time he'd seen her to now, and all that he wanted to happen. He wasn't exactly sure where he'd go from here, or if he'd go anywhere, but he knew one thing- he wanted Kacey with him, and hoped that she felt the same way.

14 Fireside Revelations

"Cookie, that was something else," Austin said contentedly. The four young wranglers and four dudes had just enjoyed a special treat in the Cow Camp mess hall. Somehow, somewhere, Rodney Watts had gotten fresh-caught ocean fish shipped all the way to his kitchen, and had prepared it in a way that was met with universal approval. It was the best fish anyone present had ever tasted, and they all said so. Rodney, typical of chuckwagon cooks, was pleased but humble.

"Shucks, folks, I'm glad you liked it," the cook responded quietly. "It seemed like a nice change of pace from eating squirrels and skunks like we usually do." His sarcasm, not understood by the dudes, set Tate into a hearty series of guffaws. Finally, after a moment, the young muleskinner composed himself enough to ask a question.

"Rodney, what type of fish was that anyhow? Didn't taste like no trout I ever caught..." he trailed off.

"That, my boy, was flounder. Kind of a funny lookin' ocean fish. Took me a while to find it," Rodney replied, trying to keep a straight face. It was difficult, though, because Tate was coming unglued with another series of laughs. This, in turn, caused everyone else to laugh, though they didn't know why. Finally, after wiping the tears from his eyes, Rodney could take no more. "Just what is so funny, Kid?" he demanded.

"I thought flounder was when your horse went lame when it ate too much grain, not a fish!" Tate said, barely able to contain himself.

"No, you dang fool kid, it's not flounder, it's founder! Horses founder on sweet feed and flounders swim and get eaten!" Now Rodney was the one who could not keep from laughing. The local girls and Austin were beside themselves and stomped the floor around their seats. They slapped their hands on the table and laughed until their bellies hurt. The two cowgirls were clutching at each other in an attempt to, somehow, stem the hilarity. But there was no halting, for every time they looked up and saw Tate's bewildered face, another wave of laughter would hit them hard. Even the dudes, who undoubtedly knew nothing of the dangerous horse ailment, thought the whole situation was hilarious. They continued to laugh uncontrollably for nearly ten minutes.

Eventually, the girls took the dudes outside to start a bonfire. Tate and Austin threw on aprons and helped Rodney clean dishes until he kicked them out of his kitchen. He mentioned something about dessert in an hour, which was music to their ears. The young men made their way down toward the fire pit, with Tate stopping along the way to grab a guitar out of the wood shed. Austin hoped he wouldn't be called upon to play- he'd done a little picking and singing, like most ranch kids, but thought that he might embarrass himself if he attempted to wear off the rust this evening.

As they approached, the group of women all turned and stared. It was another moment that made Austin slightly uncomfortable, and he reddened a little. Suddenly Kacey gasped when she saw the guitar.

"Is that my daddy's old flat top, Julie?" she asked the pretty redhead seated beside her.

"Yes, I believe it is. You remember him pickin' down at the store in the evenings?" Julie replied, knowing the answer.

Kacey's father, Lefty Loftus, was one of the first acts to play at The Lamplighter as a teenager touring the country. He'd fallen in love with the valley immediately and had taken to ranching. In order to buy his first herd of cattle, he'd sold nearly all of his instruments to other bands.

But the guitar Tate was holding, a weathered dreadnought, had been his very favorite, so he kept it. He used to sit on the front porch of the general store and entertain whoever came by. Ten years ago he'd loaned it to a ranch hand at the Hatchet Creek outfit for the summer, and the cowboy had quit on bad terms. Lefty assumed that he'd taken the instrument with him, down the road. It was a wonderful sight to Kacey, and she knew her father would be happy to hear that the guitar was still around.

The ladies from Florida sat contentedly, snapping pictures as Tate treated them to a few of his favorite songs. He was talented, they could tell. Listening to the words of the songs, songs about heartaches and God and prison and the like, each of them settled into their own mind. Sometimes they would hang on each word, other times they would not seem to hear anything at all. They were caught up in thinking about the past and the future while worrying about the present all at the same time.

Austin himself was doing some of that, too, though he had less concern than most. Long hours in the saddle each day gave him plenty of time to think about things, and he suddenly felt glad for that. *Here are these ladies, completely removed from whatever ails them, and they can't seem to shake loose and have fun,* he thought. *I wonder what it's like to be so worried that you can't enjoy a night like this!*

Quickly, he decided to help them enjoy themselves. Rising from his seat on a log, he strode around the fire pit and extended a hand to the mother, asking for a dance.

"Ma'am, will you dance with me?" he asked politely. The woman immediately blushed, then looked at her teenage daughter and smiled.

"You see, sweetie, that's what a gentleman acts like," she said to her child. "Not like those punk kids at your school. Of course, Austin, I'd be delighted."

Tate picked up on the atmosphere immediately

and began playing a swinging honky-tonk dance tune. It was just the right tempo for Austin to guide the woman carefully around the rough ground without having it be an awkward slow dance. The others watched as the young cowboy whirled her over the makeshift dance floor, and when the song ended they all applauded. She thanked him for the dance, hugging him tightly, and then retreated to her seat. The woman's daughter turned and stared blankly at her as if to say "What was THAT?" She had never seen her mother as the carefree, dancing type. It was a side of her that the girl liked immediately.

From there, the conversation picked up rapidly and so did the spirits of the worried dudes. It seemed that now, finally, their vacation could be just that- a break from it all, and a place to relax. Rodney came down the hill with a tray full of dessert plates, and as they ate he took advantage of his captive audience to tell a story.

"I's down in your part of the country once, believe it or not," he motioned toward the dudes. "There was a little Cajun queen named Clara Withers that had me followin' her 'round the country while she raced her pony. Big, lean sucker, that horse was. He'd bend 'round a barrel so fast that his head and tail would about meet." Rodney gave them a chance to soak in this imagery, then continued.

"My youthful self was plum full of vinegar, so I decided that workin' the buckin' chutes and clownin' for bulls was a good way to make my livin'. Me and Clara had a big time runnin' the Gulf Circuit. She'd pick up a check every week and I'd make a little scratch, too. We'd run 'round from rodeo to rodeo like Bonnie and Clyde, just showin' up and takin' everybody's dough."

"Eventually, though, things got kinda ripe between me an' old Clara. She'd knock over a barrel and I'd pay for it, Lordy! I'd pay. Sometimes I'd get runned over by a bull and she'd be over flirtin' with the judge. Yes sir, mighty ripe in a hurry! We decided to call it a day down 'round Orleans when I found her and my old pard' Slim neckin' behind the announcer's tower."

"Good days, though. We had us a few good days in there. I don't regret nothin' 'bout it, 'cept maybe what I did to old Slim's nose. I was angry, and I reckon he found out in a hurry. Yep, good old Slim…" the cook trailed off. Everyone was waiting for his next tale, but he neglected to indulge them.

"Reckon I oughta hit the hay," he said, picking up their dishes. Offers to help him were waved off absently, and he went back up the hill to his kitchen. Before he left earshot, though, he called down. "I'll sack out in the lodge tonight, seein' as we've got a full bunkhouse."

This was music to the wranglers' ears, as Rodney's famed snoring would have made worthless any opportunity for romance between the cowboys and cowgirls. Now, though, they could proceed with their customary, natural inhibition rather than his nasal droning. Tate and Julie exchanged knowing glances and made some noise about retiring for the evening, which urged the dudes to call it a night as well. The couple showed them their quarters, which were two finely appointed cabins tucked into the trees, not far from the lodge and mess hall.

Suddenly Austin and Kacey found themselves alone by the fire. They sat directly across from one another at first, which made Austin a little more nervous than he would have liked. Her gaze was on him and it was unrelenting. The fire's flames licked their way around a pair of large, half-burned logs, and every time he met Kacey's eyes he saw the red embers burning in their reflection.

She rose from her seat and came over to sit with him, carrying the guitar with her. It was almost perfect, he thought, this girl in this setting. With nothing between them but the night and a scant few inches of dead tree trunk, he tried to calm his nerves and make conversation. She never gave him the chance to speak, though. Instead, she took off her hat and leaned in, kissing him on the lips. It sent a chill through his entire body, and instantly made him feel at ease.

He returned her kiss eagerly, a little too eagerly, then reeled and sighed. His eyesight found the fire for a moment, then returned to Kacey. Not surprisingly, she was looking right at him. Her lips turned up into an angelic smile that caused him to grin and blush.

"Well, now, that was…something!" he said finally.

"I'll say! I've wanted to do that for a while," she replied. "I hope you don't think I'm too forward, kissing you like that. I let my feelings get the best of me."

"No, I'm glad you did it. I'm glad we're here together. You're pretty special, as far as I can tell, and I'd like to think that maybe you're in the same boat," he answered her hopefully.

"Yeah, I think maybe you and I will be good together, Austin. You're not like anybody I know, and I like it. I like it an awful lot."

"Well alright then!" he laughed, trying hard not to show completely the pleasure he took in her words. "What do you say we go curl up for the evening?"

With that, they headed back up the hill followed closely by Austin's dog. Reaching the old stone bunkhouse, they tiptoed inside and found Julie and Tate fast asleep at one end of the long, low building. Together they made their way to the opposite end and settled into a creaky bunk. The pup went to sleep almost immediately at the foot of the bed, and the teens followed suit.

Just before he nodded off, Austin took stock of the situation. Here he was, working a well-funded ranch in the high country with a good horse, a good dog, and now, a pretty girl to go with. It seemed as perfect to him as anything in the world. He kissed Kacey's forehead, smelling the wood smoke in her hair, and heard her murmur a sleepy "Good night" from where her head lay on his chest. No matter what tomorrow brought him, Austin knew that he was happy in this moment.

15 A Dream Realized

Mr. Crandall returned from his business trip to Houston on a beautiful Tuesday afternoon. He had planned to catch a ride from the airport with Mr. Loftus, who drove into the city each Monday and came back on Tuesday afternoons with a trailer full of supplies for the store. Expecting to see Kacey's father's big white pickup, Austin did a double take when he saw a rusty truck coming up the drive toward the Crandall Ranch headquarters.

As the rig neared, he could see three people inside the single cab. The truck bounced and rattled loudly as it came closer, owning its age with aplomb, but when it skidded to a stop he could see brand new tires mounted on the rusted rims. The engine sounded strong, and the body looked to be straight and complete. As he approached the passenger side door, he wondered just who in the world this was.

Suddenly, the door burst open and a slim blonde girl of fifteen was hugging his neck. She squealed in delight as she pulled on him, and Austin was nearly smothered. It was Jessie Crandall, his boss's daughter. He spun her around and hugged her back with all of the platonic brotherly charm he could muster.

Looking past the babbling teen, he saw Mrs. Crandall emerge from the middle seat of the truck. She was a fine looking woman, naturally pretty but also very well kept like most Houston oil men's wives. Her designer western clothes were tailor made for her figure, and she looked stunning, even climbing out of the rusty old truck. She approached Austin with a welcoming smile and open arms.

They embraced one another tightly for a moment, and then she spoke.

"It's so nice to see you healthy and happy up here, Austin!" she said with a southern twang that reminded the young cowboy of his home state. "Sounds like you've been quite a help up here, and I thank you for that. And for keeping my husband safe…" she trailed off. Then, under her breath she said, "I think he'd be upside down in a ditch without you!"

"Oh, Mrs. Crandall, it's been my pleasure. Mr. Crandall has been the best friend a guy can hope for up here," Austin said. He peered across the hood of the truck at his boss, who was smiling like a lunatic. "Although I think, maybe, he's gone loco today. What's gotten into him?" He asked this question with volume, so Mr. Crandall could hear. The older man kept on smiling, which caused Austin to laugh out loud.

Mr. Crandall addressed Austin casually, beckoning him over toward the driver's side. "Son, I haven't gone loco, though my wife might think otherwise. You see, the thing is…I went and did something funny. Actually, I might be a little bit crazy. For the first time in my life, I went into a car dealership and asked to see the most low down, lousy truck that they had."

"I don't know, Mr. Crandall, I think you could've done worse," he said sarcastically. "This rig doesn't look half bad."

"Well, I'm glad you think so. You see, I got to thinking about our outfit up here. And, well, the thing is…" the old man lagged.

"Daddy went and bought you this lousy truck!" Jessie exclaimed loudly. This brought a snorting laugh from Mrs. Crandall, who was listening intently. The humor was lost on Austin, though.

"Really, Mr. Crandall? You bought this truck for me?" he asked unbelievingly. It seemed too good to be true.

"Yes, Austin, it's yours. I got it in the city when I left town and had it tuned up. Put new rubber on it too. Seems like just what you'd look for in a truck- strong motor, heavy springs, and dirty. Do you like it?" the old man asked.

"Like it? I love it! Thank you so much, Mr.

Crandall!" the youth projected, extending his hand. It was the single nicest gift anyone had ever given him, and he nearly welled up in tears at his boss's generosity.

"Good, good. I'm glad you like it," the boss said, pumping Austin's hand. "You sure do a good job around here, Son, and I can't thank you enough."

Austin grabbed the ladies' luggage from the bed of the truck and carried it toward the ranch house. Mr. Crandall beamed like a proud father as he showed his wife and daughter their accommodations, explaining each room as they toured the place. The rustic house was spotless and organized and very comfortable, which met with their approval. When Austin reached his bedroom door with Jessie's suitcase, he excused himself for a moment in order to throw his clothes and toiletries into a canvas war bag.

It had been decided that, if Jessie ever came to stay, Austin would move into the old bunkhouse opposite the barn. This suited him fine. She was a teenage girl that needed her own room, and the bunkhouse was comfortable with its stone fireplace and log walls. Now she was here, and he was prepared. He had cleaned out his accommodations in Mr. Crandall's absence. This was due in no small part to his blossoming romance with Kacey: he knew that, at some point, he would want some privacy at the ranch.

With the boss and his family settling in nicely, Austin went back to his chores. It had occurred to him, while Mr. Crandall was gone, that the Crandall Ranch was a big operation for one man to run. Over the last week he'd spent time going over every corner of the property, trying to make it presentable. Mowing and cleaning and painting took up any free time that he might have had before and after his daily rides with the herd, and at the end of each day he had collapsed into bed heavily.

Austin strode past the barn and saw Wiley's head protruding into the aisle through the open top of the stall door. The sorrel nickered loudly when he spotted Austin, anxious to be let out into the sunshine. Eyeing the open front corral, Austin decided that the fresh air couldn't hurt and let the gelding out for a little exercise. The horse whinnied and threw his hind feet toward the sky after watching Austin close the gate, and then took off running around the corral.

Going back into the barn, Austin planned to let the rest of the horses out to run around as well. Then an idea struck him, one that he knew would make Mr. Crandall happy. Quickly the young Texan brought Olga, a smallish chestnut mare, out into the aisle. Her hooves had finally been shod by a determined Tate, and their clip-clopping on the concrete floor was music to Austin's ears. The cowboy outfitted her with one of the spare saddles in the tack room and tied her to the fence. He'd ridden Olga several times over the past few weeks with mixed results, but he felt confident that Jessie, who had plenty of show-jumping experience, could handle the horse's frisky behavior.

Austin ran to the house and announced his plan to Mr. Crandall, whose eyes lit up. Of course he and Jessie would like to go for a ride, he said. And no, Mrs. Crandall would not, as it had been a long travel day for her. Austin could see his boss's wife dozing on the overstuffed leather sofa, her feet propped up on the armrest. With the plan approved, Austin ran back to the barn and saddled two more horses. By the time Jessie and Mr. Crandall reached the barn with Austin's puppy in tow, their horses were ready.

The three riders headed immediately for where Austin knew the herd would be- he'd been up to the high pasture only hours before and had seen them contentedly munching grass in a nearby stand of Aspen trees. Mr. Crandall and his daughter were all smiles, and for good reason. The temperature in Houston was expected to be over a hundred degrees today, Mr. Crandall mentioned, which made the cool mountain breeze feel that much better.

When they reached the stand of trees where the herd was grazing, Mr. Crandall explained all that he could to his daughter about the livestock. She was uncharacteristically quiet, soaking up everything he had to say.

"See, baby, that's the mama cow for that calf. See how he follows her around?" Mr. Crandall said joyously. "It's just like how you and your mama were back before you discovered boys!" He was teasing her, but Austin didn't doubt that some truth backed his words. Jessie had been uncommonly forward toward Austin in the past, and he got the feeling that she was completely boy-crazy.

Occasionally she asked for more detail concerning one thing or another, and Mr. Crandall would defer to Austin for an answer. After looking over the cattle briefly, they headed for another part of the ranch- the high lookout that Austin had taken his boss to the first time they rode together.

It was a bit of a trek to the high overlook, involving several stream crossings and some technical, rocky lengths of trail. It pleased him to see Mr. Crandall and Jessie enjoying the high country together, riding confidently on beautiful horses. This was a big part of the reason Mr. Crandall had ventured into the ranching business, he knew: to spend some quality time with his daughter. Austin was happy that his boss had finally been able to see her on their family ranch. All the same, there was a slight pang in his stomach, a longing for a similar father-son experience. It would not be possible, though. His father had disappeared shortly after he was born, and he'd grown up without one. It was something that he didn't like to think about, and he sequestered the feeling quickly, refocusing on the trail.

When they reached the overlook, Jessie gasped in amazement. "Daddy, this is so pretty!" she gushed. "It's like a post card!"

"I know it, Honey. I still get chills when I come up here," the older man said quietly. "When Austin brought me up here the first time, baby, I was a puddle, crying all over the place. It's just so incredible. Now, I'm glad you're here to see it with me," Mr. Crandall continued. "We'll get your mama up here, Jessie, and show her how pretty the ranch is."

"Yeah, Daddy, maybe then she'll decide to get back into horses," Jessie said dryly. "She used to like it so much, remember?"

"I remember. She used to love to ride when we were younger. We'd go to check out new oil fields in West Texas, and sometimes we'd have to go on horseback because there weren't any roads on the place. She sure could ride!" the old man said nostalgically.

"She used to love it until we moved into Houston. I think if anything is gonna make her like horses again, this will do the trick," he continued, looking at his daughter. "Austin has a nice gentle gelding for her to ride, and it ought to be a great day out tomorrow. What do you say, Jessie? Austin?" he asked, nodding toward the young cowboy.

"Sure thing, Mr. Crandall, we can all come up about mid-morning and check the herd together. We can pack lunches in our saddle bags and make a day of it. I've got Jax ridin' like nobody's business, he'll be just fine for Mrs. Crandall," Austin replied happily. He really enjoyed the Crandall family's company, and would be glad to take them with for a day in his world.

"Well, alright then. Let's get ourselves back to the house and get into town for dinner. I wanna show the girls what our diet is like!" the older man exclaimed, winking at Austin.

"Yeah, Daddy keeps bragging about this Lamplighter place. He says the steaks are as thick as a two-by-four, and that you're the king of the dance floor or something, Austin," Jessie teased the cowboy. "I think maybe he's a little bit crazy."

"Oh, he's definitely crazy, Jess'," Austin retorted. "Crazy enough to hang out with me, anyway!" This made all three of them smile as they turned their horses toward ranch headquarters.

Suddenly a loud, high-pitched bark sounded from the stand of pines across the valley from them. Austin quickly looked around and realized that his puppy had disappeared from view. Scanning hard toward where the sound was coming from, he located a grey flash running through the underbrush, following a large tan-hided animal. Only visible occasionally, it looked as though the lead animal was quickly pulling away from the dog.

"Austin, is your dog chasin' one of our cows clear across that canyon?" Jessie asked sarcastically, thinking that she knew the answer was yes. It was a childish attempt to get him in trouble with her father, his boss, for her own entertainment. The grin on her face told the whole story.

"Nope, not unless one of our black cows turned light brown," Austin said lightly, though inside he was glad to prove her wrong. The dog gave up on his chase and began running toward them with a toothy grin on his face, his tongue lolling out the side of his mouth. They continued to watch the pine trees, looking for the large tan animal. Suddenly, in a clearing to the east, a massive bull elk appeared, his hide shining brightly in the lowering sun's rays. Just as soon as Austin could alert the others, a long and loud whistle-like bugle rang out from the animal. Even though it was nearly a half-mile away, the sound pierced the wind and seemed as loud as a locomotive's horn.

It was the first time any of them had seen an elk,

and they drank it in deeply. The horses noticed the animal as well and their ears were perked, necks craned to the east. Eventually, the bull moved back into the timber and disappeared, leaving the entire party energized. They rode back to headquarters with a happy silence among them, and arrived in the corral sooner than any of them would have liked.

16 Ready for the Roundup

The Crandall Ranch crew made the trip into town and pulled up at The Lamplighter after navigating through an uncommon sea of traffic on the main street. The weathered asphalt thoroughfare was crowded with cars parked diagonally in front of the two-story buildings that made up the downtown business district. From one end of town to the other, a disproportionate amount of shiny rental sedans and SUV's were interspersed with the locals' pickups, Austin noticed from behind the wheel of his old truck. Beside him, Jessie Crandall stared out the open window and took it all in. They were following Mr. and Mrs. Crandall, who drove the boss's shiny rig separately.

At the shared parking lot between The Lamplighter and the Loftus' General Store, Austin pulled into an empty spot in the back row. He excused himself for a moment and ran in to the store to see if Kacey was working; he hadn't seen her in nearly a week, since they had spent the night together at Cow Camp. Stepping through the door and onto the worn hardwood floor, he heard a woman's voice coming from the back of the store.

"You watch yourself, young lady," the voice said sharply. "You're too young to be getting involved with some strange Texas cowboy!" Austin could tell that the woman was in one of the rooms behind the counter because her voice was muffled. There were no windows between the back rooms and the store's interior, and this gave him more leeway in walking around the store without the woman noticing him. He didn't want to surprise a woman who was, clearly, talking about him.

With this in mind, he began walking for the aisle, but stopped short behind a tall metal shelf when he heard Kacey reply to the voice.

"Mom, I'll be fine. Austin is a perfect gentleman and he lives here, not in Texas!" the cowgirl said. "He's kind and handsome and smart and funny and he couldn't be any nicer to me, Mom. The only guy that even comes close to him, respect-wise, is Hunter Langston, and Hunter and I tried that. Remember?"

"I know, Kacey, I just don't want you to get hurt. You know that I trust you, but I also know that, at your age, your hormones will make you think every boy is 'the one.' I'm here to tell you that you'll have lots of boys after you," the woman, apparently Mrs. Loftus, said. She continued in a low voice that Austin could barely discern, "I just don't want you doing things you're not ready for."

"Oh, Mother! I'm not gonna just sleep with any

guy who smiles at me! You haven't even met Austin, you don't know him, and it's wrong of you to assume anything about him or me!" Kacey said indignantly. "He's a stand-up guy that treats me well and I really like him, so save it!" the pretty young clerk said, ending the conversation. Suddenly Austin felt very guilty for eavesdropping, even though his presence was purely coincidental and innocent. He also felt something else: a sort of pride resulting from Kacey's unrelenting defense of their young relationship.

Austin was unsure of what to do, of how to either leave the store or make his presence known. Whatever he did, he needed to do it quickly. Sliding his leather soles back to the entrance, he opened the door with a heavy pull, making sure to jingle the string of sleigh bells that hung on it. Then he closed the door loudly and strode around the shelves and into the aisle. He saw Kacey sitting at the counter, and her face showed surprise when their eyes met. This astonishment was quickly replaced by a wide smile.

"Hey, are your ears burning? We were just talking about you!" Kacey said loudly, so her mother would hear her and, Austin presumed, refrain from grilling her daughter. "How are you doing?"

"Oh, I'm good. Just came into town to get some grub- Mr. Crandall's wife and daughter came into town today, they're all over at The Lamplighter. I thought I'd take a minute to come see you, though," the young Texan said, meeting her eyes across the counter. "I kind of miss you," he said lowly, which made her smile.

"Well, I'm glad you did. I keep thinking about

you," she said, her eyes dropping his gaze. Kacey then said, under her breath, "Ever since we spent the night at Hatchet Creek, I can't get you off my mind." Austin instantly welled up with happiness. It was exactly what he'd been dealing with, trying to keep his wits about him as he went about his daily business at the ranch. Kacey was constantly in his thoughts.

"I know what you mean," he replied lowly. "We've only hung out a time or two, but I can't get you out of my head. It's a little scary-but I like it."

"Me too, Austin," she said, reaching across the counter to grasp his hand. Her touch was electric and sent a chill up his arm. Suddenly, he desperately wanted to skip his dinner plans and stay at the store all evening. He knew, however, that his attendance next door was compulsory, and he was already running late.

"I'd better get back to the restaurant, Kacey," Austin said with a disappointed tone in his voice. She nodded and climbed down from her stool behind the counter, then walked around to where he stood. "I wish I could see you again soon," he remarked.

"I'd like that, cowboy," she said. "Maybe at the dance tomorrow night, huh?" she asked in a wishful tone.

"What dance is that?" Austin replied.

"The roundup kickoff dance at the 7 Bar 7. Don't you know about it?" Kacey said. When Austin shook his head, she realized she had forgotten to mention the Langston's roundup to him at Cow Camp. It had been on her list of things to do going into the dude ranch, but her mind had gone blank when Austin showed up. He affected her that way.

"I completely forgot- I was supposed to invite you and your boss to the Langston's roundup this weekend. Sorry, sweetheart," she continued, displaying bashful puppy-dog eyes in apology. "My friend Hunter's family is pushing a herd down from Red's, which is up by Hatchet Creek, and they've decided to throw a huge party! Everyone's got their favorite dudes coming back from early in the summer, we're gonna have a big time. Wall tents and the whole bit up high, then a ranch rodeo at their ranch headquarters on the second night. It's going to be so much fun!"

"That sounds like fun," Austin replied. "Say, you said you were supposed to invite me? So I can come? And Mr. Crandall?" he questioned, his mind racing.

"Yes, yes, yes! You need to come! And your boss's family is invited too. Heck, everyone's invited that has a horse and a saddle. Like I said, there are a bunch of dudes coming back- Julie's got a family from Ohio coming out especially for the roundup!" The idea of a few days moving cattle and cowboying with his new neighbors appealed to Austin, and before she finished her sentence, he was already nodding.

"Well, I'll have to discuss it with Mr. Crandall, but I'm sure he'll be up for it," he said. "Is that why all these rental cars are around- cattle drive dudes?" Austin asked. It seemed like there were several dozen shiny rental sedans in town, more cars than the dude ranches had beds.

"Oh, no, there are lots of locals that have moved away who are coming back for the roundup," Kacey replied. "A lot of the kids in this town skip out after high school- they're not into ranching, or they marry off and stay wherever they went to college," she said matter-of-factly. "Personally, I love it here. Sure, we don't have a lot of night life or a mall, but we've got the mountains and good horses. That's enough for me."

This made Austin smile. "I'm glad to hear you say that, because I love it here," he said, peering down at her. They exchanged a look for a long moment, until she turned away.

"Well, you'd better get back to the restaurant, Austin," she said quietly.

"Yeah, I suppose so. I'll talk to Mr. Crandall about the roundup," Austin said absently. "I know we've got a wall tent up in the barn, but I assume it'll be pretty full with Mr. Crandall and his wife and daughter. Suppose I just sleep under the stars?" he asked.

She grinned devilishly and pulled him close, her fingers tugging at his belt loops. "Sure, cowboy, you can do that if you want to get snowed on! You're not in Texas anymore, hot stuff." She looked past the counter, checking to make sure her mother was out of earshot, before she made her next statement. In a breathy voice she continued, "But I'll tell you what- if you need to, you can sack out with me and my girlfriend Lisa in our tent." With that, she rose on her tiptoes and kissed him quickly. "Now go eat! You'd better come and find me at the dance tomorrow night, though," she said, steering him toward the door.

Austin walked across the parking lot to The Lamplighter, his mind racing. He couldn't wait to break the good news about the roundup to his boss, who would be ecstatic. Mr. Crandall was always up for a truly western experience, and the 7 Bar 7 roundup was bound to be just that. Austin hoped Mrs. Crandall would be up for the adventure, though- Jessie's comments about her mother's recent disinterest in horses had him concerned. He hoped that their ride the next day would be a positive experience, and that she would agree to ride at the roundup.

After finding the Crandalls in the very crowded dining room, he apologized for his tardiness and relayed Kacey's invitation to the group. Mr. Crandall was noticeably excited and asked question after question about how things would go, and Austin took this as confirmation- the Crandall Ranch would be fully represented at the Langston roundup. Together, they made a list of supplies they needed from the store along with a list of things they already had at the ranch.

The next day, Austin rose early and pulled out all of the required gear. He found an assortment of enameled tin cookware in the bunkhouse, from which he pieced together a basic camp cook kit. The few pans, plates, forks, and coffee cups he selected were wrapped tightly in a small canvas tarpaulin, and this was tied snugly with a length of baling twine. The package was tight enough to keep from rattling when tucked into a pannier.

He went on packing up everything they needed, except for the few supplies they needed to pick up at the store. When it was all piled up, there was quite a mound of camping equipment on the ground. Satisfied, Austin covered the entire pile with a large white canvas tarp, called a manty, and secured it with heavy rocks at each corner. This way the gear would remain unmolested by rain, snow, or early-morning dew, and would be ready for their departure early the next morning.

Austin was summoned to breakfast by an exuberant Jessie, who looked very cute in her cowgirl duds. She was clearly excited about their upcoming adventure on the 7 Bar 7 as well as the picnic ride they had planned for this day. As he approached the porch where she was standing, calling him, Austin could see that she had decorated her eyes and cheeks with glitter to match her shimmering belt. It was a stark reminder to him that, even though Jessie was only a year younger than Kacey, she was far less mature.

Mrs. Crandall had put out a spread for breakfast. Bacon, scrambled eggs, hash browns, and toast were piled high on plates in the middle of the long wooden dining room table. Austin removed his hat and sat down to fuel up for the day, eating several helpings' worth of everything that was offered. He'd nearly forgotten how nice it could be to have a motherly figure around the house. Usually, he just ate a bowl of instant oatmeal and drank a few cups of coffee before his day began.

As they ate, Austin described what was in store for them on the day's ride. Mrs. Crandall was still unsure about the whole plan; She expressed concern about the fact that she hadn't been on a horse in nearly a decade. Austin did his best to calm her nerves.

"Ma'am, I'm certain that you'll pick it right up again," the young cowboy said. "It's just like riding a bike, no different. Heck, Mr. Crandall hopped right on Wiley and got back into the swing of things."

"Well, we'll see, Austin. I'm not so sure about this," Mrs. Crandall said. "I got a pretty bad scare last time I rode, got bucked off and broke my wrist."

This concerned Austin. The horse he had picked out for Mrs. Crandall was a good, steady mount, one of the calmest warmbloods he'd come across, but the only thing that would cure her fears was getting her to spend time in the saddle. *Today's ride has to go well,* he thought while chewing on his last piece of toast. Finally, after considering his words, he attempted to sway her.

"Mrs. Crandall, there are a few things you'll never forgive yourself for missing- your wedding day, your child's birth, and the view between your horse's ears up at the lookout we're going to. Now, you've gone two-for-two so far. What do you say we make it a perfect sweep?" He looked across the table at her with an easy smile on his face, but his eyes were serious.

"Well...okay," she replied, blushing slightly. "That horse you've got for me had better be good, though!"

"Yes, ma'am. Old Jax, he's a peach. We'll be just fine. Now let's go ride!" Austin said.

With that, they all headed out to the barn. It was the perfect day for a ride. As Austin topped out on the lookout and spied the herd lowing contentedly in the trees below, he looked back at Mrs. Crandall. Her fears had dissipated like a spring storm cloud as soon as she set her jeans into the saddle. Now she was trotting along, joking with Jessie and Mr. Crandall, and her smile was a mile wide.

Austin now knew that they would all be going to the roundup, and his thoughts immediately turned to Kacey. He could hardly wait for the dance this evening to tell her that he would, indeed, be looking for a dry place to sleep. Austin hoped they would get a chance to pick up where they left off at Cow Camp.

17 Red's Ridge

The cattle drive started out at a leisurely pace, with everyone meeting at the Langston's 7 Bar 7 headquarters around 9 AM. Trucks and trailers streamed in through the large timber-framed gate and formed a loosely-defined line in the closest pasture, each driver taking care to leave plenty of room between their rig and the next. Horses and mules were unloaded and tied to the trailers, where they would soon be saddled or packed. Before that, though, the cattle drive participants walked through the ankle-high grass toward the Langstons' massive log barn to visit over coffee and fresh donuts.

A few of the locals turned to look as Mr. Crandall's fancy horse trailer crunched over the loose gravel driveway and into the field. Most of them had heard about the Texas oil man's purchase and resurrection of the old Kissner Ranch- word traveled quickly even in a remote community like Mirror Valley- but only a few had met him. The cattle drive would be a good occasion for Mr. Crandall and his family to gain proper introduction to their new neighbors. After parking the rig and unloading the horses, the Crandalls stepped out to begin making acquaintances.

Austin stepped lively, anxious to see any familiar face in the barn. He expected Tate and Julie to be inside, as he'd seen his friend's battered truck and trailer in one of the first parking spots, horses tied to the side. Instead of seeing the lanky horseshoer and his lady, though, Austin stepped around the barn's open sliding door and straight into a short, well-built cowboy. The men both reeled, stumbling backward from the surprising contact.

"Pardon me," Austin said quickly, embarrassed.

"No, you're alright. My fault," the shorter man replied in a low tone. He looked Austin over carefully, measuring the tall Texan. It was an oddly tense moment between two strangers with no history together, Austin realized. Slowly, the shorter man met Austin's eyes and locked them in a steely gaze.

"I'm Austin Mathers," the Texan said, extending his hand. He hoped the other cowboy would see fit to stop staring at him like a bird dog on point. His words took a moment to register with the man, but soon Austin saw a flicker of recognition in the cowboy's cold grey eyes.

"Oh, so you're the mysterious Texas hand, huh?" the man replied, shaking Austin's hand a little too firmly. "I'm Hunter Langston, and I've heard of you…"

"Pleased to meet you, Hunter," Austin said warily. "Hopefully you haven't heard anything bad."

"Nope, not yet. I've been meanin' to get to know

you, though. You've been swimmin' in some precious water, if you know what I mean," Hunter said flatly. He eyeballed the tall Texan once more, but more casually this time.

"I'm not sure I know what you mean," Austin replied.

"I'm talking about a certain young girl that means the world to me. Kacey told me all about you a while back," Hunter said.

Austin's eyes lit up at the mention of Kacey Loftus. Hardly a minute had passed that he didn't think of her. She was in his mind from the minute he rolled out of bed to the minute his head hit the pillow. *Apparently this Hunter guy feels like Kacey is his responsibility,* Austin thought. *I'd better be careful what I tell him.*

"Kacey's a nice girl. She and I get along just fine," Austin said cautiously. "I think she's got a lot going for her."

Hunter looked at him sternly. "See, that's why I gotta check you out, *hombre*. She's too good to be runnin' with any old buckaroo, only she don't know it sometimes," he said. "That's why I told her to invite you out to our little shindig here," Hunter trailed off, waving his hand toward the barn.

Now it was Austin's turn to make a mental connection: this was Hunter's family's ranch. *Now I've really got to prove I'm a good guy,* Austin thought, *not only is this guy Kacey's guard dog, but his family also owns the biggest ranch in the*

Valley.

"Well, I intend to treat her right, Hunter," Austin said. He'd done nothing with Kacey that could be considered inappropriate, and wished Hunter knew that-but it wasn't his place to tell him. It was Kacey's place.

"You see that you do, Austin," Hunter said, plainly challenging the Texas cowboy. "I'd hate to have to straighten things out."

Austin took this as fair warning. Hunter was a tough guy; Tate had mentioned that fact more than once. Not only was he from rugged ranch stock, which made him strong as rawhide, but he was an accomplished bull rider. His sort ran on hot blood and adrenaline, and viewed dangerous activities with less regard for safety than for thrill. Austin hoped he wouldn't wind up tangling with Hunter. He could scrap, and had handled fights in the past, but never against a man like Hunter.

"I don't intend to do anything I'll need to answer for, friend," Austin replied finally, looking Hunter straight in the eyes. This seemed to suffice with Hunter, who extended his hand again. The two cowboys shook and went their separate ways, having set their ground rules.

Austin went inside the barn and poured himself a cup of coffee, glad to be through with the confrontation. He grabbed a donut off the table and walked over to sit on a hay bale in the barn aisle. A familiar figure made its way over and sat down beside him.

"What did old Hunter want, Austin?" Tate

Sanders asked lowly. He had spied the two men talking from where he had stood in the chow line, and could guess about the subject matter. Tate counted Hunter as a valuable acquaintance, but not a friend like Austin was.

"Oh, not a whole lot," Austin lied. "He was just welcoming me to the ranch, mostly."

"Didn't seem too chummy to me," Tate replied. "I thought, maybe, he was hassling you about Kacey."

"Well, he did mention her, but it's not a big deal."

Tate wasn't convinced. "Yeah, he thinks she hung the moon. They used to go together some, but that was a few years back. I reckon he's a little protective of her yet."

"Tate, you ever have a horse that just wouldn't break? You know- you'd ride it and work it, buck it out every time you put denim to leather, and still it wouldn't come around?" Austin asked.

"I did, once. I had me a Pinto pony some years back that gave me fits. I'd top him out every day, ride him into a thick sweat on cows all day, and the lousy crow bait would still be rollin' his eyes back in his head at the end of the circle. I traded him off to some Amish for a set of horseshoeing tools," Tate replied. "Why do you ask?"

"That guy, Hunter. The look in his eyes is something I ain't run across in men. If he was a horse, he'd be a renegade bronc," Austin said. "He looks like he could win a fistfight with a rattlesnake in a cactus patch."

The Langston family called a brief halt to the

festivities in order to thank everyone for coming and to discuss the drive. The entire group would ride out together to the farthest end of the range, and then spread out to cover the whole pasture. It would be slow going the first day, with much of the high country ground being covered in scrubby Juniper and Aspen trees. Each rider would pick up cattle as they came to them, and would drive their small group to an ancient set of corrals built about halfway between the farthest fence line and the 7 Bar 7 headquarters.

The drive would halt at the corrals and make camp for the night, heading back out the following morning to trail the big herd to headquarters. Dudes were encouraged to try their hand at anything they felt comfortable doing, but were also called on to watch, learn, and ask for assistance whenever they needed it. This was intended to be a fun weekend, Mr. Langston said, and they wanted everyone to be safe.

With the impromptu meeting over, everyone made their way out to the trailers to saddle up. In total, there were nearly forty cowboys, cowgirls, and dudes participating in the drive. After packing the Crandall Ranch's extra mount with a tent and camp supplies, Austin led it over to where Rodney Watts had parked the Hatchet Creek Ranch chuck wagon. Rodney recognized Austin immediately.

"Cookie, would you mind if I tied our pack horse to the wagon? I'm not sure it'd be a good idea for me to pony him and try to move cattle," Austin queried politely, hoping to appeal to the cook's sense of reason.

"Pack horse? Heck, kid, that don't look like no pack horse to me- looks like a genuine Thoroughbred race horse! But if he'll follow, you're welcome to tie him on," Rodney said, smiling. "I'll even unpack that nag up at the corrals for ya, if you want, and high-line him so he don't get sour standin' around waitin' on ya."

"Thanks, Cookie, I'm obliged to you," Austin replied. With that, Austin tied the horse to a metal ring protruding from the wagon box, using a bowline knot to ensure that the horse would not come loose, and walked back over to see how Mr. Crandall was doing with the horses. He'd set out each saddle and bridle so that the Crandall family could get started tacking up. As he rounded the front of the trailer, Mr. Crandall was just tightening the cinch on Wiley. The other two warmblood horses were standing with saddles on and bits in. Austin was pleased to see that his boss had taken initiative, and had seemingly progressed in his dealings with horses.

Quickly, Austin brushed and saddled Digger. The buckskin took the snaffle bit willingly, reminding Austin of just how lucky he was to have a nice cow horse to ride. It only took the young Texan a minute to buckle on his short leather chaps, called chinks, and his gun belt. While bent down, securing a wayward spur strap to its proper place, Austin heard a horse's feet swishing through the pasture grass toward him. The shadow of a horse and rider soon blocked him from the sun's rays.

"Hey, Cowboy, how's life?" a sweet voice said. It was Kacey. Austin's heart pounded instantly, and he considered his answer.

"Just about perfect," he looked up, smiling widely. "There was only one thing missin' on this fine morning, and that was a pretty girl to ride with. Now you're here, and I'm tickled to death." This made her smile and blush slightly.

"Come here," she said warmly, leaning in her saddle toward him. He did as instructed and received a quick kiss for his trouble. "I'm so glad you're here," she said, sitting upright again. Kacey's grey mare eyed Austin warily as he took a step backwards, but stayed still under her rider's calm seat.

Mr. Crandall emerged from the trailer's built-in living quarters and glanced at the pair, smiling.

"Why, Kacey Loftus, don't you just look picture perfect?" the oil man asked rhetorically. "I'd swear you were posin' for a horse catalog photo shoot with that fancy outfit on!" Mr. Crandall spoke the truth, Austin thought, she did look perfect. "Hang on a second, darlin', and I'll introduce you to the family."

Mrs. Crandall and Jessie emerged from the rig, both wearing brand new felt cowboy hats they'd bought in town. Mr. Crandall introduced Kacey to his wife and daughter as "Lefty's daughter, from the general store." This suited Kacey and Austin both just fine, because an introduction of "Austin's girlfriend" would have been news to them. They hadn't really talked about any sort of relationship yet, though both were up for it.

Austin couldn't be sure, but he thought he saw Mrs. Crandall throw a wink his way after shaking Kacey's hand. Maybe she had been a quick study in the ways of young men and women, or maybe Mr. Crandall had been telling her what he'd heard from Lefty concerning Austin and Kacey. Either way, she seemed to sense that there was more than meets the eye going on with the pretty cowgirl.

Jessie seemed to bristle some after the two teenage girls were introduced, which made Austin nervous. He wasn't concerned about her feelings- she was a hormonal teenager that had her heart broken just about every day. She might have thought Austin was hers once, in a roundabout way, but he'd certainly never done anything to spur on that notion and he wouldn't feel sorry for bursting her bubble with the truth. No, he was worried that, possibly, he was unable to hide his affection toward Kacey.

With their horses ready to go, the Crandall Ranch crew mounted up and headed to the open pasture gate where a number of riders sat ahorseback, talking. After a few minutes, Hunter Langston rode up to the front of the group and announced that the drive was starting. He extended his fiery grey gelding into a long, level trot and didn't look back. The other riders settled in behind him in groups of two or three, with the Crandall family sitting about mid-pack. Austin and Kacey intentionally held back, riding out only when Tate and Julie joined them on their horses.

Kacey reined her mare close to Digger's shoulder and reached out for Austin's hand. He took it and the pair locked eyes for a long moment, conveying their mutual affection without words. When it was over, Austin looked up and saw Jessie turn around in her saddle quickly, her mouth agape. Apparently her fears had been confirmed.

The foursome of teenagers chatted and joked the entire way up to the far end of the pasture. It was a beautiful day for a ride, their horses were well rested, and the evening promised to be eventful. When they reached the fence, riders were already streaming out to the east and the west, directed by Hunter from atop his grey.

"Tommy, you can go two sections thataway," Hunter said to a local rancher, pointing east, "then bring your dudes through the blue flats. There ought to be about thirty head of cows in there, and they'll push real easy." The rancher nodded and relayed the directions to his guests, some of whom already looked saddle-weary.

Spying Kacey, Hunter grinned broadly. He tipped his hat to the two ladies and, spotting Tate, his eyes lit up.

"Tate, it's about time you got up the nerve to ask old Julie out!" Hunter said. News of Tate and Julie's relationship was not new, but Hunter never rejected an opportunity to give his former rodeo teammate a hard time.

"Yeah, well, she may as well have just double-hocked me and dragged me to the branding fire like a new calf," Tate retorted. "She made up her mind that she wanted to burn her iron into my hide, so here I am." This reply was followed with a wink and a smile toward Julie, who could appreciate a little joking at her own expense.

"Kacey, I had a talk with Mr. Wonderful here this mornin' on your account," Hunter continued, waving a hand toward Austin. "He and I have come to an understandin', but that don't mean I ain't gonna see what he's made of." The stout bull rider looked from Austin to Kacey and back, daring them to say something. They didn't, so he continued.

"You know, we've got near about everything covered as far as pushin's concerned. Lotta folks came out, which is great," Hunter said. "But we still need to get old Curly out from Red's Ridge, and my new *amigo* Austin is just the man for the job."

Tate and Kacey stiffened slightly at Hunter's words, though Austin wasn't sure why. He decided he would ask later, after they were out of Hunter's earshot. Julie couldn't wait that long, though.

"You mean that old Longhorn bull? He's been up here since you were wearing short pants and riding stick horses, Hunter. Never comes down except at night, and that's only to screw up the Angus line by breeding Longhorn blood into it. He's probably dead, as old as he is…" Julie trailed off. She hoped Hunter was just picking on Austin, trying to rattle him. Sending him after a wily Longhorn bull like Curly was dangerous business.

"Nope, he's up there. I seen him myself this summer when I rode up to go fishin'," Hunter replied. "He's got horns about seven feet wide now, must go about eighteen hundred pounds. It's time for him to quit screwing up our breeding program- we're gonna send him to the locker plant once old Austin brings him in."

Austin wasn't sure what to do. He was capable

with a horse and a rope, and proficient with a pistol if worst came to worst, but something told him that catching Curly might be a dangerous undertaking. Nevertheless, he had been challenged to do something, and he'd do his best to succeed. He looked over at Kacey, who was fixing Hunter with a steely gaze. She didn't approve of her friend's hazing, but knew that any vocal admonishment of Hunter would only cheapen Austin in everyone's eyes, so she kept her mouth shut.

Departing from Hunter's post, Tate led the four riders to the area known as Red's Ridge. It was a deep canyon, nearly fifty feet from top to bottom, and about a mile long. A spring bubbled out of the rocky pitch at its top and created a rippling stream that proceeded down the draw. At the bottom, the canyon was scarcely ten feet wide in some spots, with rock outcroppings all but closing off the stream's downward progress, but opened up into sizeable meadows in others. It was the perfect habitat for a wild bull to call home.

Tate reined in his bay, Whiskey, and waited for the others. From their high vantage point they could see down the entire length of the canyon. A seemingly out-of-place red spire of rock jutted high above the canyon walls from the middle of a meadow. This was the area's namesake: Red's Ridge.

When Austin came close, Kacey shot him a worried look and quickly urged him to be cautious. She and Julie would ride along the top of the canyon walls, looking for any signs that the bull may have moved. Austin and Tate decided to ride down into the deep canyon and push it from top to bottom. With any luck, the bull would make its way out onto the flats and join up with the other riders' groups of cattle. It sounded good in theory, but both cowboys knew that if catching old Curly was that simple, the Langstons would have done it long ago.

Austin and Tate both stepped down from their saddles and tightened their cinches, then picked their way down the rocky pitch and into the canyon. For nearly an hour, they saw nothing but an occasional mule deer or coyote. The girls stayed within sight most of the time, though when the canyon walls became sheer cliffs and the valley became narrow, they were not visible. It was hot in the canyon, with the tall walls robbing the riders of a cooling breeze. Sweat dripped off Austin's brow and onto his saddle horn, then slowly ran down the pommel and onto his saddle blanket.

They were approaching the tall red rock spire called Red's Ridge, riding side by side through the unusually lush grass of the surrounding meadow. Suddenly, the sound of crashing brush erupted from the base of the ridge on the right side. Snapping his head toward the sound, Austin laid eyes on the biggest Longhorn bull he had ever seen. It was a monstrous animal with a beautiful red and white coat. The bull's horns were easily seven feet wide, Austin thought, and they gleamed in the bright sunlight.

The bull stood with its rear end pressed against the vertical rock face and tipped its head from side to side, causing the massive horns to dip and rise like tree branches in a wind storm. Austin was surprised to see the animal take a stand- most cattle would simply run around the spire and keep on going down the draw. He expressed this to Tate as they rode closer, and his friend answered matter-of-factly.

"He can't go around. That red rock only lets you on down the canyon on the left. It's a natural corral on this side," Tate said.

"So we've got to get him herded around this thing without lettin' him go back up the draw?" Austin beckoned. He wasn't sure a hundred men on horses could stop this behemoth from breaking through and going back up the canyon. Certainly two riders couldn't do it.

"Well, that's the idea," Tate replied. "It ain't possible, but that's what we gotta do." The two cowboys sat silently, their horses alert to the presence of the bull. Curly was working himself into a frenzy, bellowing out loudly and pawing the ground. It seemed that the longer the two teens were in his area, the angrier the bull became. They didn't have much time to make a decision about what to do with him.

The pair had been sitting there long enough, apparently, and the Longhorn bull could take no more. He ran at the riders at breakneck pace, quickly closing the distance. Austin reacted by instinct, shaking out a huge loop in his rope as the bull continued its charge. When it came so close that he could smell the old bull, he reined Digger out of the way of its swinging horns.

As Curly passed him, Austin spurred Digger into a full gallop and tore after him. Gaining ground, he began swinging the loop above his head. The heavy rawhide reata he had tied hard and fast to his saddle horn had been hanging in Austin's bunkhouse when he moved in, and it was significantly longer than the thirty foot rodeo rope he normally carried. He was glad for the extra length now, bearing down on an animal with headgear like Curly had. Just getting a loop around the horns would take up over half the length of his normal rope.

The canyon wall was closing in on Austin quickly, and he knew that, if he didn't catch the bull now, it would disappear back up the draw, possibly forever. He would be known as a cowboy who couldn't catch, and that didn't sit well with Austin. He had to drape the heavy rawhide loop over the bull's horns, and fast.

Austin buried his heels into Digger's sides and threw the loop with all his might. In what looked to be slow-motion, the reata settled nicely over both horn tips, then tightened above the bull's eyes as the animal continued running forward into the noose. Expertly, Austin flipped his extra slack over the bull's back, so it dragged on the ground on the right side of the running bovine. He had laid his trip perfectly.

The canyon wall was getting so close now that Austin could see individual rocks and tufts of grass. Undaunted, he reined Digger hard to the left and waited for the running bull to take up all of the slack in his rope. What happened next would make a freeway car wreck look tame. The bull hit the end of Austin's rope with so much force that it didn't simply spin and fall down. Curly did a complete circle in midair, landing on his back with all four feet facing skyward. The force of the impact pulled Digger right off his still-churning hooves, and Austin was ejected from the saddle instantly. The young Texan flew face first into the canyon wall, which was only twenty feet away when Austin had reined Digger to the left.

For a long moment it looked like all three participants in the wreck had breathed their last breath. Neither the horse nor the bull stirred at all. Tate came galloping up as fast as Whiskey could run, and dismounted with all the grace that God gave a water bug. Regaining his feet, he ran past Digger and straight to Austin with tears burning down his cheeks. He thought, surely, that his friend had just killed himself while trying to prove something to some idiot bull rider.

"Austin!" Tate hollered as he ran. "Austin, can you hear me?" He pulled up short of where his friend lay in the dirt and tried to prepare himself for the worst. Gingerly, he took the final few steps to his friend. He cautiously reached a trembling hand out and touched Austin's shoulder, speaking lowly. "Austin, buddy, are you still with me?"

Austin stirred slightly, his legs weaving from side to side. Slowly he came to and realized that someone was talking to him, asking him if he was okay.

"O-o-oowwww!" Austin exclaimed, his face still pressed against the canyon wall. "What was THAT!?"

"You took a bad spill, brother." It was Tate, Austin knew.

Cautiously Austin flexed his fingers and his toes, then his legs and arms. He turned around very easily and saw what looked like a scene out of a painting. The valley they were in was absolutely beautiful, there was a gorgeous bay cow horse cropping grass, and a bull lying at the end of a rope. Digger had risen from the sandy ground he'd fallen down on and was now taking careful steps backwards to keep tension on the rope, just as he'd been trained. Tate stood close by, and Austin could see tears on his cheeks.

"What's the matter, Tate?" Austin asked. "Are you alright?" This brought on another bout with tears from the gangly horseshoer.

"Nothing's the matter, friend. I'm just glad you're okay," Tate said, hiding his eyes. "I thought you were dead. That was the worst wreck I've ever seen!"

"Heck, I'm all set. Just a little scraped up is all," Austin replied, pulling himself to his feet. He squeezed Tate's shoulder affectionately, then stepped back toward Digger.

As he walked, Austin thought about Kacey- was she still watching? She and Julie had been on the wall, riding, he remembered. Looking up, he saw her sitting atop the beautiful grey mare, her head in her hands. She was crying, he could tell. *She must not have seen me get up*, he thought. *She probably thinks I'm dead!*

Tate came plodding back to Austin's side and handed him his battered felt hat. Dusting it off, he let out a shout that reverberated off the canyon walls. Kacey looked up and saw Austin waving his hat, and she began to cry once more in earnest.

The bull was still, lying on its side in the dirt. Austin replayed the wreck in his mind and wondered if, with the severe impact, the animal had broken its neck. It took a long moment of study before he determined that the bull was still breathing, its sides heaving in shallow breaths. Austin went to his horse and, after giving Digger a reassuring rub on the neck, pulled a small coil of rope from beneath the strings of his saddle.

Austin went to the bull and expertly hog-tied one of its front feet together with the opposite side hind leg. With the hooves bound, the bull wouldn't be able to get up when it came to. Looking at the horns, Austin decided to impose another precautionary method. He pulled some slack in his rawhide reata and arranged the loop over the bull's neck, then behind the remaining front leg. Digger pulled up the slack, which pinned the bull's front leg to its neck. When the big sire came to and tried to gore Austin, it would have no leverage to do so.

Tate walked up and looked down on the bull, then let out a low whistle. It was the largest bovine he'd ever seen, a throwback to the first herds of cattle that had been brought to the area by trail drovers over a hundred years earlier. This sort of hearty animal had been brought up the trail from Old Mexico by the hundreds of thousands, long before any road existed. *It almost seemed a shame to send a relic like this one to the slaughterhouse*, Tate thought.

"Well, Austin, I don't think we're gonna get this old bull to just lead like a show pony back down to the ranch," Tate said. "What do you reckon we do with him?"

"Hunter said he wanted us to bring his bull in, right?" Austin smiled, reaching into his pocket. He removed a well used jackknife and folded out a razor-sharp blade. "I'm fixin' to bring him his bull!"

The two cowboys took pains to clean and disinfect as they went about castrating the bull. It was quite a job to do on such an old animal, and they worried a few times about the amount of blood loss that was occurring. With small bull calves, castration was as simple as making a small incision and removing the necessary parts- there was little worry about infection or blood loss. But on a big bull like Curly, they made sure to exhaust their canteens and the emergency bottle of iodine that Austin carried in his saddle bag.

Presently, the bull began to stir. Satisfied that Curly would live to see another day, they quickly pulled Austin's ropes and mounted their horses. The old Longhorn thrashed about for a while, then struggled to its feet. It took a look at the cowboys and their horses, possibly contemplating another charge, but thought better of it. With a loud bellow, the bull trotted back up the draw and left them alone.

Tate led Austin through the remainder of the canyon and out onto the flats below. As they appeared out of the steep depression, Julie and Kacey rose from their seat on a rotting log and walked to meet them. Swinging down from the saddle, Austin was nearly squeezed to death by Julie. Tears streamed down her face, and she sobbed silently into his shoulder that she was glad he was okay.

Kacey stood back from the rest, eyeing Austin warily. When Julie turned to Tate, Austin took a step toward his girl. She backpedalled a few steps, still terrified by the wreck. Austin kept walking toward her, slowly at first, then faster, until she could not back away fast enough to escape him. His eyes pleaded with her. *Please come here, Kacey,* he thought. *I'm okay, don't be scared.*

Suddenly she could take no more. She lunged at him and hugged him as tightly as possible, pushing herself into him so hard that they nearly lost their balance. Her arms began to pound on his back in an expression of anger at the fear she had felt, and he thought she might like him to release her. Instead, though, he held her tightly and let her anger subside. As sore as he would surely be after the wreck, Austin reasoned that a few more bruises on his ribs were worth the pain if Kacey felt better afterward.

Kacey finally pulled her face from where she'd hidden it in Austin's shirt, and he could see that her eyes were bright red. She had been through an emotional roller coaster, and he doubted if she had stopped crying for a single moment since he galloped after the big Longhorn. Fresh tears streamed down her face in earnest, and it choked Austin up some to see her that way.

"I- I- I thought you were…." Kacey didn't finish. Instead, she buried her face in his shirt once again. He clutched her tightly to him and tried to soothe her.

"Kacey, honey, I'm sorry to have scared you like that," Austin managed through clenched teeth. "I didn't have time to think, I just went."

"Well it scared me half to death!" she cried. "I don't get scared like this, not ever! I've seen some awful things, too, but nothing that shook me up like what you just did." Kacey was less hysterical, but still could not look directly into Austin's eyes. He kissed her forehead and ran a dirty hand through her deep brown hair, trying to calm her.

"What do you say we go down to the corrals and take care of the horses, hun? I'm sure Digger could use a rest after that spill we took," Austin suggested. Kacey didn't respond for a long time. She simply held him, her face still wet with tears. After a few long moments, Austin led her over to her grey mare and turned her to face the saddle. She slowly stepped into her left stirrup and swung aboard.

Tate had Digger ready for Austin to mount nearby, and when he swung aboard Austin detected the first hint of soreness that was sure to overtake his entire body in the next twelve hours. He'd be sure to find a bottle of horse liniment in Rodney's wagon as soon as he got to camp. Both he and Digger could use a thorough dose of the unpleasantly aromatic rub-down medicine. Disregarding the pain, Austin rode so close to Kacey on the way down to camp that their legs touched much of the time. He wanted to make sure she was okay.

They were the last four riders to make their way into camp that evening, and everyone gathered around as they rode in. Most in the group noticed Austin's torn shirt and skinned up forearms, as well as both of the cowboys' dirty, bloody hands. Hunter Langston had been holding court on a wooden corral fence, undoubtedly telling jokes and spinning yarns about horses and cattle. When the riders rode up, though, he silently watched them approach. Sizing up the situation and seeing the remnants of tears on Kacey's face, he pursed his lips tightly.

Austin rode Digger directly up to the fence and looked Hunter in the eye. From his saddle, he was at eye level with the bull rider, who sat on the top rail of the corral. Nobody, not even the old-timers in the crowd, saw fit to speak. The air was tense and everyone knew it, though they didn't know why. After a long silence, Austin reached into his saddle bag and removed a bloody mason jar containing the bull's reproductive hardware.

"I got your bull for you, and nearly got myself killed doin' it," Austin growled. He tossed the jar to Hunter. "I'll be lucky if Digger don't come up lame in the next few weeks- old Curly yanked us right off our feet. Tossed me face first into the canyon wall. Tate thought I was dead."

"Dang, *hombre*, I never thought you'd lay eyes on that bull," Hunter said, nearly speechless. He realized that his act of hazing had nearly been a total catastrophe.

"We laid eyes on him, all right, and he's a big boy. Did three flips when I tripped him, and he was out like a light," Austin said flatly. He leaned in close, so nobody but Hunter could hear what he said next.

"And you see that girl, the one with the tears still comin' out her face?" Hunter nodded slightly, knowing that he was talking about Kacey. Austin continued, "I might feel like hell in the morning, on account of the wreck, but I'd take that a hundred times over before I ever let her go through something like this again. Your little wild goose chase has got me purt'near killed, and it's got her hysterical. She's shakin' like a leaf. If you ever do somethin' like that again, I'll do to you what I did to that bull. Is that clear?" he asked pointedly, and added emphasis by pointing a finger at the mason jar, affixing Hunter with a gaze so vicious that it seemed that the cowboy might fall off the fence.

With that, Austin led Tate, Julie, and Kacey to an open corral where they unsaddled quietly. As they did, everyone else at the roundup kept their distance. They could still sense the tension in the air, and didn't want to cause any more problems. The four teens slowly walked over to Rodney's chuck wagon to see about a cup of coffee, and were appreciative when the cook simply poured their cups full without asking about the day's work. Rodney was an old-time hand, and he could see it in their faces without asking any questions.

Austin saw his boss, Mr. Crandall, and his family sitting around a fire nearby. He took Kacey by the arm and guided her over to the company of his surrogates because he did not want her to be alone. She still had a faraway look in her eyes. They sat down around the fire and Austin slowly told of the day's adventures, keeping a close eye on Kacey as he recounted his confrontation with Curly. When she started to tear up, Mrs. Crandall moved close to Kacey and held her hand in a show of support.

Mr. Crandall sat stoically through the whole tale, but had to compose himself immediately after. When he attempted to speak, his voice broke hollowly. Finally, he was able to muster a few words to his young hand.

"Son, I'm glad you're alright. We don't want anything to happen to you, and I don't care if it's my cows or someone else's- you don't need to be doin' things like that," he said, then looked away. Austin realized that his boss was dabbing his eyes with the silk wild rag that hung around his neck. Mr. Crandall was crying on his account.

Mrs. Crandall, Jessie, and Kacey were all sobbing quietly too, and Austin felt a pang of remorse for ever taking Hunter's order to catch the Longhorn bull. If he'd been a little smarter, he could have avoided all of the teary eyes. *I was just cowboying, trying to prove myself,* Austin thought. *But all the approval in the world ain't worth hurting these people. Never again.*

It occurred to Austin that he'd never felt as close to anyone as he did to the people he was with in Mirror Valley. Everyone from Julie to Mr. Crandall, even Wendy down at The Lamplighter, made him feel like he had a place with them. And Kacey, with the way she reacted to his near-death episode, had shown him the sort of devotion that he'd only read about in old paperback westerns. The realization that people cared for him like that caught him off guard, and he had to turn to his own wild rag for a moment.

18 Sorting it Out

Austin woke violently from his dream and looked around. He wasn't immediately sure where he was- all he knew is that, thankfully, the nightmare he'd been having was over with. In it, he'd been lying on the ground helplessly, and an angry bull was bearing down on him with horns as sharp as hunting knives. Just as the bull had lowered its' head to gore him, he'd woken up in a cold sweat.

He slowly sat upright, becoming aware of his surroundings, and peeled his canvas bedroll cover away from where it stuck to the clammy skin on his chest. The night air had been crisp and cool when he decided to sack out on the ground, and he'd nodded off instantly with a stomach full of Rodney Watts' tasty chuckwagon cooking. It had been a fitting end to a rough and eventful day. Now the chilly night air calmed him, but also caused him to shiver.

Kacey had not been herself since she'd seen

Austin cheat death at the end of his own long reata the previous afternoon. The 7 Bar 7 roundup, which both Kacey and Austin had looked forward to as an opportunity for some alone time, had become very somber the second he had spurred his horse after the Langston family's renegade Longhorn bull. Austin had planned to sack out in Kacey's small canvas wall tent, along with her friend Lisa, but after sitting silently through dinner and avoiding the raucous crowd around the bonfire completely, he knew Kacey was not in any mood for romance. She had distanced herself from Austin, eyeing him warily as they ate. When he'd tried to comfort her, she was cold and curt. *She's still scared,* Austin told himself. *She hates me for scaring her like I did. I'm sure she'll come around, hopefully soon.*

Austin had wisely brought an old-fashioned cowboy bedroll to the roundup, and he decided that lying out under the stars just in front of Kacey's tent was the best course of action. Lisa had sought lodging elsewhere, sensing that her girlfriend didn't need to be bothered, so it was just Kacey and Austin. If she had needed him, or wanted him, he was close by; but it would also give her time and space to sort things out. He'd given her an awkward hug after walking her to the tent door and told her to call on him for anything she might need.

The small clearing where Austin had set up the tent was out of view from any of the other roundup participants. A small stand of Aspens sat between their camp and the corrals, and past that lay the chuck wagon. All of the other riders had set up their separate camps on the far end of the clearing, and, looking out, Austin could see nothing but the silhouetted treetops and the bright stars beyond them.

Behind him, he heard a faint rustling in the tent. The door's heavy metal zipper made a loud noise as Kacey opened it and looked out. There was a long pause before either of them said anything.

"Hey," she said softly to the cowboy seated in front of her.

"Hi," he returned with a weary voice. Austin turned to look at her, standing with her upper body leaning out through the tent opening. Her wavy brown hair cascaded down over her shoulders, partially concealing the "Mirror Valley High Rodeo" logo on her oversized t-shirt. From where Austin sat, he couldn't tell if Kacey had a pair of shorts on or not.

Both of them had hung their chaps on the tent's ridge pole above the door. They acted like an awning, casting a shadow over the door even in the nearly pitch-black darkness. The chaps swayed from side to side in the slight mountain breeze, concealing and revealing Kacey's face over and over. Cowboy and cowgirl shared a long moment without talking before she pushed her way free of the canvas shelter and came to him.

"I want you to come inside," she said determinedly. Her hand reached out and tousled his hair gently. "It's getting cold out here." Austin could clearly see through her flimsy excuse, but chose not to argue. He simply did as he was told and dragged his bedroll in through the tent door. *Maybe she's through with being upset about the wreck,* he wished.

Inside, Austin struck a match and raised it to a hissing lantern. The transparent cloth mantle ignited with a telltale pop, and soft yellow light blanketed the inside of the tent. He knelt down next to a small woodstove and blew a lungful of air at the faint red embers that remained from earlier in the evening. With some dry tinder added on top, the coals began to smoke steadily, and a flame soon appeared.

Kacey was sitting on the makeshift bed that Austin had fabricated for her. He had collected a few springy spruce boughs and laid them on the uneven ground, then covered the bed with a canvas manty. It was crude, only a foot above the ground, but infinitely more comfortable than lying on the hard mountain soil. She had laid out her bedroll on the mattress and, had she not been so flustered about Austin's near undoing, would have slept comfortably with the scent of tree sap in her nose.

Still on his knees, Austin turned to face her. She was leaning back on her elbow, watching him build the warming fire. Her bare legs were extended in his direction, trim ankles crossed. The legs seemed to go on for days until they disappeared beneath Kacey's shirt, and Austin had to try hard to keep his eyes moving upward, toward hers. When his gaze fixed on her face, she met it with a pleasant smile and slid back on the bed to make room for him.

The fire inside the stove began to crackle and pop loudly as the dry chunks of dead Aspen trunk were engulfed in flame. Turning back to the stove, Austin spun the door-mounted damper until it was partially closed to slow the fire; the logs inside would provide heat for several hours without additional stoking. He rose and shut off the fuel supply to the lantern next. The tent went dark slowly as the excess gas hissed its way out through the mantle and burned off.

Twin rays of deep orange firelight were cast onto the dirt floor of the tent through symmetrical vents in the partially-open damper. The beacons brightened and dimmed as the flames licked their way around the logs inside the metal stove door, but kept their respective shapes on the ground and extended nearly all the way to the far tent wall, illuminating only a small portion of their quarters. Austin's eyes quickly adjusted to the relative darkness, and he stepped over both his and Kacey's saddles where they lay on the floor, making his way to the bed.

Once there, he sat softly and slid sideways beneath the flannel and canvas sleeping bag, coming to rest when he felt Kacey's body pressing against his. Her arm came to rest around his midsection, and when she squeezed him tightly, pain shot through his ribcage and took his breath away. He winced, his body tensing instantly. She quickly released her grasp and, after a moment, Kacey spoke.

"Austin, sorry!" she exclaimed. "I didn't mean to hurt you."

"No, no, it's okay, sweetheart," Austin said through clenched teeth. "I guess I must've busted a couple of ribs in that wreck." Regaining his composure, he turned gingerly to face her. The faint light from the stove door illuminated her pretty face and reflected in her eyes, and

Austin noticed that she looked exhausted. *She must not have slept a wink so far*, he surmised.

"Serves me right, I guess, for doing something so dangerous," Austin continued. This comment brought fresh tears to Kacey's eyes, and he immediately wished he hadn't reminded her of the wreck. He pulled her tight to him and ran his fingers through her hair as she wept quietly into his shoulder. Finally, she was able to speak again.

"Austin, I'm not sure why I'm acting like this- so sour. I've never been one to get emotional or moody," Kacey said. "But, today I was so scared! I can't explain it, and I feel terrible that I've been so cold to you tonight. You didn't do anything to deserve that," she said. Momentarily, she considered her next words. "I guess I must really care about you, more than I ever thought I could care about anybody…"

"Does that bother you?" Austin asked casually.

"It's something new, unfamiliar, but it doesn't really bother me," Kacey replied. "It's just gonna take a little getting used to, you know?"

"I know it. I've never really concerned myself with anything other than looking out for old number one," Austin said. "Now I'm constantly thinking about you, how you're affected by what I do. Me riding after that Longhorn today was my normal self, my old self. I never second-guessed it- it was just what needed to be done. But looking up at you on the cliff, seeing you crying, that hurt worse than any wreck I've ever had."

"Then, when we got into camp and I saw how worried Mr. Crandall was, it made it worse. I told myself this afternoon that I'd never do anything like that again- I'd never scare y'all like I did." Austin's voice was barely a whisper as he finished, but he kept his composure.

Kacey considered her words carefully, and then spoke. "I don't want you to stop being yourself, Austin. I like you just the way you are! But that did shake me, seeing you flying off your horse like that. It was like I'd been kicked in the stomach by a mule- I've never been physically hurt by something that happened to someone else. It's gonna take some adjustment, I think..."

"I'll do my best to stay out of dangerous situations like that from now on, Kacey," Austin promised. "I can't say it'll be all sunshine and roses, but I'll do my best."

"If we both try, we'll be okay," Kacey said matter-of-factly. "Now, enough of this somber talk- let's get some shuteye! I'm bushed." With that, the couple settled into one another's arms tightly and left their worries behind. Sunrise would see them rise refreshed both physically and emotionally. The events of the previous day were forgotten by the time Rodney filled their breakfast plates with heaping piles of eggs, potatoes, and thick bacon.

After helping Rodney with the dishes and packing up their camping gear, Austin went to the corral to inspect their horses. Despite the careful doctoring he'd received the night before, Digger was noticeably stiff and sore from the wreck. His movements were jerky, and Austin had already decided that it wouldn't do to ride his beloved buckskin on this day. He had spent some time before breakfast working with the Crandall's pack horse, which had never been under a riding saddle outside of an arena.

Austin arranged to tie his buckskin gelding to the back of Rodney's chuck wagon. The wagon was nearly empty on the way back to the ranch, all of the groceries having been eaten by hungry riders. With extra room and capacity, Rodney was happy to carry Austin's pack horse's load, freeing up the Thoroughbred for a riding saddle. Austin would ride the converted jumping horse down the 7 Bar 7 headquarters.

Hunter Langston was again delegating the work for the day, positioning riders on all sides of the herd. He rode over to the corral where Austin, Kacey, Tate, and Julie were saddling up their mounts and, in an uncharacteristic move, dismounted from his prancing grey horse. Hunter strode over to the corral fence and spoke to the two cowboys.

"Austin, Tate, I'd like it if you two would take the left point today," he said cautiously. "I'm pretty sure these cows will trail on alright, but it won't hurt to have a couple of real hands steering the ship."

"You sure?" Austin asked. "I'm not as well mounted as I was yesterday…" Austin trailed off with no inflection. His anger toward Hunter had passed with the morning sun, and he was back to his general good nature. The fact that he was on an unproven cow horse was a real concern, though, and he wanted Hunter to know all the facts before appointing him to ride point- a position at the front of the herd which required a competent horse and rider.

Hunter dismissed his concern with a wave. "I'm sure you'll be just fine, Austin." With that, he remounted the grey and loped off, ending the discussion. Austin looked over at Tate, who simply shrugged and finished cinching his saddle down on Whiskey's back. The lanky farrier didn't act concerned about Austin's horse situation, and Austin took it as a good sign. They would ride the left point and, with any luck, the Crandall Ranch would have another cow-worthy horse in the barn if the jumper performed well.

The four teens mounted and rode over to the large holding pen to start the day's drive. Julie and Kacey were assigned to ride with a group of dudes, including the Hudgens family, who had returned to the Hatchet Creek Ranch from Ohio a few days before the cattle drive. Jesse Hudgens, the family's fourteen year old son, had taken to the cowboy lifestyle with aplomb on their first visit earlier in the summer. By the time they returned to Mirror Valley, it was hard to distinguish Jesse from the local ranch kids. His horsemanship skills had improved dramatically since their first visit, and his disrespectful nature and dreadfully disheveled appearance were now gone completely.

Mr. and Mrs. Crandall's daughter Jessie had noticed the young Ohio dude almost immediately, and her misdirected angst regarding Austin's relationship with Kacey was quickly forgotten. The youngsters were seen following one another around the fire at the mountain camp, and were riding close beside one another as the herd moved out toward the 7 Bar 7 headquarters. Julie and Kacey noticed this and commented that "The Jesses" were a match made in heaven. It made the two cowgirls smile, and helped an otherwise uneventful day pass by quickly.

The herd trailed smoothly down to headquarters, and Austin had no problems with his new horse. The Thoroughbred gelding, named Pepper, proved to be levelheaded and fairly agile throughout the day, quickly heading off any cows that tried to leave the worn wagon track road they were following. The tall liver chestnut horse did not shy when pressed into thick cover or onto uneven footing. The animal seemed to cover large distances in short order, proving that his long legs and back were good for more than leaping over poles in a show-jumping ring.

As the sun began to set in the western sky, the herd reached ranch headquarters. Austin and Hunter, who had been riding on the right point, loped ahead to open up the pair of swinging gates into the alleyway between the ranch's holding pens. With each bound of Pepper's canter, Austin felt a biting pain from his cracked ribs. It was very uncomfortable, but bearable through gritted teeth and concentrated movements in time with the horse's gait. The cattle moved between the riders and spread out in the alley, calves sticking closely to their mothers' sides. When the entire herd was in the aisle, Austin and Hunter closed themselves in with the cattle, along with two other riders, to begin sorting.

Carefully, the four riders divided the cattle into eight separate pens along the alleyway, whistling and slapping their chaps when a cow or calf proved stubborn. Austin's horse worked exceptionally well, which pleased not only him but also Mr. Crandall, who sat ahorseback next to the pens. Kacey sat on the fence next to him, and the two began to talk.

"Well, Kacey, it seems that boy has no end to what he can do if he puts his mind to it," Mr. Crandall said, waving a cigar stub in Austin's direction. "It makes me mighty proud, havin' him around."

"Yes Sir, he's something else," Kacey replied, never taking her eyes off the young Texan. "I'm sure glad you decided to buy the old Kissner Ranch. Without you, I'd have never gotten to know Austin."

"It seems like things just came together, doesn't it?" Mr. Crandall asked.

"Sometimes that happens- when things are right, they just happen smoothly," she replied. She thought for a moment before speaking again, but continued in earnest. "I'm taken with him something serious, Sir, I'm sure you've noticed, and he feels the same way. Never, in a million years, did I think I'd be head over heels for some Texas cowboy, but here you guys are, and here's me turning into a puddle every time I look at him."

"He's a fine young man, Kacey. I've often thought that, if I had a son, I'd want him to be like Austin," Mr. Crandall said sincerely. "It's not just the ropin' and ridin' that I like, either. You see how he's soft on that horse, workin' with it to make the right thing easy and the wrong thing uncomfortable? That's how he goes about everything in his life. He's calm and collected, he tries hard to make things simple and easy for others, and he's got a way of relating to everything that makes him magnetic."

"I know what you mean, Mr. Crandall," Kacey said. "That horse he's riding now wasn't mean, but he was antsy as all get-out. This morning, even though Austin was stiff and sore, he rolled out of bed an hour before I did to check on Digger, and then started working with that one he's on now." She shook her head slightly, as if still in disbelief. "It's little stuff like that, putting the needs of others- even animals- ahead of himself, that makes him something altogether special. Now look at that horse- you'd think he'd been born and bred on the ranch."

The cowboys finished sorting the cattle and exited the pens for a well-deserved rest. Their horses were quickly unsaddled and turned loose in an open corral, and they rolled in the pen's short grass. When they regained their footing, the lathered, sweaty areas beneath the saddles and breast collars were caked in soothing muddy dust. A bale of hay was tossed into the pen, divided into four equal sections, and the sorting horses settled contentedly into eating a hard-earned meal.

With all of the other riders already unsaddled and working on their first round of drinks in the ranch's traditional chow hall, Austin and the other three sorting riders, including Hunter, gathered on the fence for an impromptu meeting with Mr. Langston, Hunter's dad and the ranch's owner. It seemed strange to Austin that he would be included in the gathering. *What do they want me in on this for?* he wondered. *I'm not so familiar with this ranch that they need my two cents…* Just the same, it wasn't in Austin's makeup to shirk any obligation, deserved or not, so he stood with the others dusty riders and listened to the ranch boss.

"Young man, I can see from your torn-up duds and stiff-and-sore walk that you've been through a wreck. I can only imagine that you're the hand that tripped up old Curly…" Mr. Langston said to Austin. "I'm Kip Langston, and I'm pleased to meet you," he said, extending his hand.

"Nice to meet you, Mr. Langston," Austin said, grasping the old rancher's hand firmly. "I'm obliged to you for inviting me and Mr. Crandall's family out to join in. As for Curly- well, I'm sorry I couldn't bring him in on the hoof, but I figured givin' him the knife was better than losin' him altogether," Austin said, looking squarely into Mr. Langston's eyes.

"Heck, son, I'm tickled to death that you cut him out of our breeding program. It was a stupid stunt, Hunter sending you to go chase that old feral bull,"Mr. Langston sent a sharp glance at his son, admonishing him in front of the other men. "And you didn't deserve that, but you did it anyway. Takes a lot of jam to go after a heavy set of horns like that, and even more to ride point after a wreck like you had."

"Well, thank you Mr. Langston. I'm just glad I could help out," Austin said, trying for Hunter's sake to refrain from smiling with pride. He felt it unnecessary to rub any salt in the young bull rider's wounds. "So what's our next step, then?" he asked, anxious to deflect the attention from himself.

"We're gonna relax tonight, do a little ranch rodeo in the ropin' pen after supper. Tomorrow, though, most everyone's goin' on home. I'd like for you four…" Mr. Langston motioned to the group at hand, "to stick around though, and we'll brand the slicks and cut 'em all off their mommas," the elder Langston said. "We'll throw the cows out into the main herd and ship the young ones off to a winter feed lot we've got leased near the city."

The four riders nodded their acceptance of his invitation and began to make for the chow hall. Mr. Langston hung back to walk with Austin, and the pair began discussing the next day's activities in more detail. It was Austin who spoke first.

"Mr. Langston, I'm not certain I've got a good rope horse healthy enough for work tomorrow," he said apologetically. "My cow horse, Digger, was sored up something fierce this morning on account of tangling with Curly yesterday, and that jumping horse I was sorting on tonight was new to cows this morning…"

"Oh, Austin, I wouldn't worry about it. We've got more horses than Carter's got little liver pills, and I'm sure we can find one for you to heel and drag with tomorrow. I don't expect you'll be wantin' to flank calves, being as you're hurtin' worse than you let on. Broke some ribs, huh?" Mr. Langston eyed him knowingly. He had seen the way Austin had winced in pain whenever he'd reached to open a gate from the back of his horse. It had impressed him, seeing the young man maintain composure while in pain.

"Yes Sir, I believe I might have," Austin replied calmly. "I'll try to pull my weight, though."

"I believe you'll be alright, Son, just takes some time with ribs. I'd say a stiff little rope will save you raisin' your arms as much. It might help your traps stand open, on end, so the calves can just walk into the loop. We've got some nice heel ropes hangin' in the barn. Grab one for tomorrow if you'd like," Mr. Langston said.

"Thank you, Sir. I'll do that," Austin said gratefully. They continued on in silence and entered the chow hall, where the cattle drive participants were just beginning to enjoy a fine dinner of beef steak, beans, potatoes, sourdough biscuits, and salad. It was a fitting feast, reminiscent of, but far more delicious than, the chuck that old-time trail drovers would have eaten, and the entire assembly ate until there was nothing left.

Austin joined Mr. Crandall's family at a table, along with Kacey, Julie, Tate, and the Hudgens family. They were all chatting pleasantly, leaving Austin with his thoughts. He chewed absentmindedly on a biscuit and reminisced about all of the things that had happened since he moved to Mirror Valley. Each event, each memory, seemed to begin and end with Kacey; She was the first person he had met in town. Every time he recalled seeing her, his smile grew faintly. And when he thought about the evening they'd just spent together, working through a rough situation and coming out of it stronger than they had been, he could not help chancing a glance across the handmade table at his lady. Not surprisingly, Kacey was staring right at him. She reached out and took his hand, and, squeezing it, sent him a deep look of affection and satisfaction.

For a moment, everything seemed to drift away from Austin's field of vision. All that remained was a strong, beautiful young cowgirl that he could call his own. *There's no telling what's gonna happen tomorrow, or even tonight, or once school starts up,* Austin thought. *But I know that, no matter what, this is a moment I'll be thinking about for the rest of my life. It's perfect- I'm at home here!*

With a knowing smile, Kacey let go of his hand and rejoined the table's conversation.

19 Texas Tornado

The large red and white Paint mare stood tensely with her head held high above the top rail in Bucking Chute #4, just to the side of the bright orange return alley gate. It was late May, and the day's warm sunshine had given way to a brisk mountain evening. Over the grandstand, the last hint of twilight could be seen above the high-reaching peaks that encircled Mirror Valley, guarding the winding road over Breakheart Pass like sentries on an ever-vigilant night watch. Bright overhead lights cast an intense glow on the deep, moist soil inside the rodeo arena at the High Prairie Equine Center.

Behind the bucking chutes, Austin handed his modified bronc-riding saddle up to Tate, who stood on the raised metal walkway next to the confined mare.

"Cinch 'er down tight, *amigo*," the lanky Texan

said to his friend. Tate simply nodded and turned toward the horse.

The High School Finals Rodeo was a four day event that pitted the best of the best in each rodeo discipline against each other, vying for the title of "Champion" and the gold-plated belt buckle that went along with it. In years past, the location for the Finals was determined before the season began, with the rodeo commission soliciting bids from venues in nearly every major western city. This season, however, the format had been changed: the rodeo team with the most combined points in all disciplines would play host to the big event.

Early in the season, it seemed as if Mirror Valley would have no chance at home field advantage. For a while, it looked like a long shot for the team to send even one competitor on to the national event. In fact, the first three rodeos of the year had seen Mirror Valley's entries miss the short-go-around, or event finals. Then Hunter had come home.

Hunter Langston was leading the national point standings in both bull riding and steer wrestling during his first semester at the University of Wyoming. The college rodeo circuit was no match for the tough youngster, and he had collected seven championship buckles in his first eight rodeos. It seemed that he was a shoo-in for the National Championship in both events. Then, over the Christmas break, Hunter had gone south with a few teammates to spend their vacation roping and chasing girls in Arizona and New Mexico.

After a few weeks of relaxing in the sun, their

competitive spirits got the best of them, and they drove to San Antonio to compete in the famous professional rodeo there. Since there was no rule barring college rodeo cowboys from competing in professional events, they saw no wrong in it, and simply thought of it as a way to pay for their trip with the money they would win.

Hunter did well, making the short-go in both bull riding and saddle-bronc riding, an event which he had competed in during high school. When the finals came around, Hunter got bucked off his bronc, but won the bull ride with a 90 point score in front of a crowd of more than ten-thousand fans. After the 8 second whistle, though, Hunter's bull had thrown him into the arena fence, then turned and stomped on him. Before the bullfighters could get the animal away, Hunter had suffered a concussion and a broken shoulder blade, which ended his rodeo season.

News of the misfortune reached Mirror Valley the next day, and a plan was laid out by the time Hunter got back into town. Without the ability to ride, Hunter's scholarship to the university had been suspended until the following year, leaving him with no school to go back to. Instead, Hunter was hired immediately by the Mirror Valley School District to supervise and coach the Mirror Valley High Rodeo Team. He was, they thought, exactly what the struggling team needed: A proven winner.

Hunter's tutelage provided the team with a spark, and within two weeks the young cowboys and cowgirls were making the event finals. Kacey Loftus collected a buckle in the barrel racing event the next weekend, and the team was quickly on a roll. As the end of the season rolled around, the team had strung together victories in impressive fashion, with Kacey and Austin leading the way. Their remarkable turnaround had, at the season's final rodeo, amassed the team enough points to edge out Clovis, New Mexico for the right to host the National Finals.

Austin wasn't thinking about any of that at the moment- he was simply focusing on the task ahead of him. For the last few days, he had ridden every one of his broncs. Another cowboy, Chance Rancort from Twin Falls High in Idaho, had also ridden all of his mounts, and the two of them were neck-and-neck for the national championship. Each of them had one horse left to ride, with the highest scoring ride taking home the coveted gold buckle.

The grandstands were filled to capacity, with rodeo fans from all around the nation looking on in anticipation. There were television cameras broadcasting the rodeo all around the world, and after each ride Austin had been mobbed by a sea of reporters from newspapers and television news journalists looking for a scoop on the big event.

The media had gotten wind of Austin's story thanks to a small write-up in the Mirror Valley Chronicle, and he had been bombarded with requests by journalists and fans for autographs and interviews. He handled each request respectfully and happily, though truthfully he couldn't understand what all the fuss was about. *I'm just a kid riding bucking horses,* he thought several times. *Sure, I'm having a good run lately, but that Chance Rancort is doing just as well. How come they want to talk to me?*

Finally, Austin could take no more, so he asked a pretty young reporter from the Denver Post about it.

"Well, Austin, it's because you're interesting. The whole deal- moving up here from Texas, no parents around, working hard, doing right," the comely journalist replied. "People love to hear about the best of things- the Cinderella-type story, you know? And that's you. You've got people all over the country, even people that have never seen a horse or a cow in person, asking 'Did Austin win?'"

"I'm not special, ma'am, and that's the truth of it. I'm just a high school kid who happens to buck out horses," Austin said dryly.

"It's that sort of down-to-earth mentality that makes you so appealing to people, Austin," she said matter-of-factly. "Plus," she added, "you're super cute, something that's not lost on the millions of female readers and viewers out there." With that, she winked and trotted off to her waiting news van, leaving Austin standing blankly with his hat in his hands.

Chance Rancort was the second-to-last rider on the scorecard, with Austin set to go off last. Across the return alley, Austin could see the youngster from Idaho lowering himself onto the horse he'd drawn, a sharp-looking bay gelding named Grenade. The stock contractor for the Finals was an outfit named Matchstick Rodeo Company, and the rumor was out that the company's owner- a man named Gerald Match- had sent a few of his prized professional-level bucking horses on the truck along with the other animals. This rumor was confirmed by Mr.

Match himself in a television interview the day before the finals.

"Yessir, I put a pair of horses on the truck that I normally only send to Houston, Cheyenne, and the National Finals in Vegas," the stately stock contractor had said directly into the camera. "I heard there were a couple of kids that were riding everything in sight, so I thought I'd give 'em a couple of real rank ponies to play with. There have been world championships and over a half-million dollars won on those two horses, so if these boys are up to it, they ought to be up around 95 points."

Chance's horse began to pitch inside the bucking chute, its hooves clattering loudly against the steel sides. Undaunted, the cowboy reached down and slipped his boots deeply into his stirrups, then leaned back against the carefully measured lead shank and nodded his head. In a flash, horse and rider were bounding across the arena. For what seemed like an eternity, the talented rider matched Grenade's every move, throwing his hand back over his head and keeping his balance with each jump. The horse grew more and more frustrated with each passing second, snorting loudly and kicking higher each time.

The eight second whistle blared loudly with Chance still aboard. His would be a high score, Austin knew. The pickup riders, mounted on stout and seasoned roping horses, galloped on either side of the still-pitching horse, and one of them reached out and grabbed Chance under his armpit, pulling him away from the bronc. Chance lunged and hugged the man's waist, holding on until he was clear of Grenade's churning hooves. He let go and landed on his feet, then threw up his hands in exuberance. The grandstand resounded with applause that shook the ground beneath it, where the bucking chutes were, and for the first time Austin felt a twinge of nervousness creep into his stomach.

The arena announcer sounded loudly over the speakers and over the crowd's noise.

"And…Chance Rancort… From Twin Falls, Idaho… Ninety-Four Points!" the announcer's voice boomed. The crowd noise reached another level, with cheers so deafening that Austin could scarcely hear himself breathe. Chance took his hat off and, in a traditional celebration, sent it flying toward the crowd like a Frisbee.

Sensing that Austin might be experiencing a moment of nervousness, Hunter appeared out of nowhere. The older cowboy walked to within inches of Austin and stared up at his charge.

"Austin, I know I've given you a hard time," Hunter yelled. "Truthfully, you didn't deserve it. You're a good guy, and I'm sorry for hassling you."

Austin nodded but did not attempt to speak.

"Listen, Austin," Hunter continued, yelling loudly to be heard above the crowd. "You just watched the second best ride of the night. This mare you're gonna ride-Texas Tornado- I've seen her buck. I watched old Whitey Gant win the world on her five years ago in Vegas! Now, get up there and stick with her, savvy?"

Austin nodded again. Hunter added another piece of advice.

"She rears up out of a right-hand delivery like you've got here tonight, pard'. Be ready and mark her out good, then just lift and reach like you do! You're the best bronc' rider I've ever seen, Austin, and if anyone can ride her, you can! So go do it!" He extended his hand to Austin and they shook.

Austin climbed up onto the top of the chute above his mount and began to prepare for the ride. Tate was by his side, and the two exchanged a meaningful glance, then turned to look out into the arena. The air seemed to still completely, and the crowd grew silent. Punctuating the silence was the announcer's voice.

"Ladies and Gentlemen, this is the ride you've all been waiting for…This young man…Has become a household name…Across the nation…He's a native Texan…But now calls Mirror Valley home…He's about to buck the horse that Whitey Gant won the world on five years ago…That's right, Ladies and Gentlemen…One of the top ten professional bucking horses of all time… So let's do this young man a favor…When that gate opens…Cheer for your hometown cowboy…As loudly as possible…" the voice crackled through the public-address system.

Austin lowered himself down onto the mare's back and carefully inserted his feet into the stirrups. He measured out a length of his lead shank and took a firm grip, then cocked his elbow so his hand was pointed skyward. The voice over the speakers continued.

"Here he is… from right here in Mirror Valley… Austin…Mathers!"

Austin leaned back and placed his spurs high on the horse's neck, but then remembered Hunter's advice and lowered them to just above the points of the mare's shoulder. He braced himself against the lead and nodded his head, signaling the chute boss to open the gate. When the chute opened, the Paint mare reared onto her hind legs and spun toward the open arena. Her jumps were the most impressive and explosive thing Austin had ever experienced. When the mare lined herself out into the middle of the arena and began to buck in earnest, Austin quickly fell into time with her and began to spur her shoulders. His shiny blue and gold chaps rose and fell with each move of his legs, accentuating his ride in just the manner intended.

With each kick of her hind legs, Texas Tornado raised into an almost vertical position, her nose nearly touching the dirt. Austin had to lean back as far as possible, careful to lift with his free arm until his shoulder blades met with the Paint's rump. When her hind end came down, Austin leaned forward skillfully and got his balance back. He heard nothing but the sound of the horse's hooves meeting the earth and the stifled gasping of his own breath.

Austin never heard the 8-second buzzer, and was surprised when the pick-up riders came racing up alongside him. He'd made the whistle! Casually, he had the sense to hand the lead shank to one of the pick-up men before bailing onto the back of the other rider's horse.

Instead of falling off the side, though, Austin simply sat astraddle of the horse behind the mounted man's saddle, and the tandem raced around the arena together.

"Great ride, Kid!" the pickup man said loudly over his shoulder, his horse still galloping. "Best one I've ever seen, really!" The man pulled on his reins and stopped his horse directly in front of the grandstand, then extended a hand to Austin, who had dismounted.

"Thank you, Sir," Austin said, meeting the older man's eyes. They shook firmly, and then the pickup man spurred after his partner, who was having trouble directing Texas Tornado toward the return alley. Austin was left standing, all alone, in front of the grandstand. Slowly, the noise of the crowd returned to his ears. It was the single loudest thing he had ever heard, and when he realized that they were cheering for him, he blushed a deep red.

Remembering his manners, Austin removed his hat and waved politely to each corner of the grandstand, thanking them for their applause. The announcer's voice came over the loud speaker.

"Well, well, well…Ladies and Gentlemen…What do you think of the hometown boy…On Texas Tornado…Austin…Mathers!" The crowd increased its volume even more, which Austin didn't think was possible. The announcer continued. "How about this? Ninety…Seven…Points!"

There was a roar so loud from the crowd that, had he not been holding it in his hands already, it might have caused Austin to chase his hat across the arena. There were thousands of voices screaming in unison, creating such a deafening atmosphere that Austin could not hear the announcer, who was still talking. Not sure what to do, Austin walked toward the bucking chutes. He was met on the arena floor by Chance, who extended a hand of congratulations.

"Great ride, man!" the Idaho cowboy yelled into Austin's ear as he clapped him on the shoulder.

"Thanks- you too! Great horses, huh?" Austin replied. Chance just nodded and strode away. Austin watched his rival disappear behind the chute gate, but then was nearly run over by the pickup man's horse, which skidded to a stop right in front of him. The rider dismounted and motioned for Austin to step aboard. Not understanding, Austin looked at the man quizzically.

"Go take a victory lap, Son! That was something else, and those folks up there would like nothing more than to see you run this pony around the arena to celebrate!" the man shouted over the din. Nodding, Austin mounted the horse and spurred it into a spirited lope. He circled the arena several times, pointing and waving to everyone in the crowd, which was still in a tizzy over what had just happened.

Austin reined the lathered pickup horse to a stop in front of the bucking chutes and, climbing down, was tackled by his entire team. The fact that he'd won the national championship in the saddle-bronc division also gave Mirror Valley High enough points to win the team title, and the gold buckles that went along with it. They were as happy as any group of kids could be, and for a moment, Austin thought he might never get away from the hog pile.

Presently, he was pulled back to his feet by Hunter and Tate. Austin dusted himself off casually, and then walked over to the return alley. As he walked through the swinging orange gate and beneath the grandstands, he looked around for his saddle, which one of the arena hands had undoubtedly taken off of Texas Tornado and hung on the fence. Kacey came walking toward him, carrying the tattered leather rig in her arms and wearing a big smile.

It amazed Austin that, even after all this time, the sight of her could make his head spin. As she approached, he searched for the right words. When nothing came to him, as was still often the case when Kacey was involved, he simply smiled down at his approaching lady.

As usual, she turned what could have been an awkward moment into something completely comfortable. She simply swung his saddle up onto the nearest fence rail and hugged him tightly to her, conveying her happiness and pride in him without a single word. After a moment's embrace, she pushed away from him and looked him over carefully, as if considering something.

"What's that look for, Kacey?" Austin asked. The bright lights from the arena were but shadows beneath the grandstand, only a small sliver of illumination here and there between the rails of the many chutes and gates located nearby. He noticed that she looked her age just then, younger than the woman he'd come to know and appreciate as his own. Still, her eyes were mesmerizing and bright, even in the darkness that surrounded them.

"Oh, I don't know, Austin," Kacey started. "I'm just so proud of you! Not just because of the ride, or the buckles, or the way our little town is famous. That's all wonderful, and I'm happy about it, don't get me wrong… but, that's not it." She stopped, considering her words.

"Well, I'm glad that all this has happened, too, honey. It's good for the town, good for our school. But if that's not what you're thinking of, what is it?" Austin said gingerly.

"When you rode that horse, the first thing you did afterward was shake a man's hand firmly, then get embarrassed because of applause, and then you took off your hat because there were ladies in the crowd, cheering. I saw that and came back here by the stripping chute and bawled my eyes out!" Kacey said.

"Oh, Kacey, why were you crying? That's the last thing I ever want to do, to make you cry! What's wrong?!" Austin said, ready to do anything in his power to fix the situation.

"Nothing! Nothing is wrong, Austin!" Kacey said quickly, squeezing his hands. "I'm not sad at all, I'm happy." She looked up at him then, fixing him with a warm gaze. "I'm just so happy to have you in my life; You're it. You're exactly what every woman wants, and you're exactly what every guy should be like." Tears began to trickle down her cheeks once again.

"And I'm positive that I'm the luckiest girl in the world,"

Kacey continued. "I'm in love with you, Austin. And I'm not talking about the silly, schoolgirl puppy love, either. I just plain love you, the way my mom and dad love each other. I want nothing more than to be alongside you, wherever you go, whatever the world has in store for you, for us. You're a good man, and you make me a better woman. Does that make sense?" she asked levelly, then looked away.

Austin could never have guessed that Kacey would come to him, at this moment, with something so serious. He thought for a moment, again trying to find the right words. Her feelings were his, almost exactly, and he wanted her to know. She was still looking away, almost as if she regretted letting her feelings be known. Austin squeezed her hands tightly and then, in a quick move, pulled both of them down to the ground next to the fence. She wound up on his lap, looking at him. He spoke directly.

"Kacey, I'm not sure you'll believe this, but I've been in love with you since my first day in Mirror Valley. It gets stronger every day, and I honestly can't imagine life without you. That's the truth. I'm no good at saying things like this, but I hope you know that I do love you. I'm as happy as a guy can be, and it's got nothing to do with that horse I just rode..." he trailed off.

Kacey looked up at him, unable to speak, and smiled broadly. She pulled his face toward hers and they exchanged a long kiss. After a few moments, she tucked her face into his shoulder and they sat, embracing tightly, neither wanting to let go.

"Now, Austin," she said into his ear, "we can continue this later. Right now, I think we ought to go collect our buckles!" Kacey rose from the ground and extended a hand to help Austin up. She brushed his shirt off and straightened his collar, then fixed his hat squarely on his head. The announcer's voice echoed beneath the metal grandstands, announcing the awards ceremony going on in the middle of the arena. The crowd was still wild, cheering loudly with each buckle awarded.

After a final, quick kiss, they joined hands and walked slowly out into the bright lights of the arena.

ABOUT THE AUTHOR

Sam Finden was born and raised in Farmington, Minnesota. He found his way to Arizona, Colorado and Texas before moving to Montana. He spends his spare time and money on horses and hunting.

Made in the USA
Lexington, KY
24 November 2014

The Girl in the Box
Contemporary Urban Fantasy by Robert J. Crane

Alone
The Girl in the Box, Book 1

Sienna Nealon was a 17 year-old girl who had been held prisoner in her own house by her mother for twelve years. Then one day her mother vanished, and Sienna woke up to find two strange men in her home. On the run, unsure of who to turn to and discovering she possesses mysterious powers, Sienna finds herself pursued by a shadowy agency known as the Directorate and hunted by a vicious, bloodthirsty psychopath named Wolfe, each of which is determined to capture her for their own purposes...

Available Now!

Untouched
The Girl in the Box, Book 2

Still haunted by her last encounter with Wolfe and searching for her mother, Sienna Nealon must put aside her personal struggles when a new threat emerges – Aleksandr Gavrikov, a metahuman so powerful, he could destroy entire cities – and he's focused on bringing the Directorate to its knees.

Available Now!

A Familiar Face
A Sanctuary Short Story

Cyrus Davidon gets more than he bargained for when he takes a day away from Sanctuary to visit the busy markets of his hometown, Reikonos. While there, he meets a woman who seems very familiar, and appears to know him, but that he can't place.

Available Now!

(Free for signing up for Newsletter at RobertJCrane.com!)

Champion
The Sanctuary Series, Volume Three

As the war heats up in Arkaria, Vara is forced to flee after an ancient order of skilled assassins infiltrates Sanctuary and targets her. Cyrus Davidon accompanies her home to the elven city of Termina and the two of them become embroiled in a mystery that will shake the very foundations of the Elven Kingdom – and Arkaria.

Available Now!

Crusader
The Sanctuary Series, Volume Four

Cyrus Davidon finds himself far from his home in Sanctuary, in the land of Luukessia, a place divided and deep in turmoil. With his allies at his side, Cyrus finds himself facing off against an implacable foe in a war that will challenge all his convictions - and one he may not be able to win.

Coming Fall 2012!

Savages
A Sanctuary Short Story

Twenty years before Cyrus Davidon joined Sanctuary, his father was killed in a war with the trolls and he has never forgiven them. Enter Vaste, a troll unlike most; courageous, loyal and an outcast. When Cyrus and Vaste become trapped in a far distant land, they are forced to overcome their suspicions and work together to get home.

Available Now!

The Sanctuary Series
Epic Fantasy by Robert J. Crane

The world of Arkaria is a dangerous place, filled with dragons, titans, goblins and other dangers. Those who live in this world are faced with two choices: live an ordinary life or become an adventurer and seek the extraordinary.

Defender
The Sanctuary Series, Volume One

Cyrus Davidon leads a small guild in the human capital of Reikonos. Caught in an untenable situation, facing death in the den of a dragon, they are saved by the brave fighters of Sanctuary who offer an invitation filled with the promise of greater adventure. Soon Cyrus is embroiled in a mystery - someone is stealing weapons of nearly unlimited power for an unknown purpose, and Sanctuary may be the only thing that stands between the world of Arkaria and total destruction.

Available Now!

Avenger
The Sanctuary Series, Volume Two

When a series of attacks on convoys draws suspicion that Sanctuary is involved, Cyrus Davidon must put aside his personal struggles and try to find the raiders. As the attacks worsen, Cyrus and his comrades find themselves abandoned by their allies, surrounded by enemies, facing the end of Sanctuary and a war that will consume their world.

Available Now!

Sienna Nealon will return in

Family
The Girl in the Box, Book Four

Just hours after finding Andromeda and crossing paths with her mother, Sienna finds herself back at the Directorate and up against a bigger threat than ever before. Omega, the organization that unleashed Wolfe and others upon her, has declared war on the Directorate and the first strikes have already landed. Facing the seemingly unstoppable forces of Omega and Sienna's own mother, the Directorate seems poised for defeat when a new threat rears its ugly head - a traitor in their midst, one that may mean the destruction of everything Sienna has come to care about.

Coming Fall 2012

About the Author

Robert J. Crane was born and raised on Florida's Space Coast before moving to the upper midwest in search of cooler climates and more palatable beer. He graduated from the University of Central Florida with a degree in English Creative Writing. He worked for a year as a substitute teacher and worked in the financial services field for seven years while writing in his spare time. He makes his home in the Twin Cities area of Minnesota.

He can be contacted in several ways:
Via **email** at cyrusdavidon@gmail.com
Follow him on **Twitter** - @robertJcrane
Connect on **Facebook** – robertJcrane (Author)
Website – http://www.robertJcrane.com
Blog – http://robertJcrane.blogspot.com
Become a fan on **Goodreads** –
http://www.goodreads.com/RobertJCrane

A Note to the Reader

I wanted to take a moment to thank you for reading this story. As an independent author, getting my name out to build an audience is one of the biggest priorities on any given day. If you enjoyed this story and are looking forward to reading more, let someone know - post it on Amazon, on your blog, if you have one, on Goodreads.com, place it in a quick Facebook status or Tweet with a link to the page of whatever outlet you purchased it from (Amazon, Barnes & Noble, Apple, Kobo, etc). Good reviews inspire people to take a chance on a new author – like me. And we new authors can use all the help we can get.

Thanks again for your time.

Robert J. Crane

Chapter 1

Someone Else

I wondered how many cops were within a hundred miles of me as I slammed the convenience store clerk's head into the counter. It made a satisfying thump and rebounded as he spiraled to the ground, his head hitting the shelf behind him before it made contact with the tile floor. He didn't move, which was fortunate more for his sake than mine, as I took the bills out of the register and stuffed them in a plastic bag. I fiddled around behind the counter for a minute, tidying up loose ends, then broke his cell phone and the landline, smashing the plastic into pieces. It'd be a long walk to the next one.

The smell of day-old hot dogs wafted around me as I walked past trinkets and tourist shirts that proclaimed *See South Dakota!* The slow hum of the air conditioner working overtime to keep the building cool in the prairie summer heat thrummed around me. I ripped open a candy bar and took a bite, savoring the sweet taste of the caramel and chocolate mingled with the salt from the peanuts. It was the first thing I'd eaten since I made a stop outside Gillette, Wyoming a few hours after sundown. I wondered if the clerk at that store had woken up yet. Probably. He wouldn't remember anything. Just like this one.

I walked to the back of the store and paused when I opened the cooler to grab a drink. The bitter chill of the freezer air overpowered the air conditioning, sending goosebumps up and down my arms. I threw three bottles of soda on top of the piddling amount of money I'd taken from the till; I'd thought it would be

more. I considered trying to wake up the attendant to get him to open the safe but decided he'd had enough excitement for one night.

I stepped up to the door that led to the space behind the freezers. Locked. I rolled my eyes and kicked, sending it off its hinges and into the room. It wedged in the back wall, sticking out as though it was a tombstone buried in the brick. The symbolism was obvious, at least to me. I reached over and ejected the DVD that was recording from the camera feeds all over the station, put it into my plastic bag and pondered the safe in the corner. Wasn't worth the time. I only needed petty cash for this trip and it was better to remain as off the radar as I could. Not that robbing convenience stores was going to keep me off the radar, but let's face it: it was a means to an end, not an end itself.

And the end was ahead. Far, far ahead.

Everything on the shelves looked good as I wandered back out into the store, but I didn't need much. I threw a couple packages of chips into the bag and three boxes of white powdered donuts. Way better than the chocolate ones. I took one last look around and decided to try one of the hot dogs. Sure, they looked old, but I'd been eating food that came in a plastic wrapper since I left Casper, Wyoming yesterday. And before that, other canned and plasticized food. Laying low wasn't pleasant, but living off gas station food wasn't much better.

After I finished fixing my hot dog, I took a bite and stepped outside, the flavor of the ketchup and mustard masking the chewy, rubbery consistency of the meat. The convenience store was right off Interstate 90. The nearest town, Draper, South Dakota, was a few miles away and probably deader than a prairie dog on the freeway by this time of night.

I felt the hot summer air of the planes, my little bag in one hand, and a half eaten hotdog in the other, as I walked back to my car, an older model Honda. I'd stolen it before I left Casper, but I

acquired some new license plates in Rapid City so I wasn't real worried about the cops taking an interest in me. By the time the sun came up tomorrow I'd be in southern Minnesota. I could melt away onto the back roads, pick up some new tags, maybe even a new car. This one smelled like the previous owner had a problem with Mary Jane. Actually, not so much a problem as a deeply troubling relationship.

I watched another car pull into the parking space just down from me. I caught sight of the lights mounted on the roof and realized my earlier question about cops was answered: there was one here, now. The lights weren't on, no siren was blaring and once the officer parked his car he sat there, looking at a clipboard in his lap. I sighed; the minute he walked inside he'd discover what had happened and I'd have the cops after me. I needed time.

I walked to his window and rapped on the glass with my knuckle. He made a motion for me to step back, which I did, and he opened the door. Tall, heavily built, and in his early forties, he clicked on his big, heavy flashlight before he started to speak. "Is there a problem—"

He didn't have a chance to see it coming. It wasn't his fault; he followed procedure flawlessly, but I was possessed of strength and speed far beyond a normal person. His hand had reached his holster when mine broke his nose. I brought his head to my knee, giving him something else unpleasant to deal with when he woke up. He hit the ground and I stooped over him. After I was done, I grabbed his pistol, his pepper spray and taser. I smashed his cell phone to pieces, broke his radio, then picked him up and stuffed him back in his car. He'd live, but suffer for the inconvenience he'd placed on me by driving up at this particular moment.

I got back in the Honda and caught another whiff of the reefer that permeated the seats, the upholstery, the dashboard, everything. I looked at the map sitting on my passenger seat and traced my finger along the line I'd drawn to my destination. From the

money I stole this time, I might actually be able to pay at the next convenience store. That'd throw 'em off the trail.

I stepped on the accelerator and took off, back to the freeway, back to the long ride. I was over five hundred miles from where I was going and it'd take me at least a couple more days to get there. But it'd be worth it; I'd show them all. I let a little smile of triumph float onto my face as I broke open the pack of donuts and pulled out the first powdered. I took a bite then spit it out the broken window.

Stale. I felt a flash of rage and had a fantasy about killing the convenience store clerk instead of letting him live. I threw the rest of the package out as I hit seventy, not a car on the road ahead of me. This time...this time they couldn't stop me.

Chapter 2

Sienna Nealon

My heart thudded in my ears as I ran, the green of the woods surrounding me. My breath caught in my throat; I was gasping from the exertion of running, and that wasn't easy for me. I'm a meta-human, with powers that include far more strength, speed and agility than humans. But apparently I needed more cardio in my workout.

I heard the footsteps behind me, pounding against the hard ground. I stopped, pressing my back against a tree. Scott Byerly ran past and did the same while Kat Forrest trailed a little behind him.

"Thanks for slowing down," Kat said, huffing as she came to a stop. She was taller than me, with long blond hair and green eyes. Her face was usually tanned but it was red now, spots of color standing out on her cheeks. She wore a simple T-shirt and gym shorts which seemed far too short, and socks and tennis shoes far too low for my tastes. Her long, smooth, tanned legs almost blended in with the backdrop of old pine needles on the forest floor. "Thought you were gonna leave me behind."

I grunted. It wasn't for lack of trying; we were on the run for a reason, and I had no intention of getting caught because Kat couldn't keep pace.

"Any sign of him?" Scott didn't bother to complain. He was tall, with short dark hair and a nose that was a little rounded. Kinda good-looking. Like me, his eyes were scanning through the trees around us, watching for the unseen threat that was some-

where out there. His eyes halted for a second on Kat's legs, causing me to snort, then they kept going. He wasn't breathing as hard as she was, but close.

"Not that I can see." I pushed off the tree, trying to steady myself. We had been running for over an hour before this, full tilt. I was tired; my legs hurt, my lungs hurt, and I was cranky. "But the way the three of us are gasping for air, a tractor trailer could sneak up on us and we wouldn't know it until we felt the treads on our backs."

"I'm exhausted." Kat stood up straight and her hair hung in strings over her shoulders as she joined us in looking around. "I'm in no condition for a fight; I'm not sure they're paying me enough for this."

Scott shot her a half-smile. "You don't think it's worth it to be the next generation of M-Squad recruits?"

"Not sure I wanna be an M-Squad anything," Kat said under her breath.

I had been offered a position as a trainee with the Directorate, an organization that helps track and police metahumans – metas – like me. They hoped to position me to help their agents in hunting down dangerous metas. Shortly after I'd gotten an offer, so had Scott and Kat. Their offers might have had something to do with the fact that the three of us almost single-handedly stopped a very dangerous meta who had threatened to blow up Minneapolis. I thought it was a signal that the Directorate was looking to expand their reach because of some growing threats.

"So are we gonna keep moving or wh—" Kat got cut off mid-sentence as something hit her from behind. I saw a flash of white fur, heard the WHUMP! as she went down, her hair a solid streak of blond. I was already in motion. My foot lashed out at the ball of white as she hit the ground, her shriek drowned out and muffled. I missed clean; the creature that attacked her rolled through and landed on all fours, ready to strike. I was off balance and it was

impossibly fast. I stared at it, the red eyes of a wolf glaring back at me as I tried to recapture my footing.

It was long, bigger than the dogs I had seen, and the fur was stark white, the faintest reminder of the last winter, when snow blanketed the ground in the same shade. I saw it tense, watched it shift weight from its hind legs to its front as it moved to pounce again. I had no easy defense; my leg was almost down when it left the ground and I flinched, already anticipating the pain as I saw it leap, mouth open and focused on my neck.

A solid wall of water hit the animal, causing it to yelp and hurtle sideways, knocked off course by the pressure of the blast. It slammed into a tree trunk and I lunged, foot extended in a running jump sidekick. I aimed at the neck, hoping to put the beast out of the fight. When I was a foot away from my target the hair changed color, shifting in a ripple down the fur like the summer wind had stirred it, and as it went brown the neck grew wider and longer and the shape of the creature began to change.

It stood on its hind legs, leaving all fours behind as its limbs grew longer, paws sprouting long claws. My foot hit it behind the shoulder and I heard bones cracking; a roar came from the mouth of what was now a bear. The brown mass twisted and batted at me with a paw and I dived, trying to avoid the swipe. I felt one claw hit me, raking behind my ear and drawing blood.

"Let's coordinate our attack," Scott said from my left, loosing a stream of water that missed the bear wide.

I ignored him as I rolled to my feet, already in a defensive stance. The bear reared up on its hind legs, standing an easy four or five feet taller than me. I glared at it, my hands raised, ready to try and counter whatever it tried. "You got blood in my hair."

The bear cocked its head at me, distracted, for just a second. Long enough for the blast of water to knock it over again, taking it off its hind legs and down to all fours.

"I had him!" I said. A hot flush of irritation ran through me as

I watched the bear stagger from the stream.

Scott had both hands out, the air around him shimmering as he drained the humidity from it. It was Minnesota in July; he had plenty to work with. A jet of liquid shot from his fingertips in a pressurized burst, splattering against the brown fur and driving the bear back. I'd been on the receiving end of it before; he could make it hurt, if he wanted to. "Sorry, I thought we were supposed to work as a team."

I ignored his jab and pounced while the bear was distracted, jumping on its back. I didn't pull my punches, and I landed three of them in rapid succession behind the ears. If it'd been a human, it would have been dead, I think. The bear, with its thicker skull, started to wobble and tried to bring up a paw to bat me off. I slid lower and wrapped an arm around its throat, locking it in tight while I hit it thrice more. It collapsed under my weight and fell to the ground. I hit it again and watched the tongue fall out of its mouth, unrolling on the ground as it went limp in my grasp.

"Is it over?" Kat brushed herself off as she got to her knees. "Can I get up now?"

I stared at the bear underneath me. "I don't think s—" I stopped when I heard a whizzing noise; something was coming toward us, something fast. I felt something brush past me and threw myself down. Something soft grazed my cheek and pulled at my arm as it passed. I caught a glimpse of Scott out of the corner of my eye; he went down hard, something pulling him off his feet, a net made of beams of light, shining and intertwined. It pinned him to the ground, the energy forcing his hands and arms down, mashing his face as it cut into him. Kat was similarly pinned to a tree in a sitting position; I could see her feet sticking out the bottom of the net as she hung there, limp, a foot off the ground.

"You think it's over?" A blond woman hovered in the clearing above me, her outfit a kind of shameless riff on things I'd seen people wear when riding bicycles, minus the helmet. Her hand ex-

tended, pointing at me, and I lunged as I felt another net fly past me, disturbing my hair as it missed, passing down my back. It stretched in a four foot square, holding tight to the earth like a web made of light.

My shoulder hit the ground, little pieces of rock pushing up into my clothes and skin as I rolled back to my feet. I ran, not bothering to look back as I made for the cover of the forest. I heard a laugh from behind me, heard the air move around her as she pursued me. I dodged around a tree and chanced a look back; she was lower now, only a few feet off the ground, and not far behind me.

I could smell the fresh air, feel the sun on the back of my neck as I ran, dodging past the trunks of trees and hearing the whoosh of the little nets she was sending my way. Scott and Kat were both down; they'd be okay. I just had to get away long enough to turn the tables. I had to beat her, had to win, more than anything.

I came upon a small ravine and let myself drop. I hit the ground, absorbing the impact along my legs. I had fallen next to a huge rock, at least three feet across. I smiled as I hefted it in both hands and readied it to throw. A normal person couldn't have done this; the rock was huge, almost a boulder – the kind you'd use for decoration in a garden.

I heard sound overhead as she overflew me. I watched her disappear past, and waited, my muscles straining as I held the rock at the ready. I could hear the flutter of wings, and she came back around, her head visible through the boughs above me. I waited until I had a clear view and I let the stone fly. It soared and hit her in the chest with an awful cracking noise. I pumped my fist in victory until I saw her flip over and fall from the sky.

I felt a sick sensation in my stomach as I watched her drop. She followed a lazy arc as she fell; I heard her body hit the ground, the impact reminding me of the time I'd dropped a steak on a counter; a kind of wet slap.

I ran over uneven ground, feeling the dirt kick up as I raced toward the place where she had landed. I pushed aside tree branches to find her in a creek, the water running over her. I cringed and hurried over. I felt the cool water splash into my boot (black, pleather, fairly nice until I got them wet) and soak my socks, felt the chill of it on my hands as I reached down and grabbed her under the arms to drag her to the bank. My gloves were leather and not meant to get soaked, but I dared not take them off; her shirt was sleeveless and her pants were short. My touch as I pulled her out of the water would be much worse than the damage she'd already taken.

Her hair was wet with water and just a little blood, I noticed as I pulled her onto the stony bank of the creek. She snorted and choked out clear liquid and bile as I pulled her onto the rocks. I felt the dampness make its way through my jeans and my long sleeved shirt. It was desperately hot, I was sweating, and the cool wetness was a kind of sweet relief from the heat.

"Woo hoo hoo," came a catcall from the other side of the creek. "Look at that; Sienna and Eve, getting all wet and clingy." A low guffaw came after it and I felt a bitter pang of annoyance. The speaker was a little taller than me but still short for a man. He wore a cutoff tank top and ragged blue jeans, and his hair was thinning on top, obvious since he wasn't wearing his usual baseball cap to cover it.

"She's hurt pretty bad, Clary," I said. I looked down at her and her eyes fluttered. A thin trickle of blood ran down her forehead.

"She'll be fine." He dismissed us with a wave, turning his head away and puckering his lips in amusement. "It's not every day I get to see the two of you rubbing up against each other. I might have to watch for a bit."

I picked her up and carried her off the rocks to the trail. She was wet, an unconscious, dead weight that wasn't fighting back. I

set her on the dirt, long strings of her hair tangled. They touched the ground and I saw the little granules of sand cling to them. I felt guilty; she was going to be super pissed when she woke up.

I heard Clary splash through the creek behind me as I knelt next to Eve. Her hair had gotten long; it was short when I first met her. She was very thin, her chest flat, heaving up and down with great effort; her breathing was ragged. When I pulled her shirt back to look at the damage, I heard a moan of pain from her and a deep breath of interest from Clary. I shot him a dirty look and turned back to Eve.

Her sternum was broken, a hideous blackish blue bruise had begun to spread from the center of her chest. I didn't dare unzip her shirt to look closer (especially with that pervert Clary behind me) but I knew enough that I was certain I'd have to call—

"Dr. Perugini is on the way," came the voice from in front of me. Roberto Bastian came toward us at a jog, his buzzed black hair dripping with sweat. "She'll be here in five or less. Until then, let's just assess the damage—" He halted and dropped to a knee next to Kappler. "Damn." He shot a look at me, but there was a surprising lack of guilt in it. "You're playing a little rough for a training exercise, Nealon."

"The rock kinda got away from me," I said. "It's not exactly easy for us ground-based types to take down a flyer. She was throwing her nets at me and I just..." I searched my memory, trying to make my vicious ambush seem not quite so vicious. "...figured out a way to take her down and did it."

"Boy, did you," said Glen Parks, splashing across the creek with Scott and Kat in tow. Parks was an older man, his long hair gray, mustache and beard matching it perfectly; not quite ZZ Top length, but close. He brushed the beard to the side and I could see a contusion across his neck that looked like my wristwatch. "I'm not upset that you took this exercise seriously, but next time be more careful with the neck. Even as a bear I'm not immune to

your strength."

"Sorry," I said, somewhat abrupt. I turned my attention back to Eve as Kat eased down beside me, her hands already brushing against Eve's neck. The German woman was rasping and her eyes were still rolled back in her head. "I was just trying to win."

"Damn, you sure were, girl," Clary said. "But you're gonna catch all kinds of hell from—"

"What is going on here?" The crackling of an Italian accent was laced with thunderous irritation. I blanched at the sound of it, and after examination, wondered why I was more afraid of the re-action of a human doctor than the metahumans I had been sparring with only minutes before.

Dr Isabella Perugini stopped on the bank opposite us, her dark hair pulled back in a ponytail, her white lab coat falling below her knees. She slid off her high heeled shoes and began to pick her way across the stream, trying to balance on the rocks jutting out of the water. Her dark complexion was more flushed than usual, her eyes narrowed at me. "You again?" She said it as she executed a hop from one rock to another. "I thought I sorted you out!"

"I got carried away," I said.

She made her last jump and flinched as her foot caught the edge of the rock she landed on. She cursed loudly, then covered the ground to get to us. She knelt and looked to Kat, who had un-zipped Eve's shirt to expose her bruised and misshapen sternum. "How is she?" the doctor said to Kat.

"All the problems you'd expect her to have." Kat ran a hand through Eve's hair. "Fractured skull, presumably from the landing, broken sternum." She gave the doctor a wan smile. "I'm working on it. The broken bones will be mended in just a minute."

Perugini turned back to me, one eye cocked and twitching, the other narrowed. She didn't say anything. She didn't have to.

"Training's rough," Bastian said as I avoided her gaze. He looked at me, expression neutral. "It's gonna be fine. We've got

Forrest; she'll fix it."

Perugini's mouth became a thin line. "What happens on the day she isn't around?"

Kat let out a sharp exhalation and fell back on her haunches, then lay down on the rocky shore. "That day is not today," she said with a gasp as I watched little blades of grass and weeds spring up from between the rocks she lay on, reaching up to stroke her exposed skin. "She'll be fine." Kat lifted her head to look at Dr. Perugini. "I might need a minute, though."

I heard the sound of feet splashing in the water and looked up to see Ariadne Fraser making her way across the water. She held her high-heeled shoes in her hands, and her black jacket and skirt were taxing her balance. I raised an eyebrow in surprise when she made it across the bank, her pantyhose having developed three runs along her thighs and two holes in the toes from her crossing. Her red hair was the only splash of color visible on her as she made her way over to us, serious as ever. "Situation?"

Perugini answered, frost under her words. "She'll be fine. Training exercise got out of hand."

Ariadne dropped to her knees next to Eve, looking down at the German woman, who was still unconscious but now breathing easily. "Why is she out?"

"She landed on her head," Perugini said, her eyes glancing at me for a brief second. "Kat has healed her skull fracture but I suspect she won't be awake for several minutes, possibly an hour." The doctor put on her stethoscope and placed the metal end on Eve's chest. "There doesn't appear to be any lasting damage but I'd like to do an MRI just the same."

"You're sure she's all right?" Ariadne looked back up at the doctor, her eyes slitted, her hand clutching Eve's in a way that caught my attention. I looked up and saw Clary looking back at me. He gave me a subtle nod, a wide grin on his face.

"I'm sure." Perugini wrapped her stethoscope around her

neck. "Have someone come out here with a Humvee to pick us up with a stretcher. I want to get her back to the medical unit for tests and observation until we're certain she's fine."

Ariadne hadn't taken her eyes off Eve the entire time Perugini was speaking. "Okay. Bastian, do it."

"Yes, ma'am." Roberto stood up and took a few steps away, speaking with his hand up to his ear.

"How did this happen?" Ariadne's voice was quiet, but it crackled with accusation and left a silence no one seemed eager to fill, least of all me. I started to speak, but was interrupted by Clary.

"Sienna hit her with rock while she was flying and she came crashing down into the creek." Clary's tone was purest joy, as though he were a kid tattling on his wicked sister. "She put some heat on it, too, took Eve right outta the sky like a friggin' plane comin' down—"

"Thank you, Clary." I don't want to say I was frightened of the icy edge in Ariadne's voice, but it was probably the harshest I had ever heard her sound. I didn't back away, but my eyes locked onto hers and I caught an undefinable hint of something that made my heart beat a little faster. Ariadne let go of Kappler's hand and stood. "You're all dismissed." She locked eyes with me. "You too. We'll discuss this tomorrow."

"I'm sorry," I said. "It was an accident—"

"Did you intentionally knock her out of the air with a boulder?" Ariadne's voice came out low, almost whispered. When I nodded, she followed with, "Then that tends to rule out the possibility of it being an accident." Her eyes were dark and they watched me. "We'll discuss it tomorrow. Just go."

I paused and started to reply – something about them pitting me against unfair odds, since Eve could fly and had been a member of M-Squad dealing with dangerous metas long before I even showed up, about how maybe I was doing her a favor by pointing out a pretty big vulnerability in the way she did battle – but every

one of those arguments died on my tongue. I nodded and turned away, forcing one foot in front of the other as I walked out of the clearing and into the trees.

Chapter 3

I heard the sounds of conversation die down behind me as I grew further and further from them. The heat in the woods was oppressive, even under the shade of the trees. The air didn't feel like it was moving, even when a brief gust of wind shifted more hot air in my direction, turning the sweat that was already trickling down my back into a tepid river that slid down the crease of my spine. I took a deep breath, sucking in the warm air, feeling it seem to stick in my nose and mouth, felt the perspiration drip from my forehead into my eyes, mixing with a little of the moisture already there.

Dammit. I got so caught up in the training exercise, in winning, in beating the others, that I let myself get carried away. For years I'd had no one but Mom to spar against, and now, only a few months out in the world, was testing myself against people that tracked and caught metas for a living. I felt a twinge of relief at the knowledge that Eve Kappler was going to be all right, and a little bit of pride knowing that I'd knocked her out of the sky.

Kappler was a severe woman by nature: she was thin, austere, too dry in personality and reserved in her manner to draw much attention. She had never really been nice to me (not that I'd smite her for that; there were a lot of people in the Directorate that had never shown me kindness; I'd be smiting for a long time to get to them all) but that didn't mean I wanted to hurt her. It was practice. Mom had never intentionally hurt me during practice. Well, most of the time, anyway.

I ran my sleeve along my cheek, slopping off the salty mix of sweat and the first annoying hint of tears. I wanted to believe they

were from all the perspiration that was in my eyes, but I suspected they might also have been from the pride stuck in my throat, that burning feeling that I couldn't swallow away even though I wanted to. I had just gotten called out on my performance in the midst of my peers and fellow trainees. I hated that.

I took another breath, in and out, then another. I had stopped walking and was just standing, feeling the hot air gathered around me in a wall, like some sort of fortress of heat that had enshrouded my body. My long sleeves, gloves and pants didn't help, and even though I wore tennis shoes, my socks were long. They were all soaked, some from sweat but most from wading into the creek to recover Eve. Every single article of my clothing was starting to stick to me, even as the water that had taken up residence within had matched my body temperature; only a little dash of coolness was running down and surprising me every once in a while. The rest just felt like sweat.

The first days of brutal summer had started only a couple weeks ago; before that it had been a beautiful, sunny-skied and cool-aired spring, all the way to the last of June. Since then, it was as though the weather had decided to get hostile. I had to say I preferred winter as a season to summer; it was colder, but even factoring in the number of times I'd landed in the snow while fighting, I didn't get as wet as I did sweating during these training exercises, which were an everyday thing, in one form or another.

"Hey." I had missed the footfalls behind me, caught up in my own thoughts. I turned without drying my eyes, hoping that the sweat would mask the other, marginally less stinging liquid. I doubted it would. Scott was there, along with Kat, who was leaning on him. They walked like I envisioned a couple would, her arm around his waist, her face looking more drawn than it had a few minutes ago. She rested against him, leaning her weight against his muscular chest. If we had been in a different place, and different people, she could have been a drunken sorority girl, lean-

ing on her boyfriend for support.

And I could have been a...I dunno. Something else.

"You took down Eve pretty hard." Scott stopped, repositioning himself as Kat pushed off him to stand on her own two wobbly feet.

My hands came up to cover my mouth as I wiped the sweat that was beading on my upper lip. "Yep." I let them rest there, as though I could cover the lies that were bound to drip out when he asked the inevitable question.

"Why?" It was Kat who asked it, her hair looking stringy because of the humidity, but without a hint of the frizz that was afflicting mine. Thanks, humidity. It'd take a miracle and an hour with the flat iron later to get the kinks out.

I didn't move my hands away from my mouth. "Why what?"

"Why'd you take her down so hard that I had to fix a skull fracture, a broken sternum and three ribs?" Kat let go of Scott and dropped to her rump, sitting with her legs in front of her. "I know we don't do these kind exercises where we beat the hell out of each other for real very often, but we've done it enough to know you don't lose control like that." She laughed and tossed a blond lock over her shoulder. "I mean, when it comes to the training, you're like the queen of control; it's why you're Parks' favorite—"

"I just didn't think." I was sweating even harder now, my lip pressed up against my hand, more perspiration trailing down my forehead from my hairline. I felt my shirt sticking to me and all I wanted was a shower. "It got away from me, the rock. The adrenaline was pumping after we took down Parks—"

"After you took down Parks, you mean? When you left us behind?" The accusation came out of Scott, his arms folded but his manner cool.

"I drew her away from you," I said. "I don't know what else I could have done to help you. I wanted to win, and it was just..." I

pulled my hands away from my mouth and licked my lip, tasted the salty residue of sweat.

"It's not Wolfe, is it?" Scott stared me down. His T-shirt had been white when we started, but now it was gray in the places where he had sweated through, and bore the stains of dirt and grime from where he'd been pinned to the ground. "He's not breaking out or whatever—"

"He's not," I said. "I haven't heard from the rogues' gallery in my head in months. I think Zollers and I have that under control." That was mostly true. The medication Zollers had given me was working, but I had other help as well.

"I guess it was hard for us to tell by the way you acted back there," Kat said, sarcasm oozing through her words, which were laced with a kind of bone-weariness. Her eyes flicked down, and they were lacking the brightness that was ever-present in them. "I didn't mean that. Accidents happen, especially when they're trying to train us for all the possibilities that could happen out there. It's just not like you."

"It happens." Another voice joined our conversation. My head swiveled and I saw Glen Parks, shifting out of the shape of a wolf again. "You get reckless after playing this like it's a game for too long." He got taller as he walked, leaving behind all fours as his fur receded into the long beard and hair that I was accustomed to seeing. "Too much of this type of training's not good. We need some real world experience for you three." He halted behind me. I didn't look away, even though my eyes were burning, this time from the sweat. "Especially for you, before your killer instinct gets away from you."

I felt a burning again in the back of my throat. "I...do not...have a killer instinct."

Scott coughed. "Um...haven't you already killed three people?"

My tongue seemed to stick to the roof of my mouth and my

jaw fell open. "I didn't...I mean, Wolfe was unintentional and Gavrikov...he was gonna nuke Minneapolis."

"And the other guy?" Scott stared back at me. "Henderschott? The one you tried to teach to fly?"

The angry red settled in my cheeks, burning me as I took a breath before answering. "That wasn't me."

Scott looked back the way we had come, back toward the creek, which I could still hear running in the distance. "Yeah, well *that* was all you. And Eve wasn't an enemy."

"This is a pointless discussion." Parks' voice was rough, like a flint striking a rock or a knife running over a sharpening stone. "Byerly, help Forrest back to her room. And let her rest, will you? You know how using her power takes it out of her."

The burning in my cheeks got a little worse; I was pretty sure that Scott and Kat were sleeping together, but I didn't really want to know for fact if it was true. Most of that was because there was someone I wished I could be sleeping with, but it wasn't possible for me to touch him for more than three seconds without causing him excruciating pain followed by death. They walked away, Scott half-carrying Kat toward the dormitory building, which was quite a distance.

"What's your problem, Sienna?" My head snapped back around to find Parks still looking at me, the rough, wrinkled skin around his eyes folded more than usual. They weren't quite slitted, but they were a lot closer to closed than normal. It was the same look he got when we'd go to the firing range for weapons practice and he had to focus on a target at some distance. Parks was blunt to a fault, but he didn't mean anything bad by it. He just said what he thought and let you sort it out.

"I'm just tired." I couldn't get a hand up to cover my mouth without Parks knowing I was lying. Hell, he probably knew anyway because his eyes grew more closed and he nodded. For the last six months he'd watched me as he trained all of us. We were a

class of three, so it's not like he had a ton of people to pay attention to. "We've been at a higher tempo of training lately, early mornings, late nights, all that. Like you said, it just wears on me. I'm ready to get to it." I tried to hold my head higher, look him in the eyes, all that point-the-chin-in-defiance stuff. "I've had enough of the games. I want to get out in the field and go to work chasing down rogues."

His gaze softened, the wrinkles spreading out. "Ariadne says you're not ready."

"That would matter to me if Ariadne was my training officer and worked with me every day." I found I no longer needed to fake the defiance, the chin jutting. "I'm ready. Like it or not, me and the Junior League just took out two members of M-Squad. What do you think?"

He played it cool, too damned cool, not looking away but not registering a thing until he kicked his old, brown cowboy boot into the dusty ground. "We'll find out soon enough if you're ready. I must be getting old and senile to have taken down Kat first instead of you."

"She's easier to sneak up on."

"Don't get cocky." His eyes found me again, his fingers stuck in the loops of his old jeans. "Fast way to get yourself killed, underestimating the people you're fighting – or did you not learn from my example today?"

"I got it." I cleared my throat. "I won't underestimate anybody."

"Bold statement to make. Hope you're right about that. You need to trust your teammates though, watch their backs, because they'll be the ones watching yours, not anyone else." He got a sour look and turned away from me for a second. "Get on home, then. Looks like you got the rest of the day off; might want to take your liberty when you can get it. Not much time off around here, you know."

"I know." Believe me, I knew. It'd been six months since I had a day off. I walked back to the dormitory thinking about how different training to be an agent of the Directorate had been from what I thought it would be when I started. Looking back, I felt naive, like I was a kid when I began, wandering in because I had no idea what else I should do with myself. I had, after all, been cast out into the world after the ultimate sheltered life. Sort of.

It was only a couple weeks after first leaving my house (for the first time in over ten years) that I decided to enter the training program. I hadn't even come close to living a normal teenage life when I decided to really leave normal behind and become what amounted to a paranormal cop. The Directorate paid me a lot of money to do this, all in hopes that someday I'd be a useful member of their policing force. And I was good, at least if we went by the training results. I put Scott to shame and made Kat look like a helpless little girl by comparison in every exercise they threw at us, from martial arts to weapons to chase and apprehension.

It was the "soft skills" that I lacked. Diplomacy, presenting a kind face and sympathetic ear to a metahuman who has just manifested their powers or to a human witness, freaked out by something they've seen that defies explanation. That was part of the job I was training for, being what they called a "Retriever" – trying to convince the newly powerful to come to the Directorate to get some purpose and direction in their abnormal lives. I sucked at that. Probably because it was foreign to me.

Maybe it was because I left home at a dead run with only the clothes on my back, being chased by two guys with guns and then, shortly thereafter, a crazed homicidal meta who nearly killed me. I guess after my own experience, it was hard for me to feel a ton of empathy for someone who gets a gentle knock on their door from someone without a gun who explains that they're different, they're special, and that there's a place for them, then offers them a chance to join a training program to channel their powers. It's a

little different than my first real encounter with powers, which involved me being nearly choked to death in a grocery store parking lot after watching a maniac kill two innocent people.

I entered the dormitory building and felt the beautiful bliss of the air conditioner unit working overtime, sending a sweet chill across my body. The smell of the air was even different in the dormitory than it was outside, holding some kind of magical scent, like the processed and machined smell of the indoors, so much different than the overpowering, heated and wet atmosphere of the outside. By the time I got to my dorm room all the sweat on my body had congealed, evaporated or turned to a freezing layer of moisture.

I closed the door behind me and peeled off the layers of sticky clothes. I grabbed a bottle of water out of the mini fridge by the desk and drained it on the way to the bathroom. As I stepped under the shower head I reflected that this wasn't so bad; the cool water washed down, rejuvenating me. I was in there for about thirty minutes, which was a short shower for me. When I stepped out I heard someone out in the room, and brushed open the door.

Zack was standing in front of the windows, looking out on the sun-beaten grounds. The sprinklers were going just outside, spraying the thirsty grass with water. I leaned against the bathroom door when I saw him, a smile spreading wide across my lips as I felt the wood of the frame through my bathrobe. "You're watching sprinklers water the lawn instead of me in the shower?" My smile turned wicked as he spun to face me.

Zack was tall, at least six feet, which was a bit of a stretch for me. His hair was a darkish blond, and he usually wore a self-aware smile. He was impassive now, though, with a hint of hesitation. I didn't like it when he wore that expression; it meant he had bad news. "I didn't want to gawk." I knew him pretty well by this point; he was my boyfriend, after all.

"You've got bad news?" I stepped out of the bathroom door,

taking a couple steps closer to him, waiting for him to break it to me.

"I'd call it 'disappointing', not 'bad'," he said, crossing the distance between us and carefully placing his hands on my hips as he pulled me closer. He kissed me, but only for two seconds. After three, he'd stagger and get lightheaded. At five seconds, it'd start to burn. He broke away, but kept his hands where they were, avoiding any other flesh-to-flesh contact. The effect of my powers is cumulative, so if I kissed him again, it would start to drain him. "I have to cancel our date tonight."

"Oh." I tried not to show my disappointment, but it was definitely there. We had planned to go into Eden Prairie to eat at my favorite Greek restaurant, and after that see a movie. It was my favorite kind of date night.

"Kurt and I have to go to Michigan to track down a meta that's causing a stir in Detroit." He looked pained as he said it, his handsome face pinched with the regret of having to tell me. "Not sure when I'll be back."

"Hopefully soon?" He rested a hand on my shoulder and I wished I could pull him closer, kiss him again. And again. "Maybe tomorrow?"

He grimaced. "Maybe, but I doubt it. This one sounds complicated – a couple of assaults, a robbery. Might not be that quick."

I rested my head on his shoulder for a second, smelling his cologne, then remembered my hair was wet and pulled away, my hand feeling the cloth of his black suit, where I'd left a damp spot. "I'm sorry."

There was a twinkle in his eye as he laughed. "It'll dry on the way to the airport, and if it doesn't, I'll probably be glad when Kurt and I have to haul our bags through the parking garage to the terminal. I don't know if you noticed, but it's kinda hot out there."

I ran a hand through my hair, trying to untangle it. "I noticed.

The most comfortable part of my training exercise was when I ended up having to drag Eve out of the creek."

His brow lowered as he frowned. "Out of the creek? What happened?"

I felt my teeth click together and my jaw tighten. "I... um...kinda knocked her out of the air with a rock."

"That must have been a helluva a rock."

"It was a helluva throw, actually. The rock was just average."

"It's always a helluva throw if you're doing it, Miss Meta." He found his way back to a smile. "Why did you have to pull her out of the creek, though?"

I flinched at the memory of Eve, broken, lying on the rocky shore of the stream. "I kind of...broke her sternum...and ribs...and maybe fractured her skull a little."

His right eyebrow crept up until it was an inch higher than the other. "A little? I've had a fractured skull before. It's not a minor injury."

"It was an accident. Things just got a little out of hand." I took a deep breath.

He chewed his lip, opened his mouth and started to say something, then stopped. He blinked, then started again. "It wasn't Wolfe?"

"Ugh." I turned away from him, exhaling sharply. "Why does everyone keep asking me that? It's not Wolfe, okay? He's buried, safe and sound, way in the back. It was just me, slipping the leash a little, sick of training and thinking I was actually fighting someone. It's kinda been a while since I felt a real threat and peril, you know."

"Yeah, I know." I felt his hand on my shoulder and it took everything I had not to put mine on top of his. Passing out on my floor wasn't something that would make him very happy. "Not much longer and you'll be done with training and into the real world." I turned to look at him over my shoulder. "Then you'll

long for the good ol' days of training."

I hung my head. "I doubt it. I just wish things were easier sometimes."

His eyes watched me. "With training?"

"Like...with everything. With training, with us...everything."

"With us?" His hand dropped to his side and he cocked his head. "What's wrong with us?"

"Let's see...I'd like to be able to touch my boyfriend for more than two seconds without stealing his very soul." I spat the words out like they were some kind of foul venom. He took a step back and I closed my eyes and took a breath. "I'm sorry. That's my issue, not yours."

He stared at me, almost a blank look, and I caught the subtle calm of his gaze. "No, it's an issue for both of us."

"Yeah, but it's my fault." The full meaning of his last sentence made its way through my warring emotions and I felt a sharp drop in my stomach. "What do you mean by that?"

He perked up, his mouth forming an oblong "o" as he recoiled slightly. "I...nothing."

"It meant something." I could feel the tension in my face. "It's because we can't—"

"No, I told you, that doesn't matter—"

"It matters to you like it matters to every guy—"

"—there's more to us than just—"

"*It matters!*" My shout ended his protest and he took another step back, as though he were afraid of me unleashing Wolfe on him. "It matters. I know it matters to you. I may have to wear heavy clothing but it doesn't mean I can't *feel* anything through them—"

"I was out of line." He held up his hands. "We knew getting into this that it was going to be different, because you're different. That's not bad, it's just..." His eyes went to the side as he searched for the word. "...really inconvenient at the end of the night."

"Yeah. Well." I looked at the floor. "You're not the only one it's inconvenient for."

"I just meant that—"

"You think I don't want to?" I was back on his eyes again and he grimaced, balled up a fist and looked away. "You think I don't think about it all the time? You're not the only one that feels the effects after a date. We can't even sleep in the same bed without worrying that I'll roll over and press my cheek against you in the middle of the night, making you another ghost in my head."

"I didn't come here to fight." He was focused on me, his eyes earnest, face oddly blank. "I came to say goodbye. I have a plane to catch in an hour and a half."

"Well, you better get moving, because the airport's at least a half-hour away at this time of day." I pulled my arms tighter against me and narrowed my eyes at him.

He started toward the door and I watched him go. He stopped and started to say something, his fingers and knuckles white as they held the edge. He made it through a half-spin and halted, and I heard him breathe deep as his head dipped down. Whatever he had on his mind didn't come out, though, and after a minute he turned back and walked out the door, closing it much gentler than I would have expected.

My hand went to my forehead and covered my eyes from the light. I hoped he'd be all right on his trip, but I didn't have the guts to call him and tell him that. I heard my smartphone beep – the one the Directorate had given me – and felt a thrill as I ran to where I'd left it on the desk next to the computer. I turned it on and swiped the screen to find I had a text message waiting. It appeared and I sighed – it wasn't him. My eyes played across the words and my hand went back to my forehead, blotting out the light, as if that could make the world, all my troubles, and that damned text message go away.

I'm back in town. Come over so we can talk. - Charlie

Chapter 4

About an hour later I shifted my car into park in the driveway of my house. The tree-lined streets provided a little shade, but when I opened the car door, I felt the blast of warmth and hurried to get inside. The soles of my shoes seemed to stick on the driveway as I walked to the front door, pausing in the closed-off porch to shut the outside door before I opened the door to the house. The light was dim and mostly came in from gaps in the boards that covered all the windows, just the way Mom had set them up, screening me, the girl in the house, from the world outside every time she left.

I took a deep breath and slid my key in the lock. While Mom had been missing for the past six months, Ariadne had checked the records and told me that there wasn't a mortgage on the place. I had used my ample earnings to keep the property taxes and home-owner's insurance paid and a lawn and maintenance service helped keep the place up for me. I stopped by every week or so, just to make sure everything was okay, but otherwise the house was empty.

Except when Charlie came to town.

The smell of something cooking on the stove hit me as I shut the door. The air conditioner was running and I felt the effects, the cool air filtering in like a sigh of relief after holding my breath. The alarm was deactivated; no reason to keep it active since no one was living here. When last I had left, the place was clean, a little musty, but otherwise all right. I had left all Mom's clothes in her closet, the dishes in the cupboards, but cleaned most of the food out save for the things like Ramen Noodles that didn't have an expiration date looming.

I heard her clanging some pots in the kitchen before I saw her. She peeked a head around the wall and flashed me a smile. Her hair was dark, long, and stood out against her tanned skin and white teeth. Her lips were curled, and painted the deepest shade of red the cosmetics companies made. "Hey there." She emerged from the kitchen and I almost blinked in surprise. I shouldn't have; nothing about my aunt Charlene – Charlie, she liked to be called – should have surprised me by now.

She wore a white tank top that was partially sweated through, and jean shorts that were cut off way too short. Her bare feet were leaving moisture spots on the linoleum floors as she stepped, walking delicately on her toes over to me. Her midriff was bare where her shirt didn't quite reach the waistband of her shorts, which was frayed badly and washed out, white threads where there might once have been blue, the button at the top of her fly a clash against her belly. I shook my head and she smiled wider. "Your mom didn't like how I dress, either."

"I don't care how you dress." I walked toward her, suddenly self-conscious in my heavy jeans and t-shirt that covered me to the neck.

She spread her arms wide, prompting me to give her a careful hug, avoiding the prodigious amount of skin she had exposed. "Be careful," she said in whispered caution, "you know the stronger succubus will drain the weaker." I pulled back and she made to muss my hair, but I pushed her away with a gloved hand, drawing a laugh from her.

"What brings you back to the Cities?" I asked, using the local slang for the Twin Cities of Minneapolis and St. Paul. I walked my way to the couch as she leaned against the pillar at the edge of the kitchen.

"Just passing though." She said it breezily, like she did almost everything, not a care in her world. She smiled. "Figured I'd drop in on my favorite niece."

"Your only niece, to hear you tell it."

"That too. You know, you could do a better job of stocking this place. All I found was Ramen."

"Want to go out to eat?"

"No plans with your boyfriend, the agent, for tonight?" Her leer was suggestive, in a way that if my mom had ever let slip onto her face, would have freaked me out. They were so different.

"No." I didn't look away, exactly, but neither did I look toward her.

"Uh huh." She bored in on me and stepped back into the kitchen, peering through the tiny pass-through that looked out into the living room. "You guys break up?"

I sat down and tugged at my jeans, which felt tight, restrictive and hotter than they had any right to be considering how low the air conditioner had been set in here. I'd feel the electricity bill this month, I bet. "No. Not exactly." She stared through the little square hole at me, not looking away. "We had a fight."

Her face disappeared, but her voice was still loud. "Lemme guess: about touching."

I felt my lower lip jut out, puckering. "What else would we fight about?"

"Couples fight about lots of things, sweetie." Her voice came from the kitchen, over the clanging of a pan. "But succubi tend to argue about one, if they're crazy enough to be part of a couple."

"You calling me crazy?" I said it with an air of amusement.

"Little bit. You are just like me, after all." I caught a grin through the pass-through and then I heard water pouring down the drain in the sink. A minute later Charlie emerged from the kitchen. "I mean, there's a whole world of men out there. You don't really have the luxury of sleeping with the ones you like and expecting them to be alive in the morning, so..."

I looked away from her. "Yeah. I know it, he knows it, but it still makes us both crazy." She sat down on the couch next to me,

splaying out and putting her bare feet on the glass coffee table I'd bought as a replacement for the one broken months ago. "How do you deal with that?"

She had her mouth open, her tongue rolling over her molars, the very picture of disinterest. "You don't sleep with the ones you don't want to die, and you don't get close enough to anybody to have it matter."

"I just...I'm sick of being the world's greatest tease to my boyfriend. He's a good guy, and..." I stopped as her chest jerked in a case of the giggles. "What?"

"You don't have to be a tease. I mean, there are other ways to—"

"Well, yeah, I mean, I know but—" I stuttered as I answered her.

"Just making sure. I wouldn't have expected your mom to teach you anything."

I blushed. "She didn't. But I mean, I know stuff—"

"Sure you do, sweets. Sure you do." Charlie slapped me on the thigh and clicked her tongue against her teeth. "So are we going out to eat or what? 'Cause I'm starving and I poured the Ramen down the sink."

"What?" I blinked, still thinking about what we'd been talking about a sentence before. "Oh, sure."

"Your treat, right?" She gave me a wide grin. "Not all of us have high-paying gigs with the meta cops. The rest of us have to make our money honestly, and I blew the last of my cash getting back into town. Haven't had a chance to stop by the...ATM...yet."

"Sure." I nodded at her and reached for my purse, which was hanging at my side. "My treat. There's a Greek place over in Eden Prairie that's really good—" My attention was caught by the sudden ringing from my bag. "Sorry." I grabbed my cell phone and answered it while Charlie looked on with an eyebrow raised. "Hello?"

"Are you off-campus?" Ariadne's voice was clipped, urgent, washed out slightly by the connection.

"Yeah." I looked around the living room. "I'm just at my house, checking to make sure everything's still all right."

"I need you at Headquarters immediately." Her voice was pinched, more hurried than usual. "The Director and I need to speak with you."

"Umm." I swallowed, heavy. "Is this about—"

"I'm not going to discuss it on an open line. Report to the Director's office in forty-five minutes." I heard a click and looked at the screen of my phone. She'd hung up on me.

I looked up to see Charlie staring at me, her head slanted to the side. "About this Greek place?"

I felt the tension in my guts and wondered if I was about to get a thorough ass-chewing back at the Directorate. "I can't. I just got called back to work."

Charlie's jaw dropped slightly and then twisted to a kind of cold disbelief. "I just threw out the Ramen."

"I'm sorry." I put my phone back in my purse and my hand pushed my hair behind my ears before it fell over my eyes. "I have to go." My hand came out with ten crisp twenty-dollar bills and I handed them to her. "This should cover dinner and a little more. I'm sorry to leave so abruptly, but—"

Her eyes lit up and she took the money a little quicker than I would have thought. "It happens." She tossed her hair over her shoulder and bit her lip as she counted the bills.

"How long are you in town this time?" I tried to catch her eyes, but they were on the money still.

"Not sure." Casual indifference. Great. "A day or two, maybe more, maybe less." She smiled, oddly infuriating me. "You know how it is. Sometimes I get the call and I have to get outta town."

"Yeah, maybe you can explain how that works to me sometime." I laced it with irony. "I need some help, when we get a

chance, you know, keeping them under wraps—"

"Pfffff." She turned her exhalation into a full-blown insult by rolling her eyes at the same time. "We've been over this. You absorbed them, not vice versa. It's not that hard. You just make them do what you want them to do. It's your body, not theirs. If they give you any flack, tell them to sit down and shut up, that it's your head and you'll run it however you please."

I pondered how to explain to her how powerful Wolfe could be when he wanted to assert himself. The drug that Dr. Zollers had put me on helped keep him on a leash, along with some other pointers about building a wall in my head that Charlie had given me over the last few months, but I didn't feel like it was enough. He was still back there; I could feel him sometimes, and I hated it. "All right. I gotta go."

"Call me, kiddo. We'll do lunch sometime." She winked at me and started toward the bedroom.

"Just make sure you do the dishes before you leave." She stopped in the hallway and shot a look back at me, a little frown with a slanted down eye that made me wish I hadn't said anything. "You left them in the sink last time and I didn't find them for a week."

"Ugh, fine, yes, Mom." She said it with a laugh and another roll of the eyes. "Tell your bosses I said hi."

"Yeah, right. Because you want the Directorate to know about you."

"Hell no. I'd like to remain far off their radar, if you please." She tugged on her waistband. "They've probably got a file on me. You should check sometime."

"I don't think so," I said. "They don't have any record of my mom having a sister."

"Uh huh. If you were the suspicious sort, you might think something of that – like I was lying?"

I started toward the door. "I don't think you're lying, Char-

lie."

"Why's that? Doesn't everyone in the meta world want a piece of you? Having someone pretend to be your aunt when you still don't totally know who to trust? Seems like kind of a winning strategy to get close to you, if it worked." She was stock still, waiting for me to respond.

"You're right." I opened the door. "But that's the problem, isn't it?" I smiled at her and a puzzled look crossed her face. "You may be my aunt, but I don't trust anybody."

I caught a flash of a smile from her as I backed out the door. "Heh. You really are just like me. See ya later."

I closed it behind me, stepping out onto the warmth of the porch, and felt the heat pervade me again. "Guess it runs in the family."

Chapter 5

I wondered if I was in trouble the whole way back to the Director-ate, pondering if the man in charge (Old Man Winter, we called him, because he was old, a frost giant, and his name was Erich Winter) was going to run me through the mill for what I'd done to one of his stars. I parked in the Headquarters building and took the elevator straight from the garage to the top floor, where his office was. It was still sunny out when I arrived, in spite of the fact that it was nine o'clock at night. And ninety degrees. I love Minnesota.

It was damned quiet when I knocked on the door, and a muf-fled call of "Come in," was followed by the door swinging open to reveal Glen Parks, his gray hair pulled back in a ponytail. I checked to make sure I was in the right place. Old Man Winter was sitting at his desk, his back to the window, gray hair and cold blue eyes visible even at this distance. Ariadne was at his shoul-der, but her clothing had changed since I had seen her on the grounds earlier. Her red hair was pulled back and her blouse was white.

Parks moved aside for me to enter and I blinked as I stepped into the office. Scott Byerly and Kat Forrest were seated in the chairs in front of Old Man Winter's desk, Kat still looking slightly washed out, and Scott was quiet, his fingers resting on his chin, eyes forward. "Looks like the party started without me." I clutched the strap of my purse a little tighter, wondering if I was about to get smacked down. No one said anything.

Scott stood as I approached the desk, offering me his seat. I smiled and shook my head, then turned my concentration back to Ariadne and Old Man Winter, who both stared at me, Old Man

Winter with his usual stoic calm, Ariadne intense, her eyes almost on fire. Scott found his way back into the seat and the silence continued, unabated, as I shifted my weight between my feet for the next thirty seconds or so, hoping someone would say something before I had to resort to small talk.

"I suppose you're wondering why we called you all here." Ariadne was the one that spoke, the lines visible at the corners of her eyes.

Kat and Scott exchanged a look with each other. Kat sat up straighter in her seat, her eyes a little wide. "Um...because Sienna nearly killed Eve?"

"I didn't..." I stopped myself just in time. I didn't look at Old Man Winter. "It was an accident."

"Unfortunately, we don't have time to hash over training accidents at the moment." Did I detect a note of regret and acrimony in Ariadne's voice on that one? Her mouth remained a severe line. "We have other business." She looked over Kat's shoulder to Parks.

I turned to look at our trainer and he stepped forward, a folder in his hand. "In the last twenty-four hours there were a string of convenience store robberies from Gillette, Wyoming across the Interstate 90 corridor in South Dakota that have caught our attention."

Scott snorted, and when we all looked at him, his face went red. "Sorry. It's just funny to hear I-90 described as a corridor. It's a big, long stretch of dusty plains and nothing."

Parks stepped between us and set the folder on the desk, opening it to reveal some photos. "Corridor or not, this could be a problem. No fatalities so far, but there were assaults during each of the robberies. The one in South Dakota included an assault on a local police officer. Several concussions for the store clerks, some trouble remembering what happened, including the assailant, who," he coughed, "appears to have overpowered all the victims

without a weapon." He pointed to one of the photos. "This clerk was lucky: his head nearly went through the counter, but he lived."

I stared at the picture he indicated. The shelves behind the counter were trashed, the glass broken, and blood stains ran in a circular splatter down the surface. It looked like whatever had happened had been painful. "You think it's a meta."

Parks paused before answering. "Yeah. It's the Sherriff's Deputy in Draper that puts it over the top for us. He was knocked out before he could draw a weapon or react. That's not normal. Assuming he was following procedure, he wouldn't have let someone get so close to him." He looked at each of us in turn. "We've seen this sort of pattern before. It's probably a young meta, a junior hellion who's getting hold of his oats, thinks he's a badass, not quite ready to cross into the realm of killing just yet, but getting there."

"Probably dangerous if cornered," Ariadne said, leaning on the desk with both hands. "M-Squad is being dispatched to help some of our agents from the Texas branch deal with a severely dangerous meta that's wreaking havoc in western Kansas, and our other agents are on assignments, which leaves us with no one to follow up on these incidents."

I perked up and saw Scott and Kat do the same. "No one?" My question was tentative, and I was reminded of the times when I would get Mom to break her rigid and inflexible rules. I called those occasions miracles, because they didn't happen very often.

Ariadne's mouth became a thin line. "We're strained. Meta activity is up – way up. We're spending a lot of time chasing ghosts lately – things that don't pan out." She brought a hand up to push her hair back and I caught a glimpse of something, written hard across the faded lines of her face. Ariadne wasn't old, more like middle age, but in that moment she sure as hell looked it. "We have no one else to send, and this needs to be followed up on. Congratulations." Her eyes bored into each of us in turn. "You're

up."

"This is serious business," Parks said, his arms folded as he stood apart from Ariadne and Old Man Winter. "You're not kids anymore and I vouched for you, told 'em you're ready to give it hell. Don't take any stupid chances, and watch each other's backs."

I swallowed my excitement. "What do want us to do, exactly?"

Ariadne exchanged a look with Parks. "The last robbery was about three hundred miles south of the Twin Cities, at six o'clock this morning, in Owatonna, Minnesota."

"I know where that is." Scott was awake with a little excitement. "They've got an awesome outdoors store down there—"

"You're not going down there to go shopping." Ariadne cut him off without mercy. "You're going down there to ask questions and establish a direction to head." She opened a packet and slid the contents across the desk to us. I saw my face on a driver's license, as well as one for Scott and Kat. There were also three leather holders that looked a lot like wallets, but when I picked one up and flipped it open it held the credentials of an FBI Agent named Katrina Ahern, with a picture of Kat.

I held it up and dangled it in the air in mild surprise. "Impersonating a federal agent is a felony."

Ariadne met my stare, grim and serious. "It's real. Your names and pictures are in the FBI database and you'll pass muster unless you do something deeply stupid. My advice?" She let a little half-smile loose as she said it.

"Don't do anything deeply stupid," I said, staring at the FBI ID with my picture in it. "You said these are real—"

"They'll even get you into an FBI field office if you had some reason to go there," Parks said. "I wouldn't recommend it, though, because you'll likely have to answer questions you won't want to. These are so you can bypass local law enforcement if they give

you any guff, and to get civilians to answer your questions. Now, you all look like friggin' kids, but we'll dress you up professionally and that oughta take care of most of the problem."

I stared at the Driver's License with my picture on it. I wondered idly why I'd been given it, then realized it fit my new name, Sienna Clarke. I also noticed it added about five years onto my birthdate. I tried not to think about the implications of being twenty-three years old in a single stroke.

"All this is part of your cover story." Ariadne's voice snapped me out of my thoughts. "You're rookie agents, chasing down leads on a robber that's crossed interstate lines."

"What happens if we run across the real agents who are investigating it?" I asked because I was curious. I had a feeling it would be bad.

Parks smiled. "According to the FBI's computers, agents Clarke, Green and Ahern," he nodded at each of us in turn, "are the only ones assigned to this case. Your only issues will be the ones you make for yourselves, which is why Ariadne was cautioning you not to make a spectacle."

"So you want us to track this guy down?" Kat looked a little confused. "Catch him or kill him...?"

"Capture, please." Ariadne's tone turned to ice. "If things escalate, we'll examine other options, but for now it's capture only. While the robber has used brutal means, as yet he or she hasn't caused serious, lasting harm to any of the victims. Like Parks said, we suspect a teenager, manifesting their powers and getting out of control with the taste of freedom they're experiencing."

She drew herself up, removing her hands from the desk and tucking them behind her back. "This is their tipping point. If we act quickly, we can save them and bring them back here. If you screw it up, they go the other way, become a criminal for life and either spend time in our Arizona facility or end up dead."

"You'll draw weapons from the armory in case things get out

of hand." Parks was stern as he said it. "Just make sure you aren't the ones who make it go that way."

Ariadne shot a look at Parks. "They're all qualified to carry a sidearm?" After he nodded, she went on. "Remember that your best weapon is yourselves. You'll leave within the hour. Pack a bag and be prepared to be gone for a week or more. Any questions?" She waited for us to ask anything, but none of us did. "Keep your cell phones on you at all times. I expect progress reports every three hours while you're awake, even if it's only something as mundane as 'We stopped to pee at a gas station'. If we suffer from anything on this excursion, it will be overcommunication, not under." She glared at each of us in turn. "And no fighting amongst yourselves."

"It's been like...months, since any of us fought," I said.

"And keep your temper in check." Ariadne looked daggers at me. "Are we clear?"

"Like Saran wrap, but without the flexibility." I smiled at her.

"You are being entrusted with a responsibility that is most serious." Old Man Winter finally broke his silence, leaving behind the role of set piece that he so often cultivated during meetings and gracing us with his deep, thickly accented voice. It was so smooth he could have been on the radio, but it was intimidating too, the way it spilled out, with more authority than anyone else I'd met. "This is your first step out of training. Agent Parks has assured us that the three of you are ready, but remember that you are still being tested, that you are not yet agents. Succeed and follow the rules and this can be a significant mark in your favor; fail and we will have to evaluate how effective your training has been."

His ice cold gaze fell on Kat first, causing her to shudder, then on Scott. "Be careful and achieve your objective. This is your chance." His eyes fell on me last of all, and I felt a freezing chill as he looked through me. "Do not fail us."

Chapter 6

"Can you believe this?" Scott slapped the steering wheel as we cruised out the front gate of the Directorate an hour or so later. "This is it! Finally, the big time!"

Kat gave him a weak smile from the passenger seat, but she didn't say anything. I was stretched out across the seat behind them, supposed to sleep first so I could drive later if need be. It had been a long day, filled with more emotion than I had wanted it to contain. I checked my phone for the thousandth time since Zack had left. Still not a word, a text message, anything. We'd had fights before, but this one was different. He'd never not talked to me afterward. I chalked it up to him catching a flight and hoped he'd call me when he landed.

"Isn't anybody else as excited about this as I am?" Scott's disbelief was edging into his enthusiasm. He looked at Kat, who shrugged, then turned to me. "What about you?"

I yawned. "It's a hell of an opportunity. Let's not screw it up, lest we get six more months of running around the woods, trying to subdue members of M-Squad without hurting them badly."

"About that," Kat said, turning to face me. "You got your head on straight? Not gonna go crazy and flatten this meta we're chasing, are you?"

"Let's catch him first," I said, "then I'll worry about whether I'm gonna put the severe hurt on him or not. After all, we're basically heading to some town in the middle of nowhere hoping there's a clue that will lead us on to the next place this person's gonna strike."

"Criminals are dumb." Scott turned the SUV onto US High-

way 212, heading east. "It wouldn't surprise me."

"You think he left a note that says, 'Next I turn south and drive 400 miles to Ankeny, Iowa, where I will rob a convenience store and stop to use the potty'?" I rolled my eyes.

"Why do you think they're sending us to Owatonna if there's not going to be any clues as to where he's going next?"

"He or she," Kat said.

I yawned again. "Because half of what the Directorate does is gather evidence so they can justify locking these criminal metas up when they actually catch them. I've seen the files. We'll pick up the evidence and get whatever info the locals have, and when the Directorate hears about the next attack, we'll haul ass to catch up."

Kat and Scott exchanged a look and then she turned back to me. "Wow, you've given this some thought. But what makes you think that the, uh...the meta...the criminal—"

"Suspect." Scott said it businesslike, as though he were trying to play the part of a real FBI agent. "Or perp. That's what they call them on the TV shows."

"Anyway," Kat said, "what makes you think the perp will have a destination? Couldn't they just be on a drive, or maybe running from something?"

"Maybe." I felt the cool air from the AC, slowly flushing out the humid heat that lingered even now, after the sun was down for a couple hours. The temperature display for outside still read 83 degrees. "It could be a Bonnie and Clyde-type situation, where they're just bopping around from place to place, but it seems a little odd. I'm kinda surprised there's not more information on who the perp is."

"We'll ask some questions when we interview the victim." Scott sounded self-assured.

I looked over at Kat. "You have the details on this one?"

"Um..." She fumbled for her phone and clicked it on. Peering at the screen, she tapped it a few times and then started to read.

"Yes, okay. Daniel Lideen, age twenty-five, of Waseca, Minnesota. Looks like he's worked at the store for about six years, assistant manager, was alone on the night shift...a patron found him at around 6 A.M., looked to have been knocked out for a while before he got rousted by this customer, who's a regular." She looked up. "Nothing spectacular there. Multiple contusions to the head from getting slammed into the counter, maybe a concussion or brain injury; the last report indicates they weren't sure."

"Hm." I got lost in my thoughts. "You can take a peek inside, though, right? Figure out what's wrong with him?"

She nodded. "I can probably take care of any memory loss. Was that what you were thinking?"

I smiled. "I was thinking it'd be nice to help the poor guy out since he got the crap kicked out of him, but that's not a bad idea either. After all, if he can give us a description of the perpetrator, that would make our job easier."

It got quiet for a while after that. I sat with my head leaned against the window, staring out at the darkened fields passing us by until we got into the suburbs. I recognized the familiar lights of Eden Prairie as we passed through and got onto the 494 loop, skirting the southern edge of the city. I could tell Scott was still excited, and he chattered occasionally about how great the assignment was going to go and his certainty we'd achieve success and start building a reputation within the Directorate. I was sure he was right, but was privately hoping that it would be a good reputation rather than a bad one.

We caught Interstate 35 and headed south as the clock clicked 11 P.M. The traffic on the road was light and Scott kept us well above the speed limit. Parks had mentioned before we left the Directorate that the plates for the SUV were flagged as an FBI vehicle, and there were flashing lights and a siren in case we needed them.

The land flattened out and the buildings became more scat-

tered as we passed out of the southern suburb of Burnsville. Shopping centers gave way to fields and forests, the trees becoming havens for shadow as the headlights of our SUV chased the blackness off the road ahead. Forty miles passed in the blink of an eye – I closed my eyes and was jarred awake what felt like seconds later, but I knew wasn't after I smacked my mouth and it was dry, my tongue finding a layer of film over my teeth.

I rubbed my eyes as I pushed myself off the window. Kat and Scott were talking in hushed voices in front of me. I heard him chuckle, saw her giggle and bat her eyes, watched her hand reach out and stroke his forearm. I started to ask them where we were but stopped myself. There was no reason for me to interrupt their moment.

I watched a sign pass that indicated that Owatonna was only a few miles away. I quietly pulled the water bottle I had left in the cup holder and drained it, rehydrating my mouth. Kat and Scott took no notice of me, still chatting in low voices. I could have heard them if I tried, but I made an effort to tune them out. I focused on Zack and checked my phone again. Not a text message, a missed call, a voicemail, nothing.

"You're awake." Kat's voice contained a hint of surprise and I looked up from my phone to find her tight smile looking back at me. Her eyes were slightly squinted and she appeared to be chewing on her lower lip. I felt a little bad for her, because it was obvious nerves were working on her at least a little. "The GPS says we'll be there in less than five."

I nodded as I took another drink of water and popped a piece of gum in my mouth. I had left the purse behind when I changed into a gray suit with a white blouse underneath, placing my wallet and FBI ID into the pockets of my suit jacket. I could feel the lump that was my pistol under my left arm, the weight of it against my side in my shoulder holster. I knew Kat and Scott were carrying as well, but I doubted that they knew I was carrying a backup

in an ankle holster on the recommendation of Parks. The two of them had been uncomfortable with the firearms portion of our training. I reveled in it, like I did all the other parts that involved fighting.

Parks drilled it into our head over and over to use every tool at our disposal. "Your powers set you apart from others," he'd said. "In ancient times, people with your powers could rule entire countries. In modern times, one man with a gun can hurt you more than an ancient army. The gun is mankind's great equalizer and you're a fool if you don't recognize it." He talked like a drill sergeant when he was training us. I knew he'd done a stint in the army because he'd told me so. Parks knew his stuff. He'd been with M-Squad for almost ten years, since he and Bastian had basically built the unit from the ground up.

I also carried a knife strapped to my calf on his recommendation, but that was another thing I wasn't likely to mention to the squeamish Kat especially, nor Scott. No use making them edgy. I was glad Scott was excited. I was skeptical. I hadn't done this before, and I didn't want to get into a situation I might not be prepared for while hunting down a meta I had no knowledge of.

Scott guided the car onto the exit ramp as the gentle voice of the GPS told him to turn. I could see the Kwik Trip lit up just off the freeway, a fifty foot sign out front with the price of gas in red as an enticement to save a cent over their competitors across the street. We turned into the parking lot and stopped in front of the pump. Kat and I both looked at Scott, questioning, until he shrugged. "We need gas. We can look around here and then head out to the hospital to interview Lideen, if he's awake."

Kat walked alongside me toward the door while Scott pulled out his Directorate issued credit card to swipe it in the gas pump. "Talk to the clerk while I go to the bathroom?" She said this to me as I pulled open the glass door so she could go in.

"Uh, okay." I shook my head as she veered toward the back

of the store. I watched her pass a bakery case with a wide selection of donuts. I felt my stomach rumble and realized I never did get my dinner, but I shook it off. It felt like my metabolism had slowed in the last few months, in spite of the training routine. I had to watch what I ate.

I approached the counter as the Asian kid behind it stared at me, the only person in the store. I reached for my FBI ID and flipped it open, trying not to feel nervous. After all, he was most likely going to be paying attention to the ID, not me. "Sienna Clarke," I said, just barely remembering my assumed name. "FBI. I'm here to ask some questions about the robbery."

"Uh, yeah." He nodded, his acne seeming to have reddened. "I wasn't here when it happened."

"I know that." I pulled out a small notepad and pen I was carrying in my pocket. "The victim was a Daniel Lideen, right?" He nodded at me. "You work with Dan very often?"

"Nah," he said. "He was usually mornings or overnights. I work evenings; this is only part-time for me. Dan's a full-timer. I was here before he took over last night at eleven, though."

"See anything unusual?" I was asking mostly out of general interest. I wasn't planning on spending a lot of time interviewing this kid, since he hadn't been around for the robbery, and based on our information, the perp had been in South Dakota during his last shift.

"Not really." He shrugged. "We get a lot of traffic from the interstate, so there's more strangers that come in here than regulars."

"All right, well, thanks for your help..." I looked down at his white nametag, standing out on his blue shirt. "...Shaun."

"Sure." He nodded again. He seemed to let out a deep breath and I suspected he might be a little nervous talking to the law. Couldn't imagine why.

"I'll take these." Kat appeared at my shoulder and plopped a

plastic bag onto the counter. I looked down and saw she had filled it with a half dozen donuts from the bakery display against the far wall. She looked up at me innocently. "Want one?"

"I don't think I can," I said. "They go right to my hips."

She picked up one with white frosting and multicolored sprinkles and took a big bite. "You sure?" Her mouth was full, and the glorious smell of sugary dough was in the air. "It's really good."

I blinked and shook my head. "I can't." I looked down at the bag then back up at her with a suspicion. "Are you going to eat all of those?"

"Unless Scott wants one, yeah."

I sighed and pushed my way out the exit with a forced smile for Shaun, who blanched because I caught him checking out Kat. It figures; not only does she have a body that draws the attention of every man that crosses her path, but she doesn't have to work that hard to maintain it.

Scott was screwing the gas cap on when I got back to the car. "How'd it go?"

"Fine. Your girlfriend will be back in a minute; she's buying out their entire bakery."

He frowned. "I didn't expect to turn up much here, but I kinda hoped..." He let his words trail off.

"That we'd find the meta hiding out in front of the store, wearing a trench coat, a backward baseball cap, and rapping profanities?" I cast a look back toward the entrance as Kat made her way across the parking lot toward us, a donut in one hand and the bag hanging from her fingers in the other.

"Guess this is where the real detective work begins, huh?" He opened his door and climbed in while I got into the backseat behind him again. I watched him start to fiddle with the GPS. "Let's hope the victim or the local cops can shed some light on things for us, or else we're gonna be hanging out in this town until we pick

up another incident. Hospital is an exit back, police station is east of here a little ways." He shrugged. "Hospital first?" I nodded and we were off.

When we arrived at the nurses' station and flashed IDs, a middle-aged overweight woman in pink scrubs showed us to Daniel Lideen's room. He was sleeping, his long face tilted to the side. The nurse left when Scott asked her to and I looked to Kat. "You should get a feel for his injuries before you wake him up."

She put her hand on his forehead, causing him to stir slightly. "Not a bad idea." She closed her eyes and her breathing slowed. A light glow appeared under her hand and the clerk's skin started to shine. A black and purple bruise under his eye began to fade along with a thin scab that ran the length of his cheek. I saw Scott shutting the door as Kat took her hand off the clerk's forehead and his eyes opened, blinking at the two of us. "That should do it," Kat said.

"Hello, Daniel," I said as I leaned over him. "My name is Sienna Clarke and I'm with the FBI." I halted to give him a second to process that information. His eyes blinked a few times as he tried to focus on me. "I'm here to ask you some questions about your assailant."

"Oh...okay." His voice was a little scratchy, and I couldn't shake the feeling that he was more asleep than awake. "I already told the officers what I remember."

"I know." I tried to make my reply as soothing as possible. "But they're local cops and we're here to ask because the same thing that happened to you happened to some other folks in Wyoming and South Dakota. Can you tell me anything about the person that robbed you?"

He screwed up his face in intense concentration, staring over my shoulder, then went blank. "I don't...I can't remember."

I shot a look at Kat, whose eyes widened as she put her hand on his upper arm. I saw the glow from her as I asked him another

question. "Tell me what you do remember."

"Um...I came into work at about eleven...and I did some re-stocking in the freezer." He squinted, as though he were trying to recall. "I remember eating my sandwich and drinking some coffee at about five." His face relaxed and he shook his head. "After that...I don't know."

I looked sidelong at Kat, who was taking long, ragged breaths and whose hand was at her side. She shook her head. "Can you tell me anything else, Dan? Anything could help."

His eyes were blank. "That's all. That's all I remember."

I gave him as warm of a fake smile as I could. "Excuse me while I talk to my associates." I beckoned to Kat, who followed me, shuffling along in slow steps to the hallway outside. I looked left and then right; the corridors were white, with dingy tile and little color, but empty. I honed in on Kat. "What's the matter with him? Has he got brain damage?"

"No!" She shook her head with more emphasis. "I checked him over again after the first time, and this guy is healed; he's in perfect condition. His skull is fixed, his scars are gone and it doesn't look like there was anything wrong with his brain even when I touched him the first time, let alone now."

Scott looked back at the door to the room, which was drawn. "Is it possible he's lying?"

"Possible." I nodded at him as I chewed that one over. "But I don't think so. I was looking in his eyes as he answered, and he didn't show any of the obvious signs. He was working last night, so it seems unlikely he's secretly the meta doing all this, unless he can somehow teleport to Wyoming and South Dakota on his breaks." I shook my head. "I don't think he's lying. I think there's a simpler explanation."

"What?" Scott looked at me. "You think he has some kind of neurological damage that Kat can't detect?"

I looked back at him, then to Kat, before I answered. "No. I

think that whoever attacked him..." I took a step back and looked through the semi-open door to see the clerk sitting upright in bed, blinking, looking around the room, disoriented, even though he had just been healed by someone who could fix nearly any ailment. "...took his memory."

Chapter 7

We cleared out of the hospital after some perfunctory goodbyes and thank-yous to Daniel, and checked in with Ariadne. We sat in the car, engine running to give us air conditioning to offset the heat (still almost eighty even though it was nearing midnight) while we listened to Ariadne.

"You think whoever attacked him is responsible for his memory loss?" There was a slight fuzzing in the speaker, probably the result of the air conditioner operating near full blast to keep the three of us from sweating through our suits, but otherwise it almost sounded like Ariadne was in the car with us.

"Which guarantees that it was a meta that attacked him." I was almost glum at the realization. I was kind of hoping it was going to be some petty criminal that we could slam dunk and leave to the local authorities. Part of that might be because I was checking my phone every few minutes for a call or message that I had yet to receive. I wasn't going to be the first to break the silence, that much I knew. "Any idea what kinds of metas can cause memory loss?"

"There are a few," Ariadne said. "Let me talk to Dr. Sessions and get back to you with a list."

"Any other incidents?" Scott cradled the phone in his hand, holding it just below his chin when he was talking, as though it were a tape recorder.

"Nothing at present. You still need to meet with the local cops, but the Police Chief for Owatonna is out for the night, so it's best if you wait until tomorrow to make that stop." There was a pause and a hiss on the phone before Ariadne spoke again. "Check

into a hotel and get some sleep. If there aren't any incidents to-night, check in tomorrow morning after you've stopped by the Owatonna PD."

"Understood." I tried to keep the fatigue out of my voice as Scott punched the end button on the phone after the two of them added their responses to my own. "I don't know about the rest of you, but I'm exhausted."

Scott grew a curious grin, one that cracked his ruddy face and made his eyes dance. "You can't go to sleep just yet."

"Pretty sure I can." I rubbed my eyes. "And will."

"No, no, no." The smile was getting kind of creepy. "Do you realize what we're carrying with us?"

"Guns and teenage angst?"

"Ha. No." He reached into his pocket and pulled out his wallet, dangling the new Directorate-issued driver's license in front of my face. "Fake IDs that aren't really fake."

I let my jaw drop in disbelief. "What are you thinking?"

He smiled again, then turned forward in his seat and fastened the seatbelt with one hand while fiddling with the GPS with the other. "I'm thinking we find a hotel with a bar."

I leaned back in my seat and draped my hand over my eyes. "Right. Because there's no possible way this could go horren-dously wrong."

I kept my peace on the drive, even though I was questioning not only Scott's level of responsibility but also his sanity. We found a hotel (with a bar across the street) and I shook my head as we pulled up.

Scott must have sensed my discomfort. "We all agree that the meta who's doing this is probably far from here by now, right? If he keeps to the pattern?"

"Mighty big 'if'," I said with a shake of the head. "But proba-bly."

"So if we check into the hotel and then have maybe one or

two drinks..."

I could tell by his smile he was already reveling in the freedom and there was little I could do to sway him. Still, I had to try. "What if Ariadne calls us after we've been drinking with a lead we need to pursue immediately? We're screwed. We won't even be able to drive anywhere."

"I can drive." Kat spoke, turning to face me. "I'm pretty drained from healing that clerk; I don't think it'd be a great idea for me to drink right now. So if we get a call, I can drive while you guys sober up."

"See?" Scott gave me a shrug of unworry that did little to assuage my concerns. "Got it covered."

I grabbed my bag and opened the door. "Got it covered like what? Like you had Gavrikov covered?"

"You're never gonna let me forget that, are you?" He was following behind, and I caught a hint of annoyance in his voice.

"Not so long as he's stuck in my skull, no."

We checked in, getting two rooms. I started to suggest that Kat and I could stay in one room while Scott stayed in the other, but when I handed him the cards for his room he handed the other to her and I didn't bother to argue. I preferred to stay by myself anyway.

We went up to the third floor where our rooms were side by side. "Meet out here in five and we'll head down together," he said.

"I think I'll pass," I said. "You guys go have a good time. I'm just gonna turn in; might as well have one of us be rested for the morning."

"Come on, Sienna. We've been working our asses off for months, had Parks and Ariadne breathing down our necks, had all manner of shit go wrong, and now we have a chance to unwind. Don't be so uptight."

I took a deep breath before answering so I could avoid ripping

his head off while we still had potentially weeks' worth of road tripping ahead of us. "I'm not being uptight. I just don't want to screw this up, okay?"

"I get it." He let the smile recede into a smug, almost taunting expression. "It's okay. I admire your restraint. You probably don't even wonder what it feels like."

I tensed, felt every muscle from my lower back up locking into place. "Wonder what what feels like?"

"Drinking." His half-smile dissolved into a real one. "You haven't wondered what it's like? Your boyfriend goes out drinking sometimes, doesn't he?"

I felt myself relax, but only a tenth of a percent. Dammit, I had thought he was talking about something far different, and it had let a wave of acid loose in my stomach, sending it roiling. "Yeah, Zack goes out drinking every now and again." Usually when I'm busy, but he does it. Because he's old enough.

"And you never felt curious or left behind?" He smiled, a little too innocently.

Damn his smile. I knew what he was doing, what he was suggesting. Any other day, it might not have found its mark. After all, my boyfriend was mature, responsible, secure in his job, and if he went to the bar with his college buddies, he did it on his time off (and usually when I was training.) I'd never felt left behind, not really, because I was too busy doing other things. I pulled my cell phone out of my pocket and lit up the display. Still nothing. "Fine." I looked back up at him. "One drink."

"Attagirl." He shot a look at Kat. "This'll be fun. The three of us, on our first assignment, blowing off steam, hanging out at the bar." He draped a thick arm around Kat and drew her close, giving her a peck on the cheek. "It's kinda like..." He thought about it for a minute.

"Being grown-ups?" I offered it sarcastically, but it only widened his smile.

"Five minutes." He turned and his hand fell to grab Kat's, and they walked toward their door. "We'll head down together."

I nodded and slid the card key into my door and turned the handle. When I walked inside, I flipped the switch and waited for the lights to come on. The carpet was a deep maroon and it was a simple setup – two beds, desk, dresser and TV.

I threw my bag on the dresser and retreated to the bathroom. I looked in the mirror at myself. I looked older, mostly because of the suit, but also because I had my hair back in a ponytail. I held up a gloved hand and heard the leather stretch as I clenched a fist and then relaxed it. Grown-up indeed. I pulled the glove off and started to splash water on my face to help me wake up, but then remembered that it would probably destroy the careful amount of makeup I had applied earlier, before I left the Directorate. I rarely wore the stuff, but in this case it seemed important for the role I was playing.

I looked again at myself in the mirror and wondered what I was thinking. We were on a serious assignment, the first chance we had to prove ourselves, and we were going to a bar at midnight to have some drinks even though we weren't anywhere close to done with our assignment. I sighed and looked at the faceplate on my phone again. The LED indicator that let me know when I had messages or missed calls wasn't blinking. Screw it. Screw him. We'd been working our asses off for months, Kat was going to stay sober, and Scott and I would just have one or two and call it a night. An energy drink or coffee tomorrow and we'd be ready to keep going.

I tried to remember that reasoning as we walked in the doors to the bar. The light was orange in the room, with flatscreen TVs suspended from the ceiling around the bar itself. Tables were set up to the left and right of the bar area, with a small dance floor in the far corner. Music was playing, a modern pop tune, but not a soul was dancing. I scanned the room as we walked in and the

place was only slightly packed, which surprised me given it was Saturday night.

We made our way to the bar, Scott leading us, his grin reaching an infectious stage. He bellied up and Kat sat next to him. I took the seat on the other side of him, mostly because he was more likely to talk than Kat. She was always tired and quiet after healing someone.

The bartender made his way over to us, a guy in his forties that had more than a few extra pounds. He had long brown hair in a ponytail and was happy enough after he checked our IDs. "Whaddya want?" he asked in an accent that was as far from midwestern as I could imagine.

Scott looked over to me first and I shrugged, so he turned to Kat. "Just water for me," she said. "Designated driver."

"What's good here?" I picked up the mixed drinks menu that he had proffered and thumbed through it.

"Honestly? I got some strengths; I make a pretty good Whiskey Sour, Bloody Mary, Rusty Nail, Dirty Martini...my Fuzzy Navel is the stuff of local legend—"

"You don't need to show us that," Scott said.

The bartender smiled and his face split into jowls. "I also make a pretty good Cherry Bomb."

I shrugged, without a clue. "I'll try the Whiskey Sour."

"Straight up or over ice?"

He looked back at me and I felt the fatigue of the day edging in. "Surprise me."

The bartender nodded and Scott ordered a beer, a local brand, and went to the other end of the bar to prep our order. Once he was out of earshot, Scott turned to me. "What do you think so far?"

"He seems like a nice enough guy. Kinda big, though. You think that's glandular?"

"About the case." Scott shook his head.

"I think we should not screw it up." I tried to give him my

most serious look. "Right?"

"Right." He looked back at Kat, who was resting her face on her palms. "Right?" She gave a lethargic shake of the head, pulling it off her hands to spread her palms with indifference. "It'll be fine. Just a drink or two, and we're off to bed for the night, and back to work tomorrow." He smiled again at me and I caught the first hint of nervousness. "But come on, admit it – we're out on our own, on the road, we're in charge of this thing, and we're sitting in a bar after a long day of chasing down a meta. Tell me this isn't how you imagined it."

I felt a charge of amusement. "First of all, it's been like four hours, not a day, and most of it we've been driving, so I don't know how hard it's been." I saw his nervous happiness start to evaporate and stopped myself. "Yeah, it's kinda how I imagined it. Freedom, right?" The bartender returned and set down a napkin and placed my drink on top of it, complete with a maraschino cherry, put a beer bottle in front of Scott and slid a water glass onto the bar beside Kat.

"I'll drink to that," Scott said, raising his beer up and angling it toward me. He waited for me to pick up my glass, which was a lot shorter than his; kind of a midget glass, I thought, like they didn't want me to have a grown-up's cup. I clinked it against his bottle as he said, "To us! To freedom!" and then reached around him to click my glass against Kat's. Even she was wearing a smile, as wan as it was.

"Pretty sure it's bad luck to toast with a water glass," I said to Kat as I took the first sip of my drink. Whatever she said in reply, I didn't hear. I felt my face contract as the full flavor of the whiskey hit my mouth. It was only mildly sour. What caused me to make a face like I'd swallowed battery acid was what I could only assume was the result of the alcohol. It was pungent, powerful, and I immediately wanted to spit it out and throw the cup far, far away from me. They had given me poison, I was sure of it.

"Are you all right?" Scott was looking at me with his brow furrowed. He took a swig and set his beer back down on the bar.

I swallowed the vile mixture and wondered where the barman had gone. I assumed he'd wanted to be as far away from me as possible when I discovered that his idea of a good drink was far removed from what I had thought it would be. "Is it...supposed to taste like I took a swig of household cleaners?"

Scott laughed and looked back at Kat, who feigned a smile of amusement as she rested her face on her hands. "A little strong, huh?"

"It's a little strong in the same way that compared to normal humans, we are a little strong."

He picked up my drink and took a sip. "Not bad. It'll probably take a little bit for you to get used to the flavor, that's all."

I wanted to tell him that the only way I could ever get used to the flavor would be to take a blowtorch to every taste bud in my head first, but I refrained. I stared down at the drink, looking at it like it was an adversary I was facing off with. "Acquired taste, huh?" I picked up my little kid's glass, suddenly thinking it was a lot bigger now. I didn't want to waste a lot of time on this, and it certainly didn't bear sipping, prolonging my disgust for an hour or more, a little shot of revolting nastiness at a time.

I threw it back like I'd seen on TV, trying to ignore the strong, nearly gag-worthy reflex it caused as it passed my tongue and drained down my throat. I felt the ice on my lips, and that was good, the last lingering aftertaste of the liquor still remaining on the cubes. I set the glass down on the bar and shook my head, as though I could rid myself of the tang that was still on my tongue.

The bartender made his way over, and just as I was about to ask him to make my next round a water, he set another Whiskey Sour in front of me. I looked up at him, frozen, like I had gotten caught flashing him a fake ID, except this was much worse. "The gentleman down there sent you this." I looked at the barman, and

he lifted a pudgy finger to point to a man down the bar.

He had brown hair, spiked a little in front, with a thin face and intense eyes that caught my attention even from twenty feet away. He raised his glass to me and I could almost feel the ice cubes melt in mine as I picked it up and raised it in a silent toast across the distance between us. He took a drink of his and I took a deep sip of mine, taking care not to make the face that was struggling to get out, that mixture of putrid desire to spit and horror that drinking so vile a liquid was socially acceptable.

"Picked up an admirer, huh?" I turned back to Scott to find him with a second beer in front of him, and his words were drifting a bit as he talked, slurring. I looked past him at Kat, who was shaking her head as if to keep awake, not paying much attention to us.

"I guess." I looked back to the man to find he had turned back to the bar, nursing his drink, attention focused on a soccer game on the screen in front of him. "Or maybe he just figured I was the only unattached woman in the bar." I swiveled on my stool to look around and confirmed my suspicion; most of the people in the bar were plainly coupled up.

I looked to Scott and frowned. "Why didn't he assume I was your girlfriend and send a drink to Kat?" Scott got a blank look, then hemmed and hawed. "Never mind, it doesn't matter," I said. He took a breath and lifted his second beer, draining it.

"Take it easy." Kat leaned over, crossing Scott's body to weigh in over the blaring music that filled the bar, now a classic 80s rock tune that had more metal than an orthodontic patient's mouth. "You're not going for a third, are you?"

"I've been drinking beer and wine with my family since I was like...thirteen," Scott said, his words curling as he answered, his tongue sounding like it was getting heavy. "I can handle it."

"Uh huh." Kat looked from him to me, her eyes narrowed slightly. "How much does your family usually let you have?"

"One." He swayed on the stool. "We're social drinkers, not alcoholics." He laughed, as though it were the funniest thing in the world.

She rolled her eyes and then whispered something in his ear. He straightened on his stool and turned to me. "I think we're gonna turn in for the night." He pulled a wad of cash from his pocket and laid some on the bar. "You coming?"

I felt a flush of red as I imagined what Kat had said that got him to change direction so quickly. I didn't want to be in the room next to them, certainly not for the next half-hour. "I think I'll stay a little longer."

He grinned, a goofy one. "Heh. Well, you might wanna stop after that one." He pointed to my drink. "After all, if this is your first time drinking, you need to build up a tolerance."

I felt a sway of my own in my head. "I'll work on that." I shot him a dazzling smile. "Have fun."

Kat rolled her eyes at me but smiled, a weary look that I knew contained at least a grain of indulgence; her making an accommodation she normally might not have made when she was this tired, only for the purpose of getting him out of the bar before he became too trashed to walk.

As if to illustrate my point, Scott started to stand and his legs buckled. Kat caught him with an arm around his back and I could see her help him regain his balance, her meta strength enabling her to keep him upright. They walked to the door, her steering, him along for the ride. I chuckled under my breath and was dimly aware that the room had a gentle bob to it that could have been my head rocking back and forth. I knew that my best bet was to avoid drinking even one more drop of the suddenly much tastier drink in front of me.

When I turned back to the bar, I started because there was someone in the vacant seat to my left. He caught my eye, those intense blue eyes locked on mine, and he gave me a disarming smile

that somehow got me to giggle, which came as a great shock to me. "Sorry," he said. "Didn't mean to startle you."

"I didn't mean to be startled." I took a deep breath and closed my eyes, shaking my head that I'd said that. "Sorry, I just didn't expect—"

"Do you mind some company?" He caught my gaze and held it, and his smile went beyond the realm of disarming and into charming. He was wearing a button-up shirt that was unbuttoned at the top, giving me a glimpse of the beginning of some well-defined chest muscles.

I caught my breath and it held for a minute before I could squeeze out my answer. "I don't mind."

"My name's James. James Fries." He held up his drink, a tall, clear glass with some sort of garnish being the only hint it wasn't water, and took a leisurely sip, not breaking eye contact the whole time he was drinking. "And you are?"

"Sienna." I thought about it for a second, remembering that my identification had a drastically different name on it than the one I'd grown up with. "Sienna Clarke."

"What brings you to the mighty town of Owatonna, Sienna Clarke?" He leaned against the bar, the angle of his body making him look very cool, his laid back attitude drawing my interest.

I took another breath and caught a whiff of a musk, something that left me wanting to take another breath so I could smell it again. "I'm here for work." I blinked a couple times and the room swayed pleasantly. "You?"

"The same." He took a sip and I admired his lips as they caressed the glass. "What do you do for work?"

"I'm..." It took me a second to remember my cover story. After all, I wouldn't have wanted him to think I was some sort of person with super strength and powers that defied reasonable explanation. "I'm with the FBI. I'm doing some...investigating."

"Investigating. How mysterious."

My hand found its way to my glass, which found its way to my lips for another sip. "I do like to keep a certain mystique about me." This time it didn't taste too bad. In fact, it was almost good. "Do you live around here, James?"

"No." I watched the sweat drip from his glass, leaving little blotches, like inkblots on the napkin as the dark wood of the bar bled through. His hand swirled his glass, slow. "I live in Minneapolis. I'm here for work."

"I see. What do you do for work?"

He smiled. "Recruiting."

I laughed, light, and I had no idea why. "That was vague."

There was a glimmer in his eyes. "I have a mystique to keep up, too, you know."

"Fair enough." I put my empty whiskey down and watched as the bartender slid by and snaked it, replacing it with another. I started to protest but he had a wide grin on his fat face and nodded at James as he headed back to the other end of the bar where someone waited with a hand raised in the air. I looked at the new drink and felt a certain pressure in my chest at the realization that this could not end well. "I can't drink this," I said to James and watched him half-smile.

"Why not?"

"I'm a lightweight." I said it with the air of someone making a confession. "And I have to work tomorrow morning, which means I kind of need to call it quits for tonight if I'm going to be at all able to think or drive tomorrow."

"Acetaminophen and ibuprofen are your friends," he said. "And lots of water."

"I think moderation might also be a swell idea."

"Much less fun." His hand moved, very casually, across the bar and came to rest on my own. I could feel the gentle weight of it through the glove, the very slight warmth, and it caused me to redden, a heat rising in my cheeks that might not have been no-

ticeable had I not been drinking. He watched my reaction. "Is that too much, too fast?"

"What?" I had been in a little bit of a daze, staring at his hand on mine. "No. Not really."

"No?" He picked up my hand and cradled it in his, rubbing it. "Not this either?"

It felt strangely good, even through the glove. "No. That's fine." His eyes were on mine, staring, with a warmth that I found compelling, drawn to, and I couldn't quite explain it. I found myself leaning closer to him.

He leaned in and kissed me. It was sudden, and caught me by surprise. My eyes widened when he did it, but it felt so good, the pressure, the warmth of his hand as it touched my cheek, and rested there, his lips on mine. I kissed him back, the haze in my mind so agreeable, and I felt his tongue part my lips and swirl. I let him hold my face in his hands and he kept them there, pressing his lips on mine so firmly—

I opened my eyes in shock and with the realization that I couldn't, wasn't able to—

I pulled away, broke from him with sudden violence, standing so abruptly I knocked over both my stool and my drink, trying to get backward, away from him, him who didn't know what I was—

He looked at me with vague amusement. "So that was the line, huh?"

"What?" I looked around to see everyone in the bar staring at me, and turned back to him, still sitting on his stool, the same little smile crooking his lips. "No, it's fine, I just...can't..." I let out a breath in frustration. "Are you okay?"

His eyebrows arched upward. "I'm fine. Are you?"

"Yes. I'm fine. I'm sorry." I cocked my head and tried to give him my most regretful expression. "Thank you for the drinks, James. You're a really nice guy – and a fantastic kisser, by the way – but I have to go."

He stood and tossed some bills on the bar. "Why don't I walk you out?"

He took a step toward me but I held a gloved hand out and rested it on his chest. I let it linger there; damn, it was firm. "I don't think that's a good idea, for a lot of reasons."

He seemed to be suppressing his grin, but nodded. "Fair enough." He reached into the pocket of his pants and came back with a business card. "If you're ever in Minneapolis, give me a call."

I straightened my blazer and nodded, feeling the holster against my ribs. "I'll keep that in mind." I nodded toward his stool. "You might want to sit down for a few minutes." He gave me a quizzical look. "Just a suggestion. Nice to meet you, James."

I walked from the bar and tried really, really hard not to look at him as I pushed my way out the door. It didn't work, and he gave me a sizzling smile that made me want to go back to him, and kiss him until his eyes rolled back in his head and his face melted off. I shook my head in disgust at that thought and walked out into the parking lot. It felt like I was being weak when I thought it, weak and casual and flippant, endangering James's life so I could feel...something. I was lucky that the eternity that it felt like he kissed me was less than I thought it was, or he would have made a hell of a scene pitching over in the bar.

The parking lot lurched as I was about halfway across it. I stopped, regained my balance, and kept going. Once I reached the elevator after passing through the hotel lobby, I leaned against the wall and felt my head spin. Those Whiskey Sours weren't so bad.

When the elevator door dinged I opened my eyes to find the doors still closed. I heard another ding and stared, waiting for them to open. On the third ring I realized it wasn't the elevator: it was my phone, and I scrambled to grab it out of my pocket. I thrust it up to my ear after hitting the talk button, not even looking at the caller ID. "Hello?"

The elevator dinged, the door opened, and I heard Kat's voice on the other end of the line as well as in person. She stood in the hall and turned her head in surprise when she saw me stagger out of the elevator. "Get packed." She pulled her phone away from her ear and I got a good look at her face, which was still drawn, but now more serious, her blond locks twisted and mussed around her. "Ariadne called. There was another robbery."

I dropped the cell phone back in my pocket and my hand went out to the wall automatically to support me. "Where?"

"Red Wing, Minnesota." She started to hold out a hand to help me but I waved her off. "It's north of here, a little over an hour, on the Wisconsin state line. We need to move now." A little hint of a smile peeked at me, understated, on her tanned and pretty face. "If we hurry, we might be able to catch up with them."

Chapter 8

A few minutes later our SUV was back on the highway, doing about a hundred miles an hour, barreling north on the interstate with the siren blazing. Kat was at the wheel and I was in the passenger seat. Scott was passed out in the back seat, his head against the window. We hit a bump and he didn't stir. I rolled my window down and let the warm night air blow in my face.

"How are you holding up?" Kat didn't take her eyes off the road. I could tell she was tense, white-knuckling the wheel. I would have been too. Scott had learned to drive years ago. Kat and I had learned in the last six months, with Parks as our instructor, in an intensive driving course that the Directorate gave us to teach us how to drive both offensively and defensively. Now I could run a car off the road at eighty miles an hour easier than I could parallel park.

"My world is in motion," I said, as I swallowed heavily. I didn't quite feel sick, but I certainly felt the first strains of it. "I could do with a little less of that."

A tight smile made its way onto her face and a few of her teeth peeked out from between her lips. "At least I didn't take the back roads route the GPS suggested. All those twists and turns..."

"Bleh." I shook my head. "Drinking is bad for you. Also, I think I came close to kissing a guy to death in the bar."

"What?" Her head snapped over to look at me.

"He's fine." My eyes pointed straight ahead, and I was trying to watch the road in order to avoid getting motion sickness. "I mean, he seemed fine, so we must not have kissed for very long."

"Um, wow." Her eyes were not on the road, which became

obvious a moment later when she had to swerve after the tires started bumping on the strips at the edge of the highway. "Sorry. Wait, so what happened? I mean, aren't you and Zack..."

"I don't know." I pulled out my phone and pushed the button again. The screen flared to life, giving me a perfect view of the background, but there were no missed calls or waiting text messages. "We kind of had a fight."

"Oh." She turned to look at me, then swiveled her gaze back to the road. "What about?"

"Pretty much about what you and Scott were doing just before we left."

"Sleeping?" She turned to me and then reddened. "Oh. Before that."

"Yeah."

She let the silence hang for a minute. "Because you guys can't...?"

"Yeah."

I think the edge in my response put her off, because she got quiet before she spoke again. "Not even a little? Like maybe being really careful, with some clothes on, and—"

"No." I tried to end her inquiries, but I felt my frustration bleed over. "I don't have much margin for error, Kat. A little unnoticed skin contact in the throes of passion and a few seconds later he's dead." I felt the breeze run through my hair. "That's not really how I would want it to go. It's not a turn-on, having impending death hanging over you during sex. Especially..." I swallowed heavily again, this time unrelated to that slightly sick feeling that was growing in me. "...you know. The first time. Or hell, any time."

"I guess it sort of kills the romance, huh?" She looked at me again, and her face turned sympathetic, her eyebrows arched in concern. I found it annoying, especially since I knew she and Scott were having plenty of sex; scads of it, loads of it, probably every

single night of the week, and I couldn't even get a kiss in without worrying about hurting someone. "So, did you and Zack break up?"

"I don't know." I frowned. "We didn't really resolve anything, and he hasn't tried to talk to me since we fought, so maybe." I looked over at her. "Why?"

She didn't look at me, just shook her head, and when she answered, her tone was completely casual. "No reason. Just wondering." She chanced a glance at me, then half-shrugged. "Well...you were kissing some other guy in a bar..."

"Oh." I felt a dull pain in my head, and then I slapped myself right on the forehead. "Oh, damn." How could I have been so stupid? "I didn't even...it didn't even occur to me about Zack. Damn, I have a boyfriend. Damn damn damn."

"Well, maybe." Kat wasn't exactly reassuring, even though I knew she meant well, so I spared her the glare.

The trip passed uneventfully, though by the time we reached the sign indicating Red Wing's city limits, I was feeling a little more ill and had the beginnings of a headache. We pulled up in front of a gas station that had a police car parked outside, lights still flaring. My feet hit the pavement and I steadied myself, my FBI ID already in my hand as I crossed the pavement to talk to the two cops that were standing behind the yellow tape that cordoned off the door.

"I'm Agent Clark and this is Agent Ahern," I said, my ID wallet unfolded as I ducked under the tape and joined the officers behind the line. "What can you tell us about what happened here, Officer..." I let my eyes find the silver nameplate of one of them. "...Olmstead?"

The one I had spoken to was a bald guy, dark skinned. "We responded to a 911 call a couple hours ago from a customer that came into the station and found the clerk unconscious behind the counter. The guy had been smacked around pretty hard. We sent

him to the hospital and started looking over the scene, but we didn't find much of anything."

"No forensics?" Kat chimed in, catching the attention of both officers, drawing it away from me. I hated how she could do that, but it was the least of my problems now.

"Nah," Olmstead answered. "The store serves a couple thousand people a day during the summer, more on a weekend like this. There's enough hair and fingerprints in this place to start a new civilization in a petri dish, but nothing we can tie to anybody."

I looked over his shoulder and saw a camera hanging from the awning above the gas pumps. I pointed at it. "What about that?"

"Nothing," he said with a shake of his head. "Perp took the recording and smashed the system. Most of these smaller stations don't bother with off-site data backup because they use the cameras more for people who drive off without paying for their gas."

"Thanks for your help, Officer Olmstead." I smiled at him and he nodded back, slightly tense from what I presumed was being questioned by the FBI. "We'll need the name of the victim and which hospital you sent him to."

"Sure." He pointed to the road we had just been on. "Hospital is that way. We only have one. Follow the signs and you can't miss it. Victim's name is Roger Julian. He was pretty messed up when they carted him away. Couldn't remember a damned thing."

I exchanged a look with Kat. "Nothing?" When I turned back to the officer, he shook his head. "How bad was he hurt?"

"Not bad," Olmstead said. "Scrapes and bruises, lost consciousness for a while. Paramedics said he looked like he'd be just fine, but they wanted to get him an MRI because of the disorientation, the loss of consciousness and the head wound. Thought he might be concussed."

"Uh huh. Thanks for your help, Officer." I nodded at him, and Kat and I walked back to the car. I heard him say something under

his breath to the cop that was with him about the FBI recruiting toddlers, but I pretended not to hear it. Once we were in the car, I turned to Kat. "Sounds like this one might have the same issue."

"Yeah." Kat started the car and put it in gear. "I'm not healing this guy unless he's got major problems, but I'll take a look and see how hurt he is. I'm guessing if he can't remember anything about the attack, he's suffering from the same kind of memory loss as the last guy."

"You sure you can't heal him, just to be safe?"

She let out a slow breath. "I don't think so. I don't want to push it. After we get to the hospital, we seriously need to find a place to crash for the night or else you need to take over driving."

I did a little head shake of my own. I couldn't tell if I was sober yet, but I doubted it. "We should just find a hotel. I'm not in any condition to drive yet."

We went a little further down the road, turning when we saw a blue sign with a white H on it. After another mile, the hospital came into view and we parked. It was a predominantly brick building with white trim and an enormous, multi-story octagonal entry. I felt the warmth of the air as I stepped out onto the pavement. I looked into the car before I closed the door; Scott was still passed out in the back, snoring.

I shook my head to clear the cobwebs as I followed Kat across the parking lot and through the sliding doors. The hiss they made as they moved, coupled with the cool air conditioning hitting me in the face, gave me a half-second of disorientation. I'd started sweating, just a little, on the walk from the car. I wished this damned state would come to some sort of happy equilibrium in regards to the weather; but no, she bitterly clung to her extremes.

After inquiring at the check-in desk we were routed up a couple stories to the critical care unit. The tile floor clicked under Kat's heels and I heard the squeak from the soles of my flats as we walked along. She had slowed her pace so that I would trail behind

her. The air bore the familiar smell of disinfectants and I heard raised voices ahead of us. We came around a corner and found a nurse's station with three security guards surrounding someone.

"Sir, I'm going to have to ask you to—" One of the security guards stepped forward, blocking my view of the person that the three of them had surrounded. A couple nurses were behind the desk in the station, backing away.

"I don't think you realize the depth of your mistake here." The voice was familiar, but I still couldn't see the speaker.

"Sir, we're going to have to call the police." The lead guard's hand rested on his holster, and I could see that he was tensing on the grip.

"That's a shame." Cold, bitterly ironic, the speaker didn't sound at all regretful. I couldn't shake the feeling that I knew that voice and I adjusted my position, crossing in front of Kat. I caught a glimpse of him over the security guard's shoulder.

He was in profile to me, looking at the guard closest to him, and didn't see me. His hair was long, brown and hung almost to his shoulder blades. I saw that his face was red, though it was hard to tell through his swarthy skin. I knew his eyes were brown, though I couldn't see them from this distance. I quickened my pace and drew my FBI ID.

"Gentlemen," I said, holding it open. "Sienna Clarke, FBI. This is Agent Ahern." I nodded to Kat. "What's going on here?"

"Ma'am." The lead security guard peered hard at my ID while the other two watched their subject with undistilled suspicion. "This man was trying to access patient rooms long past the end of visiting hours."

I turned to the man they held captive. "Is this true?"

He folded his arms and stared at me with barely disguised disbelief. "I just came here to talk to the guy who got robbed." He nodded at the lead guard. "This clown gave me the party line and I was about to give him the party platter."

Kat squinted. "What...what that does even mean? Is that a threat?"

"Absolutely not," he said. "A party platter filled with meats and cheeses is a generous gift, and he should be damned happy to get it."

"Ma'am?" The head guard got my attention turned back to him. "What is the FBI doing here in the middle of the night, if you don't mind me asking?"

"The same thing your troublemaker is doing," I said. "We need to have a conversation with the patient. He's a witness in a series of robberies that have crossed state lines." I nodded to Kat. "If you could show Agent Ahern to his room while I deal with your interloper..." I gestured with my hand toward the man standing between them all and he rolled his eyes and nodded back, with the greatest reluctance. I locked eyes with Kat. "We'll be outside when you're done."

"Ma'am?" The head security guard spoke up again. "Would you like us to come with you, keep an eye on him?" He said it as the troublemaker walked past me, already on his way back to the elevator.

"Him?" I turned to follow him as he walked past. "If he gives me any problems, I'll just shoot him."

I heard the security guard behind me, a warble of uncertainty as he whispered to his colleagues. I followed the long-haired man back to the elevator, stopping in front of the door after he pressed the down button. "I didn't need your help," he said, stepping into the box.

"Of course you didn't," I said with an easy nod. "You were about to lay waste to three local rent-a-cops and probably a couple nurses because you had it all well under control."

"Damned right." His sullen look finally cracked and I caught the shake of his head that was followed by a grin. "How have you been, Sienna? I haven't seen you in my dreams lately."

I blew air noiselessly between my lips. "Honestly, I've been too busy to think about you, Reed."

"Ouch." He ran a hand through his long hair. "So you're a full-on Directorate agent now, huh?"

"Nah. I work for the FBI. Longer hours, worse pay."

He rolled his eyes. "Sure. Should we play the game of denial about why each of us is here, or can we cut the crap and get right to the truth?"

"I will if you will."

"You're here because of the guy, right?" He stared me down. "The guy going around treating convenience store clerks like he's Chris Brown?"

I started to lie, but he was watching me. I'd known Reed longer than just about anybody, though I hadn't spoken to him in months. "Yeah. We figure this is a new meta, just manifesting, that needs a serious reining in."

"Yeah?" He tugged on the front of his shirt. He was wearing a nice one, a white dress shirt that was untucked, with a suit coat over it and dark jeans. "You talk to the guy in Owatonna?"

"You mean the guy with a big hole in his memory?"

"He was kind of a dead end, wasn't he?" Reed smiled. "The ones in Wyoming and South Dakota had the exact same problem, oddly enough. How big of a believer are you in coincidence? Because I'm not much of one; and head traumas don't typically cause that much memory loss."

"What kind of meta would be able to do that?" I folded my arms, felt the familiar lump under my left arm as I rested my hand on my pistol.

He shrugged, looking for all the world like he was a man unconcerned with anything. "Well, the beatings could be caused by just about any type...as for the other, there's a few that could cause that, but one in particular I'm thinking of."

I waited a minute for him to answer. "I thought we weren't

gonna do the mystery game."

"I said we weren't gonna do the denial game – I never said I was gonna tell you everything I know." He turned and pushed the button to call the elevator and stared at me, puzzlement brewing on his face. "Why Clarke? Why not just go with Nealon?"

I rolled my eyes and lowered my voice. "Because if you're going to commit a felony, it's best not to use your real name, especially if said name is being entered into the FBI database as an agent. That tends to leave a pretty exact record if anything goes wrong."

He frowned. "Well, wouldn't they have had to put a picture of you into the database in a personnel file?"

"I—" I stopped and thought about it. "I don't know. Maybe. I'm not planning on making a major problem of it."

"Huh." He stared back at me with cool amusement. "I might worry about that a little bit if I were you, especially given who you work for."

"Oh yeah?" We both looked up as the elevator dinged. "Care to share what you mean by that?"

He smiled as he stepped into the elevator. "Nope." His hand reached out to hold the door as Kat came up to join us. "What's the word, blondie? Does this guy have a swiss melt for a memory too?"

Kat had the rarest of expressions cross her face, irritation, as she shot me a look, as though she were asking permission before speaking in front of him. I nodded at her. "Yeah," she said. "He's perfectly healthy, his brain is fine, but the memory's just gone, like it never existed."

"Same old story." Reed pulled his hand back and the elevator door started to close. "See you ladies down the road. Oh, and Sienna? You smell like whiskey. Just FYI."

The elevator doors closed before I could snap back a reply. I looked to Kat, who was slightly flushed. "Of course I smell like

whiskey," I said. "I've been drinking whiskey." Kat shrugged as I pushed the elevator button to call another one. "Ass," I said, lowering my voice.

"Who was he?" Kat waited until we were walking across the parking lot to ask.

"Him?" I chucked a thumb toward the hospital building. "When Zack and Kurt came to my house for the first time, they ended up drawing guns—"

"What?" She looked at me with incredulity. "Really?"

"Really. I kinda got into a scuffle with them first. Anyway, I ended up running when Kurt started shooting, and Reed was waiting outside and offered me an escape route, so I took him up on it."

"They shot at you?" She stopped and grabbed me by the arm. I felt the strength in her grip; it wasn't quite as much as I could bring to bear, but the girl was no slouch. "With real bullets?"

"Tranquilizer darts. But I didn't know that until later."

"So who is he?" She stared at me evenly, and had the slightest smile. "He's kinda cute, you know."

"I had noticed that, yes." I pulled my arm gently from her grasp. "And if he'd ever stick around for more than five minutes without disappearing, that might matter."

"Oooh," she said in a somewhat high and floating voice. "A man of mystery?"

"The very definition of it." I opened the passenger door to the SUV and climbed in, tossing a glance back to confirm Scott was still snoring softly in the back, head against the window and mouth open wide. "I bet you could do with a little bit more of that in your life right about now."

"Huh?" She cocked her head at me, question written on her face, then swiveled to look when I indicated the backseat. She saw Scott, shook her head and stuck the key in the ignition. "So what did he tell you?"

"Not much. Said he'd interviewed the victims out in Wyoming and South Dakota, that they had the same memory gap as the guy in Owatonna." I leaned back against the headrest. "So now we've got four people who got the holy hell beat out of them and they don't remember a thing about it. We've got no idea where they're going and no clue who's doing it – except..." I frowned.

"What?" She was at rapt attention, looking at me.

"Reed confirmed one thing." I chewed my lip. "He said a meta was definitely causing the memory loss – and I think he knew which kind of meta it was."

Kat looked at me blankly. "So what kind of meta causes memory loss when they attack you?"

I looked out into the black night, and I racked my brain for something, anything, I'd learned in my studies, anything at all about metas that could make memories disappear. Without that clue, we were without anything to do or any lead to investigate until the next call came in. "I don't know," I said. "I just don't know."

Chapter 9

Someone Else

The heat was near unbearable. Somehow I'd done it again, scored the crappiest possible car I could get my hands on. I'd stopped in some half-assed town called Ellsworth just over the Wisconsin line and stolen an old Dodge that was sitting overnight in a grocery store parking lot. The reeferhead's Honda had started making gawdawful grinding noises in southern Minnesota. I tried to make it last, filled it up in Red Wing, but no, it started going into catastrophic failure mode after I crossed the river. This is what happens when you have to choose between buying weed and performing regularly scheduled maintenance, I suppose.

I thought maybe I'd get lucky this time, but I wasn't. The Dodge was older and the air conditioner didn't work, which might explain why it was left in a parking lot. It was after midnight, and still pretty damned stifling out. I wished for the millionth time that I had made this little trip in winter, then remembered what winters were like in the upper midwest. Spring would have been the time for this. Or fall.

My shirt was dripping with sweat by the time I hit the first exit ramp in Eau Claire, Wisconsin. The home of pretty near nothing, the city of Eau Claire had still somehow managed to attract over sixty thousand people to live within its limits. I'd been here before; I couldn't see the appeal.

The night was dark, but the yellow light of the moon was in the sky as I rolled through a commercial district. There were a line of little stores and I followed the thoroughfare until I reached Fleet

Street, where I turned left. I was going by directions I had memorized before I left Gillette, but they were as fresh in my mind as if I had them with me on a piece of paper. I eased the car down the road, squinting to read the house numbers by the moon and the streetlights.

8453. I stopped when I saw them on the front of a white house, the little bronze numerals barely visible in the dark. I climbed out of the car two blocks down and started to walk back. I felt a grin split my lips and I barely restrained myself from wanting to run.

The house was older, built in the seventies, a little one-floor rambler on a city lot, the grass now overgrown by a week or more, weeds sprouting up all over. The aged wooden siding looked like I'd get splinters just from touching it, and I had a suspicion that the dark lines on the roof meant that this place couldn't hold its water. A red door was the single spot of color on the exterior and a wooden fence higher than my head partitioned the backyard off, hiding it from view.

I cleared the fence with a jump, felt the shock through my knees as I landed and cursed under my breath. I'd been jumping through a lot of hoops the last few days, had been on the receiving end of some rough luck, and whoever crossed my path next was going to be the recipient of all my frustrations for those setbacks and reversals. It was going to be sweet.

I walked slow, letting my eyes make sure the path in front of me was clear. I could see a light on in the back of the house as I came around the corner, crouched in a defensive posture in case someone was waiting for me out back. It never pays to be surprised.

The back of the house was one long, straight line, and I could see a couple people in the kitchen window, having a conversation. Both were men, one older than the other. The younger one looked to be in his late teens, while the older appeared to be in his forties.

Looks could be deceiving, though, because I knew he was at least a millennium old if not older. Franklin Beauregard, he was named. He was the reason I was here.

I ducked under the kitchen window and crawled through the grass on my hands and knees. The wet of the dew was the only coolness I had felt since I left the Honda in Ellsworth. I felt it on my knees and the temporary pleasure of the temperature change gave way to annoyance at getting wet – those fellas inside were really gonna suffer for all this crap.

I stood once I was clear of the window and climbed the step to the back door. I braced myself and took a deep breath before lifting my foot and kicking. I hit the door and felt it splinter as my momentum carried me through, breaking it into four pieces. They should have used a steel door; that would have at least slowed me down as I ripped it from the hinges.

I heard raised voices and the young man who I assumed was Franklin's son entered the back hallway first. He uttered a cry of warning when he saw me and whipped a fist through the air. I reached out, caught it and tugged him forward, ramming his head into the wall.

I was past him in a half a heartbeat, looking through the narrow kitchen at Beauregard, a smirk on my face. "Hello, Franklin. What brings Omega to Eau Claire, Wisconsin?"

He clasped one hand over the other at his midsection and I watched his face become calm resignation. "As if you don't know."

"Oh, I know. I just wanted to hear you say it." I took two steps toward him. He didn't move. "Tell me where Site Epsilon is."

His eyes widened and I watched his aged hands turn white as they clenched each other. "How...?" His face went back to relaxed. "You...are batting at shadows."

"Nah, I'm batting at the things that cast shadows." I took an-

other step. "Site Epsilon. Andromeda. Where? Last chance." I angled a hand toward him in warning. "And don't even think about coming at me with those—"

His battered jacket burst open, the ripping of the fabric like a thunderclap in the quiet summer eve. I jumped forward and hit him three times in the face before he landed the first attack, a hard bite on my shoulder. I grunted in pain and slammed his head against the wood floor. Two gargantuan snakes extended from his body, one from behind each of his shoulder blades. I snatched a butcher knife from the block next to the sink and cut into the first as it struck at me, splitting the head from its body. It went limp and dropped, flopping on the floor behind him.

I got to my feet, knife in hand as Beauregard struggled to his knees, the remaining snake head giving him license to do so. It extended five feet from his body, keeping out of range of the knife, hissing and striking every time it got close to me. I feinted toward him and it snapped and came at me. I reached out with my free hand and wrapped my arm around it, trapping it in a headlock as I drove the blade through the top of its skull, slicing the head off. Without so much as another sound, it fell still and quiet, and I turned to Franklin, who was on his knees, both snake bodies limp and hanging from his shoulders.

"Andromeda," I said as I dangled the knife before his eyes. "Would you care to guess what you lose next?"

He bowed his head, and I heard a whisper. "Decorah, Iowa. It's in Decorah."

I knelt and dropped the blade to the ground, clucking my tongue. "Why do you have to lie to me, Franklin? It demeans us both."

"I'm telling the truth." He looked up at me, his fingers resting on the floor as though he were drawing strength from it.

I reached up and my hand wrapped around his neck, applying only the slightest pressure, forcing him to look me in the eye. "Site

Epsilon is not in Decorah, and we both know it. You've certainly got an Omega safehouse there, but that ain't where Andromeda is." I smiled at him. "So...the hard way, then."

He gasped as the pain began, my other hand holding him tight on the cheek. "But...you...would have done this anyway..."

"Of course," I said, my hands holding him as he started to grunt, then let out his first scream. "It's not like I trust you." I felt the surge begin as his life, his soul, drained out of him, my hands pressed tightly to his cheeks. His memories flooded into me, into my mind, causing it to swirl, a fresh infusion of life into my brain. I let his body drop to the floor and I stood up, looking down on him in pity. "Now that you're in here," I tapped the side of my head, "you can't lie to me anymore, Franklin."

I heard something move behind me and I turned. His son (I knew because of his memories now in my head) was stirring, moving from where I had put him down against the wall. I walked to the back door and knelt next to him, flipping the boy over. He still looked young, but I'd put a nice gash on his forehead. His eyelids fluttered and he mumbled something. "Shut up," I said. I stared at him for a minute, then shook my head, letting out a sigh of impatience. Too young.

"This is your lucky day," I said as I pressed my hand against his face. Even unconscious, I felt him squirm when the pain started. I held contact for another couple of seconds and then pulled my hand away. I could see the rise and fall of his chest, the regularity of his breathing a sign of the mercy I didn't even know I had in me. "Don't worry," I said. "You won't remember any of this."

Chapter 10

Sienna Nealon

I awoke to a headache that felt as though a lumberjack had decided to chop down my skull. Light was shining through a window and there was a faint rattling that I was sure was between my ears, the remnants of my brain trying to escape its own stupidity for drinking too much last night. I groaned and realized that the buzzing was not in my head: it was in fact to the left of it, on the nightstand next to the hotel bed I was sleeping in.

I rolled over and grabbed my phone, slapping the talk button without bothering to check the display. I wondered for a half-second if this was what life had been like before Caller ID. "Hello?" My voice was little more than a croak.

"Hey." I heard the quiet voice of Zack on the other end of the line and sat up, far too fast for my own good.

"Owww," I said, my hand rushing to my temple, which felt as though it were about to explode.

"You okay?" Zack sounded a little resigned. Or cautious. Actually, it was hard to tell because the pain in my head was so sharp.

"Yes. Just...have a headache."

"Hm. First night on a mission, away from the Directorate..." He sounded like he was brainstorming. "Let me guess, they gave you cover as an FBI agent, complete with an ID that said you were over twenty-one."

"Should I worry that you immediately assume the worst about me?" I tried to cram some reproach into my words, but I'm pretty

sure it failed. I dangled my legs over the edge of the bed. Apparently I hadn't managed to shed my suit before I passed out.

"You should assume that I've been a college student at roughly your age. My fake IDs weren't as realistic as what the Directorate can produce. Also, I've been on some of those 'sit around and wait' assignments. They're moments of excitement followed by long stretches of boring nothing."

"That sounds familiar." I stood up and hung my head, because it felt better for some reason. I paused, trying to string together some thoughts. "About last night..."

"It's all right, you don't have to apologize. I know it's been tense for you lately." His voice was soothing.

"Yeah, I...wait, what?" I bristled, every muscle in my body tensing as the meaning behind what he said made it through my fog-addled brain. "What did you just say?"

There was a long pause on the other end of the line. "I...I said..."

"Did you just say '*I* don't have to apologize'?" I felt my jaw clench. "I know damned well I don't have to apologize. I was just minding my own business in my room when you came in and we had a lovely conversation about how you secretly resent the fact that I can't put out, which is something that you've never had the balls to say to my face."

I waited for a response, and when it came, there was a little heat on it. "This isn't the time to have this conversation."

"Really?" I almost yelled at him. "When's a good time to discuss the fact that we've been dating for months and can't touch for more than two seconds per day? Wedding night? Golden Anniversary? When would be the appropriate time to talk about the fact that we can't have sex, Zack? Please, tell me so I can write it into my schedule!"

There was the barest gap of silence on the other side. "Fine, you want to do this now? Yes, it's grating on me, okay? But that

doesn't mean—"

"It's grating? Grating?" I let fly with my disbelief. "Just say it, okay? It's frustrating and it's never going to get any better! Unless you really love the touch of heavy leather gloves, you'll be enjoying a nice embargo of skin-to-skin contact for the rest of your life."

"I – what? Touch of leather gloves? You mean, like—"

"I mean it's never going to get better, Zack." I was firm, final.

"So, what?" He didn't even sound real on the other end of the phone. "You want to be done? Finished with me?"

It felt a little like someone was choking me, and the pain in my head was splintering, telling me to say something I didn't really want to. "I think we've gone as far as you can go with me, Zack. If you ever want to have anything approaching a normal life, yeah...I think we're finished."

There was a smoldering quality about the way he said his next words, like there was a fire underneath every single one of them. "If that's the way you feel—"

"It's not the way I feel, Zack." I should have been on the edge of panic, ending things like this. It's not like I set out to do it the day before, when I was content on the campus, in training, and with my boyfriend. "It's the way it is. You're too big a boy to keep holding back; time to grow up. My life is solitary confinement – it's a prison sentence, and you don't deserve it, even if you do act like an ass sometimes."

"That's it?" I could hear the edge in his voice. "It's over?"

"Yeah." I didn't have an edge in mine. I was just tired. "It's over. Be safe in Michigan." I pushed the end button on my phone without waiting for his reply and sagged back onto the bed, taking a deep breath. I felt a burning at the corner of my eyes, and I couldn't believe what I'd just done.

In a way, I was sorry I hadn't done it sooner. I mean, I kissed another guy at the bar last night, and almost got carried away.

That's not the strongest sign that things were going well in my relationship with Zack. In fact, it was probably a sign that there were some deep, serious, underlying problems. Well, one anyway. And just because I had to live the rest of my life to less than the fullest didn't mean he had to.

There was an insistent knocking at my door and I levered myself back up and opened it to find Kat waiting. "Ariadne wants us all on the phone in an hour to make our report."

"Fine." I massaged my temples. "You want to come to my room or what?"

She shrugged. "Sure. I think I can have Scott up and moving by then." She looked down at my attire and made a face. "You might consider showering and changing your clothes. You look—"

I looked down at myself, at what I was wearing. "A little ragged, yeah. I'll do that. See you in an hour."

I shut the door and got to work. I rummaged in my overnight bag and found pain relievers and the other drug I was taking. I popped the acetaminophen, then an equal dose of ibuprofen, then got my syringe ready for my morning injection of chloridamide. The injection was critical because if I didn't take it, the souls of the people I'd absorbed tended to get a little...feisty...in my head. I took a deep breath and plunged the needle into a vein. I was fortunate in that I was a meta; if not for my continuously regenerating vein structure, I'd likely be out of places to inject the drug by now.

The shower brought me back to life, and after I spent a few minutes getting my hair straightened and had changed into a fresh suit, I felt worlds better. The pain was still lingering behind my eyes, but it was in the recesses of my mind rather than front and center. And it didn't hurt to blink.

An hour later, there was a knock on my door and I opened it to find Kat, who was as sunny in her disposition as ever, and Scott, who wore sunglasses and looked as though he'd had an anvil

dropped on his head. He grumbled some sort of greeting as he slouched into the room and flopped in a chair at the table. Kat sat across from him, a small smile seeming to be her only defense against laughing at both of us.

When Kat's phone rang, I caught a nearly imperceptible twitch at the edge of Scott's eyebrow. I might not have noticed it but for the fact I felt one myself. "Just a second," Kat said to whoever was on the phone. She pulled it away from her ear and pushed a button. "You're on speaker, Ariadne."

"Get packed and get moving," came Ariadne's voice over the phone. "Early this morning a car was reported stolen from a parking lot in Ellsworth, Wisconsin, just across the river from you. We flagged it as a suspect vehicle on a hunch and it was found abandoned an hour ago by a police patrol in a neighborhood in Eau Claire, Wisconsin. I'm sending you the address."

"How do we know that the stolen car is linked to our mystery robber?" The question occurred to me even through the haze in my head.

"We don't." Ariadne sounded tense. "But we've got nothing else to go on and car thefts aren't exactly a common occurrence in Ellsworth, where the dairy cows outnumber the people twelve to one. Get moving, all right? I'll check in with you in a few hours; we're managing a crisis with M-Squad so I may not be quite as quick to respond right now. Stay out of trouble." There was a click and the phone shut off.

"Ah, words of confidence and encouragement," I said, lighter than I felt.

We were in the car and moving a few minutes later, leaving the town of Red Wing behind. We rode through downtown, which seemed to be mostly brick buildings, and got on a bridge that stretched across a wide river. On the other side a sign proclaimed that we had entered the state of Wisconsin. If I hadn't been so hungover, I might have rejoiced at crossing my first state line. As

it was, I sat in the back and tried to keep my eyes hidden behind my dark sunglasses.

After a few minutes we cleared the low lying river country and found ourselves zipping down a road with farms on either side. Cattle grazed in the pastures as the sun beat down overhead. One cow was lingering so close to the fence I could see her jaw moving while chewing her cud as we passed.

Towns and fields streaked by as I thought about Zack. I closed my eyes and tried to imagine what he was doing right now, facing off against some meta in Detroit. I truly cared for him, which was why I had to let him loose. At least, that's how I justified it as I stared out the window, watching the endless fields of green go by. I felt like a glutton for pain, like I wanted to clutch the misery close to my heart and let it sit there. It was all for him, I told myself, and somehow that made it hurt all the more.

We took Interstate 94 east to Eau Claire, Kat driving the whole way. She didn't have the siren roaring for this trip, though she did strategically flick it on a few times when we were caught behind slow moving cars on two lane roads. And once for a tractor.

When we got off the freeway, we followed a main thoroughfare into a stretch of commerce, and then turned onto a side street. It was past noon, and the sun was directly overhead, bright and glaring. Kat kept the car under the speed limit as we followed the GPS to the address Ariadne had sent us. There was a car, an old Dodge, parked on the curb. We came to a stop behind it and I looked around. There was no sign of movement, nothing.

I opened my door and stepped out into the boiling midday heat. The humidity once again gave my skin an immediate sensation of moistness and I felt the beads of sweat start to gather on my forehead. "Never thought I'd wish the sun away," I muttered under my breath. I caught a chuckle of appreciation from Kat. Scott just grunted.

The three of us approached the Dodge the way we might have approached a corpse; slow, tentative, and with undue caution. "No one inside," I said. "We'll need to check the trunk." I looked around the street once more. The residents of Eau Claire clearly had enough sense to stay in during this awful weather, though a lawn sprinkler was going off a couple doors down.

"You think there's anything here?" It was Kat that answered. Her blond hair was up in a tight bun today, and her petite frame and dark sunglasses coupled with her black jacket really did make her look like an FBI agent. I felt another tingle of annoyance; the girl could just look good regardless of circumstances.

Scott leaned over the passenger window and reached his hand through. "Glass is broken here." He pushed a button on the dash and I heard the locks disengaging and the trunk springing open.

I walked to the rear of the car, my hand hovering just over my gun. I edged around the trunk lid and sighed when I looked down. "Nothing. A blanket, a spare tire and a jack."

"Sounds like all the ingredients for a redneck first date—" Scott said with a smile that was cut short by a sizzling sound. His body jerked, his face drew tight and his sunglasses flew off as he spasmed, a peculiar blue light dancing over him like little bolts of lightning running across his suit.

"Kat, down!" I shouted and barely had time to hit the pavement before a bolt of electricity shot past me and hit the car. I rolled across the lawn and came up with my pistol, a Sig Sauer P250. I loved my meta powers, but they weren't a hell of a lot of use at range – or against something that shot lightning bolts.

"Too late." The voice was low and gravelly. I saw Kat lying on the street behind the car, splayed out on the ground with three guys in black tactical vests huddled around her and Scott. Two others stood at either bumper of the car, covering me with weapons of their own, big shiny silver ones that reminded me of the kind the Directorate used to bring down stray metas. Their leader

was standing over Kat, an assault rifle in his hands and pointed at me. "Now are you gonna give yourself up or are we gonna be leaving your body to go rancid in the heat?"

Chapter 11

I stared him down, my gun aimed at his comrade who was standing to my right. Assuming they were human, even my meta speed and my skill with the pistol wouldn't be enough to save me from getting blasted by at least one of them. I took a closer look; their vests were bulky, which told me that they were likely kevlar. I considered trying to aim for their heads instead of center mass, but dismissed it as a bad idea. Aiming for a small target in my first combat shoot seemed like a recipe for failure. Besides, even with a vest the bullets would put a full grown man on the ground in a world of hurt.

"So what are you gonna do?" Their leader spoke again, and I saw the others flick their eyes toward him. "Live or die, your choice."

"I'm somewhat attached to the former," I said, keeping my gun trained on the rightmost enemy.

"Then you might wanna put the gun down, real slow." His voice was rough and used to issuing commands. "Otherwise we're gonna have to cut that loose, pretty quick."

On one knee as I was, I couldn't see Scott or Kat, and I wondered if they were still alive. I had seen what hit them, and I hoped that the weapons they'd been shot with were no more fatal than the Directorate equivalent. "All right," I said, not really sure if I was going to follow his command or shoot, but knowing I didn't have much time to make a decision.

"Put the gun on the ground in front of you. Go slow." There was that command again.

I felt my jaw tighten and I started to inch the gun lower, keep-

ing the bearing on my target. I'd be less accurate firing from this position, but I still felt confident I could put him down. The other two...well, that was the problem, wasn't it? That was why I was even considering surrendering. I started to say something but I heard the squeal of tires at the end of the street to my left and it took all my training to keep from jerking my head to look in the direction of the noise.

They were not so well trained, and all three of them turned, giving me an opening. I fired a double tap on my target, two quick shots that sent him over backward, gun skittering away. I changed targets quick, drew a bead on the leader and fired twice more. I knew they were bound to be less accurate than my first shots, and one of them went wide, but the other hit him in shoulder and knocked him over. I started to change targets again to the last guy, but he had heard me firing and had drawn a bead on me. I knew I wouldn't make it in time.

A car slammed into him, bumper smashing him against the stolen car. I watched his body fold at the knees, a scream from him faint in my ears after the echoing of the gunshots nearly deafened me. He was pinned between the cars, legs crushed, and his upper body had fallen into the open trunk. I could hear little cries coming from within; likely the sound of him screaming, but from where I stood it was muffled. I opened my mouth and closed it, trying to restore my hearing after the trauma of firing a gun repeatedly with no ear protection.

I knew there were two more enemies behind the car where I couldn't see them, and I wasn't about to stick my head up to see. I looked at the car that had crashed into the stolen one, but the front window was spider-webbed, the cracked glass obscuring the identity of the driver. I thought I heard the sound of fighting from the other side of the car, where Scott and Kat were laying, but I couldn't be sure through the ringing in my ears. I edged toward the hood, away from the crashed rear, and raised myself up, gun

pointed. My eyes widened at what I saw and I hesitated.

"You're just like me; you know how to get yourself in trouble," came the soft voice of the woman standing in front of me, holding the bodies of the two remaining assailants by the back of their collars. Both appeared to be unconscious. She was wearing a red tank top, cut off jeans again, and flip-flops. Her dark hair was hanging around her face and she dropped the bodies to the ground. "What would you have done if I wasn't here to save you?"

"Charlie?" I stared at her in near disbelief. I heard a grunt from the first guy I had shot, laying about a foot to my right, lanced out a foot and kicked him in the head, causing him to go limp. "What are you doing here?"

She shrugged. "I was bored in Minneapolis, so I came looking for you."

I stood slowly, looking around the street, which was quiet save for the ticking sound from the engine of the car that had crashed. "And you decided to go looking on a random street in Eau Claire, Wisconsin?"

She laughed. "No, I absorbed the mind and soul of a tech geek a few years ago. I tracked your cell phone's GPS."

I looked down reflexively at my pocket. "Really?"

"It's not as hard as you'd hope it would be." She shrugged. "Looks like my timing was good. What'd you do to provoke an Omega sweep team?"

"Omega?" I felt a thrill as I made my way around the car to check on Kat and Scott. "These guys are from Omega?"

"Uh huh." She leaned down and grabbed one of them by the chest, ripping open his collar to reveal a small tattoo of the Greek letter Omega. "See?"

"Curiouser and curiouser." I bent over Kat, trying her pulse (not an easy task with leather gloves on). She stirred at my touch, causing me to sigh in relief. I reached out and shook Scott, causing him to groan, his eyes fluttering. "Omega must be tracking our

robber, too."

There was a sound from behind me of metal stressing and squealing and I was back to my feet, gun drawn again. The door of the car that had crashed was opening. "I thought you drove that?" I asked over my shoulder to Charlie.

"Nuh-uh," she said without concern. "I parked down the street and hustled up when I saw these guys ambush you. I thought it was one of your guys driving."

"Whoever's in the vehicle, hands up and come out slow," I said. "No sudden moves."

"Uggghhh." The moan was not subtle, and was followed by the sound of a body hitting pavement. I saw the head and shoulders of a man, his long, dark hair tangled around his face. "I save your life and this is the gratitude I get?"

"Reed?" I stared at him before holstering my gun and running to his side. I rolled him over once I reached him; his nose was bloody and he had the start of a bruise forming under his right eye. "What are you doing here?"

He coughed, then grimaced. "There's an Omega safehouse just down the street. I was surveilling it; figured it might be a nice, boring place to keep an eye on while I waited for word on another robbery. Then you and your pals go and get bushwhacked by an Omega sweep team, and suddenly my life gets really interesting."

"Can you walk?" After I said it, I heard Charlie approach behind me, her flip-flops smacking against the pavement. The ringing in my ears had begun to subside.

"I think so." He took my hand and I pulled him to his feet. "We need to get out of here before the law arrives. Doubtful they're gonna ignore a scuffle this big."

"I need to get a look at this Omega safehouse," I said. "Preferably before the cops get here."

Reed waved his hand in the direction that his car had come from. "Down the street. 8453 is the house number." He clutched at

his side and his face was a mask of discomfort.

I looked at him, then Charlie in turn. "Can you get Kat and Scott into my car and meet me in front of the safehouse?"

She got a lazy grin on her face. "You just need all kinds of help today."

"Can you do it or not?"

She shrugged. "Sure. Keys?"

"Kat had them last," I said, already turning to run down the street. "Check her pockets – and, Charlie..." She turned and I shook my head at her attire. "Remember to touch them only on the clothing."

"No problem with the blond girl," she called back. "But the boy...I might touch him some other places."

I ignored her and ran down the street at full clip. I saw faces staring out of the windows of houses, saw curtains rustle in others as I passed. I watched the house numbers decrease until I reached 8453, a nondescript single story white house. I decided to avoid the front door and instead jumped over the wooden gate to the backyard. I listened over the slight ringing that persisted in my ears as I came around the corner and saw the back door kicked in.

I drew my gun, changed to a fresh magazine and stepped inside. The door led into a small hallway. I could see a kitchen to my left, along with a body and a lot of blood. Straight ahead was a family room, and off to the right was a hallway leading to several bedrooms. I went into the kitchen first, which had a nasty green tile backsplash over orange countertops and beige linoleum floors. Those were distracting, but the body in the middle of the kitchen was more bizarre than the horrific 70s color scheme.

First of all, it was obviously dead. There was enough blood on the floor to fill three bodies, and his face was frozen in anguish. He was elevated slightly off the floor by something on his back.

Worse than him were the remains of two enormous snakes lying on the kitchen floor. I shuddered. I do not care for snakes. I

kicked at one of them to make sure it was dead. It didn't move, but that didn't make me feel much better. While I knew logically that they weren't slimy, I couldn't shake the feeling that if I touched it, it'd be slick and disgusting. I leaned in to look at the dead man, adjusting the body to see what was causing his corpse to incline.

When I lifted him, I almost retched. I saw what was holding him up, and it looked as though the snakes had been growing out of his shoulder blades. I dropped him and stood, stifling an urge to vomit. I kept my gun in hand and stepped over him, coming around the corner of the kitchen into the dining room to find another man on the couch, this one much younger, and with no obvious signs of snakes growing out of him.

He was also quite alive, though he was limp, arm hanging off the edge of the sofa. His chest moved up and down, eyes closed. I heard the faint sound of sirens outside and walked over to him, shaking him with one hand while keeping the pistol pointed at him with the other. He didn't stir, and after two more attempts I left him and took a quick look around the rest of the house. Two bedrooms were pretty simple and a cursory look under the beds and in the closets didn't reveal anything. The third bedroom seemed to be set up as an office, and I grabbed the laptop computer for later analysis by someone who'd know what to do with it.

I started to leave but paused as I headed toward the front door. There had to be a basement, didn't there? I started to set down the laptop when I heard an urgent series of honks from a car horn, just outside. I clutched the laptop tighter and with a last look at the young man unconscious on the couch, I ran out the front door.

The Directorate SUV was next to the curb, and another violent blast from the horn issued forth as I went down the front steps. I saw Charlie in the driver's seat and Reed's long hair through the tinted window in the backseat. I jumped in the passenger side and Charlie gunned the engine, not even waiting for me to shut the door. She slowed the car at the corner, which was fortunate, be-

cause two cop cars went shooting by, sirens blaring, and my aunt gave me a grin. She made the car take a leisurely turn to the left, and off we went.

Chapter 12

"Where to?" Charlie asked as we headed down the road. I saw a couple more sets of cop cars, lights flashing, go past.

"I don't know." I held the laptop tight, almost as if I were afraid to let it go, lest it vanish. "We need to lay low."

"I thought you were with the FBI?" Reed spoke up from the backseat, his voice laced with sarcasm. "Why didn't you just stay on scene?"

"Because while I and my colleagues might well be from the FBI, I'd have had a hell of a time explaining you two." I looked from him to Charlie, who still wore a grin. "If I'd had to, I would have, but let's just say I wanted to make that Plan B."

"That coulda been a lotta fun," Charlie said. I shot her a look of disbelief and she shrugged. "Come on, lying to the cops? Talk about a thrill."

"So is this your aunt?" Reed asked.

Charlie looked back with a faint smile of pleasure. "You know me?"

"Charlene Nealon, A.K.A. Charlie," Reed said. "Didn't know you were still around, but yeah, I've heard of you. I particularly enjoyed reading about your exploits in Nevada."

I saw a subtle change in Charlie's persona then, a subtle clamping of her jaw as her smile disappeared and she turned back around to focus on the road. "That was a while ago. I barely re-member Nevada."

I watched Reed, and he smiled. "There's some other people that could probably say the same."

"How are they doing?" I caught Reed's attention and nodded at Kat and Scott, both unconscious next to him. Scott was leaned

up against the window like he had been the night before when he passed out, and Kat was lying gracelessly across his lap. I would have cringed for her, but, frankly, it wasn't as though she'd never been in that position before.

"They're out." Reed illustrated his point by reaching over to give Scott a gentle slap across the face. Scott moaned, but did not wake. "The sweep team hit them with an amped-up version of a taser. No wires needed. I'm told they got the design from the Directorate after you guys left one behind at your house."

"One of those things put Wolfe down on the ground," I said. "I can't imagine it felt very good for either of them." I turned around to talk to him. "Who is Omega?"

He kept a cool dispassion as he stared back. "You don't know?"

"The Directorate knows next to nothing about them." I ran a hand through my hair. "Old Man Winter knows something, but he's...not telling." I frowned. "It's above my pay grade."

Reed shrugged. "I can't help you, then. Sounds like something you'll figure out when your pay grade goes up." He gave me a maliciously self-satisfied smile. "Of course, if you want to leave the Directorate and join me, I could answer your questions instead of keeping you in the dark like they do—"

"Oh, for crying out loud," Charlie said. "They're the gods, okay? The old ones, the ones from the myths, or what's left of them." She turned from driving to focus on me. "The Greek gods, the Roman ones? Persians, Norse, all else? There's a reason there are some commonalities: it's because they were all part of the same group. They ruled the planet for thousands of years, through their intermediaries, and vassals, and kings, and whatnot." She turned back to the windshield as she made a turn, then glanced back at me. "You've gotta at least know that much, right?"

I squinted at her. "You mean...like Zeus and Poseidon and Thor and Odin and all that jazz?"

"Well," she said, "Zeus and Poseidon are good and dead; so's Odin. Not sure about Thor...but anyway...yeah, those guys. What's left of the originals, and quite a few of their descendants. It's kind of a cabal."

I let out a snicker, more from disbelief than anything. "And they're...what? Out to take over the world?"

Charlie shrugged, and I turned to Reed, who rolled his eyes. "Probably not in a literal sense," he said. "Not anymore, at least. But yeah, like she said, they're a cabal, and they have a ruling council and a pretty strong organization. At this point they're collecting metas, building their strength, and...given their history, probably up to no good."

"No, seriously." I let out a short laugh. "What are they up to? What's their objective?"

Reed sighed. "I don't know. No one does. We just know they're making power moves, collecting metas...kinda like the Directorate, but even more shadowy, if that's possible."

"I don't love the sound of that," I said.

"You're telling me." Charlie spoke up, bringing the car to a squealing stop at a red light. "I've tangled with their sweep teams before – they're the ones they send out to bring in metas they want to talk to." She laughed. "They're a fun bunch, but they oughta stick to catching newbies; kids that have just manifested and don't know what they're doing."

I stared at the laptop cradled in my hands. "Why does Omega have a safehouse in Eau Claire?"

"Because the Twin Cities is too hot for them." Reed's answer came with a cringe in his voice. "Minneapolis or St. Paul would be too close to the Directorate. Eau Claire's only an hour away, and a few hours from Chicago, where they have a lot bigger presence."

"But why?" I asked. "Why have a presence up here at all? What are they hoping to accomplish?"

"Tracking metas," Charlie said. "Just like you guys. Track

'em and collar 'em, recruit the ones that seem promising. It's all anybody does nowadays, keep snatching up every unattached meta out there."

"What'd you find in the safehouse?" Reed leaned forward and I felt his hand on the back of my seat.

"A guy with a couple snakes lying on the kitchen floor, dead."

Reed frowned. "The guy or the snakes?"

"All of them," I said. "Looks like the snakes grew from his shoulder blades. Kinda creepy."

"Sounds like a Zahhak," Reed said, exchanging a look with Charlie, who nodded.

"What's a Zahhak?" I wrinkled my forehead.

"Look it up on Wikipedia sometime; it's a pretty scary meta to go up against." He entered a pensive state, his fingers resting over his mouth. "They're pretty rare, but I heard Omega has one – or had one, I suppose."

"Why have they been after me?" I turned to question Reed on this one, and when I looked at him, his expression was suddenly pained, a twisted grimace. "You know, don't you?" He nodded, slow, not looking away. "Why are they after me?"

"They're not after you, specifically." He took a deep breath. "You've never been the end to them, always the means. They're after your mom."

I exchanged a look with Charlie, who seemed surprised. "Why?"

He shrugged. "I don't know for sure, but I think she knows something...something from when she was with the Agency – you know, the government group that was destroyed before the Directorate came onto the scene?" I nodded. I knew Mom had been at the Agency with Old Man Winter before I was born. "Anyway, something happened that has a lot of people scouring for her."

I turned back to Charlie. "Do you know what it is?"

She let out a long cackle. "Your mom and I aren't on what

you'd call 'speaking terms'. I haven't talked to her since way before you were born."

"What happened?" I asked.

She turned the steering wheel to bring us into the parking lot of a hotel that was shaped like a giant, round cylinder. "She didn't like the way I did things and I didn't care for the way she told me to run my life." She pulled the car into a parking spot just outside the lobby and gave me another lazy shrug. "So I told her what she could do with her opinions and we didn't really need to talk after that, cuz it'd all been said."

"Can't imagine what she might have taken issue with," Reed said under his breath.

Charlie shot him a searing look and jerked her head toward the lobby. "We should get rooms here for the night, unless you want your friends to continue sleeping in the back of the car." She turned around and saw Kat's head in Scott's lap. "Although she seems comfortable there."

I checked us in to four rooms, using the Directorate credit card for two of them and my personal card for the other two. As I swiped it through their reader, I was reminded that I needed to call Ariadne and make a report, since Scott and Kat were unlikely to do so in the next few hours. Once I was done, I hurried back to the car and Charlie drove us to the outside entrance nearest to the rooms. She and I each grabbed one of the unconscious members of my team and dragged them into the building while Reed walked ahead to make sure we didn't run into anyone. Fortunately, the hotel seemed quiet.

We made it to our rooms without incident, and after depositing Kat and Scott onto the king-sized bed in their room, Charlie grabbed the key for her room and left. Reed lingered, watching the door to the room until it shut. After it did, he remained silent for almost a minute, listening. When I started to say something to him, he held up a finger to his lips and then opened the door, looking up

and down the hall. He shut it and walked back to me, stopping only inches from my face. "How well do you know your aunt?" he asked in a low whisper.

"Not well." I looked into his concerned eyes and felt a tremor within. "I met her about six months ago when she tracked me down, and we've been in contact on and off ever since, meeting whenever she's been in town."

"Do you trust her?" He didn't break eye contact.

"Only a little," I said. "I don't exactly know her well."

"She didn't come on the mission with you?"

"No." I shook my head. "She said she tracked my cell phone GPS."

"Uh huh." He licked his lips, thinking. "Sounds a little funny."

"Why so suspicious? You think she has something to do with Omega?" He stared back at me, as though waiting for something. "What? What am I missing?"

He turned a slight smile, and looked at me with expectation. "Come on," he said. "You know."

"Come on, what?" By this point I was just annoyed. Kat and Scott were passed out on the bed behind me and who knew when they'd be coming back to consciousness. I had to report to Ariadne that we'd gotten in a violent clash with Omega forces, ending with two people not associated with the Directorate getting involved to save our bacon, in an incident that would certainly have drawn more than a little attention.

"Nothing," he said. "I'm gonna go...recover for a bit. Let me know if anything major happens."

I shook my head, feeling my annoyance fade at the remembrance that he'd wrecked his car to save me from the Omega sweep team. "Reed..." He looked back over his shoulder, almost out the door. "Thanks."

He nodded, a little smile breaking on his face, and left.

Chapter 13

I tried to reach Ariadne, but her cell phone went straight to voice-mail. I tried her office, but her assistant told me she was out and unable to be reached for several hours. When I asked her to connect me to the Director, she informed me that he, too, was unavailable. I sighed, told her to have them call me urgently, that I had run afoul of Omega, and left it at that.

I stayed in Kat and Scott's room, watching the light fade outside the beige curtains as the day ended. I looked at a clock when the last rays of sunlight were still visible, and it was just after 9 P.M. Neither of them had moved, but their pulse was regular, they reacted to prodding and other stimuli; they just...didn't seem to want to wake up.

There was a knock on my door and when I looked through the peephole, Charlie grinned back at me, her smile overlarge and distorted by the glass as though I were looking at her in a funhouse mirror. Her cutoffs and tank top were gone, replaced by a red dress not unlike the one I had seen her wear when we first met, something with very little length and quite a bit of cleavage exposure. I tried to smile, but inwardly grimaced as I opened the door. "Hey."

"Hay is all around us; this whole damned place is a farm town." She made a slight gyration, as though she were dancing to music only she could hear. "What do you say we go find a couple cowboys to while away the dull hours with between now and morning?"

"Sounds like a great idea," I said. "Because we don't have enough carnage on our hands already without killing a couple of poor locals that are just out for a good time."

"It's not about killing," she said in a soothing voice, "it's about having some fun. Unwinding." Her smile was oddly infectious. "You've been watching these vegetables all day. You need to get out and let loose. Have the other guy watch them for a while." She strolled over to Scott and brushed his cheek with her hand, letting it linger a moment longer than I would have, and a slight shudder ran through her body. "Ooh. Is he a Poseidon type? Tastes like the ocean to me."

"Tastes?" I'm pretty sure my face was locked into disbelief. "You touched him."

"Yeah, it's a sense you start to develop with maturity." I felt a rough swell of annoyance as she walked to the other side of the bed and let her hand drift onto to exposed cheek of Kat. "Mmmm. Persephone type? If you ever get a chance – you know, maybe tangling with one that's a 'bad guy'," she used air quotes, driving my eyebrows up almost to my bangs, "you need to take a drink of a Persephone. They are double yum."

I closed my eyes and felt a throbbing in my temple. "I know you did not just suggest that I drain—"

"A bad one," she said, her voice suddenly higher. "I'm saying that if you run across a bad one cuz I know how focused you are on that sort of thing, catching 'bad guys' – you should definitely drain them dry, because they are all kinds of tasty, let me tell you." She did a pirouette and came around the bed, then brushed my hair out of my eyes, careful not to touch my face. "Come on, get the other guy and get ready. We need to go out, niece."

I sighed. "Go out where?"

She leaned her head in close to me and gave me a mischievous smile. "The bar, here in the hotel."

"I went to a bar last night. It didn't end well. I almost killed some guy."

She raised an eyebrow. "Was he cute?"

I felt a pang as I remembered, not for the first time in the last

few hours, that I had broken up with Zack only this morning. And had kissed James last night. "Yes. He very much was."

"Sounds worth it to me." She looked me up and down. "You change and get ready, I'll go knock on the other guy's door and get him to watch the kids." She turned and headed for the door.

"His name is Reed, you know."

She waved a hand carelessly behind her as she walked out. "I've already forgotten it again."

I stood there in the middle of the floor for about ten seconds, pondering my options. I could sit in my room, avoiding the horror that was drunkenness, the searing pain of a hangover and the loss of judgment that resulted from it, or stay here and stare at the walls. I had almost convinced myself that that was the wisest course, the soundest of ideas, when Zack wandered across my mind again, and I realized he'd be doing that for the rest of the night – just like he had been all day – and I'd have only the unconscious bodies of my two colleagues to keep me company.

There was a knock at the door, and when I looked through the peephole, it was Reed, looking a little cross.

"Your aunt just told me to get my ass over here and watch over two sleeping Directorate agents," he said, nonplussed. "You can't be serious."

"I need to get out of here for a while," I said. "We won't be gone long." I started toward the door, my bag on my shoulder, intending to go to my own room, which I hadn't yet seen.

"What am I supposed to do if they wake up?" He looked at me in near astonishment, mouth slightly agape.

"If Kat wakes up first, explain the situation to her," I said. "It's not like you haven't met before."

"And if he wakes up first?"

I shrugged. "I don't know. Get creative."

I closed the door, which muffled his reply. I'm pretty sure it was a curse, and I'm equally sure I didn't care. I went to my room

and took a shower, a long one. When I was done, I dressed in a slightly looser suit, the most comfortable one I'd brought with me, straightened my hair and applied some makeup. When I came out of the bathroom, Charlie was waiting, lying on the bed, watching TV. She perked up when she saw me, and I stared at her, question on my face.

"They gave you a spare key," she said. "I pocketed it when you handed me the packets. Figured I might need it later." She smoothed her dress, which didn't show even a sign of wrinkling, and smiled at me. "Ready to have some fun?"

"Sort of."

"But not too much fun, because that's probably against a Directorate rule of some kind."

She dragged a little smile out of me with that one, and we were off. We crossed the lobby, an open air, ornate space with leather couches and decor that looked like it might be just as appropriate in a manor house as it was here. As we walked, I couldn't help but notice heads turn to watch Charlie. Male heads. Lots of them.

We bellied up to the bar, and after I'd shown my ID, the bartender, a skinny guy this time, asked us what we wanted.

"What do you think, daahhhhhling?" Charlie said it with an exaggerated English accent, like she was a duchess or something.

Why break a winning tradition? I only knew one kind of drink, anyway. "Whiskey Sour."

The bartender nodded and Charlie said, "Make it two." He walked off.

"So," I said. "What now?" I swiveled on my stool to take in the whole place. It was Sunday night, and there weren't too many people around. There was a cluster of guys dressed professionally in the corner, ties loosened, sleeves rolled up, lots of laughing going on. I caught a furtive glance from a couple of them at Charlie, who, unlike me, was facing away from the bar and leaning back,

her legs crossed and cool indifference beneath her slight smile.

"Now, my dear," she said after a long pause, "we have fun." The bartender set her glass at her elbow and she grabbed it, slow and smooth. "Keep 'em coming." She pressed it against her lips as she stared at the guys in the corner, taking a long, measured drink.

I picked up my whiskey and felt the chill of it in my hand, then took a sip. It still gave my mouth an involuntary spasm, but not as bad as the night before. I almost enjoyed it this time. It burned, though. I took another, and when I finished, I caught Charlie looking sidelong at me with amusement. "First time?" she asked.

"Second. I did this last night, too."

"Ah." She finished her drink and signaled to the barman. "It's my second time, too." Her eyes fixated on the guys in the corner. "Tell the bartender to send my drink over there." She blinked, then looked at me as though she'd forgotten me somehow. "Actually, just come with me; he'll figure it out."

I looked over at the men she was talking about. Not a one of them was under thirty, and I doubted more than one of them was under forty. "I, uh...think they might be a little out of my age demographic."

"Older men have their advantages. Experience, patience..." She grinned at me wickedly.

I stared back, and I felt the flush come to my cheeks. "How can you...I mean...you could kill someone."

"Pffffft." She waved her hand at me. "First of all, it takes a while for your touch to kill someone; you oughta know that. Second, you just have to be careful, making sure that things are as covered as you can get them...after that, it's all about using strength and muscle control." The bartender set another drink next to her and it was in her hand, then in front of her mouth, hiding her grin. "Just because you're a soul-draining succubus doesn't mean you have to live some kind of virginal life as a nun. I mean, even

your mother didn't buy into that idea, and she was the most stiff, serious—"

"Ah, okay." I cringed, interrupting her. "I could have done with a little more exposition and a little less color commentary on that one." I let my expression soften. "But thanks for the info. I was...struggling with some of that."

She pulled the glass from in front of her mouth after taking a long drink. "That's what I'm here for, niece: to teach you all the things that Mommy can't." She giggled. "That's why I'm the coolest aunt. Now, how about we take your newfound knowledge over to the table in the corner and you can find out what I mean?"

I looked back at the guys she was indicating. I felt a reaction, a wave of no, no and hell no. "Um, no. There's not one of them that's my type."

She shrugged, indifferent. "Suit yourself. Sit over here and be a black hole of excitement. In a place like this, you take what you can get. Sometimes it surprises you what you'll find." She stood, draining the last of her drink, and walked over to the table with the guys. When she was a few feet away, they all sat up and took notice of her, especially when she leaned over once she reached the table. I heard her tone, not her words, and it sounded conversational, almost confessional, like she was telling something to an old friend she hadn't seen in a long time. One of them got up and dragged a chair over for her. She sat in it, giving him a smile and running a hand along his exposed forearm, eliciting a shiver from him.

I turned back to the bar and stared at my drink, wondering why I couldn't do what Charlie could. I wasn't that outgoing, that confident, that fearless. Sure, I didn't have any interest in any of those guys because they were way too old for me, but even if they'd been a table full of guys my age, all hot, I still wouldn't have had the guts to do what she did. I turned and watched the easy manner with which she wrapped them all around her finger,

with a joke that had them all laughing, with a gentle caress on the back that left the man on the receiving end wanting more.

All I'd had thus far was Zack, and he wasn't exactly wrapped around my finger. I mean, I'd pretty much driven him away because I was afraid I'd hurt him. Even the revelation that Charlie had given me, that there were ways we could be intimate without him getting hurt, sounded awfully risky (not to mention fairly devoid of any romance), maybe moreso to me because I wasn't really sure how it all worked. I mean, I'd only ever kissed him for three to four seconds before I had to stop, and she was talking about protection and muscle control – it was bizarre and exciting and scary as hell all at once, but I didn't know which feeling was heaviest.

Also, I'd let him go. I felt a twinge of guilt and pain, and took a drink to bury that feeling under the rush that the liquor granted, that heady sensation that would be making me drift oh-so-pleasantly in just a few more minutes. Of course the aftereffects would suck, but since when do teenagers worry about consequences? I took another drink, trying to banish that thought. Self-awareness was a curse, a terrible curse. The ice clinked in the bottom of my glass and I realized I had downed the whole thing without noticing.

I started to wave over the barman, but he was already coming with another. His face was almost gaunt, his eyes sunken when he set the Whiskey Sour in front of me. "Here you go," he said.

"Okay, but after this I'm done." I picked up the drink and took a swig.

"And your friend?" He nodded toward Charlie and I turned to see the whole table laughing again, every one of the men paying rapt attention to her, leaning over each other to tell her something, to catch her attention. I watched the way she twirled her hair, the way she laughed at them, smiled. "You gonna keep paying for her?"

I handed him my credit card, the personal one, not the one from the Directorate. "I'm gonna go out on a limb and guess she can probably convince those guys to buy her a round or two, but give her one more on my tab, then close it out."

He smiled at me. "Done deal."

I looked down at my drink, studying the amber liquid in my glass broken by the white of the ice cubes and the red of the maraschino cherry that floated on top. I pulled out the cherry and popped it into my mouth, leaving the stem on the napkin that held my drink. I took another long sip and thought again about Zack. Maybe I'd been hasty. Or maybe I'd been sane. I looked back at Charlie and wondered how she could be so cavalier, so quick with her touch when it could be so harmful, so deadly if she wasn't careful.

"You're prettier than her." There was a voice at my elbow and I looked to see a familiar face. His hair was spiked, and his handsome features looked slightly more rugged tonight, though his shirt was still unbuttoned at the top. James smiled at me, and I couldn't help but smile back. "Don't doubt it for a second; she may have the attention of those geezers, but you're the knockout in this bar."

"James." I said his name with a certain amusement that was probably fueled by the drinks that I was starting to feel the effects of. A little tinkle of suspicion was present too, far back in my mind. I think I might have let slip the barest hint of a smile as I looked back at him again.

"Sienna." He dazzled me with his in return. It started slow, but got pretty powerful pretty quick. I ignored the flutter in my stomach. "Mind if I sit with you?"

I waved a hand vaguely at the stool. "Yesterday you're in Owatonna, today you're in Eau Claire. Are you following me?"

"Can I be honest?" He took off his suit jacket and hung it on the back of the seat before sitting down next to me.

"I'd prefer it, actually. What kind of a girl says, 'No, please lie to me'?" The suspicious part of me was gaining traction.

"A surprising number, actually," he said, keeping it cool. "Though usually not in so many words. Anyway, I'm here because of you."

"Oh?" I took a sip, a very small one, and kept my hand ready in case I had to reach for a weapon. "I have a stalker?"

The bartender set a beer in front of him and he took a long pull. "Nah. I told you I was a recruiter, didn't I?"

"Hmmm." I thought about it. He probably had, but all I remembered was his lips. "I believe you did. So you're here to recruit me?"

"If I can." He had stopped paying attention to the beer.

"You recruit a lot of people away from the FBI?" I turned on my stool to face him, letting my arm rest on the side of the bar.

"No," he said. "But I've recruited a few people away from the Directorate." He kept his body facing toward the bar, but his eyes were on me.

I felt a chill, a little one, and I knew my eyes widened. "How did you find me here?"

He looked away. "Not the hardest thing to do. Go to a town where an Omega safehouse gets hit in the morning, go to all the hotel bars and look for the prettiest succubus around." He looked back at me, and was smiling again.

"You are quite the charmer," I said, vacillating between confusion and feeling flattered. "What will you do if I do say no to your offer?" My hand clenched tighter around my drink, and my breath caught in my chest.

"You haven't heard it yet." His smile took on an otherworldly quality, getting brighter. Or was that the alcohol? "Listen, this is just like Red Rover as a kid. You picked the wrong side and I'm just asking if Sienna can come over."

I looked at him and cocked my head. "Red what?"

"Never mind," he said with a shake of the head. "To answer your question: if you say no, I'll learn to live with my deep, bitter disappointment and hope that you'll still be okay with me trying to seduce you." His smile grew wider, and I found for a flash that I wanted to slap it off him. But just for a second, because damn...he said it with a hell of a lot of charm.

I let go of the breath I had been holding and turned back to the bar, allowing myself just a sip of the whiskey. "You might not be glad if I go along with that. Don't you know what a succubus does to a person?"

He chuckled dryly. "I do. I'm very familiar with it, in fact."

I reached down and pulled off my gloves, slowly, as he watched, then took my drink in my hand and felt the perspiration of the glass mingle with my own and slide down my fingers as I pressed it to my lips and took another swig. "Then are you really sure you want to try that?" I set the glass back on the bar.

He moved fast, faster than I would have given him credit for, probably because I could feel the second whiskey already taking effect. His hand slid across and grabbed one of mine and I felt his skin against mine, slightly warm, mine a little sticky from the light layer of sweat that came from always wearing a glove. I didn't pull away and he cradled my hand in his, bringing his other around, holding it.

"Please," I said after a moment. I started to tug my hand away, but he held onto it, staring into my eyes. I started to count in my head, knowing it wouldn't be long before he'd get weary and pass out. 1...2...

I pulled at it again and he didn't surrender it, instead leaning closer to me. "It'll be all right," he said, bringing my hand to his lips for a gentle kiss. ...3...4...5...6...my eyes widened as he looked back up to me, cradling my hand in his. ...7...8...9...

"You should let go," I said again, more urgently this time, but I didn't pull away. ...10...11...12...

"I don't want to," he breathed, his face next to mine, the smell of his cologne mixed with the beer on his breath in a medley of strong and sweet, and he brought his lips to mine. ...13...14...15...16...17...18...I couldn't remember what came next and it didn't matter: there was just the smell of him, the taste of him...

He pulled away for just a second, looking me full in the eyes. "I'm like you...and you can't hurt me. We...are made for each other, you and me."

I took a breath, a word filling my mind with possibilities, with a legend I'd only heard of and never given much thought to; of a type of meta, my equal and opposite, the only one who could keep my powers at bay. I felt it in my head, in my heart, and on my lips, and it was beautiful; a breath of hope for someone who'd been hopeless for far too long.

"Incubus."

Chapter 14

He didn't let go of me, not across the lobby, not in the elevator, when the passion was rising and we kissed again, a roaring chorus of excitement building in my head and body. We didn't part when it opened to my floor, nor when we hit the wall of the hallway. I fumbled for my room key as we staggered, blindly, one of us walking backward nearly all the time, to my door. I threw it open and we were in, the lights already on dim, as though they were set in anticipation of our arrival.

My jacket was shed instantly, so seamless I hardly noticed it come off and wondered if it had been he or I that had done it. I tossed my gun and holster onto my open bag, followed by my shoes as I ran a hand over his smooth chest, reveling in the fact that I could touch him without fear. We broke apart, breathing heavy, and he smiled at me as I fumbled to undo the buttons on his shirt. He reciprocated, much more smoothly than I, and we hit the bed, lips once more intertwined.

I felt the weight of him on top of me, his chest pressed against mine, his fingers working on the snap and zipper of my pants. No sooner had he gotten them undone than my jacket began to ring. Loud, musical, the tones a perfect distraction to the symphony of touch and sensation that was going on a few feet away. He caressed me, running a hand along my side, making me shudder while I wished he would finish what he had started and get my pants off. I let the tips of my fingers slide over the smooth skin on his back, holding him in place, pulling him closer to me.

His lips pulled from mine for a second. "Is that your phone ringing?"

I craned my neck to kiss him again. "I don't know, and I don't care." My hands reached up to the back of his neck and pulled him closer. I felt his tongue in my mouth, tasted the beer flavor, and then he pulled away, running gentle kisses onto my chin and then down my neck. I felt his hands as they ran over me, the touches a delight, all different kinds of pleasure running through my skin. The phone had stopped ringing, wherever it was, and I couldn't be happier as I lay there, breathing heavy while he touched me.

The first heavy knock on my door jarred me, causing me to jerk in surprise. I looked at him, locked eyes, and I shook my head. "Just ignore it," I said, running a hand through his hair. A second knock came, louder and more insistent than the first. I leaned back, letting my head fall against the pillow as some of the heat left me. "Oh God, why now?"

He chuckled and lay his head on my belly. "Because it's the worst possible time."

The knocking came again, sustained, persistent and louder. "Sienna?" I heard Kat's voice, then knocking again. "I know you're in there; your phone's GPS is still transmitting."

"Go away!" I cried. "Come back in an hour!"

"I can't!" she shouted back. "Ariadne just called, and we've got things to deal with!"

I felt a kind of surly whine come from my lips as James laughed softly against my stomach. He kissed me on the belly and rolled off me, allowing me to get to my feet and stagger to the door. It took all my restraint, once I had opened it just a crack to see Kat, not to reach out, grab her by the head, and slam it in the door for interrupting my efforts to lose my virginity. "What?" I felt the acid drip from my tongue, looking daggers at the pretty cheerleader who didn't have any problems at all sleeping with her boyfriend.

She looked paler than usual, but then again, she had looked like that a lot on this trip. "Ariadne called."

"Yes, I heard you the first time."

She looked to either side down the hallway, then back at me. "Can I come in so we can talk?"

"No," I said. "You can leave so I can get back to doing what I was doing!"

Her brow crinkled and she looked mildly offended. "What were you doing?"

I let out a heavy exhalation and felt my hand go to my forehead as I bowed my head. "Ugh, never mind. What did Ariadne want?"

"She got your message and was calling you back." Kat looked at me with wide eyes. "Also, leaving us with that Reed guy while you went to the bar? Not cool. You're lucky I woke up first."

I felt a wash of chagrin. "What did Scott say when he woke up?"

"He's still kind of out of it, but he didn't seem too happy." She shook her head and glanced past me, suddenly stiffening. "Is there someone in there with you?"

I opened the door wide enough to show her that I was in my bra with my pants unzipped, then shut it back to only a crack. "Yes," I said with some urgency.

Her eyes widened in alarm. "Won't that...you know," she lowered her voice to a bare whisper, "kill...whoever you're with?"

"Apparently not," I said. "But the mood? The mood is officially dead, thanks to you."

"I'm sorry, but Ariadne wants us on the phone right now." She stared at me, and I knew the firmness in her voice didn't come from her.

"Just give me half an hour," I said, pleading. I started to shut the door.

"Now." She reached out and grasped my wrist, giving it a squeeze, then letting go immediately. "She's in Kansas, and things have gone very, very wrong. She only has a short window to talk

to us. She's waiting for you."

I buried my face in my hands and took a deep breath. "I'll be there in a minute."

I closed the door and felt James's hands slide across my hips, teasing and promising more touches, more caresses. He kissed the side of my neck and I squirmed; it hit the right spot. "I have to go," I said, my eyes closed, my words heavy with the regret I felt over every inch of my body – some inches more than others. I slid free of his grasp and turned to kiss him again on the mouth. I broke away after a moment. "I promise I will be right back after this call is over."

I saw his eyes go cool in the half-light. "All right. I can wait." He cracked a smile as his fingers stroked my bare arms and grasped my hands in his. "I think you're probably worth it."

I pulled away, giving him a coy smile before I stooped to pick my blouse off the floor. "Probably?"

He gave me a noncommittal shrug and went back to the bed as I threw my arms through the sleeves of my blouse. "I guess we'll see."

I sat on the edge of the bed and he leaned over my shoulder, kissing the back of my neck as I buttoned my shirt. "You never did tell me who you work for."

"I doubt you'd have heard of us," he said, nuzzling, his tongue on the side of my neck. "But if you're interested, I can give you the whole pitch of why you should join us...after."

I felt a little amusement as I slipped on my shoes. "So recruiting me isn't your first priority anymore?"

"Nuh-uh," he grunted. I gasped as his fingers tweaked me.

I stood and brushed his hands off. "I'll be back as soon as I can." I picked my holster up off my suitcase and put it on, followed by my jacket. I took a last look at him once I was at the door, gave him a weak smile, and closed it behind me.

I leaned against the wall in the hallway, trying to catch my

breath. After taking time to compose myself, I walked two doors down and knocked. The door cracked open to admit me and Reed stood there, looking much less beaten up than he had a few hours ago.

"Is that Sienna?" I heard Ariadne's voice crackle from the speaker of the phone sitting on the bed.

"It is," I said. "Sorry for the delay; I was just—"

"It doesn't matter," Ariadne cut me off. "I only have a few minutes. Our operation in western Kansas has gotten complicated; M-Squad has been ambushed by some heavy-hitting metas, and we've lost half the team from our Texas facility. The Director and I need to manage the fallout from this, but I wanted to get back to all of you first."

"Things have gotten a bit complicated here as well," I said, feeling a little catch in my voice.

"Yes," Ariadne said, "Kat and Scott have explained. We'll have a conversation later about how you've been keeping quiet about your aunt, but for now let's talk about your friend Reed."

I locked eyes with Reed, who looked unconcerned. "You know he's standing right here, don't you?"

"He's offered to help us," she said, "with some additional resources from his organization. He's also shed a little light on what we're dealing with down here in Kansas." I heard the tension in Ariadne's voice. "Omega seems to have chosen this moment to launch a surprise attack against the Directorate. We think they drew M-Squad down here for the express purpose of putting them out of commission." Ariadne's tone was flat. "I'm afraid this little chase we have you on, trying to track down this meta that's robbing convenience stores, is going to have to wait. Reed told me you've captured a laptop from Omega?"

"Yes, I have it right here." I pointed to Kat's overnight bag, prompting a quizzical look from her. I pointed again, and she went over to it, opening it and digging around until she came out with

the laptop. "It's password protected, though, and I didn't want to chance digging around in it because...well, because I'm terrible with computers. Figured I'd leave it to the pros."

"I want that computer in the hands of our techies right now," Ariadne said. "How fast can you get it back to the campus?"

I looked to Scott, who cleared his throat. "If we drive fast, with the sirens on, we're a little less than two hours away."

"If there's any hint of what Omega is up to or what their next move might be, we need to know now," Ariadne said. "Get that computer in the hands of our tech support immediately. Do whatever you have to do." She paused. "Reed, is there anything else you can tell us?"

Reed looked like he'd been disturbed from slumber, moving after being still for several minutes. "I can't tell you much about what Omega's up to down there because it's out of my territory, but I can tell you that there's at least one more facility they have here in Wisconsin, something that's a lot more secret than the Eau Claire safehouse. One of our sources called it Site Epsilon, and it was where they were working on something called 'Project Andromeda'. Our agent was tasked to find it and get inside, but they, uh..." He shrugged. "...disappeared."

"Where is this?" Scott asked, his arms folded in front of him.

"Eastern Wisconsin, not far from Eagle River." He shrugged. "I took a preliminary look around after our agent didn't report in, but there was no sign – no trace of his cell phone, nothing. Of course, I'm the only meta my organization has in the upper midwest, and I've got about a million things to do, so it hasn't been something I've been able to get to; Wisconsin's just been too quiet in terms of Omega activity to make it a priority."

"If Omega has a secret facility here in the state that far off the beaten path," Kat was thinking out loud, "that means it's probably something important, right? Something secret?"

"How sure are you about the location, Reed?" Ariadne's

voice came off a little tinny, and I heard something in the background over the speaker, some kind of commotion.

"The search radius is about 100 miles," Reed said. "But I have to be honest, we don't know what's waiting, which is another reason I haven't checked it out. I mean, it could just have an Omega sweep team or two, or it could have one of the guys that used to be called a god hanging around, working security."

I heard silence from Ariadne, as though she were pondering her response. "Omega's made a very bold move in their attack on us in Kansas. It's already bad enough that we're not going to be able to keep it quiet from anyone – not the government, not the press and not the public. I doubt they would have made this move if they weren't prepared to follow up with additional attacks, and frankly, we still don't know a damned thing about them.

"We need something, anything. I want one of you three, Kat, Scott or Sienna, to rent a car and get the computer back to Headquarters for analysis. The other two, go with Reed and Sienna's aunt, if she's willing to help, and find that Omega facility, infiltrate it if it looks lightly guarded. If not, put it under surveillance and we'll hit it as soon as we get M-Squad out of this fight in Kansas. We're completely blind here, fighting an enemy we know nothing about."

There was a stark silence broken only by a little static from the phone's speaker. "And if we can't? Can't find anything, I mean?" Kat asked.

"Then we'll need you back at Headquarters as quickly as possible," Ariadne said, voice taut. "Because I think we can safely say that Omega has declared war on the Directorate – and we have no idea where and when they'll strike next."

Chapter 15

There were a few seconds of quiet after Ariadne had hung up, as the four of us stared around the room at each other. Kat was withdrawn, staring into space, while Reed and Scott were watching each other out of the corners of their eyes, occasionally looking like they were going to throw down right there, glares in the quiet speaking louder than anything else.

"All right," I said. "Who wants to take the computer back to the Directorate?"

"I can do it," Kat said, stirring. "I'm the least useful in a battle anyway, at least from an offense perspective."

"Yeah, but having someone who can heal fatal wounds is sort of a nice card to have in your hand," Scott said.

"I agree with the waterboy on that," Reed said, drawing a scathing look from Scott. "We're going into an uncertain situation against potentially deep odds and gods know what kind of metas."

I put my hand on my head, massaging my temples. An hour ago, I hadn't pictured things going this way. I thought of James, still in my room, and my head spun from the ten thousand questions I had no answers to. I needed to know things, and I needed to know them now. My eyes snapped open and I focused on Reed. "Who are you working for?"

He tensed and a pained expression grew on his face. He nodded slowly, and spoke. "I guess if we're gonna work together, I have to explain a few things, don't I?"

"Yeah, playing the man of mystery isn't gonna do much to endear you to us at this point," Scott said.

Reed seemed to consider that very carefully before he spoke again. "I'll give you some basics. The organization I'm with has

one purpose: countering Omega. That's it. We know who the Directorate is because they're a big player in the meta game, but we've got no quarrel with you. The only reason I was after you," he said with a nod toward me, "is because Omega was and we were trying to beat them to you."

"What about a name?" Scott looked at him expectantly.

"I'm Reed, and you?" Reed shot him a smarmy smile, then rolled his eyes when he caught my glare. "Fine, but don't laugh. We call ourselves Alpha."

"And the prize for originality goes to...someone else," Scott said, his lips crooked in amusement.

"I didn't come up with it," Reed said. "Our founders are former Omega, but they got disillusioned with what the old gods had done and decided to band together to stop them. We've been around for a few hundred years, and we've kept them in check during that time."

"Alpha and Omega," I said under my breath. "So, what? They're the end and you're the beginning?" He gave me an oblique nod. "Of what?"

Reed let out a sharp exhalation. "I don't know. I mean, I've seen what Omega does, and it's not been pleasant. This little war they've started with you, it's nothing compared to some of the dirty tricks they've pulled. They've got people working for them that are worse than Wolfe. That should give you an idea of what they're like."

"And what could I tell about you by seeing who you work for?" I stared back at him, watched him stiffen, a resigned look on his face.

"You could see that we've got a common enemy," he said, "and if you keep watching what they do, you'll see why."

"All right," I said. "So what powers do you have?"

His eyes closed and he bowed his head, shaking it like a kid who was asked to give back a toy he really didn't want to let go of.

"You're killin' me, Nealon. Can't I keep any secrets?"

"You can keep all the secrets you want," I said, not taking my eyes off him. "You just can't keep them and expect to go into the fight with us at your side."

His eyes came up, burning, finding mine. "Let's get this straight: right now, you need me a lot more than I need you."

"And if we're going into a battle," I said, keeping my tone even, "how are we supposed to work together if I don't know what you bring to the table?"

He squinted, as if he could shut out my damned, unreasonable request, then relaxed and opened his eyes again. "I'm an Aeolus, okay?"

"A what?" Kat asked.

"Like on a breast?" Scott looked at him in confusion. Kat buried her face in one of her hands.

"Like a windkeeper, you jackass." Reed stuck a hand out and I felt the currents of air in the room shift, my clothing starting to flap in a growing breeze. Reed pulled his hand back and the air stopped stirring. "I can control the movement of air, attracting it to me or pushing it away."

"That could be really useful," Scott said, "if we're on a sailboat and the wind dies."

A flash of annoyance crossed Reed's face. "And I'm sure your power is only useful if a small fire breaks out."

"All right, boys, enough of that," I said. "I think we have to send Kat to the Directorate." I looked between the three of them. "We'll need all the offensive power we can get if we're going to assault what could be an Omega base." I looked to her. "But you should get any additional help you can from the Directorate and rendezvous with us as quickly as possible. Depending on how our search goes, you may catch up with us before we even find the enemy."

She nodded. "All right. I'll need a car."

Reed shot her a cool look. "I can help with that."

I took a deep breath and looked to Kat. "Hurry." I shifted my glance to Reed and then Scott. "Bring the car around and meet me outside the lobby in ten minutes." I turned and walked to the door, Kat and Reed a couple steps behind me.

I parted ways with them in the hallway, sliding the card key into my room door. I paused and took a breath before I pulled the handle, wondering if I'd find James still inside.

I did. He was lying on the bed, the covers pulled up to his waist, his shirt still off. He greeted me with a warm smile which I didn't quite match. "I waited," he said in an enticing voice, something that called out to me, urged me on. I wanted to throw off my jacket and blouse and crawl under the sheets with him and stay there for the rest of the night. To hell with the Directorate, Omega, Alpha and all else; forget metas and humans. I wanted them all to go away and just leave me alone with James. Maybe not forever, but at least until morning.

I breathed in deep, and let it out slow. "I'm sorry. I have to go."

He sat up, an awkward discomfort on his face. "What?"

"My office called, and I have to leave on an assignment right now." I tried to convey regret, but I couldn't tell if it was getting across, because his face had gotten red.

"Wow, that's dedication," he said, voice tight. "But you know, there are alternatives." He pulled back the sheet and I looked away. He wasn't wearing anything beneath it, and I was suddenly very uncomfortable. I became even moreso when he walked around the bed, rested his hands on my cheeks and gently pulled me in for a kiss.

I returned it, but without the heat, the passion that had consumed us earlier. This one was slow, methodical – enjoyable, sure, but without the possibility of going anywhere. He increased the pressure of the kiss, and I felt the heat from his side, the desire,

and broke away, turning from him, groaning as I did so. "I'm sorry, I can't. I have a job to do. I have responsibilities, commitments." I was breathing much harder than I would have thought I would be after one kiss. "I have to go." I looked back at him, and he seemed so solitary, standing naked in the middle of my room. "When I get done with this, I'll call you, I promise. I'm..." I searched for the words. "...I...want this. I wish I could stay right now, but I just can't."

He was silent for a moment, then turned and stooped to pick up his pants. I watched. "Where are you going?" he asked.

"I...can't really get into it. Secrecy and all that."

"I could help, maybe." He stared at me as he put his pants on, then zipped them up. I felt a tremor of regret. Trying to be a responsible adult and do my job really sucked right now.

I sighed. "I don't think so."

"I'm pretty strong," he said with a teasing smile. "You probably know something about that."

"I do know something about that." I tossed the clothes I'd left out into my bag, then pulled my syringe and a vial with my daily dose of psycho-suppressant out.

James's eyes caught the syringe as I injected the vial into my arm. "What's that?"

"That," I said, tossing the empty vial in the trash, "is how I curb the voices in my head." I felt the familiar rush of sleepiness that followed an injection, and shook it off. It barely affected me anymore. "How do you do it?"

"Not like that," he said with some disapproval. "You do it with your mind, not with drugs. If you've got a strong will, you barely feel it with most people, and it gets easier as you learn to control it."

"Ah," I said, slightly sarcastic. "That's where I went wrong. See, when I first absorbed someone, it was a crazed psycho beast who was bent on killing me. I shoulda picked a weaker target I

guess, worked my way up to the monstrous, but I didn't really have an option at the time."

"You absorbed Wolfe?" He shook his head and let out a small gasp of amazement. "Wow. I did not know that. I heard you beat him but I assumed you did it some other way." He cringed. "That's a rough way to start out." His face slackened and was overcome with genuine curiosity. "How old were you when that happened?"

"Seventeen," I said. I thought I caught a flash of surprise from him, and I gave him a reassuring smile. "I'm eighteen now. Don't sweat it, okay?"

"Eighteen and headed into trouble," he said. "You sure I can't help?"

"I think my bosses at the Directorate are going to be upset enough with the people I've already dragged into this," I said with a short laugh as I closed my bag and hefted it onto my shoulder. While I did that, I felt his arms wrap around me at my waist, slipping under my untucked blouse and touching my skin, giving me a thrill that ran up my spine.

He kissed my neck again, then whispered, "Surely one more won't matter to them; but I might make all the difference for you if you get in a tight spot."

I pulled away. "Pretty sure it would matter to them." I smoothed the wrinkles in my pants and pulled down my shirt to cover my midriff. I hesitated, staring at him, his muscled chest catching my attention. "I could certainly use some more help, but I can't..." I sighed again. "You seem pretty resourceful, so I'll tell you this much. I'm going east. If you show up, I won't be upset to see you there."

He smiled, a growing, widening one that made me feel a warm flutter. "You might just see me there, then."

I walked toward the door and opened it, casting one last look back. "I kinda hope so."

Chapter 16

I suspected Reed was stealing a car for Kat to use since there wasn't a rental place I knew of that would be open in the middle of the night, at least not in Eau Claire. I crossed the lobby of the hotel with my bag on my shoulder, heading toward the bar. I hoped that Charlie would still be there; no one had answered her door when I knocked.

The five of them were still clustered around the table, still laughing. I checked the clock on my cell phone; it was close to 3 A.M. One of the guys had passed out, his head down, and another was leaning heavily on his arm, eyes shut, keeping his face propped off the table. "Another round!" one of the two that was still fully upright called out to the bartender, and he stepped into motion behind the bar, his skinny hands grabbing bottles off the shelves.

I made my way through the tables and over to them. My aunt was laughing, hard, when I got there, but I hadn't caught the set-up or the punchline, so I was still serious. She caught my eye as I approached, and stopped laughing when I got close. "This is my sister," she said to the two men who were still awake. They both turned to look at me, and at least one of them came up with an idea that was so obvious it was written all over his sodding-drunk face. His leer made me uneasy, as though I were being undressed by his eyes. "Come on! Drink with us," she said.

Oddly enough, being literally undressed with James, a near-stranger, had been far more comfortable than this.

"Hey," I said, leaning over to Charlie. "I have to go."

"Go?" She looked around in confusion and laughed, a deep,

drunken laugh. "You just got here!"

"I have to go to Eagle River tonight," I said, keeping my voice low. I heard the men muttering to themselves, something about me that I ignored, otherwise I might have had to smite them. "Will you come with me? I could really use your help."

She met my gaze, her eyes looking into mine, and I caught a fleeting hint of concern that passed in about a second. "I don't think so, sweety." She reached up and patted me on the cheek twice. "I'm not done here yet."

I knelt down next to her. "Charlie," I said, catching her attention again as she was reaching for the glass the bartender had just set in front of her. "I'm serious. This could be really bad and I need all the help I can get."

"I said no." She took a drink, draining half her tallboy glass in one gulp. "God! You're all work and no fun, Sienna."

I felt the sting of her words curiously more given what had happened only minutes before, with James. "All right. I'll leave you be, then." I stood and started to walk out.

"Hey, wait!" She stood, almost turning over the table, and staggered over to me, shaking her head as though she could get rid of the effects of her drunkenness that way. "You're just gonna leave me here? In this town?"

I stared back at her, dully. My aunt, my blood. The person who I thought would be in my corner for sure, especially heading into this mess. "Yeah. You said you didn't want to come with me."

Her head rocked back and she looked offended. "Well, I don't have any money to get home."

I stared at her in disbelief and shook my head before reaching for my wallet. I pulled out five crisp hundreds and handed them to her. She flashed me a bright smile. "Good luck," she said. "I'm sure you'll knock 'em dead, kiddo." She rolled up the bills and slipped them down the front of her dress, then turned and walked

back to the table, where she was greeted with laughter and cheers.

I was still feeling burnt as I walked out the doors of the lobby into the stuffy, hot air of outside. The SUV was only a few feet outside the entrance, already running. I walked over to the passenger door and got in, took a quick look to confirm Reed was in the back seat, and nodded at Scott, who put the car in gear.

"I take it your aunt's not coming?" This from Reed, who was bathed in the shadows behind me.

"No," I said, voice tight. "She decided she'd rather drink with her new friends." I rubbed my face, still feeling the effects of the whiskey I'd had earlier in the night. Maybe one of these days I could actually go out and have a couple drinks without it backfiring on me, but apparently now was not the time in my life when I could pull that off.

The road went by, on and on as the GPS guided us onto the freeway and we headed north. My head swam with thoughts of James and Zack, Zack and James. I had been so close with James, so close to something I doubted I'd ever be able to have with Zack. Or anyone, actually. On the other hand, I knew almost nothing about James; in fact, all I knew about him was that he seemed to be the only man I'd met that I could touch without harming.

Plus, I knew how he looked naked. And it was...not bad. Not bad at all.

I cursed my responsibility again, and thought about Charlie, sitting in the bar even now, doing what she wanted to do when she wanted to do it. She blew through town when she felt like it, hung out with me when she wanted to, and, like some kind of idiot, I gave her money pretty much any time I saw her. Maybe I felt guilty because I thought I had it so much better than her, like I'd gotten lucky. Hell, I probably had. But she didn't even seem like she was trying, just doing whatever she wanted.

Meanwhile, I had just put off something I wanted more than almost anything else in favor of doing something I had to do.

I fell asleep sometime after passing a sign that read Chippewa Falls and when I woke up there was light on the horizon. Reed was talking to Scott in a hushed voice, and I heard them both share a chortle. "Where are we?" I asked.

Scott looked over at me. "About five miles from Eagle River. Directorate analysts went over property records in the area and found a few anomalies for us to check out."

"Oh?" I blinked my eyes. "How far behind us is Kat?"

"At least four hours," he said. "She's got some agents with her, and they're going full tilt with the sirens on, but they're just west of Eau Claire now."

"Maybe we'll get lucky and come up empty the first few places," Reed said from behind us. I looked back at him in askance and he shrugged. "It could happen."

We followed the GPS, passing through the town itself and out a side road, stopping at an old building on the outskirts, an aluminum shed that looked a little like a barn. After taking a hard look around inside, we found nothing. The next stop was an abandoned farm on the other side of town. By the time we got out of the car, the sun had been up for a little while and it was already hot. I left my jacket in the car and rolled up my sleeves, shedding my gloves. Reed and Scott shared a look and steered well clear of me as we walked up the dirt road toward the farmhouse.

My holster was solid against my ribs, and, I realized about halfway up the drive, quite visible since my jacket was gone. I felt for my FBI ID and remembered I'd left it and my wallet in the jacket. I shrugged and looked at Scott. "Got your ID?"

"Yep," he said, patting his back pocket.

"Good. I'd hate to get shot by some old farmer because I couldn't properly identify myself."

"As a fake FBI agent, you mean?" Reed cracked a grin when he said it.

We walked up the dusty road, my shoes picking up an accu-

mulation of particles as we went, a fine sheen of light brown earth on the black surface. "How many more of these property anomalies do we have to check?"

"Three more," Scott said as we reached the farmhouse. The screen door was open, hanging off its hinges. The door behind it was cracked and didn't look to be in much better condition. The white paneling that was wrapped around the house was in shambles, and looked like it had been there since the early 1900s, gray in some places, cracked and peeling. The shutters were off all but a few windows and the glass was broken out of those that I could see. "I don't think we're going to have to deal with anyone living here," Scott said in dark amusement.

"I don't know about that," Reed said. "This looks like a fine place for some snakes to nest; or maybe a posse of angry badgers."

I looked at him in confusion. "Badgers form posses?"

"They do in this state."

Scott led the way through the door, his hand extended in case trouble presented itself. He paused and looked at Reed. "You want to check the barn?" Scott turned back to look into the house. "It's not looking like much in here."

"Sure," Reed said, and looked at me. "You?"

"Yeah, I'll go with you," I said.

Scott frowned, looking back over his shoulder at us. "That's okay. I'll just check out this creepy old farmhouse all by my lonesome."

"That's the spirit." I gave him a barehand slap on the back, causing him to jump and then look at me with a stern face. "We'll meet you outside."

Reed and I walked to the barn, an old, decaying structure that looked to be in just about as good a repair as the farmhouse. The silo looked as though it had collapsed years ago, now nothing more than a bed of concrete blocks laid out across an overgrown field, green grass sprouting around the white of the blocks like

tombstones in a graveyard.

"You think this is it?" I looked at Reed to see how he was holding up. He looked calm enough.

"Probably not," he said as he opened the barn door wide, letting loose a foul, disgusting smell that caused me to cover my nose and gag.

"What is that?" I asked

"I think something died in here." He tucked his shirt over his nose and walked forward, looking around until he stopped in front of one of the animal stalls. "Yep. Something died here."

"Ugh." I retreated from the barn, moving back to a comfortable distance where the smell started to fade. I could still see him looking around within, but after about a minute he came back to me, popping his head out of his shirt and taking a deep breath. "Why did you think this wasn't the place even before you opened the door?" I asked.

He pointed to the ground in front of the barn. "No sign of vehicle tracks or footprints, here or in the main driveway. I don't think anyone's been here for a long time. Now, it could have been Omega doing a really excellent job of covering things up, but now that I've looked around, I'm inclined to believe it's just an old farmhouse." He wrinkled his nose. "Complete with remains of an old farm animal."

I stared off into the distance, where the sun was up off the horizon, casting its light on the green, rolling fields that surrounded us to the trees that covered the horizon. "We've got a few more to check. I kinda hope the next one is it, though; I'm sick of these dead ends." I turned and started walking back to the farmhouse, where I saw Scott emerging from a side door, brushing his shoulders off with enough emphasis that I suspected spider webs might have entangled him.

"I don't know," Reed said, taking one last look at the barn. "It might be the next one, it might be the one after that, but I kinda

hope it's none of them. I know Omega, and I shudder to think about what kind of secrets they're hiding out here." He made a face. "I suspect it'll make us long for an abandoned farmhouse with old rancid animals."

"Maybe," I said. "But whatever they're hiding, I need to find out." I took a deep breath, trying to enjoy for just a moment the feel of the sun's rays beating down on my arms and my hands. I felt like I was soaking them up, taking in the heat. "There's a lot riding on this, a lot we've sacrificed to be at this point, to take the assignment this far." I tried to hold my chin up. "Whatever's waiting for us, we'll find a way past it."

"You sure about that?" He raised an eyebrow at me. "You're talking about the organization that threw both Wolfe and Henderschott at you. I doubt they're gonna just let you waltz into one of their most closely guarded secrets."

"I doubt there'll be much waltzing, at least not until afterward," I said. "But whatever they're going to throw at us, whatever's waiting, we'll get through it." I smiled. "After all, how bad could it be?"

Reed rolled his eyes at me. "Jinx."

Chapter 17

Someone Else

It was bad. Worse than I expected. Guards walked the perimeter of their so-called Site Epsilon, black-clad figures that wore tactical vests and hid behind tall chain-link fences with barbed wire stretched across the top. They probably weren't visible to the naked human eye, but a meta would see them if they paid close attention, their black standing out against the green of the woods like tar smudged onto a painting of a summer field.

There was a fairly obvious cluster of them hanging behind the trees just off the driveway, behind the gate. I watched them for a little while, saw them with their underslung submachine guns, and worse, knew they were probably itching for a fight after being stationed out here for so long.

The main gate looked abandoned. I had parked my stolen car a good distance down the road, out of sight. This one had a decent radio but no air conditioning, and I had resolved that the next car I stole would be a new model Mercedes, if possible. The good news was, I had enough money that I didn't have to rob any convenience stores on the way out here. Progress at last.

I took another look at the gate, trying to figure out what their game was. I assumed that they were aiming for the abandoned look, but the gate was too well kept up, without rust. The gatehouse had dark tinted windows, but the paint was peeling. Based on the size, I had to guess there were at least three human guards inside at any given time, plus others lurking nearby. Every last one of them that I could see looked to be geared like a sweep team, not

rent-a-cops with batons and pepper spray. Omega was taking their security here very seriously, unlike the safehouse in Eau Claire. They'd even made sure this property was a half-mile off the nearest road.

I slunk through the grass, keeping close to the ground. I hate getting dirty, but this was one case where I had no choice. I had other suspicions about what kind of security I'd find behind the fences; motion and heat sensors, cameras, and a bunch of trigger-happy sweepers who probably had a very aggressive kill order, one that probably transcended attempts to surrender.

I stared at the seemingly impenetrable fortress and it stared back at me. I hoped not literally. If they were watching me already, this was going to be even tougher than I thought.

I was a half-dozen yards off the driveway when I heard the sound of a vehicle. I crouched lower and saw an SUV approaching. I huddled even closer to the ground and tried to hide my face as they passed. They were headed straight for the gatehouse, and I watched as movement started in earnest on the other side of the fence. The squad of guards I'd seen earlier were moving through the underbrush, coming toward the gatehouse. I waited for the SUV to turn around, to throw gravel and spin out, hauling ass out of there, but they didn't. The guards crept closer in position, weapons raised, and I wondered how long it would be before they opened fire.

Chapter 18

Sienna Nealon

We rolled down the driveway of the next potential base for Omega, this one an old factory. We'd turned off the road almost a half-mile back, and were surrounded by tall trees and heavy underbrush. I was trying to keep an eye out for whatever might cross our path next, but I kept getting distracted by movement in the forest. After the third time, I chalked it up to sunlight coming through the trees in the distance, but I couldn't quite go along with that explanation, not wholeheartedly anyway. We came up on a gatehouse, with a fence that was at least ten feet high and ran as far as I could see in either direction.

"It would appear they're serious about keeping us out," Reed said from the backseat. "Of course, we could almost jump over the fence..."

"I don't know that I could jump that," Scott said, staring straight ahead.

"Well, some of us could jump it," Reed said, prompting Scott to turn and shake his head, amused. "I'm kidding. I could help you clear it."

Scott raised an eyebrow. "And my landing on the other side?"

"As gentle as being tossed over a fence by a tornado."

I watched out the windshield. The gatehouse was in bad shape, looked to have gone years without painting, but the windows were tinted and I couldn't see anything inside. "Something's different about this place."

"It looks pretty abandoned to me," Scott said.

"No, she's right." Reed was leaning between the seats, looking forward. "There are fresh tire tracks leading up the drive, the fence looks like it's in pretty damned good repair, and some parts of that gatehouse look like they've been artificially aged." He pointed at the windows. "Look at those. If the rest of the place is cracked and peeling, why do those windows look new? They're tinted so dark you can't see in them." He squinted. "I think I see some really small security cameras, too. Why wouldn't they remove those if the place is abandoned?"

We had come to a stop about a hundred feet from the gate, just looking. "Well," Scott said, a little tense, "if we want, we can go check it out nice and slow, or we can start our trespassing with a little breaking and entering."

I caught movement off the path behind the gate, but I couldn't tell what, just a black blur. "I think we're gonna need to start with a bang."

Scott looked across at me, then back to the windshield. "Okay. You might wanna brace yourself."

I heard Reed buckle his seatbelt in the back as Scott gunned the engine with his foot still on the brake, the sound of gravel hitting the back of the SUV drowning out any possibility of further conversation. He let loose the brakes and we surged forward, racing toward the gate. I saw it get larger, saw a head peek out of the gatehouse and then dodge back in as we collided with the chain link fencing. I heard the smash of metal on the hood, and the top of the gate whipsawed down and hit the roof of our car with a clash so loud I ducked in fear that it would buckle.

We continued to drive, the gate lodged on our car. I saw men in black uniforms on either side of us, diving for cover. I watched as two of them were hit by the edges of the gate and flew through the air as Scott continued to push the car forward, his teeth gritted and his hands clenching the wheel as he tried to steer.

We came around a bend and I had to catch my breath. At least

a dozen guards were in the road in front of us, but that wasn't what got me. It was one of them, with a long tube slung over his shoulder, down on one knee, the tube being fiddled with by one of the other guards as the man stuffed something onto the tip – a roughly potato-sized object. I watched him start to pull his hand away, his task completed. I yelled and my hand flew to my seatbelt, unfastening it. I could hear Reed in the backseat, already moving, doing the same.

"RPG!" I shouted and reached over to Scott, slapping the release on his seatbelt. "BAIL OUT!" I waited a half-second to see him grab the door handle and start to open it before I did the same. I saw Reed going out the back on the same side I was, and I hit the ground at a roll. There was an explosion as the car was hit with a rocket-propelled grenade as it sped forward, the chain-link gate still on the hood.

The explosion was loud and it felt like my hearing cut out when it happened. I felt the sting of rocks and sticks stabbing through my blouse as I rolled across the dirt sideways, a fern catching me in the face and blinding me. When I came to a stop I spit out leaves and pushed to my feet. The first time I had decided to roll up my sleeves and not wear gloves, I had to bail out of a vehicle into the woods at high speed. Ouch.

"You okay?" I heard Reed's voice and nodded, still trying to get my bearings. We were slightly down from the road and I could hear distant shouting.

"Yeah," I said, ignoring the ringing in my ears, "but we need to get to Scott."

"And cross the open road where the men with guns have a clear line of sight on us?" Reed looked at me in disbelief.

"We'll be careful," I said, moving toward the embankment that led to the road. I bent over and climbed, poking my head up and looking the direction the car had gone. I hoped that it had wiped out the roadblock of guys they'd left for us, but when I

looked I realized we weren't that lucky. I saw guys swarming all over the SUV. It was still mostly intact, though it was burning, a small fire on the hood keeping the guards from going into the front seat, which looked to be filled with smoke.

The gate hung off the front about four feet on either side, but it had bent badly upon impact and mangled it further. One of the guards was barking orders at another, but my hearing had suffered from the explosion and my ears were ringing enough that I couldn't tell what he was saying. I watched three of them point in our direction, and I heard the whistle of gunshots over my head.

I reached down and drew my pistol, firing two quick shots, more to discourage them than anything; I wasn't likely to hit them at this range. Something big moved to my left and I realized with a shock it was Scott, running across the road. He jumped, sliding down the embankment next to me and I was following him a second later, running away from the road, Reed just behind me.

By unspoken agreement, we cut a ninety degree path away from the road for a couple hundred yards before halting. None of us were breathing heavy, and I stopped to listen. Behind us, I could hear the shouts of guards; with our superior speed, we had left them behind. Also, I could have sworn there were some coming from our right, toward the perimeter fencing. "We need to head this way," I said, pointing away from the fence.

"You don't think maybe we should get out of here for now?" Reed's head was swiveling around and suddenly his eyes widened. "Never mind, I hear it now. Guard squad coming from that direction."

"Yeah," I said. "If we're gonna escape we'll need to run parallel to the fence for a while. But I don't want to try and get out of here until we know a little more about this place."

"This place has some stiff security," Reed said, pointing back the way we came. "That's not just a sweep team; they don't get armed with rocket launchers. This is a serious installation, and

they clearly mean to keep whatever's here protected. We may want to retreat and come back with more forces because with just the three of us, this could get really ugly."

I heard the logic behind his words, knew he had a good point, but I heard Ariadne's words echo in my head, about Omega and fighting blind, and as I thought about it, something occurred to me. "If M-Squad is stuck down in Kansas, our only backup will be human agents. Not good enough to assault this place without a lot of casualties."

"Yeah," Reed said, "but it would be us plus them. Right now, it's just us."

I thought hard about what he said. "But it's our responsibility."

He let out a long sigh. "I get the feeling you'll be the death of me, Nealon."

"There are worse reasons to go," I said to him with a wink. He grimaced and I shrugged; guess I can't pull it off like Charlie can.

"You got your gun?" I asked Scott, who stood behind me, looking dazed. He nodded, reaching under his jacket to pull out his Beretta. "You might be able to take them out at range with your powers; I can't."

"Gun's gonna be more effective than a blast of water at the range we're dealing with," Scott said. "But they look like they're carrying submachine guns and rifles, so they've got the advantage over us."

"Yes, let's all not get shot," Reed said. "That sounds like a winning strategy."

"I have a backup gun." I looked at Reed. "Do you want it?"

"Nah," he said. "I've never used one; I'd probably end up shooting one of you. Besides, I'm gonna see if I can make things a little more hostile in here for gunplay, maybe level the playing field." He closed his eyes for a moment and the wind picked up

around us, howling through the trees. I heard the branches stir and bend, and a strong gale nearly knocked me over. Reed's eyes opened. "Sorry about that," he said to me. "I can control it well enough if I'm paying full attention, but since we're gonna be running, you might get hit by a few unintended breezes."

The wind was roaring now, I heard branches cracking and falling through the forest, and the shouts of the guards were inaudible under the rushing of the tempest. "This way," I said, struggling to be heard as we headed away from the fence. The rattling of the trees and force of the winds blowing past us was an absolute contradiction to the blue, sunny skies above us and the sweltering heat that pressed in as tightly as the countless turtleneck sweaters I'd worn since discovering my powers. It was almost otherworldly, being in the midst of a veritable hurricane in the middle of a hot summer's day.

I could feel the sweat running down to the tip of my nose and rubbed it against my shoulder, trying to dry it. The heat was intense, the humidity drowning me. The beads of salty liquid were springing out on my forehead more from the weather than the exertion. The winds that Reed had stirred were hot, like the breath of hell itself was chasing us through the woods.

The smell of the greenery was carried on the wind. I could taste the salt from the sweat that was dripping onto my lips as we tore through the woods, three metas outpacing the humans that were pursuing us. I hoped that there weren't any of our own kind hunting us; that would suck. A break in the trees ahead of me gave way to a view of a concrete wall. As we emerged from the trees, I saw that the wall was part of a sprawling building in front of us. It was two or three stories tall, though it was hard to tell because there were no windows. There was a loading dock to our left, pavement running all the way around it. To our right, a smooth, empty wall was unbroken by anything but a small, square vent cover.

"There," I said, pointing to the vent cover. "Entry point."

"So in we go?" Scott asked as the wind howled around us. "Maybe we should contact HQ and wait for reinforcements."

"Whatever this Andromeda project is," Reed said, "it's sensitive. Omega will either evacuate it from here or destroy it by the time we get back. Hell, they may already have started to do so." He wore the look of a man doing something he desperately didn't want to. "This is it. We do it now or it'll be gone."

"I guess it's now, then," I said. "But we do this as a team and stick together, coordinating our attacks."

Before they could respond, I heard the squeal of tires and a Jeep came to a halt about a hundred feet away from us, not far from the loading docks. I counted four guys that jumped out, every one of them carrying an AK-47 assault rifle. The winds around us started to whip harder and I looked over at Reed, who was deep in concentration. Rather than powerful, straight line winds, I watched the dust on the pavement begin to swirl in circles, gathering power as it made its way toward the Jeep.

The twisting currents of wind formed a funnel cloud just in front of the Jeep, catching it and swirling it around within. I watched the vehicle buck and twist, hitting two of the men taking cover behind it, hard. One pitched over, blood splattering on the ground next to him. The other went flying, landing on his neck. The other two seemed to be holding onto the sides of the Jeep as it spun into the air, higher and higher, cresting at almost a hundred and fifty feet before the tornado dissipated and the car came crashing to the ground with joint screams from the men holding onto it. I didn't watch.

I looked back to where it had landed and saw red on the pavement, then turned away and started toward the vent. I heard tires squealing in the distance and hesitated.

"Go!" Reed gave me a gentle push. "We're committed now, we can't go back!"

"At some point we have to deal with all this security," I said, my feet pounding against the asphalt. "They're not just gonna assume we left, they're gonna keep looking until they find us."

"Or until we kill every single one of them," Scott said, exchanging a look with Reed. "And it seems like you don't have much problem with that option."

"Omega's at war with you guys," Reed said as we came to a halt in front of the vent, which was a rectangular solid metal panel that fit into the wall flush. "They've been at war with Alpha for years, so I've learned not to show a lot of mercy, because they're not renowned for showing it to us." He held out his hand and the panel started to rattle, then burst from its mounting. "Ladies first," he said with a cocky smile.

"Ass," I said, but didn't argue. "I'll go first because the range of my powers is limited, not because I'm a lady." I bent nearly double and stopped. A long metal duct ran in front of me, and off to my left. I felt a flash of familiarity, looking down the metal tunnel, and my breath caught in my throat. It was like the box.

But it wasn't, not really. I could feel air circulating through, and over it I heard more tires squeal and looked back to see two big trucks full of guards, unloading on the pavement about a hundred feet in front of the panel. "Let's go!" I called to Reed and Scott.

"Shall we hold them off?" Reed said to Scott, who had his gun in one hand and his other fist extended.

Scott fired a couple shots. "Seems the gentlemanly thing to do. Got any ideas for that?"

"Elementally, dear Watson," Reed said, another tornado forming in front of him. "Elementally."

I heard Scott give off a cackle and I started to say something smartass and join them, my gun drawn. I stopped when I saw one of the guards on the truck aim an RPG launcher right at me.

"GO!" Scott shouted, launching himself to the left. I saw

Reed go right, leaving the RPG pointed at me. I saw the flare of the tube as I dived into the duct, running as fast as I could whilst bent double.

The RPG exploded behind me, the force of it yanking me off my feet. The ductwork took an abrupt, ninety degree right turn that I couldn't quite make as the explosive force drove me forward into the metal. I burst through the soft aluminum, my head ringing, and realized I was hanging, suspended in mid-air for almost a second before gravity caught me. I fell, dropping, down, down, down into the darkness of the room below me.

Chapter 19

I hit cold metal, my shoulder landing first, then my torso, and all my breath left me. I gasped, pain shooting through me. I couldn't hear anything but ringing in my ears, again, only worse this time, like someone had set off a fire alarm in my brain, rattling the damned bell so hard I couldn't concentrate on anything else. One by one, little agonies began to work their way into my consciousness; a searing pain in my shoulder, a feeling in my knee like I'd been hit with a hammer, and the taste of blood flowing in my mouth.

I worked my way to my knees and opened my eyes. I'd landed on a metal catwalk and below me was inky blackness. I looked above, to where I'd come from, and far up there I could see a smoking bit of ductwork, mangled by the explosion and my passage through the metal. Tracing it back toward the wall, it was ballooned comically, as though someone had pushed the sides out with all the ease of crumpling tinfoil. I wondered if Scott and Reed were all right, but something told me that even if they were, I wasn't going to be seeing them come down the way I had.

I gripped the railing of the catwalk, trying to force myself to my feet. It seemed to be harder this time than I could recall it being in the past. I had pains everywhere, but after a minute of solid effort I made it to my feet, leaning on the railing for support. I looked both directions the catwalk extended, and decided I needed to pick one. I finally decided on right, not totally at random, but close. Why? Because it was the *right* way. I couldn't bring myself to even chuckle at my horrible pun, such was the pain in my body.

I staggered along, my right leg starting to numb the more I

walked. I didn't think it was broken, but I knew I was going to have one bitch of a bruise on it later. I kept my right arm close to my body because the shoulder cried out in anguish anytime I moved it. I had lost my main gun in the explosion and fall, but I had pulled my backup, a much smaller weapon with a smaller magazine, a Walther PPK. Unfortunately, all I had was the seven shots it gave me, and then I'd be out.

My shoes clanked on the catwalk, and I hoped there was no one hiding below that could hear me. It was so dark underneath that it would be near impossible to tell. I took a fragment of duct that had blown loose from the explosion and dropped it over the side of the catwalk. I listened, but either because of the ringing in my ears or the distance it fell, I didn't hear it land.

Ahead I saw the outline of a door, a big, heavy metal one. I urged myself forward, resting more and more weight on my wounded leg. It still stung, but I knew now that nothing was broken, which meant that all I needed to do was fight through the pain. The bad news was, there was quite a bit of it to fight through.

I reached the door and grasped the handle, turning it slowly. I pushed the heavy metal with my shoulder, trying not to rush or fall through. I cracked it and looked inside, finding a concrete room with some lockers along one wall and a set of double doors that went on into the room beyond.

I led with my gun, limping into the room. Some caution signs were posted on the double doors, but they didn't stop me. The doors swung open for me, and I found myself in another room, walking on metal catwalks that led to a center platform with something sunken in the middle. I felt a chill; the room was like nothing I'd seen before in anything other than a movie. Large, cylindrical metal tanks were clustered below in hexagons, ominous chemical configurations written on the sides with warnings not to disturb the contents.

The whole room was cold, bitterly so, as bad as winter, and I

wished for the first time that day that I'd been wearing my gloves and jacket. I felt goosebumps rise on my arms as I approached the center of the room. The catwalk gave way for the circular platform, which looked like it had a segment of metal in the middle that was removable. Exactly what it slid away for, I wasn't sure, but it was obvious that it was patterned differently than the rest of the platform.

"Sienna?" The man's voice caught my attention, turning me around. He was behind me, in front of the doors I had just come through, his face barely visible in the dim light of the room. He was wearing a tight shirt, no buttons, and jeans that would have stirred my imagination even if I hadn't seen him naked the night before.

"James?" I let out a deep breath, all tension. "You found me."

"It wasn't that hard," he said. "There's only one Omega facility in eastern Wisconsin – or anywhere east until New York." He walked down the catwalk, approaching slowly, his hands extended. "God, it looks like they tore you up...what happened?"

I brushed a strand of bloodied hair out of my face. "They fired an RPG into the duct I was using to enter the building." I laughed under my breath, a dark chuckle without any real humor. "I wish I'd stayed in Eau Claire with you. I think it would have been less painful."

"No kidding." He was only a few feet away now, easing closer, when he came to a stop. "I don't mean to be rude, because I know we're in the middle of kind of a hostile place here, but are you gonna keep pointing your gun at me?"

"For now, yes," I said, and the playfulness was out of my voice. "Sorry, James. I don't really know you all that well, do I? You turn up in an Omega base at a convenient moment, and although you may genuinely be here to help me, I can't rule out the possibility that you're working with the enemy."

He flushed but managed to keep his expression under control.

"Ouch. So our time together doesn't count for much, does it?"

I stared at him evenly. "Our time together was less than a cumulative hour. So, no...I don't entirely trust you. I'm sorry if that offends you. If you turn out to be on the level, I promise I'll make it up to you in spectacular fashion, but you're going to have to forgive me if I don't trust you with my life yet."

He looked at me in cool amusement, hands at his sides. "You were going to sleep with me not twelve hours ago."

"I was. I might still, depending on how this turns out."

"Do I need to point out how screwed up that is?" he asked.

I cocked my head at him. "I've yet to touch another human being for more than ten seconds without killing them. Just because I wanted you badly doesn't mean I unconditionally trust you. My life is on the line here. Respect that, and we can see what Omega is up to together."

"I'm afraid I can't respect that," he said, one of his hands coming to rest on the railing. His face was calm, still, almost a mask compared to the sly, seductive man that had been unable to keep his hands off me for the last two days. "It hurts, Sienna." He turned his face away, clutching the railing with both hands. "It really hurts." He looked back at me and I caught a glimmer of something that scared me. "But not as much as it's going to hurt you."

The railing snapped off in his hands and he whipped it at me. I fired, missing him twice before the metal rail hit me in the hands, jarring my gun out of them and sending it spiraling away. The end of the rail hit me in the side of the face as I tried to dodge, drawing a cry of pain and causing me to fall down, landing on my back, the metal of the catwalk clattering as I landed.

I felt the pain running down my spine, but I only had a moment to feel it before he was there, grabbing both my arms and forcing me down. He was strong, and his face was twisted with rage. All the handsomeness that I had admired was gone as he put

his weight and strength into holding me against the catwalk. He slammed my head into the hard metal and I felt the room spin. "You should have stayed with me in Eau Claire." He was spitting as he said it, little flecks dropping onto my face.

"I can't tell you how glad I am that I didn't," I said as I brought my leg up and hit him on the side of his thigh. I aimed for the groin but he had angled himself so that I couldn't. He grunted and slapped me, hard. I gasped at him in surprise and bucked my entire body, flexing the muscles in my abdomen, bringing my forehead up fast. I felt it make contact with his nose, and I heard the break, felt warm blood wash down my face as he rolled off, shouting and cursing.

"You bitch!" He was clutching his face, a splatter of red smudging his mouth as I struggled to my feet. He rose, a few feet away, glaring at me, his eyes on fire with rage, a world of difference from when he had been kissing and caressing me only the night before.

"So, you're with Omega?" I kept my distance; my right shoulder still in agony, my leg hurt unbelievably and was slowing me down. In addition, I had a host of aches and pains that filled my body, and made me want to just lay down and die. "They sent you to sleep with me?"

"No, they sent me to recruit you," he said, holding his nose with one hand while he watched me. "The sleeping with you would have just been a bonus. I usually don't get to take my time with a woman, you know. They all die so quickly, and it's not much fun then. I mean, don't get me wrong, the rush from the absorption is amazing, it's like a drug, but when that's done they just lie there—"

"You're quite the disgusting pig." I felt a shudder of revulsion run through every part of me. I wished I could parboil my skin off and replace it with a new set. For all I knew, I could and it would just grow back.

"I preferred the sweet nothings you whispered to me last night," he said, jumping at me, swiping out with his hand to grab me. I dodged and maintained my footing, just barely, but my leg screamed in pain. He came at me again, grasping with his hands, and I caught one of them and pulled, taking him off balance. He started to fall and dragged me down with him. Had I been in peak condition, I would have been able to avoid it; as it was, I just tried to land with a knee in his belly. He grunted and slapped me again. I felt a sharp pain and blood started to trickle down my lips as I landed on him.

I tensed my guts, trying to protect myself, and tucked my elbows close, using my left to hit him across the face. He took another swipe at me but I fended it off, keeping my elbows locked and my hands up, guarding my face. I hit him in the nose twice, causing him to cry out, then his whole body heaved as he bucked and threw me forward. I tried to catch myself and roll out of it but my head hit the metal of the platform and I saw stars. My body came to a landing, pain racing down my back, and while I was trying to shake the colors out of my vision he got on top of me and punched me in the face twice.

I was stunned and he grabbed hold of me by the front of my blouse, holding me up while he hit me again. I heard the cloth tear and felt my head hit the cold metal, a fog surrounding me. "It could have been really nice between us, Sienna, but you just had to go and screw it all up." He was pacing around me now, and I saw him raise a leg and then felt a searing pain in my ribs. "Now you've exposed our location, you've ruined any chance of us having a pleasant evening, and what am I supposed to tell my bosses when I bring you to them? I was supposed to deliver you alive, but honestly, I don't think that's gonna happen now." He kicked me again, and I heard a scream, and it took my sluggish mind a minute to work out that it was my voice doing the screaming.

"I mean, look at this." He grabbed me by the face and shook

me, forcing me to look at him. "You broke my nose. Sure, it'll heal, but *nobody* does that. Not to me. Especially not some little teenage bitch that should have been grateful I even took the time to pay attention to her." He punched me in the face again, but I could barely feel it by this point. "I mean, it would have been good between us. Better than you'd ever have again, that's for sure. But you had to go and—"

I had steadily inched my left leg up, resting the bottom of my foot on the ground. I hoped he would just assume I was trying to curl up in the fetal position. I wasn't, although I was sure that'd feel better than the way I was laying presently. My hand reached down, grasping, trying not to be obvious, while he was directing all his hatred at my face. I pulled the knife Glen Parks had told me to carry as a backup out of its strap. I was grateful, not for the first time in the last few minutes, that James had never gotten me out of my pants, or he would have seen it.

I brought the knife across his face with a blind stroke. I had aimed to land it in his temple, but he moved at the last second and I caught him with a jagged slash just under his left eye and punctured his nose. He let out a cry and screamed as he dropped me, my shoulders hitting the metal catwalk again, but without much pain this time. I rolled to my hands and knees, still clenching the knife. "I had to go and what? Save myself from doing something I'd regret?" I spit blood in his face as I got to my knees. "Thank God. I can't believe I let you touch me, you soulless piece of filth—"

He yelled and jumped from where he lay to come at me, grabbing my hand that was holding the knife before I could attack him with it. He slammed me down again and I struggled, but I felt him reversing the grip. I poured the last of my strength into it, but he was too strong, too vicious. I stared into his scarred face as blood dripped down from his nose onto my forehead, smelled his breath, the foulness of it, all trace of sweetness gone. I felt the very

tip of the knife against my belly, felt the first sting of pain as it pierced me, just a centimeter, as I fought to keep him from killing me.

He wore a satisfied leer, and the darkness and shadows made him look demonic. "You could have just had me inside—"

Something hit James in the side of the head with devastating force and he flopped off, unconscious. I was breathing deep, panting, and a gloved hand reached down, offering me help. "I wouldn't worry about it," Charlie said, looking at the little bit of blood running down my belly where he'd stabbed me. "I've been with him; you're not missing anything."

Chapter 20

"Charlie," I said, breathing the word like it was the sweetest thing I'd ever said. She helped pull me to my feet. "Please tell me you're not with Omega too."

She laughed. "I'm not with Omega. I'm not with anybody."

I found the strength and balance to stand on my own, and she let me go. She was wearing a man's jacket, which she had kept between us while she was helping me up. I saw a watch on her wrist, a shining, gold one that looked like it was at least a couple sizes too big. As I stared closer at it, I realized it was a man's watch. She caught me looking and glanced down. "Oh, yeah, this? From that guy in the bar last night."

"Oh?" I didn't really care. My head was still spinning. "That was nice of him." I looked around and saw a small control panel a few feet away, built into the railing, almost nondescript. "I thought you were gonna stay in Eau Claire?"

She shrugged. "I did, until I got bored. Then I just looked you up through your phone's GPS and headed this way. Things got a little dicey when I found your flamed-out vehicle, but the guards were all pretty distracted by something going on over on the other side of the building. Sounded like a tornado or something."

I hobbled to the nearest railing and leaned against it. "Sounds like Reed. How long ago was that?"

She shrugged again, uncaring. "I dunno. Ten minutes? I came in through one of the unguarded doors while it was going down. Looked around the building until I stumbled in here. Looks like my timing was good. What are you doing here?"

I wondered how long I had been down here. I looked at the

panel again, sliding down the railing toward it. "Omega attacked the Directorate. We came to find out what they were hiding here."

"Oh?" She made her way over to me, leaving James unmoving in a pile on the platform. "So what is it?"

"Something called Andromeda."

"Huh," she said, disinterested, as she looked over the edge of the platform. "Sounds boring. And old."

"I don't know what it is, honestly." I stared down at the panel, trying to make sense of it. There was only one button lit up, and it was an option to unlock something, a thought which made me uneasy. I took a deep breath and thought it over. I was here to find out what they were doing, but what if it was a monster of some sort? Between Wolfe, Henderschott and James, Omega certainly loved their monsters. I stared at the unlock button until a finger came down from behind me and pushed it.

I turned and Charlie was there, smiling at me, impish. "No guts, no glory, kiddo."

A slight rumble ran through the room and lights came on, casting it in blue and orange light. There were four different catwalk bridges that led to the central platform we were standing on. Below us, there had to be at least a hundred chemical tanks surrounding an oversized apparatus that was circular, and lined up perfectly so that something could be raised from the top of it into the center circle of the platform.

The control panel lit up, giving me a host of options. I stared at it, trying to take it all in. Charlie peered over my shoulder, her breath heavy and kinda sour. "What's this one do?" She pushed a big red button, and I heard a rumbling from below us as machinery sprang to life. The circular grate in the middle of our platform squeaked and retracted to the side, leaving a hole in the middle of the floor.

"Stop," I said.

"Soooo cautious," she said. "Boring, boring, boring. You

need a little metal in your life, kid, a little action."

I felt the result of all the action I'd experienced today in my bones, in the pains, the aches and blood that still ran freely from different places on my anatomy. "Actually, I could do with a little less action at this point."

"Boooring," she said again. "Why must all you people lead such mundane little lives? I thought maybe you were different than the rest. I thought you were like me."

"Umm." I tried to focus on the panel, tuning out her prattle, ignoring the fact that she sounded almost offended. "I don't know what to tell you. I have a job to do, and it's pretty serious—"

She grabbed me by the shoulders and spun me around, causing my head to wobble, as she slammed my back against the railing. "Hey, kid! Wake the hell up!" She slapped me for good measure, not hard, but enough that I felt it and it pissed me off. I stared back at her, at the intensity in her eyes as she glared at me. "We're at the top of the food chain, darling. Ain't nobody can stop us: not Omega, not the Directorate, nobody. Women want to look like us and men want to grind up against us. You can have anything you want, take what you want, and nobody can stop you, and you're killing time with these white hat Directorate wankers." She let out a sigh of disgust. "Stop wasting your time doing all this crap when you could be having fun."

She slackened her grip on me and started to back off, but I grasped the watch on her wrist and held it tight in front of her. "Ow! What are you doing?"

"What happened to the man who had this on last night?" I twisted her arm to put it right in front of her face. "Where is he now?"

"Who cares?" She said, ripping it out of my grasp. "They're all interchangeable, men. They only last a very short time," she got a wicked grin that I found damned unsettling, "so you have to use them wisely – and I do mean *use*. I keep looking for a man who

can last longer, but even he couldn't—" She waved at James. "Though obviously for different reasons, in his case."

I felt a pit of disgust in my stomach. "You're like...you're a serial killer."

"You're so immature." She made a noise of disgust, waving her hand as though she were dismissing me. "We're succubi, Sienna; draining men's souls is what we do. They're there for us; it's why we have the thrall, the dreamwalking, all of it. The world of men is our cup: we're supposed to drink it, and you're afraid to even take a sip." Her face twisted into a humorless smile. "Just like your mom." Her dark hair fell around her shoulders, framing her face in a different light than I'd seen before; she looked almost cronelike, emaciated. "Well, I'll drink enough for all three of us, I don't care. I'm not scared. I'm ready for all of it."

I leaned on the railing for support, trying to edge away from her. "Why?"

"You know. Haven't you ever felt the rush?" She looked at me in disbelief. "I know you've taken souls; haven't you felt it? When you take them, how they scream and rattle in your head at first, how it spins you around? It's the greatest high you'll ever feel, trust me, way better than anything else. I mean, I know it's tough the first few times, like losing your virginity, but it gets so good, so powerful, it feels so right." She let out a little sigh and had her eyes closed. "You have no idea." Her eyes opened and she focused on me.

"I don't want to have any idea what you're talking about," I said. "I'm not a murderer."

"Don't play games with me," Charlie said, a smile on her lips. "I know you've killed."

"Twice," I said. "Once to save my own life with Wolfe and once to save the city of Minneapolis from Gavrikov."

"Oh, right." She pirouetted and sent me a mischievous glance. "Why would you bother doing a thing like that?"

"Because I owed them," I said, trying to catch my breath and push the pain away. "Because it was the right thing to do. I don't kill in cold blood. I might not even have killed Wolfe, but I was so afraid of him I couldn't let him go."

"And what about the other guy? The one you sent for a long fall off the IDS tower?"

"That wasn't me." I grabbed a segment of rail in my hand, wondering if I had the strength to rip it loose and use it as a weapon like James had. I looked around for my knife, but it was far behind Charlie; she'd kill me long before I reached it. "That was Wolfe."

"You're weak," she said, spitting the words at me in disgust. "You're supposed to control them. They're your souls, your puppets, but you can't even keep what you've got in line. No wonder you can't bring yourself to do what's fun, what you should be doing. You're pathetic." She kicked out faster than I could have anticipated and knocked my legs out from under me, sending me to my back. I looked up and saw her face, nothing like the easygoing Charlie I'd seen; her eyes were wide, her mouth twisted in cold disdain. I felt a deep, powerful dose of fear as she said, "You're nothing like me."

"Thank God for that." The voice came from behind her, strong, fearless, and I saw Charlie's eyes widen in fright, her expression chilled as she turned to face the new threat, a woman standing at the edge of the platform, staring her down. Her dark hair was long, but pulled back in a ponytail, and she wore a simple t-shirt and jeans that had some dirt on them, as though she had been crawling around on the ground. "Get away from her, Charlie, or so help me I will crush the very life from your body the way I should have years and years ago."

I felt a swell of emotion deep inside at the sight of her, something I didn't even know I still had in me. Little tears sprang up in the corners of my eyes and I blinked them away, blinked again to

be sure what I was seeing was true. It was. She was there. I opened my mouth, and amazingly, a single word fell out.

"Mom?"

Chapter 21

She attacked Charlie without warning, reminding me of a thousand sparring sessions in the basement. My aunt staggered back under the fury of my mother's assault, kicks and punches blurring through the space between them so fast I couldn't count. I saw Mom jump-kick and catch Charlie underneath the chin, sending her reeling, and followed it up with a flurry of punches that brought my aunt to her knees.

"Wait..." Charlie gasped. "Sierra, wait..." My mother stood above her, hands still raised, ready to rain down a killing strike while looking down at her sister with cold indifference. "I was trying...trying to help her..." Blood ran freely from Charlie's nose, and one of her eyes was already swelling shut. I didn't think she'd even managed to land a blow on my mom.

Mom reached down with a gloved hand and picked Charlie up by the neck, holding her out at a distance, as though she didn't want to get to close. "Help her what? Die?" She threw Charlie to the ground, her face scraping against the grated metal platform as she landed.

Charlie lifted her head and rolled over, holding a hand out as though she could ward off my mother's cold fury with it. "Please...please, Sierra...please!"

My mother halted. "One chance, Charlie. Why should I let you go?"

"Please." Charlie propped herself up, both hands behind her back. "I won't come anywhere near her again, I swear. I swear on my life."

My mother's face twisted in disgust. "You picked the right

one to swear on. Heaven knows you've never cared about anyone else's."

"That's not true!" Charlie shook her head, her normally calm or sly expression completely consumed by fear, stricken by the uncertainty of whether she'd live or die in the next moments. "I came to help her, Sierra, I came to teach her because I knew you weren't around! I knew she needed help!"

My mother halted her advance, hovering menacingly over her sister, her face a mask. She stood there, staring down, her expression impenetrable, for a very long moment. "Get out of here," she said, growling. "If you ever come near my daughter again, Charlie, I will kill you. You know I will; and it won't be pretty, or quick."

I saw Charlie slide back, pulling herself to her feet, then turning to see her sister, and she nodded, quickly, all trace of the carefree, cocky woman my aunt had been gone as though she had never existed. "I swear. She'll never see my face again." Charlie turned and began to walk out, down one of the catwalks toward a door on the far side of the room.

"She better not see any of you again, Charlie." My mother's voice was hard, sharp as glass, and unforgiving. "If she sees so much as an eyelash of yours, you won't have time to blink before I drain you into nothingness." Charlie stiffened but did not turn back at my mother's threat.

I watched her leave, the doors swinging shut behind her, and then turned to my mother to find her looking at me, her face the same mask of fearful indifference that she wore when talking to my aunt. "Mom," I croaked. She took a few steps toward me, then stopped at my side. I looked up and saw she was using the console next to me. "Mom?"

"It looks like you haven't been following the rules," she said, voice hollow. "You're not in the house, you're not wearing gloves, a coat." Her gaze hardened on me, leaning against the railing. "Actually, it looks like you're wearing hardly anything." My mouth

opened and I tried to say something, but nothing came out. "You're a Directorate Agent now, you're living on your own and you've had a boyfriend." Her eyes narrowed and focused in on mine. "Yeah, I heard about that. You're a big girl, in other words. Big enough to deal with the consequences of your own mistakes."

She knelt next to me, her face hovering a foot away from mine. "You're going to make more mistakes, I know it. But that's your problem." She stood. "Not mine. Not anymore. Time to grow up." She punched a button on the console and a deep rumbling filled the entire room. She turned her back on me and started to walk away.

"Mom, wait!" I tried to use the railing to stand again, pulling myself up. "Wait!" I slumped, putting all my weight on the console as the rumbling noise that filled the room centered on the middle of the platform. A cylinder rose up, sliding through the hole, black, sleek metal that extended six feet above the platform before it stopped moving. "Mom? Help me," I said, my words coming out in a tumble, desperation lacing every one of them. "Help me, please, Mom."

She didn't stop, didn't turn around, didn't even slow her walk as she moved toward the doors I had entered through. "I just did."

The doors swung shut behind her.

Chapter 22

"God, am I glad she's gone." The voice was solid, strong, and so damned alarming. I turned my head to see James pushing himself up onto all fours. "Both of them, actually." He shook his head as he got to his feet. "Now..." His face was bloody, his nose a shattered mess with a hole in it, crimson running down his cheeks and lips. "Where were we?"

Something clicked in the cylinder in front of me, and a hissing sound came as it seemed to depressurize, fissures appearing in the surface of it. I watched James, whose eyes widened when he saw it, and his face snapped back to me. "Dammit, I guess I'll have to make this quick—"

The cylinder opened, a door sliding back, light shining out of it in a pale yellow across the platform. A face appeared first, followed by the rest of a body. James didn't watch, he didn't delay: he came right at me and I reached out to grab hold of him, struggling as he pushed me to the ground, his hands trying to grip my neck. "Stop fighting me!" he raged, forcing my arms down. "This will all be over in a few seconds."

"That's what you tell all the girls." I rocked my hips to dislodge him, but to no avail. I was too weary, too beaten. Everything hurt, every part of me now, and what didn't hurt just felt weary. All I wanted was to sleep, to not be a big girl, to just be back home with Mom and not have to worry about any of this—

A screech came from behind James and he paused, a look of panic crossing his wrecked face. "Uh oh," was all he had time to say before a woman came out of the cylinder, her eyes tightly shut, a scream on her lips. She was staggering, naked, trying to catch

her breath, her dirty brown hair tangled in wet ringlets around her shoulders. Her eyes opened and caught sight of him and me, on the ground, and she screamed again, this time not from fear but rage, and she attacked him, her hand coming down in a hard swipe that caught him by surprise and sent him flying over the edge of the railing, down into the darkness below.

I turned my gaze from where he had fallen to her, glowing brown eyes giving me a sense of deep unease. I had no defense against what she'd done to him; I only hoped that if she sent me over the edge I'd be able to land 1) softly and 2) on him, because I didn't know if I could take any more pummeling.

"Are you okay?" she asked in a throaty voice, a little hoarse, like she hadn't used it in a long time.

I flinched at the sound of her voice, mostly because I was expecting an attack instead. "Do...do I look okay?"

The naked girl studied me, her eyes assessing. "Not really."

I worked my way to sitting again. "Who are you?"

She looked lost in thought, far away, drifting, and I almost thought maybe she'd passed out on her feet, as though the trauma of being released from a big black cylinder was too much for her. She paused, looked across the room, then turned back to me, still almost uncertain. "Andromeda," she said finally. "My name is Andromeda."

I heard voices, raised, from behind me, and crooked my head to look. Andromeda tensed, as though she were ready for battle. The doors on the far end of the room burst open and Reed and Scott came through them, followed by two guys in tactical vests carrying submachine guns. Neither wore masks, and I knew them instantly. One was Kurt, the other was Zack.

"Sienna!" It was Scott who shouted, his hands pointed at Andromeda, who pointed her hands back at him. "We thought you were dead."

Reed matched Scott's position, though his expression was a

bit more wary. Both Kurt and Zack had their weapons pointed, and I held up my hand to stop them, and felt myself sag against the railing as they came onto the platform. "Me? Not so much. Everybody calm down," I said. "This is Andromeda." She looked at me, then at them, and began to relax. "Andromeda, this is... everybody."

Scott inched his way around the platform, still keeping his hands up, eyes fixed on her, though they looked down more than once to take in her nakedness. "So Andromeda is not a project...it's a person?"

She cocked her head at him, her pale skin giving off a briny smell, now that she was closer to me. "Perhaps it's both."

"We don't exactly have the perimeter secure here," Kurt said, scanning the room. "We need to find what we're here for and leave."

"She's it, I think." I said this as Zack made his way forward, easing past Andromeda, and grasped me under the arms to help me stand. "She's the reason we're here; though I'm not sure how much she can tell us about Omega."

Her eyes followed mine, and I caught a hint of deep intelligence in them. "Everything," she said. "I can tell you everything about Omega. Who they are, where they started, why they're here and what they're after."

"Then we need to get her out of here," Scott said. "Back the way we came?"

"No," Andromeda said. "This way." She looked at me. "Let me help." She put her hand on me and I started to protest, but something in her eyes silenced me. Her hand was on mine, and a second passed, then five, and nothing happened.

"What...are you?" I asked, staring back at her.

Her eyes glowed and I felt strength course through me as she pulled me along, almost effortless. "Something new. I am a sacrifice made by Omega to bring about change."

"Oh, good, cryptic," Scott murmured from behind me. "You'll get along well with Old Man Winter."

"Are you all right?" Zack whispered next to me, trying to keep up as Andromeda pulled me along. I noticed that all my pain had receded; the wounds were still there, but they seemed not to hurt.

"I think I'll be fine, once I get a day to heal," I said. "Did you drive here from Detroit?"

"All the way through the Upper Peninsula at about a hundred miles an hour." He gave me a tight smile. "Ariadne said you were headed into trouble."

"I was." I tried to smile at him. "I found my way out again, with a little help. What about you?"

His smile disappeared. "We'll talk about it later."

"No, wait," I said. "They sent you after a meta, didn't they?"

"They did."

"So what happened?" I asked.

"Omega jumped ahead of us, bagged 'em." Kurt was the one who answered, and I got a glimpse of him behind me. He had a bandage across the back of his head, and it was bloody. "Happened all across the country last night. The Directorate got a big fat sucker punch to the side of the head."

"Sucker punch?" I shook my head, trying to clear it. "I mean, we heard about Kansas, but you're saying they tried to what? Catch your target before you could?"

"They tried to kill us, Sienna." Zack's eyes were serious. "They damned near did. They've killed a lot of our agents in the last twenty-four hours. Kansas was a war zone; the west half of the state is on fire from the battle."

We made our way down a hallway and through a set of doors to find ourselves in a loading dock. "Your vehicle is just outside," Andromeda said. "It may be a tight fit to get all of us in it."

Kurt looked at her in suspicion. "How did she know that?"

Andromeda's voice dropped to a hushed whisper, and her eyes seemed to focus on something in the distance. "Because I see." They dropped back to looking at Kurt. "It is one of my talents."

Scott rushed forward and hit the loading door, causing it to slowly clank open. Sure enough, when it was up a small SUV was sitting in front of us, the road to the gate visible behind it, complete with the wreckage of the car we drove, gate still mounted on top of it. A few black-clad figures were visible around the yard and I watched Zack and Kurt unload on them at distance, dropping a couple while Reed stirred the winds and sent another tornado toward the largest concentration of Omega agents.

"I think we've worn out our welcome," I said as Andromeda guided me to the car and pushed me into the back seat, squeezing in next to me. Zack and Kurt got in next, firing rounds all the way up until they shut the door. Kurt rolled down his window and pulled a pistol, discharging a half-dozen shots.

Reed slipped in next to Andromeda and Scott piled in after him, slamming the door as Kurt hit the gas. "Might want to call Kat and the others," Zack said as we sped toward the gatehouse. "Warn them off. We can meet them in town and convoy back to the Directorate together."

"Okay," Scott said, already dialing his phone.

"I hope nobody minds if I sit in the hatchback," Reed said. "It's nothing personal; I just feel weird squeezing in this close to a naked girl I don't know." He blushed as he looked at Andromeda, and I realized that I hadn't even noticed that she was still wearing nothing. Of course I also felt very close to passing out now that she had taken her hands off me.

Reed went over the seat into the hatchback, giving Scott and Andromeda a little more room. Scott pulled his phone away from his ear and looked down, messing with the touchscreen. "I can't seem to reach her."

"Think she's out of cell phone service?" Zack said, looking back at him.

"It is a little spotty through here." Scott stared down at his phone. "I'll try again, but take the quickest route back to town. They should be nearly here by now."

Zack turned to talk to me. "What happened in that room?"

I searched my memory and tried to come up with a coherent explanation. "Um, well...one of Omega's lackeys got the better of me after I got blasted through a wall by an RPG. Then I got saved by my aunt—"

"Your aunt?" Zack squinted at me in the backseat.

"Yeah." I nodded. "Then she turned on me when I figured out that she had been killing people just for the rush of absorbing them." I took a breath. "Then my mom saved me from her and unleashed Andromeda."

Zack's jaw dropped. "Your mom?" He looked at me with great uncertainty. "Are you sure you're all right? I mean, no offense, but it kinda sounds like you're hallucinating. Maybe we should call Perugini or Zollers."

I shook my head. "She was real, and she was there."

He got that look on his face that he puts up when he doesn't want to argue. "If you say so."

"What the...?" Kurt slowed the car as we approached the end of the dirt road, ready to turn onto the highway. Off to the side, a car was wrecked against a tree, the hood crumpled, smoke pouring from underneath. "Hope they've got AAA."

"Look further," Andromeda said, "and you will see."

"What's she talking about?" Kurt asked.

"Over there." Zack nodded his head in the opposite direction, where there were two bodies laying on the ground, wearing black suits. "Are those ours?"

He was out of the car, Kurt and Scott a few steps behind him. Scott ran the fastest, pounding across the pavement and off the

road. I followed, aided by Andromeda and Reed. When I came up over the edge of the road, I could tell it was definitely Directorate agents, prostrate in the grass, tire marks in the dirt around them. One of them was stirring as Zack slapped him gently across the face.

"Jackson!" Zack shook him, and the agent blinked his eyes a few times. I recognized his face, but didn't know his name. "What happened?"

The agent named Jackson blinked again, staring up at him. "Zack? Where am I? What are you doing here?"

"You were supposed to be backing us up at the Omega site," Scott said. "What happened?"

The agent looked surprised, then pondered that. "I...don't know. I don't remember." He looked around, startled. "I have no idea how I got here."

"Where's Kat?" Scott was looking around, frantic. "Where is she?" He went back to Agent Jackson. "Where'd Kat go?"

Jackson stared at Scott blankly. "I don't know. Was she with me?"

"Wake the other one," Kurt said.

"It won't do any good," Reed said. "He'll have had his memory drained too."

Something vague and totally improbable caused the wires in my brain to cross. "Just like those convenience store clerks."

Reed raised an eyebrow at me. "Finally getting it now?"

Scott stared back and forth between the two of us, impatience on his face. "So who did it? What kind of meta can steal memories out of someone's head?"

"A succubus or incubus." Reed stared back at me, not breaking eye contact. "But only one that's disciplined enough that they don't want to kill."

I thought about it again, about the whole trail. A willingness not to kill innocent people even when it was inconvenient. Disci-

pline. That ruled out Charlie, and James as well, actually. Only one left. The rest of them were staring at me, but Reed was the only one who did it knowingly.

"Mom."

Chapter 23

Someone Else

I kept calm all the way out of the room, able to keep myself from looking back at Sienna only through years of ridiculous, rigorous discipline. After I was through the doors, I started to run, making my way through Omega's labyrinthine base. I burst through the exit and smashed the window out of a car that was parked outside. This one looked like something one of the Omega guards might drive, a sedan that didn't look too old. I hotwired it, and it started without a bit of fuss. The engine roared to life, and I paused, taking a breath after what I'd just accomplished.

"Good luck, kiddo," I whispered as I put the car into reverse and made a three point turn, angling it toward the road that would lead me off the premises. "If anyone can do it, you can."

I gunned the engine, scaring the hell out of a few guards. I picked up a few bullet holes on the way out, but nothing too serious, I thought. Then I felt the pain in my shoulder. I looked down, and sure enough, blood was streaming down my arm. Dammit. I hoped my daughter had better luck than I'd had. She should. After all, now she had Andromeda looking out for her.

I swerved as I made my next turn; the wheel was getting harder and harder to control and I felt a little faint. I shook my head, trying to clear the little sparkles of light from my vision. Something was in front of me though, big and black, and very close. I jerked the wheel to the right and my car went off the road. After all this time, I finally had a decent car and I ended up—

I woke up after a few seconds, I thought. I was still bleeding

out of my shoulder. I forced the door open and pulled myself out, to my feet. I snuck a quick look in the rearview mirror; at least I didn't look as bad as Sienna had when I left her behind.

I walked across the road in as close to a straight line as I could manage. I recognized the car when I got closer; government plates, men in suits in the driver and passenger sides. The first one was getting out as I got close and I used my meta speed to cut the distance between us, putting my hands on his face. I heard a scream from the back seat, and I could see the other agent pull his gun, aiming it at me, too scared to shoot through his partner. I pulled the pistol out of the holster of the agent I had in my grip and shot the other in the chest, twice, aiming for the kevlar vest I knew he was wearing.

He slammed against the door behind him with each shot, and I let the first agent drop. The door to the backseat of the SUV opened and a blond girl stepped out, flushed and angry. She was tall, willowy, pretty in that annoying kind of way a cheerleader is. I rolled my eyes when I saw her, and she put up her hands, as though she was ready to fight. I grabbed her fist when she threw her first punch, and held onto it until her expression changed.

It was kind of funny to watch. She grunted and strained, and even with my shoulder oozing blood, I still managed to keep a grip on her until her eyes rolled back in her head. I felt good after, which was normal, but when I moved my shoulder, I realized it didn't even hurt. "Persephone," I whispered as she dropped to the ground.

I went to the passenger side and pulled out the agent I'd shot. He was still breathing, so I touched his face, draining him until I was sure he wouldn't remember anything. "Sorry," I said to his unconscious body, "but it's best you don't remember running into me." That done, I pulled the blonde girl into the passenger seat and slid into the driver's seat myself. I started the car and let it run for a second before I put it in gear and pulled back onto the main road.

When I went to make the turn to the right that would take me back to town and eventually an interstate, my eyes caught on the Persephone. I didn't owe her an explanation, not really, especially since she was unconscious, and it was pretty unlikely she would remember. Still, I looked at her, and she reminded me a little of Sienna, mostly in the age, and I told her anyway.

"Sorry, kiddo, but I need you." My eyes traced the lines of her face, the slack, relaxed musculature that reminded me of a little girl who used to be so innocent...but most of that was gone when I'd left her behind just minutes earlier. I wondered when it had gone away, and who had done it. I felt a flash of anger, and knew who to blame. "He doesn't give a damn about human agents, you know, but I bet he'll care about you. That's how he always was. Metas first." I shook my head. "Not that you care, but that's it. That's why I took you with me. You're my insurance, for when we collide...because it's coming soon. I can feel it. Real soon, and after all, I'm just one girl, alone against the whole Directorate. So I'm gonna need some help, and that's you, blondie. You're it. My fulcrum.

"You're my leverage for Erich Winter."

about things that I wondered about (for Sienna, not for me). That help was much needed, and my thanks go to her for it. Any medical errors that remain are probably there because I should have listened closer to her rather than tried to go with what was best for the story.

The cover was designed by Karri Klawitter (Artbykarri.com). Exceptional covers, exceptional prices.

Thanks also to Nicholas J. Ambrose of www.everything-indie.com, who did the edit and format work here once more. Nick is truly a titan, and one of those most responsible for my work upholding the level of professionalism that it does. During the final phase of publication of this book it was driven home to me in a very obvious fashion how much Nick has contributed to every one of my books, and for that, I thank him.

And in the last part of the roundup, thanks to my mom and dad, wife and kids. You know who you are.

Acknowledgments

Third time around, and thrice charmed I have been as an author of this particular series. There are again thanks aplenty to be doled out, and here are the responsible parties:

Heather Rodefer, my inestimable Editor-in-Chief (she keeps earning that title) once more deconstructed this manuscript from top to bottom, from left to right. She has my thanks for keeping me between the (electronic) lines.

Shannon Garza gave me feedback on the emotional highs and lows of this piece (in addition to searching tirelessly for all those pesky errors I sneak in to give her something to hunt for) and helped it achieve whatever emotional resonance it may have (for me it held a lot, your mileage may vary).

Debra Wesley once more assisted me in finding errors, eliminating inconsistencies, and picking up little details that I hope my more eagle-eyed readers find (hints for the future, so read close).

Calvin Sams also read over this particular work, giving me some notes on his thoughts, and for that, I thank him.

Robin McDermott also provided a great deal of editorial input, helping to shape the way this manuscript was written, and helped me catch some very important errors.

Wendy Arnburg took time to help me figure out exactly which guns Sienna would find most comfortable. She would want me to tell you that the choice of Sienna's back-up gun (a Walther PPK) was totally the author's choice, and a nod to the world's most famous fiction user of said firearm, and was against her advisement.

Janelle Seinkner took time to answer a few medical questions

SOULLESS

THE GIRL IN THE BOX, BOOK THREE

Robert J. Crane
Copyright © 2012
All Rights Reserved.

Contact Robert J. Crane via email at
cyrusdavidon@gmail.com

Layout provided by **Everything Indie**
http://www.everything-indie.com

SOULLESS

THE GIRL IN THE BOX
BOOK THREE

Robert J. Crane

SOULLESS

…touched by that dark miracle of chance that makes new magic in a dusty world.

Thomas Wolfe

January 18, 1991
San Bernardino, California

Dear Alex,

I wish you could have known your great-grandparents. I mean my parents, Charlie and Bertie Lawton. They've been gone a long time now—Mama for over 50 years and Daddy for over 30—and I still miss them every day. They didn't get a chance to see your smiling face, your chubby cheeks, and your twinkling blue eyes. Had they had that chance they would have noticed immediately what I saw when I met you this morning. You have Mama's nose and otherwise you are the spitting image of my daddy—or so a wistful old woman at the end of her life chooses to believe.

Of course, you'll never know me either, since I am in my last year on this world and you just turned two yesterday. But somehow, I feel that you are the one I'm supposed to give this to. So here it is.

In the summer of 1940, I was home from college and Mama was dying of cancer. I was 21 years old then and I thought of Mama as an old woman. She was 39.

Mama was very proud of me then. She and Daddy had made great sacrifices to enable us to go to college, Alex. She wanted us to have the education that fate had denied her. Remembering how hard they worked for us brings tears to my eyes even now. Only Mary Ann and I ended up going. Billy stayed home and worked the farm and Betsy (your grandmother) ran off and married Danny Powell. But they could have gone too if they had wanted to. Mama and Daddy would have done anything to make that happen—even though it was a time when few people, especially daughters of farmers, went to college.

I spent most of the last week before I returned to school in Mama's room, trying to keep her comfortable. We both knew that once I left, I would never see her again this side of Eternity.

She was weak and frail, but her mind was sharp. We reminisced about old times, we laughed, and we cried. Then, a few days before I left, I asked her how she and Daddy met. In hindsight it's hard to believe, but at the time I knew practically nothing about her life before us children were born.

I was amazed by the extraordinary story that Mama told me over the next two days. I sat and listened for hours, coaxing more out of her. Then at night I spent hours writing it all down—trying to keep it in her words as best I could recall them. A month later, she was gone.

I moved on, Alex, just as my parents knew I would. I moved as far away from tobacco fields as I could. I was determined to get more out of life.

After I graduated, I rarely came back home and that is now a source of great regret for me. It was only when I started to grow old that I finally realized that the things I had run away from were more beautiful than the things I had spent my life chasing. It's funny how that happens. I hope that you will not make the same mistake.

I wrote Daddy a few times each year. Every once in a while, I'd call him, but long-distance calls were expensive in those days and he always rushed through the conversation, reminding me repeatedly that long distance calls were "high" and that the phone company was charging me "an arm and a leg." In every letter and on every call, I invited him to come visit me. I was just being polite. Daddy worked every day from dawn to dusk and I'd never known him to be away from the farm overnight. So, I was stunned when I got a letter from him (the only one he ever wrote me) that read: "Coming on the bus. Be there in two weeks. Will call you when I'm there."

That was in 1956. He stayed five days and was nervous the whole time. When the time came for him to leave, I offered to buy him an airline ticket, but he declined it. Instead, he rode the bus all the way back to Virginia.

I probably spent more time alone with him that week than I had in the rest of my life combined. There were many things about my life of which he did not approve, but he chose to be gentle. It was a precious time.

Daddy seemed surprised when I told him that Mama had told me the story of how they met—and the story of her life before she knew him. And in turn I was surprised when Daddy laughed and said, "She did, did she? Well, I'll bet she didn't tell you *everything*." Intrigued, I suggested that maybe he ought to give me his side of the story. "I reckon not," he answered. "I reckon you might as well stick with what Bertie told you."

I let it drop. But the next night after dinner, he surprised me again. He started talking. We stayed up past midnight and what he told me was even more amazing and remarkable than the story Mama had told me in 1940. After he left for home, I wrote it all down.

As you've probably guessed by now, that's what this bundle of papers is—it's those stories.

And now, having been fated to have the same cancer that killed my parents, I am facing the end of my life. Just as it was with them, the end I face is certain, but it will not come suddenly. The fact that, like them, I will be killed slowly, at least affords me the opportunity to wrap things up—to make careful dispositions. In my final days, Alex, I imagine that I have become wiser. Whether that is true or not, I regard this bundle of pages that I am passing on to you as my most treasured possession.

I have left this package with a colleague who is under instructions to give it to you when you are 25 years old. I hope you will pardon me for making you the custodian of these stories, a responsibility you did not invite. Please know that I do not give them to you in order to put you under any obligation. Do with them what you wish. I only ask that if you do not presently see the value in them, then set them aside for a while and come back to them some years later. See if they make a different impression on you then.

You will see that I have left the telling of Bertie and Charlie's life stories in their own words, up until the time they met. After that, I've taken the liberty of blending their versions, allowing my imagination to fill in some gaps and putting the story in my own words. Mama and Daddy didn't entirely agree on the events that happened between the time they met and the time they were married. That's understandable. Often in my professional life I have had to try to make sense out of how two witnesses to the same event can describe it so differently, while both being completely honest and truthful. That's just how real life and memory work. I'm satisfied that what I have written here is as close to the truth as we are now able to get.

Alex, I am what would have been called in my parents' time an "old maid" (although old maids in those days were never federal judges). As such, the natural objects of my bounty are more distant than those of most women my age. You are just a baby as I write this, but I am satisfied that you will do.

May your life be blessed, Alex. You come from good people.

With love,

Aunt Flora

Bertie

1

We met at the mill. When we was both working there. I bet you didn't even know your daddy worked at the mill. Did you? Well, he won't there long.

Maybe you didn't even know I worked there. You didn't? Ha! Y'all probably think I was a farm girl my whole life.

Truth is I hadn't never lived on a farm until after I married your daddy. Farm life ain't easy, child. I reckon I don't need to tell you that. But it was a dream come true for me.

I remember the first day I saw Charlie. I noticed him because he was new. You know what he done when he saw me? He smiled at me. Smiled right at me like I was somebody worth smiling at. I don't reckon anybody had ever looked so sweet at me. Child, it like to scared me to death.

When I saw Charlie that day, I had been working at the mill for eight years already. I was seventeen years old, skinny, and uglier than a cake of homemade soap. But here come this handsome man that I ain't never seen before and he smiled at me. Law child, I thought about that man all the time from that very minute on.

Ha! You're right. Charlie must not have thought I was as ugly as I felt like I was. You want to know why

I thought I was so ugly? One reason is because I probly was. But the main reason is because I can remember my mama telling me so. Yep, it's the truth. Bout one of the only things I have a memory of her ever saying was look at how strange and ugly this child is.

Yes, I was an orphan. But that don't mean I don't have no memory of my parents.

Naw, I ain't never talked about them to y'all.

Tell you about them?

That means going back to the beginning, Flora. You want to hear all that? From the beginning?

Well, all right. I reckon I might as well.

2

I won't but nine years old when I started work at the mill. They put me in the spinning room. I had to stand on a box to reach my spindles. My folks was dead by then. And so was my Grandma Bovry. She was a kind woman and never would have put me to work like that. It was my Aunt Sue who done that. Let me tell you about that first.

I was five when my daddy died. That broke my heart, let me tell you. He was a good man, Flora. A good and gentle man.

My Grandma Bovry, that was Daddy's mama, she come and got me. Me and Daddy was living in town, but Grandma she lived way out in the country, in a big old white house near Wentworth. It was a farm, where she lived, but it won't like our farm now. She lived in the house by herself until I got there, but she had other folks that lived on her farm and took care of it.

Everybody was real nice to me there and Grandma she carried me with her everywhere she went. She talked real proud of me, cause I could read and write some and I won't but five. Daddy had taught me how.

Grandma was feeble, but she did her best for me. There was an old man that drove her around. His name was Uncle Toy. It mighta been something else but it sounded like Toy to me. He couldn't hear a lick and I didn't never see him do nothing but sit in the kitchen eating and then when Grandma wanted to go somewhere, he'd take her. He rode her in a buggy that she called a carriage. He would carry her down to the store or to town or to church or the graveyard sometimes. He seemed like a nice old man to me. I remember he always called me Miss Bertie and that made me smile. After Grandma died folks claimed Uncle Toy's people had been stealing from her and it might have been true. But I ain't never been able to believe that Uncle Toy stole nothing.

Grandma's house was big, but it was kindly like falling down. Her husband had been dead a long time and she didn't have no chillen except for my daddy and he lived in town so I reckon there won't nobody to look after the house for her. She was old and feeble, like I said, so maybe she just won't able to make the people there work hard. I really can't say.

After she died it turned out she didn't have no money and I heard Aunt Sue and the others claiming that her help stole all her money but I don't believe it. I think she was just a poor old woman living in a big old house. Just because you got a big house don't mean you got a big pile of money somewhere, specially if the house is all falling down like that.

There was one thing about Grandma that bothered me, not at first, but after a while. She put on airs, if you know what I mean. She acted like there was something special about me, and it was because I was kin to her. She talked like her daddy had been some kind of big wig and her husband too. She had pictures of them in the old house and she would say things like, don't never forget you are a Wiatt and a Bovry. Well, that ain't the way she would've said it, or me neither back then. I learned to talk different when I got to the mill and it stuck with me. But back then I didn't talk like this. Back then I talked just as good as you do. Grandma would've said, don't *ever* forget. She didn't talk country.

Grandma didn't never tell me why being kin to her and to my granddaddy was supposed to make me special and I didn't never ask her. I reckon I was scared to. But I thought of that a lot after I had to go and live with Aunt Sue. Cause she said just the opposite. She made it very plain that I should be ashamed of being named Bovry. Seems like she told me that near about every single day until she finally sent me off to the mill and I didn't have to see her no more.

One morning when I come down to breakfast Uncle Toy was sitting there at the table and he'd done been crying. He looked up at me when I come in the room and he kinda shouted out, cause he talked real loud on account of being hard of hearing, oh, law, Miss Bertie, bless your heart, your grandma done passed.

I didn't never know Grandma to be sick. She was just real old, I reckon.

They didn't have no funeral for Grandma. Least not that I went to. They just buried her in the graveyard behind the old house. Won't hardly nobody there. Uncle Toy was there and I remember he held my hand while the preacher talked. That was a sad day, let me tell you. I loved my grandma. She was a sweet woman. I didn't know till later how she and my daddy had done had a falling out, but if she was mad at him, she didn't never take it out on me.

It was after the burial that Uncle Toy took me into the kitchen and gave me a piece of pie to eat. He was trying to get me away from the grownups who was having an argument in the front room. They was arguing about me. I knew that.

There was a few folks at the graveyard that I hadn't never seen before. I later figured out that they was some of my mama's people. One of em was Aunt Sue. After Grandma was buried, they come up to the house and was talking to the preacher about me.

I don't recollect how much of this I heard at the time and how much I heard later, but the long and the short of it was that some of them was saying that I ought to be taken to the orphanage in Raleigh. But Aunt Sue was saying no, she would take me, and they was arguing about it. See, Aunt Sue didn't have no husband and no young'uns and they was saying what do you know about raising a chap, Sue. But she kept on saying that she wanted to take me and the preacher said it was best for the child to stay with her family, so they all agreed and somebody come in and told me that I was going to live with my Aunt Sue now.

Before that day I hadn't never laid eyes on Aunt Sue. Turns out that she figured that if she took me she would have a better claim on Grandma's money when they found it.

And that's how I come to live with her.

3

Aunt Sue was my mama's half-sister. She was right much older than my mama and as far as I could tell she didn't know her too good. I can tell you one thing, she didn't like her a'tall.

She lived on the other side of the county in a little house by herself. She done sewing and washing and stuff like that for folks and that's how she made her living. She was poor, I reckon, but not as poor as she made like she was.

At first, she didn't treat me too bad. I reckon she was still hoping to get Grandma's money. But it won't too long fore she figured out there won't gonna be no money and after that she took to treating me meaner and meaner. Every time we ate, she would tell me how she was spending her little bit of hard-earned money to feed me and how she reckoned she would be plumb broke fore too long thanks to me. And, law, heaven help if I needed me some clothes or shoes. She'd go on and on about how much money she was spending on me and how if it won't for her I would have starved and been naked. She made me feel right bad, let me tell you. I reckon that's what she wanted to do.

And she didn't have nothing good to say about my mama and daddy. Oh, law, did she bad mouth them.

At first she kindly like hinted about them. She might be getting on me about something and she would say, not that I would expect your parents to teach you no better. Or she might say, I ain't surprised, seeing as who raised you. But it won't long fore she come right out and said the ugliest things, like your mama won't nothing but a cheap whore, and your daddy was sorry and no count. It especially hurt me to hear her talk so bad about my daddy—he was a good man—but I was too afraid of her to talk back. I didn't have no other person in the whole world I could go to, so there I was I reckon.

I hate to talk so ugly about somebody, but the honest truth is that I can't remember a single kind thing that woman ever did for me. She'd go around acting like she was some kind of saint for taking me in and folks acted like they believed it too. But the truth was that she didn't give a hoot about me. Once she saw that she won't going to get nothing out of it, I know she was mighty sorry she ever agreed to take me. Don't it all sound like some kind of sad fairy tale? Well, let me tell you child, that was a hard life for a little girl.

Then there come a time that made things even worse than they already was. One day Aunt Sue walked to the store and she took me with her. She took me with her usually because I think she liked reminding folks what a good deed she was doing and because she thought I might steal some food if she left me at home. She told me bout the stealing once and I just figured the other one out on my own. Anyhow, at the store, Mr. Brock, was his store, he said Sue, you got a card here, and he handed it to her. See, he was the postmaster too and his store was the post office. This was before they brought the mail out to country people. You still had to go to the store to get it then. Anyway, Mr. Brock asked Aunt Sue if she wanted him to read the card for her. And that's when I got the bright idea to pipe up and say I can read it for you, Aunt Sue.

And Mr. Brock and the other men in the store got to laughing and saying yeah, Sue, Bertie can read it for you. And she got mean and huffy and said y'all stop. Y'all know that child can't read, she said. She's just being spiteful to say such a thing.

And I said but I *can* read, Aunt Sue. My daddy taught me how.

And Mr. Brock he handed me that card and he said why don't you read it for us then, Bertie? He was laughing at me.

It was a postcard somebody had done sent her from Mexico. It had a picture of a bullfighter on one side. I took the card from him and I read out loud what was wrote on the back. I can still remember it. It said, Hey Sue. Having a good time. Wish you was here. Hahaha! Tommy.

Then them men all got to whooping and laughing and Mr. Brock he said well don't that beat all! That's a right smart little girl you got there, Sue. What's it say on the front, Bertie?

I turned it over and read off the front: Greetings from Mexico City, and they all got to whooping and laughing again.

You know Flora, I honest to goodness thought that Aunt Sue might think better of me if she knew I could read. But oh, law, did it make her mad. She just snatched that card outta my hand, grabbed me by the wrist and drug me outta that store. She was squeezing my wrist real hard and yanking on me all the way home and I kept saying what did I do wrong, Aunt Sue? And she wouldn't say nothing but stuff like you think you're something, don't you? Well, I'll show you.

When we got in the house, she dragged me into the kitchen, and she got out this big wooden spoon and, law, did she commence to beating me with that thing. She was holding me by my wrist with one hand and whipping me with that big ole spoon with the other. She hit me on my legs and on my backside and I was crying hard and then she cracked that thing down on the top of my head and drew blood. She kept on hitting me till she wore herself out I reckon then she just dropped me to the floor.

She said, real hateful like, so you think you're special cause you talk like a city girl and cause you know how to read, do you? Well, you ain't nothing but a sorry, stupid, ugly little chap. She was hollering by then. She said, your mama won't nothing but a cheap whore and your daddy was a sissy and a dope head! And the apple falls next to the tree!

She made me wash the blood out of my clothes and she made me wash that big spoon.

That was the first time she ever hit me, but let me tell you child, she took to beating me regular after that.

I saw later that it must have shamed her for me to read that card, seeing as she couldn't read herself. But child, with God as my witness, I won't trying to make her look bad. I honest to goodness thought she might think better of me if she saw that I could read. You know, something just like that happened to me at the mill too. You reckon I would have learned my lesson.

I can't help but wonder sometimes what my life might have been like if my daddy hadn't a died. I can tell you right now that he never would have whipped me for no good reason, and he wouldn't a sent me to work in the mill neither. But I reckon if a frog had wings, he wouldn't bump his tail when he jumps.

Aunt Sue didn't never take me out with her after that day. She always made me stay home if she went anywhere. By then she'd done taught me how to mend and wash clothes and I was doing her work so when she went out she'd give me a big pile to do and tell me if it won't finished when she got back she'd give me a whipping. She would always check the cupboard when she got back to make sure I hadn't got me nothing to eat. As hungry as I was, I didn't dare touch no food with her out or she would've wore me out good.

Them was sad days, Flora. I lived with her for almost three years, from when I was six years old.

I wanted to go to school real bad, but when I got up my nerve to ask her about going she just hollered at me and said who did I think I was and she won't gonna work all day so I could lay around doing nothing. When I promised that I would do all my work same as always if I could go to school too, she whipped me for it.

Then was one day somebody from the school or the county or something come to the house and knocked on the door. He said he was inquiring about the little girl Bertie and wondered how come she won't in school. I've always imagined it was Mr. Brock who told them about me, but I really don't know. Anyway, my Aunt Sue she told that man that I was retarded. He asked to see me and she let him come in the house. I had heard what she said and I was ready to prove to that man that I won't retarded at all, but when she called me in the room Aunt Sue said the child don't hardly ever say a word. She ain't right in the head. She can't hardly talk a'tall. And she was staring at me with her eyes shooting flames, let me tell you. The man was looking at me real kindly and smiling but Aunt Sue was standing behind him and she was giving me a look that said she would beat me half to death if I talked to him.

So, he kept asking me questions and talking real sweet but I was too scared to open my mouth. I reckon that after a while he must have thought I was soft in the head cause he just quit trying. He turned to Aunt Sue and he said thank you, ma'am, sorry to have bothered you, and then he left.

Law, Flora, let me tell you, child. I dreamed about that man. I prayed and prayed and prayed that he would come back and take me. I'd be sewing or washing or cleaning and in my head I'd be thinking about him coming and taking me off to a nice place with nice people and me going to school. And in my head, I could see him arresting Aunt Sue and hauling her off to jail. I'd get so happy thinking them thoughts that I'd just start crying sometimes. I really truly believed it was going to happen. I begged God every night to let him come back. I promised that if he did, I would say right out loud, I ain't retarded and I can read and write, and this woman beats me and she is ignorant and mean! And then he would rescue me just like in a fairy tale. But all that praying and crying and dreaming didn't get me nothing, Flora. That hateful woman just kept me hungry and ragged and working all the time and not a day went by she didn't tell me how stupid and ugly I was and how I should be thankful to her for not leaving me to starve in the woods somewhere. And that man never did come back.

It hurt me for a long time. I quit praying after a while. Maybe a year, I don't know. One night I said God, I'm asking you one last time to please send that man back here. If you do, then I promise I won't never ask for nothing else ever again. And if you don't then I reckon you don't care about me and I ain't never going to bother asking you for nothing else ever again. And so that was the end of that.

I reckon things turn out the way they was supposed to and the good Lord just didn't see fit to let me go to school. But let me tell you child, it hurt me then and it still does now. We've lived through some hard times since you young'uns was born and there was plenty of times when it seemed like we won't gonna have enough to get by. But no matter how hard times was, me and Charlie made sure that y'all went to school and Flora, I swear to goodness I'd take my last nickel and give it to you if you needed it for school. I'm so proud of you for what you've done and I don't mind saying I'm a little proud of me and Charlie too.

So, I reckoned I was just gonna be there sewing and washing and cleaning and getting beat by Aunt Sue until I was old enough to run off. Then one day Patsy told her about the mill in Danville.

There won't but one person that ever come over to visit Aunt Sue. Was a mean old hag named Patsy that was just as hateful as she was. Them two would dip snuff and gossip and Patsy was just as mean to me as Aunt Sue was. Aunt Sue would always go on with her about how much I ate and how lazy I was and how she had to spend all of her money taking care of me cause my mama and daddy had been sorry and no count, and how ungrateful I was, and so on. And Patsy she would nod her head and say it just ain't right Sue, you ought to let the state take care of her insteada you having to spend so much money on her and this, that and the other, like I won't even there. And Aunt Sue she'd make like she was doing something good by keeping me, when by then I was making her money by doing her work for her and she hadn't hardly ever spent one thin dime on me.

Well, was one day in nineteen and nine when Patsy was over and they was going on and on about what a burden I was and Patsy up and said if I was you I'd put that girl to work in the mill. Aunt Sue, she looked kindly like surprised and asked her what she meant and Patsy she said, law Sue, they's hiring chaps like her at the mill in Danville all day long and pays them good money too.

Now I could tell that Aunt Sue had done got real excited to hear that, but she was letting on like she won't. Law, Patsy, she said. Won't no mill take a stupid little chap like her. And she ain't but nine.

Patsy she laughed and said that's plenty old enough for mill work. And they done hired lots of young'uns from out here. Oliver Anderson done sent all of his girls and so has Nancy Boswell. And they're getting good cash money every week for em.

I could see the gears turning in Aunt Sue's greedy head and she said do they come and get the chaps?

Patsy she said, naw, they done hired Bibb Hancock some kind of way to round em up and bring em in. He comes out and get the young'uns and takes em to Danville and the mill pays him by the head as long as the chaps stay on past four weeks or something like that.

Seems like I can remember that conversation perfect. If I close my eyes even now I can see them two sitting there planning on how to send me off. Now let me tell you Flora, leaving there didn't sound too bad to me, didn't make no difference what they was sending me to do. But I tried not to act like I wanted to go, cause Aunt Sue was so hateful she'd a probly kept me there just out of spite if she thought I wanted to go. But maybe not, cause it was the cash money that made her the most interested.

She asked Patsy, how much are they paying the chaps? And Patsy said she heard they was paying spinners four dollars a week as long as they was over ten. Aunt Sue she frowned and said Bertie ain't but nine and Patsy she laughed at her and said law Sue, all she's got to do is say she's ten and ain't nobody got no way of knowing no different. She said they's plenty of chaps that ain't but eight or nine spinning there.

And so Aunt Sue told her to send Mr. Hancock out and that's how I ended up working at the mill.

Law Flora, I can't remember the last time I talked so much. I know you don't want to hear all this old stuff. Well all right, but first go in yonder and fetch me a cup of water. I done got all dried out.

4

All right. I was telling you about when I first went to the mill. Mr. Hancock came by with his wagon one morning and picked me up. Aunt Sue had took my other dress and bloomers and wrapped them up in a rag. That's all I had with me other than what I was wearing when I left that place. That and a little piece of cornbread she gave me. There was three other girls in the wagon already. I didn't know none of them. One of them, bless her heart, she cried the whole way there. We was all four nothing but young'uns.

I don't know how long it took us to get to Danville, but it seemed like a mighty long time to me.   I had done ate my cornbread by the time we got there, and I was getting hungry again.   When Danville come into sight it made my heart hurt. I had so many memories, good and bad, of that town.

What? Oh yes, I had been in Danville before. Flora, I was *born* in Danville. That's where we lived before my mama and daddy died. You didn't know it? Well, fore I'm done you're gonna hear a whole bunch of stuff you ain't never heard before.

Anyhow, Mr. Hancock drove us right down to the mill office and took us inside. Was a man there who must have been expecting him. Mr. Hancock said he'd done brought four more spinners for him. Said we was all ten years old and already knew some about spinning.

Me and them girls was looking at each other, knowing he was telling stories. But didn't none of us say nothing. We just stood there holding onto our little bags.

The man, I come to know him later to be Mr. Muse, he come over and looked at us girls like we was merchandise in a store. He squeezed my arm, he made me open my mouth so he could see my teeth, and he made us all take deep breaths so he could listen to see if we had the consumption, I reckon. After it seemed like he was satisfied with us, he told Mr. Hancock to take us down to Floyd Street where our house was going to be at. See we didn't have no girls' dorm like they got in Schoolfield. For Mill Number One they just put the girls into little mill houses in Mechanicsville.

Ended up being six of us in that little house. All chaps. There was one little coal-burning fireplace to keep us warm, was all. We had a outhouse in back that we shared with another house.

The mill didn't care how many people was in a house, long as they all worked at the mill. Rent was a dollar a week for the whole house, so the more girls we had in a house the less each one of us had to pay. Money was tight, let me tell you. We didn't make but four dollars and fifty cents a week and Mr. Hancock and Aunt Sue took half of mine. He'd come around on Saturdays and collect the pay, leaving a little for us and taking the rest of it for himself and for the ones who sent us there. The mill took our rent out of the pay, and money for the food we bought at the store and for our coal. Most times won't nothing left a'tall.

But I'm getting kindly ahead of myself. Fore I ever drawed the first penny I had to work for four weeks. That's what they called the training time.

They set me to work in the spinning room right off. Lord have mercy, child. I know you don't think much of farm work but let me tell you what. You might not be so down on it if you had ever worked in a cotton mill before.

It was so loud in there I couldn't hardly hear nothing. And the air was just clouded with cotton dust so that it got all over you and even up your nose and in your eyes. I learned to stuff cotton balls into my ears to keep the noise down but there won't no getting away from all that dust and lint. Every time you come out of that place of an evening, you'd just be covered head to toe in it. That's how come the town people called us lintheads. I imagine we must have been quite a sight for them.

My first day there was plenty scary. The boss man was yelling at us to tell us what to do. He had to yell in order for us to hear him. But if we didn't understand him right off then he'd yell and sometimes shake you real mad like. I remember that one girl who had cried all the way on the wagon. She cried so much in the mill and that just made the boss madder and madder and he shook her till she cried even more. Then one time he slapped her across the face and law, that poor child cried so hard it like to broke my heart. It was only about a week before she run off one night. I ain't got no idea what ever happened to her. Bless her soul. She didn't have nowhere to go and no money neither. I hate to even think about it.

Anyway, I won't tall enough to work the spindles yet, so one of the other spinners got me a box to stand on so I could reach them. I should tell you that there was so many good people in that mill—kind, Christian people. It had been a long time since anybody had treated me decent and it felt mighty good to be back among good folks. Even the boss who slapped that poor girl was most of the time a good man. He helped me over the years and I think he was just having a hard time that day. But the best people were the spinners who was already there. They took us new chaps under their wings and looked after us. Taught us how to do things and what to watch out for. Law, they even showed us little girls how to dip snuff. Ain't that funny, Flora? I been dipping since I won't but nine years old.

In them days we worked from sunup to sundown, every day but Sunday. We had us a dinner break for 20 minutes every day at noon. Otherwise we ran them machines all blessed day. Later on we went to ten-hour days, which was a whole lot better, let me tell you.

When I first got there, I didn't have no friends and I didn't know a single soul there. I was mighty lucky to get put in a house with all good girls though. We all got to be great friends and we would do anything for each other. We had two little beds in each room and we slept two to a bed. The girl I slept with was named Anna Johnson and she was nine like me. As little as I was, she was even littler. We had been working a few days and I noticed that she went off by herself during dinner break. It was a while later that I realized she had her a little corn husk doll she was playing with when we was on break. Bless her heart. I saw that she was kindly like ashamed that I saw her doll. So, when we was getting ready for bed that night I said Anna, that sure is a purty doll you got. She seemed embarrassed at first but when she saw that I won't making fun of her she smiled a little. Can I see her, I asked and she took the little doll out of her apron pocket and handed it to me. I asked her had she made it and she said no that her daddy made it for her to bring with her. I had figured that all the girls there got sent by mean hateful people like Aunt Sue but I come to learn most of them was just trying to help their families get by. Anyway, Anna told me all about her family and that they was poor and needed what she earned to help take care of the young'uns that was younger than her cause her daddy didn't make hardly nothing from farming. It's the honest truth that I wouldn't have minded sending home my pay to help out my family if I had one that was like Anna's. But it sure galled me to know that Aunt Sue was getting half my pay and not giving a hoot about what happened to me nor ever so much as checking up on me even one solitary time. This might sound ugly Flora, but I don't know what ever become of Aunt Sue and I don't care.

Anyhow, that night I asked Anna what her doll's name was and she said her name was Becky and that Becky was her best friend. I told her that was about the sweetest thing I'd ever seen and she was lucky to have a doll like that. Then she smiled and said I've got another one, Bertie. Another what I asked her and she brought out another corn husk doll and said I could have her if I wanted her. Law, let me tell you Flora, that just made me start to bawling. She asked me what was the matter and I told her that I ain't had no doll to play with since my grandma had passed. She made me take that little doll and I was one happy little girl that night, let me tell you. She had done already named the doll Susannah, but she said I could name her anything I wanted to and I said Susannah was beautiful and I wouldn't dream of changing her name. I asked her did her daddy make Susannah too and she said he did. I just cried and cried. After that me and Anna would take our dolls with us to work in our apron pockets and during dinner break we would go off into a corner and play with them. Then later on we found us a spot down by the river where didn't nobody go cause it was so close to where they dumped the dye in and we would play there. I loved that doll so much. She would've been my best friend except for Anna was. After about three or four years Anna went back home and I would lay in my bed at night (there was a different girl sleeping with me then) and think about Anna back on her farm with her big family, happy I hoped.

Look over yonder on my dresser, Flora. See there behind that little silk pillow? Go get it and bring it here. Oh, thank you child. Here she is. My sweet Susannah.

No, I'm all right. These old memories make me cry but it's a good kind of crying. Here you go. Please put her back where I can see her from here. That is one of the most special things I own. I wonder what ever happened to precious little Anna? I hope and pray she's happy.

I just thought of something I ain't thought of in a long time. I told you how Aunt Sue sent me off with nothing but a little piece of cornbread. Well she didn't send no money with me a'tall. I don't know how she figured I was supposed to eat. Maybe she thought the mill would feed us. Maybe she didn't care. Either way, I didn't have no food and no money and I was too scared to say nothing about it.

When we took dinner break my first day, I was so hungry and light-headed that I felt faint. One of the spinner girls noticed me sitting over by myself and she saw that I didn't have nothing to eat. Didn't you bring no dinner she asked me and I just shook my head no. Law, Bertie, she said, you gotta eat something girl or you're liable to pass out. She offered me some of her little dinner and I was scared to take it, but she kindly pushed it on me and child, let me tell you, I gobbled it down.

She asked me did I know about mill money and I said I didn't. Then she told me how you got to go the office and get some script that you can use at the store and then the mill takes it out of your pay on payday. They don't like giving it to the girls on training time, but after I told them I didn't have no money they let me have a little. I told the other girls and we all had us a regular supper that night.

We didn't eat like we do now though. One thing about this farm life, child, it keeps us fed good. You know that even when times was the hardest, we might not have had no money a'tall, but we always had plenty to eat. Well, us mill girls usually had enough but it won't nothing to get excited about. We would take us a piece of cornbread with us for our dinner, maybe with a little grease on it. Back at the house we'd keep us a pot of pinto beans cooked, or sometimes turnip sallet, and that's about all we ate. Now and again on a Sunday, if we had enough money left over, we might have us some fatback. I recollect one time that Anna's folks sent her a chicken and oh my goodness did us girls have us a feast then.

But I reckon I would have slap starved to death if it won't for that mill money I took that first week. Course that first mill money started me off in hock to the mill and I stayed that way mi' near the whole eight years I worked there.

Yep, eight years. Eight solid years. After a while, maybe a year or so, I didn't need to stand on my box no more. I remember the day I come in and said, box, I ain't standing on you no more. Well, it won't really like that exactly. What happened is they brought in some new girl, some poor little chap that won't tall enough and I gave her my box. And I helped her learn her job. By then I was one of what we used to call the old girls. Ain't that funny? I was probably only ten or eleven then.

We girls stuck together, but most of us didn't know diddly squat about nothing. I went through the change right there on the spinning room floor and it like to scared me half to death. Hadn't nobody never told me nothing about that. Law have mercy, child. What times those was.

I forgot to tell you that I was kind of famous in the spinning room at Mill Number One. Yep. Well, maybe famous ain't the right word. Maybe I should say special. Anyway, I was the only girl in the spinning room that could read and write some. So, during dinnertime or after work right often one of the other girls would ask me to read something for her, like a letter, or to write something. I'll be honest, Flora, it made me feel good to do it. I told them I hadn't never been to school, but the girls didn't believe it. They all spread the rumor that I had finished third grade and was just too humble to admit it. Ain't that funny? I spect didn't none of them have a daddy who could read and write, and they just couldn't believe that it was my daddy who had taught me how. Anyway, I liked it when one of the other girls would ask me to read or write something for her. It made me remember my poor daddy and it made me happy to help the girls. But it did cause a problem for me once.

There was a mean old heifer named Tildy who worked in the spinning room and she didn't never like me for some reason. When she found out I could read and write she just poured it on me all the time. She would say ugly things like, Bertie thinks her stink don't smell—but she used a cuss word instead of stink. She would say Bertie ain't nothing but a little trained monkey. She said, just because a hillbilly linthead can read and write a few words don't mean they're better than any other mill rat, and more ugly stuff like that. But law child, what really made her ride me was the way I talked.

My daddy was an educated man and he had taught me to talk proper. My grandma, kind as she was, would have whipped my bottom if she heard me talking the way I do now. So, I didn't sound like the other girls in the mill—I mean I didn't talk the way they did. Tildy told the other girls that I was pretending and putting on airs and doing it to make myself better than them and to make them look bad. Won't a nary word of that true, but the more I denied it the worse she rode me about it.

You know what hurt the most, Flora? I could start to tell that those other girls *were* starting to act ashamed of their way of talking. Or else they stopped talking to me, some of them did, so they didn't have to hear me, I reckon. Tildy was turning them all against me on account of me talking like my daddy had taught me instead of like they did. I didn't have nobody in the world but those other spinner girls, so I determined to change my way of talking to talk like they did. It was hard at first, but after a while it came right easy. The only people I heard in them days that didn't talk country like them was the boss and the preacher and I sure didn't want to sound like neither one of them. Fore long at all I sounded just like the other girls did. And I reckon I still do. Hahaha.

Of course, that was all the proof that Tildy needed that I had been faking it and she laughed at me and teased me and regular put me down near about every single day. So one day during dinner break when one of the girls asked me to read a letter, Tildy took off with her stuff about me pretending and being a liar and all that and I just up and told her off. Yep. Blessed her out like there won't no tomorrow. I said you shut your mouth you blankedy blank such and such. I called her a stupid sow and every cuss word I'd ever heard. Let me tell you Flora, it felt real good to say all that to her, till she tore off my bonnet and grabbed aholt of my hair with both her hands. Lord have mercy, she flung me around tearing my poor hair out by the roots, just a hollering and screaming at me. Won't nothing I could do but hope she didn't kill me. The other girls just watched. Some of them later told me that they wanted to help but they was scared to get in trouble. I didn't never hold it against them though. Fore too long the boss man come over and pulled Tildy offa me. He sent me to the mill doctor who put some mercurochrome on my poor tore up head and sent me back to work.

The boss told me later that he knew I had started it, but that the other girls told him how Tildy had been egging me on. He told us both that if there was any more trouble between us we was both going to be fired. Didn't neither one of us want that, so we just ignored each other from then on. Was less than a year after that and she was gone. Somebody told me that she and some boy had run off, but I don't know for sure. I don't know who would've wanted somebody like her.

I shouldn't have said that.

Here I am fixing to die and I ought not to have no bad feelings in my heart, should I?

Oh, yes I am. I know it, Flora. And it's all right.

Now you stop that. I don't want no crying right now. Just give me a hug and let me rest.

I'll tell you the rest of the story tomorrow, if you still want to hear it.

5

You mean you ain't heard enough already? Ha! You wanted to know how your daddy and me met and I ain't even got to that part yet. My parents? Well, I told you a little bit about them. The rest of it ain't easy to tell, Flora. Naw, that's all right. I reckon I ought to tell you everything I know. You should know about your grandparents even if the story ain't a good one. And I spect it might do me some good to remind myself of it. Me and your daddy has had us a fine life, child. We ain't never stopped loving each other for even a minute and ain't neither one of us never on purpose done nothing to hurt the other one. I have been blessed. My poor daddy won't so lucky, let me tell you.

My daddy was a doctor. I don't mean no crazy-like conjurer doctor neither. I mean he was a real honest to goodness doctor. Ain't no sense in looking so surprised like that. You might be the first one from your daddy's side of the family to get a college education, but you ain't the first on my side. My daddy went to the university in Chapel Hill and that's where he got his doctor training. His name was Charles. Charles Bovry. So my daddy was a Charles and I married a Charles. How about that?

I loved my daddy very much Flora and he loved me. I don't believe my mama loved me though, I'm very sorry to say. It's a sad, sad story, child, but I might as well tell it to you.

Now I won't but five years old when Daddy passed, and I couldn't have been no more than about four when my mama died. First, I'll tell you what I remember, then I'll tell you what I found out later.

I don't have many memories of my mama. I remember that she was pretty and that I wanted her to love me more. I can only remember two specific things she said to me. One was that I was ugly and strange. Can you imagine saying that to a little child? The only other time I remember plainly was when I was trying to hold her, and she pushed me away. She hollered at me, leave me alone! And when she pushed me, I fell into a chest of drawers and cut my cheek. She was sorry she done that, and she picked me up and was crying. But even at that age I knew she pushed me away because she didn't want me.

Like I said, I must have been about four when she passed. I remember knowing that something was wrong, and I remember seeing Daddy crying. Somebody told me that Mama had gone away on a trip and I wondered why that made everybody so sad.

My daddy had always seemed happy and jolly to me before then, but he was very sad after Mama died. I won't nothing but a chap so I can't be sure how much of what I think I remember is real, but it seemed like to me that after Mama died, Daddy spent a lot more time with me. He would sit me on his lap and show me picture books. He taught me how to read and even how to write a little and that seemed to make him happy.

I don't know how long after she passed that I found out Mama was dead. Maybe it was when the tombstone came. See, Daddy bought this great big tombstone for Mama and had it put on her grave, which was in the graveyard behind our house. He had a bench put in out there too and he used to take me out to the grave seemed like every single evening. He would just sit on that bench and cry, holding my hand. It made me sad too, but the honest to goodness truth is that I was sad because it made him sad. I'm mighty sorry to say it, but I didn't miss my mama. Even now it breaks my heart to say that. But I gotta tell you the truth. I hugged my daddy and I cried with him, but I won't crying about her. I was crying about him.

Now after a while there won't no housekeeper helping Daddy no more and it got to where he won't doing much of nothing. Even a little girl like I was knew something won't right with him. Sometimes he wouldn't remember to make us nothing to eat and I'd be so hungry. But I was scared to say anything because of how sad he was. I remember Grandma coming and fussing at him and she wanted to take me and he was going to let her but I cried and then he told her she couldn't have me and that made her real mad. Seems like to me she said some mean things to Daddy then, but Grandma was always good to me, so I try not to think bad things about her.

Ain't that a sad story, Flora? Thank the good Lord you didn't have to grow up like that.

Well, I ain't told you about the saddest day yet. I remember it was warm and birds was singing, and I was playing in the dirt. Funny how I can remember just perfect what a pretty and peaceful evening it was. Daddy was sitting on the bench at the cemetery in his same old sad way and I was playing in the dirt and listening to the birds. Then after a while it was getting dark and it was past the time we usually went home. I asked Daddy when was we going to go home for supper, but he didn't say nothing. He was leaning back with his eyes closed and his mouth open. I thought he was being silly and playing with me. So I went over and I pulled on his arm and said come on Daddy, let's go home, and when I pulled on his arm he just fell off the bench and on to the ground. Law, child, it still hurts my heart to remember that day. I didn't know it right away, but my poor daddy had done passed sitting right there on that bench.

I was so scared, and I didn't know what to do. So, I run over to the house of the man that lived next door to us, and I told him something was the matter with Daddy. It was all terrible after that, Flora. Lots of people come over and they was passing me around not knowing what to do or say. When I figured out that Daddy was gone like Mama oh my little heart did break, and I cried a river. I wanted to be dead too. My daddy was such a good and kind man and he loved me very very much. I just couldn't stand the thought of not having him. Oh, law, I do still miss him. He had a sad life, Flora. Let me tell you about him.

Grandma never did say much to me about my parents. She had the decency to keep it from me. But not my Aunt Sue. She was more than happy to tell me what sorry people they were. She had done told me the whole story, her version of it anyway, before she sent me off to the mill. Was a long time later that I found out somebody there knew the story. I reckon it must have been a big deal in Danville when it all happened. She told me what she had heard and then I got the rest of it from other folks over the years.

My mama run around with men. It's a terrible thing to say, Flora, and it still hurts my heart to say it, but it's the truth. Daddy met Mama when he went out to her daddy's farm to set his broken leg. That was after his first wife had died. Mama lived on a farm and she didn't have no education. I met her daddy one time and he seemed like a nice man, but folks said he liked to take a drink. I heard he was crippled and old by the time Grandma died, but I didn't never see him but that one time. Anyway, it won't too long after Mama and Daddy met that they got married. Daddy was living in Wentworth then in Grandma's house. I think Mama was fine with that at first, seeing as she come from a poor family, but fore long she commenced to nagging Daddy about wanting to live in Danville. So after a while they moved, and he started doctoring in Danville.

After they moved to town, Mama started spending Daddy's money faster than he could make it. She bought fancy clothes and stuff for the house and I reckon he just let her cause he was such a kind man. And then she started borrowing money on my daddy's name and got so deep in debt that he didn't have nothing left that they couldn't take from him.

I heard she run around with lots of men. I don't know how much of that is true. I'm right sure she ran around with this rich man in town and then later with a doctor in Milton, but I don't know how many others. Folks say just about everybody in town knew what was going on except for Daddy.

You want to know how she died, Flora? She killed herself. Ain't that awful? Folks say when she found out they was going to auction off everything Daddy owned to pay her bills, she was so ashamed that she ate rat poison. Poor Daddy never did know what killed her. It didn't come out till after he had done passed and the man who gave her the poison admitted to it.

Well, here Daddy was with his wife dead and him so in love with her and not knowing she had been running around on him all over the place. Then he come to find out that she had done spent all his money and he was losing everything he owned. It ain't no wonder he took to drinking and taking opium, if he did. Folks say he did and that it was real bad at the end. I was just a little girl and I didn't know nothing about that. I will tell you though, Flora, that my daddy never said a mean word to me, he never hit me not once, and I know he loved me with all his heart. He was a good man, Flora. A good man.

He was heartbroke when Mama died and he even kept some of her hair. Law, child, he was holding that hair of hers in his hand when he passed. Poor Daddy didn't never once doubt my mama. Well, some folks say that right before he died, he did find out about Mama running around and that's how come he died like he did. I don't know. I hope it ain't true cause that poor man sure didn't need one more heartbreak.

Now ain't that about the saddest story you ever heard? Ain't that a rough way for a little girl to get started in life?

My mama? Her name was Emma. Like I said before, Aunt Sue was her half-sister.

6

I still ain't told you about meeting your daddy. I was seventeen years old. I had been working in the spinning room for eight years by then. I loved the girls that worked there and even if some of the men who worked in the mill was rough, by and large it was all good people. We looked out for each other. If somebody needed help, then they could be sure the other workers would help them out. We was like a great big family.

But I got to tell you, child, I was mighty lonely there too. The other girls my age had beaus or was married even, and I didn't have me nobody. It didn't seem like to me that nobody would ever want me. I reckon you could say I didn't think too much of myself. There was a couple of boys who was nice to me, but I was so bashful that I wouldn't hardly talk to them and I reckon they figured I won't interested. So, I just made like I didn't want no boyfriend.

When the other girls my age took to courting of an evening or on Sundays, I just took to walking down by the river. That was how I found my secret place.

Ain't that a funny sounding thing? My secret place? But that's what it felt like to me and that's what I called it. I found it one Sunday when I was walking along the river and come to a place that was all growed up with briars. I thought I saw something shiny over in them, so I worked my way around them until I found something like a little rabbit path. I took a stick and pushed back the briars just enough to let me squeeze through and I followed that path a little ways and low and behold it turned out that it led to a little stretch of sand about ten feet long and maybe five or six feet wide right on the river bank, completely boxed in by them briars. It was just beautiful there, Flora. I sat down on the sand and looked out across the river. Won't nothing on the other side there in them days but woods. It was so purty and quiet there that it made me cry. I sat there all afternoon, just having peace and quiet to myself. When it started to get dark it made me sad to have to leave. But I had done already decided to it was going to be my place—my secret place. So, after I squeezed back through them briars, I pushed them back together with the stick so couldn't nobody else tell how to get in there.

After that I snuck down to my secret place as often as I could. After a while I cleared out the entrance better so the briars wouldn't tear my dress when I went in. I got me some brush that I piled up against the entrance when I left and I had another pile that I could push into it from the inside, so in case somebody walked by they wouldn't see me. Law, child, that place was so special to me and I didn't never tell nobody about it. I used to sit in there for hours on Sunday afternoons and just dream big dreams. I remember one time wishing I had me some paper and a pencil so I could write down some of the stuff I dreamed about in there, but I didn't never do that. There was plenty of times I sat in that little space looking out over the river and feeling sorry for myself. I would think about all the

happy things in other folks' lives and how it seemed
like I didn't have none of them—no family, no home,
no beau. But sometimes, child, when I was sitting in
that secret place, I'd feel so happy it would make me
cry. Like if I saw some ducks fly by or if the birds were
singing real pretty or if I just felt happy because I had
a place like that. And I'll go on and tell you the truth,
Flora. I usually took Susannah with me and me and her
would talk in there like best friends. I reckon if
anybody had been able to see me, they would have
figured I won't right in the head. Ha! Maybe I won't.

It come a time one night when I was feeling real
blue after work. I went out back of our little house just
to get some air and the moon was full and it was bright
as day out there. Then I thought to myself, why not go
on out to my secret place? See, I hadn't never been
there at nighttime. But that particular night I decided
to go, even though it won't safe for a girl to walk
around alone at night like that, especially down by the
river. But law child, I was so lonely and sad I felt like I
just *had* to go there. So, I did. I snuck on down past the
mill fence, then down to the riverside. I could see just
as plain as day, so finding it won't no trouble. I just
kept looking around to make sure won't nobody
following me and thinking to myself you're liable to get
yourself killed, you crazy girl. But I made it there safe
and let me tell you it was so beautiful when I got inside
that I couldn't hardly stand it. The moon was shining
on the river and lighting it up and it was so peaceful
there. I stayed there a long time that night. Too long,
cause the morning whistle comes early when you ain't
had a good night's sleep.

Well, after that I kept on going back after dark now
and again. I got to where I could find my way even if

there won't no moon out. And those were the very best nights. On a good night I could see about a million stars and me and Susannah loved to look at them. Ain't that silly, child? We loved to look at the Dipper, the Hunter, the Snake, the Bull, and them like that. You know all them stars, Flora, cause I taught them to you when you was just a little girl, just like my daddy had taught them to me. Remember the Seven Sisters? The most beautiful stars in the sky. Me and Susannah dreamed us up lots of stories about them sisters—who they was and how they got there. I knew they loved each other so much. And oh law child, it made my heart ache wishing I had me sisters like that who would love me too. But the one I loved the most, the one I can't never forget, is the Lady of the Chair. I get goosebumps thinking about it even now. The Lady saved my life, Flora. And I reckon she saved yours too.

Well shut my mouth, I done got to talking so much about those silly things that I plumb forgot to tell you what you asked about to start with.

It was the summer of nineteen and seventeen. I was still living in the same little house on Floyd Street where they had put me when I had showed up eight years before and I was still working in the spinning room. Them had been eight hard years, let me tell you. But I ought not complain. I know of women who worked in the mill every day for 50 years or more. Anyway, there was all the time new people moving in and out of the mill houses up and down the street. If somebody quit or got fired, they had to leave, and the mill would move somebody else in. Same if somebody passed away.

Well there was a house right down the street from ours that always had unmarried men in it. Over the years a few of the men from that house ended up marrying girls that lived in our house. It was funny like that. So, us girls was always on the lookout for any new men moving in. Now I won't looking for a man myself, mind you. I don't want it to sound like that. I just mean we was real curious like to see the new ones when they showed up and it might have been true that some of the girls was always hoping to meet a nice boy that way.

Charlie had been in that house a day or so before I

knew about it. It was during dinner break one day that some of the girls started talking about there being a new boy in the house. I remember they said that he won't from the mountains like most of the men was. They said that he had come from out in the country nearby and that it looked like his arms was too long for his body. Ha! Ain't that a funny thing to say about a man? That's all I can remember them saying about him and I didn't think no more of it. It won't so unusual for a new boy to move in that house.

Well, we was all walking back home after work that evening and was just about back to our house when one of the girls—it was Lucy Lou Daniels, bless her heart—she poked me in the side and said look yonder Bertie, there's the new boy. So, I looked up and I had to kindly like step to one side to see better and when I spotted him, Lord have mercy, he saw me looking right at him. It was like we was looking right straight at each other. I was so embarrassed to be caught staring at him and I must have turned just as red as a beet. But before I turned away, he just smiled this great big smile right at me. I couldn't even hardly believe he was looking at me to smile like that. It was just about the friendliest and prettiest smile I reckon I had ever seen and I didn't stay looking at him for more than a second or two before I turned away and hurried out of sight. My heart was beating like a drum, let me tell you. That night I snuck down to my secret place and stared up at the stars and in my mind I kept seeing that handsome face, smiling at me. And don't you know that thinking about it just made me cry and cry. And I'm telling you the honest to goodness truth Flora Belle, that hadn't never ever happened to me before—I mean being all tore up over just seeing a man smile. I reckon it must have been love at first sight, but when it happened, I didn't know that. I just knew that I couldn't stop thinking about him smiling at me that way.

So that's how we met.

Ha! And that's when the interesting part begins.

Charlie

1

You say Bertie told you about how we met and how we got married? Well, I doubt she told you everything. Me and Bertie shared our secrets before we got married. It's a wonder she would even have me after I told her mine. And after the way I behaved. I spect Bertie held that part back. See Bertie knew things about me that didn't nobody else know. And I'd bet she didn't tell you. I'd bet she didn't never tell nobody.

Me and your mama was made for each other. I believe we were meant to find each other the way we did.

You said she told you we met at the mill. Well, that's the truth. She told you about her mama and daddy, didn't she? I figured that. But did you she tell you how come I was at the mill? Did she tell you what I told her before we got married? Did she tell you what I told her right after we got married? Did she tell you about the time I.... No, never mind. Instead of you telling me what she told you, how bout if I tell you everything? If Bertie told you her story, then I might as well tell you mine.

See, Bertie knew something about me that nobody else ever knew. She knew it because I told her. And I'll bet she took it with her to the grave. I don't believe Bertie told you, Flora, because she wouldn't do that without knowing if I would want you to know. And she wouldn't ask me because we only spoke about it one time, then never again.

What Bertie knew about me was that I once killed a man.

See? I told you she didn't tell you everything.

It hurts me to confess what I done, even after all these years. There's a lot to it, Flora. It's complicated. I near about lost Bertie over it. Over how I handled it, I mean.

I'll explain it to you. It will help you to understand your mama and me better.

2

The first thing you need to understand is that my mama was a saint. A saint, Flora. There ain't never been a better woman than her.

I brought a lot of trouble on her in my life. There ain't a day passes that I don't regret that.

My daddy was an old man when Mama married him, and he already had two grown sons from his first wife that had died. You remember your Uncle James. He was my half-brother, and he was nine or ten years older than Mama. Ben was the other one. He was a couple years younger than James, so he was seven or eight years older than Mama.

Being there was such an age difference, she didn't think of them as stepsons and I didn't think of them as brothers. They were more like uncles to me.

I always thought of James as being rich. When his grandma Talbert died (she was Daddy's first wife's mama), she left him and Ben the Talbert place. James and his wife didn't have but one young'un and he always seemed like he had plenty of money and nice things. I remember he had a fancy buggy and a pretty horse and sometimes he'd come by and pick up Mama and take her to church in it. But I'm getting ahead of myself.

Anyway, James and Ben was better off than their own daddy cause of them getting the Talbert place. Ben lived by himself and didn't never marry. He kept mostly to himself. And James, he lived like a big wig.

Well, anyway, after his first wife died, Daddy married Mama. She was 22 and he was 50. I don't know anything much about why Mama married him, but I remember a time when Maggie Ferguson died and Mama's sister, Aunt Eliza, said don't let Betsy go to the funeral cause she might feel sorry for old Bill Ferguson and marry him. That made me think maybe Mama felt sorry for Daddy after his wife died and that's why she married him. But you know, a woman needed a husband in them days. Maybe he needed a wife and she needed a husband, so they just got married.

Mama was so much younger, it seemed to me she always treated Daddy like he was her boss. She called him Mr. Lawton most of the time and he called her Lil' Betsy. They won't lovebirds like me and your mama was. But they must have liked each other well enough, seeing how they had nine young'uns together.

No, it was nine. You only know of seven, but that's because Mama had two sets of twins before I was born. Both times one of the babies died. So, you only knew your Aunt Polly and your Aunt Sally, but they both had twin sisters who died. If you ever come home again, and if I'm still here, I'll show you where those two babies are buried.

So, anyway, it was Polly, then Sally, then me. I was born in eighteen and ninety-seven. After me come Kate, Jane, John and Jillianne. Them was a lot of mouths to feed, but it was a good farm and Daddy took good care of us. We was doing fine, I reckon, until he started going blind.

I was in school then. I finished the second grade before I had to quit. I'll tell you that story.

The schoolhouse was less than a mile from our house. Old Mr. David Holmes had built it and put it by the road on his place so the young'uns out in Raye would have a school to go to. It was just one big room with a pot belly stove in the middle. The teacher, it was Miss Foster when I was there, taught all the grades at the same time. We sat on these benches and did our work on slate tablets we held in our laps.

Anyway, most of the boys didn't like school and a lot of them just didn't go. But I liked it and I did good. I liked it a lot better than John, but he got to go and I didn't. I reckon the Lord knows what's best.

Well, I had to quit when Daddy started going blind. For the longest time he wouldn't admit it, but after a while it got to where he couldn't see hardly nothing. After he shot Harry, there won't no denying it no more.

See, there was a mad dog about, and everybody was on the lookout for him. It was one evening just right after suppertime when Daddy heard a dog out in front of the house, and he figured it was the mad dog. He took his gun down and went outside and shot the dog. But it was my poor dog Harry that he shot. And that broke my heart, let me tell you. Harry was the best dog that ever lived. It tore me up bad when that happened, and Daddy felt mighty sorry about it. That's when he had to admit he was going blind. If you ever come home again, and if I'm still here, I'll show you where I buried Harry. He sure was a good dog.

So, after I finished the second grade, I didn't go back to school no more. I won't but eight years old but I was the oldest boy, so it was my job to take over doing most of Daddy's work on the farm. He didn't like that, but there won't no choice back then. Daddy would still try to do things even though he couldn't see a lick. He made us run strings tied to trees or poles or stobs all over the place so he could hold on to those strings and make his way around. He even tried to plow when he was slap blind. He would have me walk along beside him while he was plowing, and I was supposed to tell him when to straighten up and whether he was deep enough and all like that. The old mule didn't know what to make of us. After a while he had to give it up and just turn it all over to me. Come a time when he went from insisting on doing all the work to when he didn't do nothing a'tall cept chew tobacco and play his fiddle. But I ain't knocking him, Flora. He was a blind old man and even after he first went blind he kept on trying as hard as he could to work the farm. When he finally gave up, he gave up all the way. But it won't before trying just as hard as he could. He was a hard worker.

Now there's one more thing I ought to tell you about my daddy. He would take him a drink now and again and that was something that come between him and Mama. Daddy won't no drunkard, mind you, and he didn't never beat Mama or us chaps or nothing like that. But ever so often he would have a drink, and now and then he'd get just as high as a Georgia pine. Mama was dead set against drinking. In fact, she and Daddy both was regular going to temperance meetings and such as that. But Daddy would fall off the wagon sometimes and when he did Mama would get all over him about it and then the next day he'd be all guilty and he would mope around for days.

When I was just a little boy Mama made me promise her I wouldn't never let whiskey pass my lips. I don't know how many times she made me promise that. It was like one promise won't good enough. Every time she made me promise, I did. And as I sit here right now, I'm 59 years old and I ain't never tasted a drop of whiskey in my life.

By the time I was nine or ten years old, Daddy was plumb blind, and I was doing near about all the man's work on the farm. Of course, Mama, Polly, and Sally was working too, and as soon as they was old enough the others did their part. But it seemed like it mostly fell on me. That's how it felt to me anyway.

You know how much church meant to your grandma. Well, she was always that way. Most Sundays we walked to the church. It was a few miles away by road but was a lot closer if you walked on the path through the woods, which is what we usually done. Unless it was winter, we would tote our shoes and walk there barefoot. We would wash our feet in the creek below the church, the one they used for baptizing folks, then we'd put on our shoes and go up to the church. Mama made us tote our shoes so they wouldn't get dirty. I remember she had these pretty little shoes she made for herself. She'd carry them in a little sack then put them on after she had washed her feet in the creek. I used to think it was funny that right after we had done washed our feet in the creek we'd go to church and if it was communion Sunday then we would do foot washing. One time was I was just a little chap right in front of everybody I asked Mama how come we have to get our feet washed since we done just washed them in the creek. I can laugh about that now, but boy was she mad at me.

Daddy didn't never go to church with us, even when he could still see. He claimed it was because he was a

Methodist, but he didn't go to their church neither. He might not have gone to church, but Daddy was a good man. Other than him taking a drink now and then, he seemed to live a good Christian life.

But not like Mama. Like I said a little while ago, Mama was a saint.

Mama saw to it that we young'uns was raised up to be good Christians and I've always tried my best not to disappoint her. Or the Lord neither. Well, I take that back. There's been plenty of times I shoulda tried a lot harder than I did.

Mama being such a good Christian is what makes my sin all that much worse.

I reckon you're wondering when I'm going to get around to telling you about that. Well, all right. Here's what I done.

3

It was late August, a dog day. I had picked a watermelon and was toting it to the creek, so I could cool it off. I was just about there when I heard Polly crying and sorta like choking and gagging. She wasn't saying nothing, and I don't know how exactly, but I could tell it was her. The sound was coming from up on the little bluff over the spring. I could tell that it was Polly and that something was the matter.

I hollered Polly. Polly, is that you? Are you all right? Then I heard a bunch of commotion and rustling around, and it sounded like Polly was crying but trying not to. My heart started racing and I went scrambling up the hill, but I lost my footing the first time and come sliding back down it. You know how steep that bluff is next to the spring and it was all covered in leaves. Anyway, I charged up there again, grabbing on to saplings to pull myself up and when I got to the top and could see, there was Polly leaning up against a big tree and her head was dropped down and she was spitting and I run over towards her then I noticed there was a man running off through the woods and he was sorta like stumbling and trying to hold his britches up with one hand. I froze there for a few seconds not knowing if I should go help Polly or go chase after that man. Then I run over to Polly and I kept saying Polly, are you all right Polly, and she wouldn't look at me, and she kept on spitting like she was trying to get something out of her mouth. It didn't take me but a few seconds and then I took off after the man. He was way up ahead of me but I could still see him and I was chasing after him and hollering and then he cut through some blackberries and by the time I got to there he was out of sight.

I run back to where Polly was, but she was gone and then I heard some crying from down by the spring and I ran down the hill and there she was leaning over the creek and she was down on her knees by the water and she kept on washing her mouth out over and over again. I said what happened and who was that man, but she wouldn't look at me and she wouldn't answer me. I said do you want me to go get Mama and then she looked up at me, her eyes were all red and she looked terrible, and she said real firm don't say nothing to Mama about this. I said why not, what's the matter Polly and she said Charlie, don't tell nobody nothing about this. She said it a few times and at first it was like she was bossing me—she was 17 then and I won't but 13—but then all of sudden she changed and she said oh please, Charlie. Please don't tell. Please promise me you won't tell. And she reached out and took a hold of my hand and she was crying, and she looked so pitiful I was fixing to cry too and she said please, oh please, Charlie. Please don't tell. And I couldn't stand it, so I said all right I won't tell. Then she said promise, Charlie. Cross your heart and hope to die. So, I crossed my heart and I promised her, and she seemed better then. And I said, who was that Polly. Who was that man? And she just looked away and wouldn't answer me.

But I knew who it was. I knew it was Ben.

4

After Polly settled down, she made me promise one more time, then she started out back to the house. I went on up to where I had seen the man running and just like I thought, he had ripped his shirt when he cut through those blackberries. I found a little piece of white cloth in the briars and I took it and put it in my pocket.

Now I just said I knew it was Ben that was running away, but I really didn't know for certain. He was a good ways away from me and all I could see was his back. The man was wearing dungarees and a white shirt, but there won't nothing special about that. I was pretty sure it was Ben, but I won't real sure. Not yet.

Him and James both lived on the Talbert place, but James lived in the old home house, you know where he lived, and Ben lived on the other side of the place in a little house. He hadn't never married, and he lived by himself. He raised a crop with a colored family and one of the colored women kept his house for him. But we didn't never see much of him, sept on holidays or when we was killing hogs or shucking corn and he'd come over and help.

For the next few days Polly wouldn't never look at

me. It was summer so we was real busy on the farm but whenever I was around her, like at dinner and supper, I could tell that she was on purpose not looking at me. Then one day I caught her by herself. I was on my way to the barn when I saw her hanging up clothes, so I went over to her and asked her real quietly, was it Uncle Brother Ben. That's what we called them back then—Uncle Brother James and Uncle Brother Ben. They was more than 30 years older than us so we couldn't just call them James and Ben. They won't our uncles, they was our half-brothers. But Mama and Daddy made us call them "Uncle Brother." I quit calling James that when I was grown, but back when I'm talking about, they was still Uncle Brothers to us. So, anyway, I said was it Uncle Brother Ben and Polly wouldn't look at me and she wouldn't answer me. I kept on asking her was it, Polly? Was it him? And then finally she turned and looked at me and her face was all red and she was mad and she said it won't nobody, Charlie. You just need to forget about that. Don't ask me about it no more and don't never say nothing else about it. Well, I could tell she won't going to admit it was him, but I felt right sure it must have been. I didn't promise her nothing this time, but I just nodded my head and went on.

Now, I still won't a hundred percent sure it was Ben, and I hadn't seen him since that day. I had just broke a hook on a singletree and I needed to borrow one until I could get it fixed, so I decided to go over to Ben's house and ask to borrow one of his. There was a path from our house to Ben's that went through the woods. You couldn't ride there that way, but it was the fastest way to walk. The path come out behind Ben's house, not too far from his well. Ben kept a big mean dog and it run loose at his place. When I come out of the woods that morning that dog come running at me barking and snarling and slobbering. I knew about that dog, but it still always scared me. As long as you walked kind of slow he wouldn't bite you, but he stayed right on you barking and raising cane. I reckon Ben didn't have to worry about nobody sneaking up on him.

After a minute or two Ben come around the house, to see what his dog was barking at I reckon. He called the dog off and he hollered what do you want. I thought it was funny that he didn't come over to me or say good morning. He just stood off in the distance and hollered what do you want. So, I acted like I didn't suspect nothing. I said, morning Uncle Brother. Hook broke on our singletree and I wondered if I could borrow one of your'n till I get it fixed. He hollered go on and get it yourself and then he went back around the house. Now that won't like Ben a'tall. He woulda normally gone in the tack room and got it himself, then he woulda fussed at me some for needing to borrow it. He ain't never before just let me go and get what I needed.

Anyway, I went on in and found a singletree and while I was in there, I peeped out through a crack in the boards and I could see Ben out front and he was hitching up his wagon. I didn't see his dog nowhere so I went out the door, laid the singletree down, then walked over to him, as quiet as I could. He didn't hear me coming and when I was pretty close, I said out loud, much obliged Uncle Brother, I'll bring it back soon. When I spoke it looked like it scared him some and he spun around and he said what do you want and I said I just wanted to thank you for letting me use the singletree. Then he kind of grunted and said all right.

He didn't say nothing about me bringing it back or being careful with it or nothing, which won't like him. He just said all right. Thanks again I said and then I turned and walked back to the barn door, picked up that singletree and headed home. I'd done seen what I needed to see. His shirt sleeve had a rip in it.

5

I was satisfied that Ben was the man I had seen with Polly that day at the creek. But I think I was still trying to find a way to get out of having to do anything about it.

See, even if I knew for sure it was Ben, and by then I was pretty sure of that, I really didn't know for sure what he had done to Polly. Well, maybe I did know but didn't want to admit it to myself. Anyway, Polly wouldn't never say and I didn't actually see nothing cept for him running away trying to hold his britches up and Polly trying to clean out her mouth. Was that enough to know for sure? But the truth is that in my heart I had no doubt what he had done, and I wondered if that hadn't been the first time.

Then I got to wondering what if Polly didn't mind. She was older than me and she hadn't told nobody so why should I? If she didn't want nothing done about it, then why should I? Of course, I knew in my heart that he had forced her. I had heard her crying and I had seen what she looked like. It was tearing me up, Flora, but I had done decided that I wasn't going to make it my business. I'm a little ashamed to admit it now, but I think I was trying to find a cowardly way out.

Then one night I was laying in bed, a few days after I had been over to Ben's and seen that he had a rip in his sleeve. I had been worrying about it same as I had ever since that day, but I was about at the place where I decided I ought to stop worrying. Then it hit me like a load of bricks and I sat up in the bed suddenly wide awake. Sally! If Ben done that to Polly and got away with it, maybe he would do it to Sally next! Maybe he already had! I knew right then that Ben had to be stopped and that I had to be the one to do it.

But what was I supposed to do? Polly had made me promise not to tell, but I reckoned that kind of promise wouldn't be binding if it put others in danger. But who could I tell? I couldn't tell Daddy. What good would that do? What was he going to do about it? He was blind and besides that Ben was his son. I figured he probably wouldn't believe me anyway.

For the next few days all day long while I was working and even while I was trying to sleep, I kept thinking about what I was supposed to do. I knew in my heart it was my responsibility. I imagined going over to Ben's house, calling him out and whipping him. That's what I wanted to do with all my heart. But I knew that won't going to happen. I won't big enough or strong enough to whip him. And, truth be told, I wasn't brave enough to try.

The longer I hesitated the worse I felt. I knew that my family was at risk, that it was my place to protect them, and that I wasn't doing it. Finally, I got up the nerve and I made a vow to myself that I wouldn't back down. I knew what I had to do, and I set out to get it done.

I decided to kill Ben.

That evening after supper, I took the path through

the woods to Ben's house. When I come to his place his dog came running over barking and carrying on like usual. When he got to me, I reached in my pocket and brought out a chunk of fat meat that I had done fished out of the pot of greens and I gave it to him. Then I walked back home.

The next few nights I done the same thing—went over there just after dark and when the dog came after me, I gave him a chunk of fat meat. By the fourth night the dog was waiting for me. He didn't bark at all.

6

The next night I waited until it was plumb dark, then I slipped out of bed and snuck outside. I had done hid the shotgun and a hambone in the barn. I went and got them, and I headed over to Ben's house.

There was enough of a moon that night that I could see without a lantern. When I got to Ben's place I whistled for the dog and he come running over and I give him the hambone and he run off with it. Then I sneaked on over to the barn, slid the door open and went in, then slid it back shut. I climbed up into the hayloft and found me a spot where I could see down to the milking stand and I just made me a nest there and settled down.

I don't reckon I slept five minutes that night. I just worried and fretted. Lord, was I tore up. I kept thinking what a cowardly thing it was to ambush a man, but I also kept thinking what an evil man Ben was and how he needed killing. Whenever I got to thinking about getting caught and likely getting hung, I just pushed that right out of my head. I figured first things first. Kill Ben, then worry about the other stuff later.

Well, that was one long night let me tell you. Funny but I can still remember how a possum come through the loft that night. Walked right past me like I won't even there. Probably not even thinking there might be a person in the loft in the middle of the night.

Finally, it was getting close to daybreak. The rooster started crowing and before too long I could hear sounds from up at Ben's house. I heard the back door open and some water splash on the ground, from him throwing out some water or maybe emptying a chamber pot. Then after a little while I heard him coming and he was calling up his milk cow. As Ben was coming in the barn, I heard the cowbell and then I saw the cow coming right on in to the stand. It seemed like everything was happening real slow and my ears were ringing and, honest to goodness, I could hear my own heart beating fast and hard.

Ben pulled a stool out the corner, set out his bucket, and commenced to milking. My hands was shaking so bad that I had to settle down. I closed my eyes and I prayed for strength. Then, when they weren't shaking quite so bad anymore, I lifted up the shotgun and aimed it at Ben. I cocked it and I put the bead right on the middle of his back. I could feel that I was starting to shake again so I knew I couldn't wait no more. I made sure I had a good aim, then I closed my eyes and I started squeezing the trigger.

But at the last possible moment, I stopped.

I lost my nerve. I just didn't have the heart or the guts to do it—to shoot him in the back while he was milking, even though he deserved it.

I lowered the gun and I cussed myself. Then I tried to raise it again but by now my hands were shaking again and I knew I wasn't going to shoot him.

I had to be quiet, but I'll tell you the truth, Flora, I started crying. I'm an old man and I can admit it now, but that crying made me more ashamed than anything else. I even thought about taking that gun and shooting myself with it.

When Ben left carrying his pail, there I was up in the loft shaking and crying like a little baby—too scared and weak to protect my family. That may have been the lowest I ever felt in my life. No, wait. There was a time much lower than that. We're coming to it.

I waited until I was sure Ben wasn't around, then I snuck down out of the loft and went on back home. When I got there everybody was wondering what had happened to me, so I told them a lie. I said that I had heard something in the hen house and had come out and found a fox carrying off a hen and that I had done followed it and spent all night and half the day looking for it. Busy as we was with tobacco that story didn't make no sense but it was all I could come up with. Mama looked at me kind of funny, but she didn't say nothing. I put up the gun and went on back to work like any other day. I was still aiming to kill Ben, but I had done come up with a different plan.

I sure hate telling you the rest of it. But here it goes. What I done is, I put it on God.

See, when I was walking back home that day it dawned on me. I had done already satisfied myself that either God wouldn't mind me killing a sinner like Ben or else he would probably forgive me for it, being as Ben was so bad. But then I got to thinking about it and I realized that God could kill Ben a lot easier than I could, so why didn't he do it instead of me? And if God killed him instead of me it would save me a lot of trouble and keep my neck out of a noose to boot. So, I made a deal with God. I said God, I'm going to give you a week to kill Ben yourself, but if you ain't killed him by a week from now then I'll take it as a sign that you want me to do it. I have to tell you Flora, that might sound crazy to you now, but it seemed like a real good plan to me at the time. I was careful not to *ask* God to kill Ben—I just said I was going to wait and give him time to do it. I just took it for granted that God wanted Ben dead just like I did. The question was who was going to kill him—me or God? But I knew that God would see into my heart and know that I was really hoping he would do it so I wouldn't have to. But I didn't pray that. All I prayed was, God I'm going to wait a week so you can kill him yourself if you want to.

I went back to my regular work that week and I slept good for the first time since that day at the creek. It felt like the weight of the world had been lifted off of me. When we all went to church that Sunday, I believe I sang better than I ever had before in my life. I wouldn't have come right out and said it, but I just felt deep in my heart that God was going to kill Ben that week.

I was expecting every day to hear that Ben was dead. I wondered how God was going to do it. One good thing about being God is that you have lots of ways to kill somebody. Maybe he'd strike him with lightning, or burn him up in his house, or visit him with the plague, or have the earth swallow him up. God had a lot more options that I did, and I was mighty anxious to find out how he'd done it.

Then it got be the sixth day after I made the deal and I ain't heard nothing about Ben being dead. I wondered if maybe he was dead but hadn't nobody figured it out yet, so I went over to his house and watched from the woods till I saw him come out and go to the privy. I went on back home and I wasn't feeling so relieved anymore. It felt like that awful weight was coming back to my shoulders. My deal with God was that if he didn't kill Ben in a week, then I would do it. It was sure looking like God wanted me to do it, and I sure didn't want to.

Well, that night I prayed hard, Flora. There was only one day left, and I was mad at God for not killing Ben yet. It looked like he was going to make me do it. So, I changed my prayer that night and I said God please take this cup away from me. Please kill Ben so I don't have to. I prayed that for a long time. I told God that I would still do it if he didn't, but I told him I didn't want to and I begged him to kill him instead. Ain't that shameful, Flora? Well, I think it is.

8

So, then the seventh day came. It was God's last chance before he put it back on me. I kept on praying that day while I worked, but since it looked like God won't going to do it, I started planning on how I was going to kill Ben. I figured I might as well shoot him while he was milking, like I had set out to do before, and that I might as well go on and get it over with. That evening, right before suppertime, I snuck the shotgun out the house and hid it in the barn.

We was eating supper when James rode up and gave us the news that Ben was dead.

Lord have mercy, I just about fell over. God had spared Ben right up till I prayed for him to kill him, then he had struck him down. You would think I'd be happy Ben was dead. Truth is, I did feel relieved. But I also felt guilty for having killed him.

Oh, yes I had, Flora. You don't need to try to tell me I didn't. I done had almost forty-six years to think on it and I know I killed Ben just the same as if I had shot him in his barn. You keep saying that Flora, but that just shows you don't understand the power of prayer.

Ben was bad and I still believe he deserved to die.

He was dangerous and I reckon I don't mind taking the punishment for killing him. Truth is, if all I had to be guilty about was killing Ben, I would have been over that a long time ago. But you see Flora, God taught me an awful lesson. Prayer is a powerful thing. Man ought not try to make deals with God. It's too complicated and too much outside of our control. See, I just prayed for God to kill Ben. I never prayed for him to do it in any particular way. I figured I ought to leave that up to God. So, God answered my prayer. He said, Charlie you cowardly sinner. If you ain't got the guts to go through with it, then I'll handle it. And I'll show you why you never should have run away from your responsibility. That's how it seems to me, at least.

For a long time, I wondered if I should hate God for what he done. It seemed to me to be the worst possible thing he could have done. It seemed to me to be cruel and unfair.

But I reckon we ain't supposed to question the Lord's ways, Flora.

9

James told us didn't nobody know what killed Ben. He said that Aunt Shirley June, that was Ben's colored housekeeper, had found him dead in the bed and that she saw that he had been sick and had thrown up.

Daddy was right tore up by the news. Ben didn't come around much but he was still Daddy's son. It broke my heart to see him crying, tears streaming down out of his old blind eyes. James came over and hugged him and Daddy kept on saying how Ben was his mama's favorite and how he had been such a good boy.

I stole a glance over at Polly and she caught me looking at her. She just turned away without showing any sign one way or the other.

James said that his wife Annie was over at Ben's house and her and Aunt Shirley June was getting him ready to be laid out. Mama said Polly come on and go with me to help and James said he'd carry them over there.

I always wondered how Polly felt about helping to lay him out. I wondered if she was glad he was dead. I hope she was. It makes me feel a little better about things to think I saved her from him. But we ain't never to this day talked about it.

That afternoon, once they had Ben all laid out everybody went over to his house. You know how we do in the country. All the people came over and brought food, even though there won't no family there that needed helping.

There won't but three rooms in Ben's house and he didn't really have no parlor, so they had done just laid him out in his bedroom. I reckon they could have carried him over to James' house, but maybe didn't nobody think of it. Anyway, everybody crowded in there to look at him and to help themselves to the food.

Lord have mercy, Flora, I was sick to my stomach. I just couldn't stand the thought of looking at him. Here I was even kind of like feeling sorry for him, after wanting so much to have him dead. Anyway, when we got there and everybody else started piling inside, I just went off to the side some and then I found me a spot under the porch where I could sit and wouldn't nobody see me.

I don't know how long I'd been sitting underneath the porch like that, but it was a good long time. And after a while…

Abruptly, Daddy stopped talking. He was staring off into space and I knew he was reliving that moment. His eyes filled with tears, and that frightened me. I had never seen that happen before. He stayed silent a long time and I was afraid to speak— almost even to breathe. Finally, a single lonely tear slid down his suntanned cheek and he quickly reached up and brushed it away. That seemed to break the spell he had fallen under. He took a deep breath and then he started talking again.

Flora, I ain't ready yet to tell you what happened then. It was something terrible. Terrible. Maybe I'll tell it to you when I get to when I told Bertie. She's the only person I've ever told it to, and I'm sure she didn't tell you. But what I found out that morning put a weight on me much worse—much, much worse—than what I was already carrying. And I been carrying that weight all my life since.

And so, there I sat under that porch, 13 years old, realizing what God had done.

10

Well, Ben was dead. James took his farm and got even richer. At the same time, things got harder and harder for us on our farm. Daddy couldn't do nothing by then. He had done quit.

As Daddy got older and more feeble and quit doing much of anything around the farm, he at least stopped being so sad all the time. He loved to play his fiddle and most of all he loved it when the young folks would come from all around to hear him play and to dance. Now Mama, being Primitive Baptist and all, she didn't approve of no dancing and fiddling. But she put up with it and didn't never do nothing to try to stop Daddy from having his fun. I spect it was on account of him losing Ben like he did.

But, let me tell you, she durn well made sure I knew what she thought.

She would all the time tell me, when Daddy won't around, how fiddling and dancing and merry making was the work of the devil. She would ask me if I agreed with her and I would say I did, even though at first I kinda liked the music and didn't see no harm in it. But I had done made up my mind by then that I won't ever going to go against nothing Mama said or wanted. I felt like I owed her that. Which is why I ain't never cared for music.

That's a shame in one way. Bertie told me that she loved to dance. But I didn't never take her dancing. Not even once. I sure do wish I would have. I spect that it would have made Bertie real happy if I would have. Wouldn'ta hurt nothing.

11

About a year after Daddy died, John decided he had done had all the school he wanted. I never could understand that. I wanted to go to school but won't able to. Here John was, able to, but he didn't want to. Anyway, John was as big as me and he was able to do all the man's work that needed doing on the place. Money was always tight with us, so I figured it made good sense for me to go to town and work in the mill. Plus, I knew that there was a real good chance we were going to lose our farm—and if we did, we would need something to fall back on.

Mama won't real happy about me going and she was still the boss. At first she said no, and that was that. But there was more and more country people taking mill jobs then and we could all see how the money they sent home was helping. So, after a while Mama said all right. I think it was probably because of all the pressure James was putting on her.

See, ever since Daddy had passed, James had been after Mama to sell him our farm. Daddy had made sure that it went to Mama when he died, and I reckon James figured it was going to go to Mama's children someday instead of him and he wanted it. I don't know why. He already had a big farm, plus he got Ben's place. And he didn't have but one daughter and it didn't seem like she wanted to live in the country. But whatever the reason, he wanted our place and he kept on and on worrying Mama about selling it to him. He would say stuff like, y'all can barely kept the taxes paid and food on the table, Betsy. Sell the place to me and you can buy y'all a place in town and you won't have to work so hard. Or he might say, sell me the place and y'all can go on living here as tenants. That way you'll have enough money to get by and you still won't have to leave. I heard him say things like that all the time. He didn't never talk to me like I was a grown-up man. He didn't pay me no mind a'tall. He just talked to Mama and she would just keep on telling him no. We're doing fine, James, she would say. Ain't nothing we need that we ain't got. But then he'd get on her about us needing a new mule or the roof needing fixing or how the bill at the store needed paying or how she needed money to pay for school and this, that and the other. Mama would just politely thank him for his concern and say she reckoned she didn't want to sell the place.

But the truth was, we did need more money than we was making off the farm. We raised good tobacco, but it didn't bring in much money since we had to do all the work ourselves and could only put up so much. Mostly what was eating us up was our bill at the store for our guano and seeds and such as that. Once we got behind at the store it seemed like we just couldn't never catch up and what we owed just kept getting bigger and bigger.

So finally I just told her, Mama, John can do all my work here now so I might as well go to town and make some extra money. And when it come time to start worrying about the taxes and the store bill that year she finally let up and said she reckoned I was probably right.

One of the other boys across the hill had done already started working there. He would stay all week then come home Saturday night, spend Sunday at home, then go back to Danville every Sunday night. He told me that mill work won't no worse that farm work and he felt like it would suit me good. I asked him would he check with his boss and see if they was interested in hiring me on and he come back the next week and said they would. So, I started making plans to go the next week. Lord have mercy, Flora, that's when Mama started getting on me real good.

She made me promise I wouldn't never drink no liquor. She made me promise I wouldn't play cards. I didn't mind that too much. I ain't never had no desire to drink liquor and I ain't never learned how to play cards. But mostly what she rode me about was the dangers of mill girls.

Yep. It seems funny now, but let me tell you, she was dead serious. She'd say, don't let any of them mill girls get you alone, Charlie. That's how they'll catch you so that you have to marry them. Just keep your distance, son. She must have told me that a hundred times: don't let a mill girl get you alone. Seems like she was sure they was all just gonna jump on me like flies when I got there—trying to get me alone so I'd have to marry one of them. I can laugh about it now, but I won't laughing then.

Mama had done hovered over me so close that I hadn't never even had me a girlfriend. You're a grown woman, Flora, so I'm gonna tell you straight. Please forgive me and remember that I was a young man then—not much more than a boy really. I'm a little bit ashamed to say it now, but I have to admit that I laid awake many a night thinking about mill girl delights. Seems foolish now. Anyway, I solemnly promised Mama that I wouldn't drink liquor, play cards or let myself get trapped by a mill girl.

As soon as we got the crop planted, I turned it over to John. And on Sunday evening, May the twentieth, nineteen and seventeen, I went with Ricky Gresham down to the Raye station and caught the train to Danville. The next day, I was an employee of the Riverside Cotton Mills.

That Sunday before I left, Mama made a great big dinner for us after church, with all my favorite food. I could tell she was sad, but she was trying to keep up a good face. You would have thought I was fixing to go off to the war from the way she was acting.

Well, it was a couple of days after that, after I had done spent ten hours busting cotton bales, that I come out of the mill with the other boys and headed toward our house on Floyd Street. Up ahead I saw there was two girls standing out in the road looking back at me and Jimmy Key. When I looked up at them two girls, I saw one of them looking me right back in the eyes. I knew right then that there was something special about that girl. It was your mama—my Bertie.

I reckon that was about the luckiest thing that ever happened to me.

Bertie & Charlie

1

When the mill whistle sounded the shrill blast that signaled quitting time, Charlie didn't hear it. He never did. Folks all the way on the other side of Danville could hear the whistle plainly when it blew every day at six o'clock, but in the breaker room at Mill Number One nothing could be heard over the roar of the bale breaking machines, into one of which Charlie had been feeding armloads of raw cotton for the past ten hours. But, whistle or not, Charlie knew his workday was done when the ravenous machine slowly powered down, screeching and grinding to a reluctant halt.

"Well, I reckon you've done ate enough cotton today, old girl," Charlie said to the machine, as he dropped the dusty white sheet of fiber he had just pulled from the bale. "Me too," he added with a chuckle, pulling the cotton balls from his ears as he turned and joined the crowd of men shuffling toward the exit.

Jimmy Key hurried over and threw an arm across Charlie's shoulders. "Another day, another dollar," he said with a wide grin. "I'm heading out that door and right straight to the closest drink of whiskey."

Charlie smiled and shook his head.

"Come on and go with me, Charlie. Ain't no telling what kind of trouble we might be able to get into," Jimmy said cheerfully.

"Not me, Jimmy. I keep on telling you I ain't a drinker," Charlie said.

"And I keep on telling you I aim to make you one," Jimmy fired back. "That's the best way there is to wash all the cotton dust out of your throat."

"I'm sure you'll manage just fine without me," Charlie said as they stepped into the late afternoon sunlight, which, after ten hours in the dim light of the breaker room, was blinding.

Charlie and Jimmy joined hundreds of other workers spilling through gates all along the fence that surrounded the mill, crowding onto the hard-packed red dirt road that would lead them to the millhouses of the working-class community called Mechanicsville, or, for those who preferred, to the clandestine saloons, gambling dens, and brothels on Craghead Street.

"Last chance, Charlie," Jimmy said with a laugh as they reached the Craghead intersection.

"See you later, Jimmy," Charlie said, turning away.

Suddenly Jimmy stopped. He poked Charlie in the ribs, laughing. Gesturing up the road, he said, "Hey, Charlie. Looks like them girls up yonder are trying to get a look at us."

Charlie looked up and saw Jimmy's meaning. About a block away, two lint- and dust-covered girls were standing side-by-side in the road, looking back toward him and Jimmy. In a moment Charlie could see that the girl on the right was trying to catch his eye. Almost a head taller than the other girl, she was smiling broadly, her dimples so big they were visible even at that distance, a strand of her black hair falling fetchingly across her pretty face. In that same instant Charlie noticed the smaller girl beside her. Her grimy face and the streak of machine grease across her dress evidencing a hard day's work, the smaller girl's brown hair was pulled and tied atop her head and her dark eyes were squinting, straining to see, as if she had just been told to look and wasn't quite sure where.

Seeing Jimmy and Charlie looking their way, the taller girl giggled and pulled the other girl's arm. At that moment, the smaller girl seemed to notice the boys for the first time. Charlie was looking directly at her. It was fleeting, but their eyes met briefly. Involuntarily, Charlie smiled. The girl blushed and turned away quickly, as the taller girl flashed another toothy smile, then made a little wave and spun around, laughing. She grabbed the smaller girl by the hand, and began to run, pulling her along.

"Woo doggie!" Jimmy exclaimed. "Ain't she an angel?"

Charlie was silent for a few moments before answering quietly. "Yes. She is. She sure is."

2

Lucy Lou Daniels grabbed her friend by the shoulder. "Look, Bertie!" she exclaimed, turning the girl around. "Yonder comes that new boy I been telling you about."

Bertie squinted, trying to discern who exactly she meant among the crowd of millworkers trudging along the road as Lucy Lou drew up straight, smiling invitingly.

"See him, Bertie? Him and that other boy yonder?" Lucy Lou asked.

At that distance Bertie couldn't see anything clearly, but among the crowd she eventually noticed the two boys toward whom Lucy Lou had gestured. As they came more clearly into focus, Bertie saw that one of the boys was looking right at her. And then he smiled.

Bertie knew instantly that the boy wasn't teasing her, mocking her, or laughing at her—the reaction she expected from boys, the reaction she feared so much that she had for years carefully avoided making eye contact with any of them. Nor was it a flirtatious smile, like Lucy Lou's reply to it. Instead the boy smiled warmly and kindly, and Bertie was swept by a sensation like none she had ever before experienced. It was as if this boy's smile was not a greeting offered by a polite stranger, but rather an acknowledgment of some profound ineffable connection. She had never seen the boy before in her life, but his smile seemed to say to her, "Hey, Bertie. I see you. I understand you." That is, at least, how she would always remember that moment.

As Lucy Lou beamed and shot a little wave of her hand at the boys, Bertie flushed and turned away quickly, embarrassed and troubled. Lucy Lou giggled, grabbed her by the hand and pulled her down the road at a trot.

"His name is Charlie Lawton and he's staying in the house where Eddie Cox and them other boys live, right down the road," Lucy Lou said excitedly as they walked toward home. "I heard he comes from a farm out in the country near here and all the girls who've seen him say he's as cute as can be."

Bertie didn't answer, keeping her head down as she shuffled along beside Lucy Lou.

"Did you see him smile at me?" Lucy Lou asked with a mischievous grin. "I shoulda just run right on over to him when he did that."

Lucy Lou stopped suddenly, her eyes widened and bright. "I know what we ought to do! Let's just wait across the road from his house and see if he comes over to talk to us."

Bertie shook her head rapidly, still looking down at her feet, a chill of anxiety rushing over her at the thought of it. "I'm going home," she muttered.

"Oh, Bertie, quit being so shy. How are you ever going to get a beau if you act like that?" Lucy Lou said. "That other boy with him wasn't half bad. Let's go wait for them and maybe he'll come over and talk to you."

Trembling, Bertie began walking faster, continuing to shake her head. "I'm going home," she said again.

Lucy Lou stopped, stamped a bare foot down on the road and said in frustration, "Bertie! What kind of friend are you!" She raced to catch up with Bertie, took her by the shoulder and changed her tone. "Please," she said pleadingly. "Pleassssse."

"No," Bertie answered firmly. "I'm going home!"

"All right," Lucy Lou said with a whine, following Bertie. Then she brightened, as if something important had just dawned on her. "You know what, Bertie? You're right! It's best to play hard to get. I'll bet you anything that boy will come over and talk to me the very next time he sees me. He might even come on over to our house. Maybe even this evening."

Bertie shuddered, and walked faster.

3

Jimmy abandoned his whiskey plans, instead following Charlie back to their house on Floyd Street, chattering about the girl the whole way.

Charlie lived with five other men in a three room mill house. Four of the men slept on small cots that were in two of the rooms—two cots to a room. In the front room, where Charlie and Jimmy slept, there was a little cookstove and a small coal-burning heat stove for the winter. Charlie and Jimmy slept on a pallet, which they kept rolled up and moved out of the way until bedtime. The pallet was less comfortable than the cots (which were awarded based on seniority) and the front room was hot and stuffy on nights any cooking was done. But Charlie's housemates assured him he'd be happy to be on the pallet when winter came around.

"I think she's one of the spinners that lives down the street," Jimmy said. "There's a whole passel of 'em living in that house, Charlie. Must be a dozen or more. Now I ain't noticed that any of the rest of 'em is much to look at it, but dang if that one ain't a peach."

Charlie just grunted, acknowledging only that he had heard Jimmy's words, not that he agreed with him.

He knew Jimmy meant the taller, black-haired dimpled girl, who was, Charlie agreed, indeed a pretty girl. But Charlie couldn't shake the image of the shorter dark-eyed girl in the grease-streaked dress—her bashful response to his smile replaying in a continual loop in Charlie's mind as they walked.

"Let's go on down there and say hey," Jimmy said.

"Naw, I don't want to," Charlie answered. "Right now, all I want to do is wash the lint off my face and get something to eat."

"Well, I'm sorry to say today was Johnny's day to cook the beans, so good luck trying to choke them down," Jimmy answered.

Charlie laughed. "That just proves how hungry I am."

"Well let's go see if we can't work us up a better appetite down at them girls' house," Jimmy said.

Charlie shook his head and chuckled. "Boy, I believe if we had a young bull acting like you, we'd put him in a different pasture. Or make a steer out of him."

"You ain't no fun a'tall, Charlie. All I'm saying is that we ought to be good neighbors and go say hey," Jimmy answered with a snort.

"Good neighbors would leave them poor girls alone, Jimmy. Just settle down, boy. That girl ain't going nowhere and neither are you. You'll have a chance to say hey soon enough," Charlie said.

"Well, then I reckon they'll just have to wait to get to know me better," Jimmy said with a grin. "You go on and try to stomach Johnny's beans. I'm going down to Craghead Street."

As Jimmy bounded away whistling, Charlie climbed the rickety steps to the house. Eddie Cox, one of his housemates, was sprawled across the porch, an arm thrown over his face.

"Hard day, Eddie?" Charlie asked.

"Same as always. A devil of a way to earn my daily bread," Eddie answered.

Eddie was the oldest of the residents—about 30 Charlie guessed. He shared a room with his cousin Tom, both men having come to Danville years ago from some place in the mountains Charlie had never heard of. Eddie and Tom worked as carders and were bachelors.

"If you hear they're hiring any more carders, I'd appreciate it if you'd let me know, or put in a word for me," Charlie said.

Eddie grunted, a response whose meaning was lost on Charlie.

"I don't want to have to bust bales any longer than I have to," Charlie added.

"Ain't nothing wrong with breaking bales," Eddie answered, his arm still thrown across his face.

"Don't pay as much as carding or weaving though," Charlie said.

"You trying to get rich?" Eddie asked.

"I ain't never heard of nobody getting rich working in the mill," Charlie answered. "I'm just trying to make as much for my family as I can. By the time I pay my share of the rent and food and buy my tickets home and back, ain't gonna be much left for them."

Eddie responded with a grunt.

"You got any family, Eddie? I mean besides Tom," Charlie asked.

"Not especially," Eddie said from beneath his arm.

"So, what you doing with all that money you're making?" Charlie asked, playfully.

After a few moments of silence Eddie said,

"Minding my own business."

Charlie flushed, realizing his mistake. "Right. Sorry, Eddie." Standing up, he added, "Reckon I'll go check on that pot of beans."

"They like to put new boys in the breaker room to see if they mind hard work," Eddie said, still not having moved an inch. "After a while they'll move you out of there, as long as you work hard. And when you end up carding or weaving or whatever, then you'll work for four more solid weeks without no pay while they say they're training you. You'll get your wish soon enough." Eddie lifted his arm off his face, opened his eyes, and looked at Charlie. "As long as the breaker room don't break you."

Charlie smiled and said, "Thanks, Eddie."

Eddie dropped his arm back over his eyes. Then he grunted.

Charlie stepped inside the house, pulled off his cotton cap and tossed it over onto the pallet rolled up in the corner. He thought about what Eddie had said and it made him smile. He knew that if anything in the mill did break him, it wasn't going to be hard work. He didn't mind hard work. He didn't know any other kind. He'd been doing hard work since he was old enough to walk, and mill work, even breaking bales, was no harder than farm work. But Charlie did wonder if something else might break him—the noise, the dim room whose stagnant air was clouded with cotton dust, the mind-numbing monotony of the job, the conditions that combined to give him a dull headache that seemed to never fully go away, and a ringing in his ears that never stopped. Working sunup to sundown is natural, he thought, but not inside a cotton mill.

He walked over to the stove, wrapped his

shirtsleeve around his hand, and lifted the top off the simmering pot. A chunk of fat meat lay atop a bubbling brown mass of pinto beans.

A ladle hung from a nail in the wall, flanked by six tin bowls hanging from nails of their own, three on each side of the ladle. Charlie took down the ladle and his bowl and scooped his supper from the pot. Although he knew there was no cornbread left, he looked anyway, feeling disappointment when he saw that none had miraculously appeared.

Charlie dropped down into one of the two chairs at the small pine table and lifted a spoonful of beans into his mouth. Jimmy was right. There was something about them that didn't taste right. How can someone mess up a pot of beans, Charlie wondered.

Just then Johnny and Ward Dillard burst into the house, arguing loudly about something. Brothers from the hills, the teenagers announced their arrival not only with their rowdiness, but also with their pungent stench. Charlie wondered if they had ever bathed in their lives.

"You ain't got no idea what you're talking about Johnny," Ward shouted, pronouncing "idea" as if it ended in a "r." "You're full of mud, as usual."

"I seen it with my own eyes, you durn fool," Johnny answered. "And if you're calling me a lie, I'll give you a good lickin' for it," he added as he snatched a bowl down off the wall.

"Just go on and try it, John-boy," Ward fired back, pulling down his own bowl. "I'll learn you a lesson you won't never forget."

During the few days Charlie had known them, it seemed the brothers were always arguing, always on the verge of a fight that never happened.

"Evening, fellas," Charlie said, as he took another bite, wincing again at the strange sour flavor. It was as he swallowed that he noticed Johnny's hands.

Johnny was standing just a few feet away, waiting his turn as Ward lifted his ladle-full of beans out of the pot. Johnny's hands were grasping his bowl, right at Charlie's eye-level. They were the filthiest hands Charlie could ever remember seeing—stained, greasy, and grimy. As Charlie pondered the fact that his supper had been prepared by that disgusting pair of hands, he felt his appetite vanish.

4

"Where you going, Bertie?" Lucy Lou asked, coyly. "Seems like you're always sneaking off by yourself. Makes me wonder if you ain't got a beau you ain't told us about."

"I done told you before," Bertie answered wearily. "I ain't 'sneaking off.' I just like going for walks by myself, is all."

"Mm-hmm," Lucy Lou said, her eyes twinkling with skepticism. "Well go on then. I'll let you know if that new boy comes around while you're gone." She finished with a laugh.

Bertie sighed and rolled her eyes as she walked away.

Many of her friends and coworkers complained about the heat, but Bertie loved this time of year, the long days allowing her the chance to enjoy at least a little sunlight after work. As she strolled down the dusty street, neighbors lounging in front of their houses shouted greetings. She had not gone far before a little boy rushed out from in front of one of the mill houses, grabbing her by the hand. "Hey Bertie!" he cried. "Come on and play with us! Davy has some marbles."

Bertie smiled and pulled the boy up into a hug. "Not today, Gem," she said. "Maybe next time. How's your daddy doing?"

"He says he's almost well," Gem said with a smile. "Did you know that two new men moved into our house? Their names are Tick and Tom and they're from North Carolina."

"Your mama told me about that," Bertie answered. "What do you think about it, Gem?"

"I think it's just fine!" Gem exclaimed. "Me and Purl get to sleep with Mama and Daddy now, on the floor next to their bed. I like that."

"You want to come and sit awhile, Bertie?" a woman called out from in front of the house.

"No thanks, Rose," Bertie answered. "I feel like going for a walk."

"Girl, I wish I had your energy," Rose answered with a laugh.

"Well, I ain't got two young'uns pulling on me," Bertie answered.

"Well, just let us know if you ever need to borrow a couple," Rose replied with a laugh.

"Is there anything I can do for y'all, Rose?" Bertie asked.

"Much obliged, Bertie, but we're doing all right," Rose answered.

Bertie kissed Gem on the cheek and set him back down. The boy grinned then dashed back toward his house, as Bertie waved and kept walking.

Rose and her family had been on Bertie's mind a lot lately. Rose came to work in the spinning room just five months after Bertie had started, she and her husband Samuel having arrived from somewhere in the mountains. Ten-year-old Bertie had helped train fourteen-year-old Rose. Since then they had worked side by side for the past eight years, becoming good friends along the way. She knew Samuel to be a friendly, good-natured, always-cheerful man, who was deeply devoted to his family and proud of his job as a weaver. To Bertie, they were a perfect family and she envied what she saw as their happy little world. But Samuel had been seriously and painfully injured on the job about six weeks earlier and the young family had been struggling to get by ever since. The inability to provide for his family weighed heavily on Samuel and had diminished his cheerfulness and, lately, his optimism. Bertie knew how much it must have hurt his pride to take in the boarders.

Bertie's walk took her east, back toward Mill Number One. She crossed Main Street, crowded with horses and wagons, then continued down Bridge Street, past the mill gate and toward the spot where the mill race rejoins the river. The sun was sinking rapidly toward the horizon when she reached the river's edge. It wasn't a safe place to walk alone. Bertie knew that. But she'd done it so many times now that she'd become inured to the risk. She walked confidently, in the belief that refusing to acknowledge the danger somehow lessened it. When she reached the water's edge she stopped and gazed across the river, knots of waste cotton floating by her like rag islands. After a moment or two she picked up a rock and tossed it into the water, brown with mud and streaked with dye. This was her routine every time she came here. In case anyone was watching her, she wanted it to appear that she had only come to look at the river. After a few more seconds she turned around, glancing all around her to make sure she was alone. Once she saw that she was, Bertie ducked under a low branch and into the dense, tangled overgrowth along the water's edge. She followed a narrow path, crouching and weaving to avoid the thorns on the bramble vines that flanked and crossed above her as she squeezed through. After about fifty yards the foliage became so dense it blocked her path entirely. She dropped to her knees and carefully pulled back a tangle of brush, revealing the mouth of a narrow opening. Bertie ducked her head and crawled in.

She emerged onto a little spit of sand, a tiny beach on the river, completely enclosed by brambles. Since discovering it three years earlier, Bertie had visited the spot hundreds of times. It had become a refuge for her. She called it her "secret place."

Once inside, Bertie slid a pile of brush over to block the entrance. She sat down on the sand and looked across the river at the woods on the other side. It was a sight she'd seen many times, and its beauty still made her sigh.

After a few seconds Bertie reached into her pocket and pulled out a corn husk doll, setting it up in the sand in front of her.

"Hey, Susannah!" Bertie said excitedly, looking at the doll. "We can't stay long, but I just had to tell you about today. Something real nice happened to me today, Susannah, although you might think it's just silly. Do you want to hear about it? All right, then. Well, me and Lucy Lou was walking home from work and she said look yonder at that new boy and I looked up and, well you know I can't see good, but once I finally figured out who she was talking about I looked right straight at him and you know what? That boy he was looking right back at me! Like there won't nobody on the road but me and him. It like to scared me to death, Susannah! And I was so embarrassed and just about to look away and guess what? That boy, he smiled at me. Smiled the prettiest, friendliest smile you ever saw. And all the time Lucy Lou was fussing over him (and her being so purty and all) and there he was, looking at *me*!"

The words were pouring out of Bertie—words she would never have had the courage to say to anyone else.

"Why do you reckon he looked so nice at me, Susannah? I know right sure that I ain't never had no boy look at me like that before.

"I'll tell you something, Susannah, but it's got to be our secret," Bertie lowered her voice to a whisper and continued, "My heart jumped when that boy smiled at me. I felt warm all up and down my body."

Bertie blushed deeply, then she picked up the doll and stood up, holding it out in front of her at arm's length. "Now Susannah, don't you laugh at me, but I just want to know what you think. Do you think that boy might think I'm nice to look at? Even as nice as Lucy Lou? You do! Oh, that would make me so happy."

Bertie pulled the doll to her chest and spun around on her toes. Stopping, she pushed the doll back out to arm's length and continued speaking to it.

"You know I love you, Susannah, and we'll always be the best of friends. But I have to admit something I ain't never told you before. I get blue sometimes when the other girls start talking about their beaus and I feel like ain't no boy never going to want to court a skinny little ugly ignorant girl like me. You're nice to say that Susannah, but I do feel that way. I feel real lonely sometimes.

"Well, here's what I been wanting to tell you ever since I saw him. Now please don't laugh at me Susannah, but you know what? I just have a feeling that something good is finally going to happen to me."

Bertie sighed, lowered her arms, and dropped back onto the sand, setting the doll out in front of her.

"I don't know what I'd do without you, Susannah. Let's just look at the river for a while, then we've got to go home."

Bertie fell silent and closed her eyes, listening to the water rushing by and to the cry of a distant whippoorwill. After a few moments he opened her eyes suddenly, looking at the doll.

"Do what?" she exclaimed. "No, Susannah. There ain't no point in me asking *him* for nothing. I don't think he likes me."

Bertie sighed deeply, then picked up the doll. "All right, my dear little friend. It's time for us to go back home."

She slid the doll into her pocket, pulled back the brush and crawled back through the tunnel.

5

The last two days of his first week at the mill crept by for Charlie. The monotonous grind of hour after hour of feeding cotton into the bale breaker, and the incessant roar of the machines, wore him down and left him with a headache that wouldn't go away. He couldn't remember ever being happier about the arrival of a Saturday. As he marched through the mill gate that morning, Charlie smiled, knowing that he only had to serve his mechanical master ten more hours and he would finally have a day off.

To his disappointment, he hadn't seen the intriguing little dark-eyed girl again. Walking home with Jimmy the day after first seeing her, they did see the taller dimpled girl. She was standing on the side of the road, talking to a tall gangly boy who was smoking a cigarette. The girl smiled and waved when she saw them, causing the boy she was with to shoot them a fierce glare. Charlie pretended he hadn't noticed them. Jimmy was glum the rest of the evening and gave up suggesting they go search for the girls.

When six o'clock finally arrived and the machines slowed to a halt, Charlie felt like shouting for joy. He followed the other workers as they lined up in front of a table behind which sat two men, one with a ledger in front of him and the other a cash box. The queue inched forward as the men collected their pay and wandered off. Eventually Charlie reached the front of the line.

"Name," the man with the ledger said.

"Charlie Lawton," Charlie answered.

The man dragged his finger down the list before him, then stopped and looked up at Charlie.

"You're on training," he said.

"Only training I got was for about 5 minutes on Monday," Charlie replied. "Tear off the cotton and throw it in the machine. I got that. I been fully trained."

"First four weeks is training time. Unpaid," the man said.

"But I didn't get no training," Charlie protested. "I been working all week same as every other man in here."

"You're on training time," the man replied flatly. "Didn't anybody tell you about training time?"

"Well, yeah. But I didn't figure it applied to busting bales. Maybe for weaving or carding, but not for breaking," Charlie said.

"You figured wrong," the man said brusquely. "Now step aside. You got three more weeks till you get paid."

"That ain't right," Charlie said.

The man looked up at him, unsympathetic. "You don't like it? Well there's plenty of boys who will be happy to take your place."

From behind him someone hollered, "Come on, buddy. You're holding up the line."

Charlie stood there, his temper rising, unwilling to back down but unsure what he should do instead. The man behind the ledger met his stare.

The standoff only lasted a moment or two. The man behind Charlie leaned forward and said softly, "Just step out Charlie, and wait for me over yonder."

Charlie hesitated, then stamped his foot in frustration before stepping out of the line, burning with anger. After a few moments, the man who had spoken to him walked up.

"Don't nobody get paid for the first four weeks, Charlie. It's a load of bunk, but that's the way it is."

"It ain't right, Press. Training time? I didn't get no training," Charlie protested.

"What you mean, boy? I trained you myself," the man answered with a smile.

Press Dinwiddie had indeed trained Charlie, just as he had trained hundreds of other new bale breakers over the years. Probably in his 30's (no one knew for sure, including Press), Press had been one of the earliest employees of Mill Number One and he had been breaking bales ever since. He had a hunched back and legs that weren't the same length, so that he walked with a crooked and exaggerated gait. Because he was (in the vernacular of the day) a "cripple," Press wasn't considered capable of any other job at the mill. He was destined to spend his working life breaking cotton bales.

"You know what I mean, Press," Charlie said with a whine. "Four weeks? And then after four weeks of working for free, all I get to make is five dollars a week?"

"Yep. That's about right," Press answered with a smile. "Welcome to the Riverside and Dan River Cotton Mills."

Charlie shook his head and stamped his foot.

"Look boy, you ain't no different than anybody else here," Press said. "Ain't nobody making you work here, but at the same time I know you're only here 'cause you ain't got no choice. Same as the rest of us. But trust me, Charlie. After you've been here as long as I have, you won't even remember them first four weeks no more."

"Do you reckon they'd give me a little advance on my first pay?" Charlie asked.

"Yeah. Probably. They like having you beholden like that. But what do you need?" Press asked.

"I'm supposed to be on the train to Raye tonight and I ain't got no money for the fare," Charlie answered.

"I'll spot you," Press said. "What is it? About fifteen cents each way?"

"Naw, Press! That's right nice of you and all, but I can't take nothing from you. I'd feel better borrowing it from the mill," Charlie said.

"Don't worry about it," Press answered. "Here's a dollar. I ain't got nothing to spend it on. That will carry you through till you get paid. You can pay me back then."

"Dang, Press. I don't know what to say. Tell you what, if you'll help me with the train fare home tonight, I'll see if my mama can give me what I need to get back," Charlie said.

"Now look boy, you're fixing to hurt my feelings. Take the durn dollar. You can pay me back when you get paid," Press said firmly.

Charlie nodded and took the bill Press held out to him, a lump rising in his throat. "Much obliged, Press. I promise I will pay you back just as soon as I get paid."

"All right, boy. Now go catch your train," Press

said, as he turned and limped away.

The last train out on the Richmond and Danville line was the Number Eight, which left at eight p.m. Among those waiting to catch it were a few dozen millworkers, recognizable by the cotton lint they carried out of the mill in their hair and on their clothes. After buying his ticket Charlie spotted his neighbor from home, Ricky Gresham.

"Howdy, Ricky," Charlie said, striding toward him.

"What do you say, Charlie?" Ricky answered with a smile, extending his hand.

Charlie shook his hand and answered, "I say I'm mighty glad to be going home."

"Trust me, Charlie. Your mama's cooking ain't never gonna have tasted so good," Ricky said, laughing.

"And my bed ain't never gonna have felt so good neither," Charlie replied.

"Oh shoot, boy. They done probably gave your bed to one of the other young'uns. I 'spect they'll put you out in the barn," Ricky said, laughing again.

Charlie laughed with him, but his stomach fell. What if Mama *has* given away my bed, he thought.

Ricky looked around then pulled a bottle out of his coat pocket and pushed it toward Charlie. "Want a little nip for the ride home?" he asked.

Charlie shook his head. "No, thanks."

"Suit yourself," Ricky said before taking a deep draw off the bottle, recorking it and returning it to his pocket.

A few minutes later the train whistle screamed. An elderly porter stepped out onto the platform and shouted, "All aboard!" and the crowd of men began to shuffle into the passenger cars.

The ride to the Raye station took twenty-five

minutes. As the train chugged along, Charlie stared out the window. Along the way, in the fading light of dusk, he saw familiar sights—tobacco fields, pastures, corn patches, hog pens, barns, and farmhouses—the sorts of things he'd been seeing his whole life without ever realizing how much he loved them.

A handful of passengers got off at the Volney station, the train's first stop and the only stop before Raye. Charlie knew some of them—farmers' children, like him, doing their part to add to their families' meager incomes. The train stopped only long enough to deposit and acquire a few riders, then it chugged on toward Raye. Toward home.

Charlie, Ricky, and a few others stepped out onto the station platform at Raye, where a knot of people were waiting to greet the arrivals or to board themselves. Charlie saw his brother John beside the station, waving and holding a mule's reins. "See you tomorrow, Charlie," Ricky said, as he turned and walked off into the dark, toward his farm about two miles distant.

John smiled as Charlie approached him. "Welcome back, brother. Glad to see you made it through the first week alive."

"Thanks, John. It's good to be back," Charlie said.

John sidled up to the mule as Charlie bent over and locked the fingers of his hands together, forming a step. John put his foot into the step and Charlie lifted his arms, while John threw a leg over the mule's back. Once mounted, John reached out his arm. Charlie took it by the elbow and John pulled him up onto the mule behind him. John gave the animal a little kick in the side and it started walking.

The brothers rode quietly for a while, until John

broke their silence. "I hope you ain't weighing old Jack down with all that money you must be toting," John said with a chuckle.

"Ain't no risk of that," Charlie replied. "I'm in training, so I don't get paid."

"Durn. You don't say?" John said. After a pause he added, "Wish I had that excuse."

Charlie didn't respond. After another few minutes of silence, he said, "Is Mama waiting up for me?"

"Probly," John replied.

"Did y'all give my bed away?" Charlie asked.

"Ha!" John laughed. "Now that was a sore subject today. The girls took it when you left, but this morning Mama told them they can't sleep in it when you're home. They got sent back to their pallet."

Charlie didn't like the idea of displacing his younger sisters, but the thought of sleeping in his old bed after a week on the floor was comforting. "I hope they won't mind it too bad," he said.

In about an hour, the mule ambled onto the wagon-rutted road that led to the house. As they neared the place Charlie could see a light through a window—a candle burning on the table. When they reached the porch, he hopped down. "You gonna put Jack up?" he asked.

"Yeah, I'll do it. You go on. I'll be in directly," John replied.

As John led the mule toward the barn, Charlie stood in front of the porch and looked at the house, the place he'd lived every day of his life, save the last six. The front of the house was built from logs, chinked with mud—one large room, with a big rock fireplace on one side. Originally that room had been the entire house, back when Charlie's great-grandfather had built it.

Charlie's grandfather added two clapboard-covered rooms to the back of the house, with a fireplace between them. There was a privy out back.

Modest by comparison to the homes of a few of their neighbors, it was bigger and sturdier that most of those in the community. After Charlie moved out, there had been seven people sharing the three rooms. His return crowded his two youngest sisters out of a bed and brought the number of residents back to eight.

Charlie looked the old place over and smiled. It felt good to be home.

The front door suddenly flew open and Betsy Lawton stepped out onto the porch, carrying a lighted candle. "Charlie? Is that you?" she shouted.

"Yep. Here I am, Mama. Home at last," Charlie answered, before bounding up the stairs and wrapping his mother in a hug.

Betsy laughed and returned the hug, then suddenly pushed Charlie away from her and exclaimed, "Boy, what is that all over your clothes?" She ran the candle up and down, looking her son over, then said, "You are filthy!"

Charlie laughed. "Sorry, Mama. It's lint and cotton dust. I went straight to the train after work and didn't have time to clean up."

"All right," she answered, "We'll get you cleaned up in the morning." Turning and walking through the door she asked, "Are you hungry?"

"I wouldn't mind a bite," Charlie answered. "I ain't had no supper."

"What?? All right then, sit down and I'll get you a ham biscuit."

Betsy walked over to the cupboard, opened a door and took out a pan of biscuits. She was slicing off a piece of ham when John came in the room.

"I'll have one of them too, Mama," he said.

"My foot you will," she answered, without turning around. "You done already had your supper."

John kissed her on the back of her head and said playfully, "You always did care more about Charlie than me. Here's more proof."

"Pshaw!" the woman replied, bringing Charlie his biscuit.

"Much obliged, Mama," Charlie said, before beginning to wolf it down. "Where's the girls?" he asked, between bites.

"They done all gone to bed," she answered. "The little ones are gonna sleep on the porch tonight."

"Are they mad at me for coming back to my bed?" Charlie asked.

"Naw," his mother answered. "They said to tell you they was letting you sleep in *their* bed tonight."

Charlie smiled as he finished the biscuit. "That sure was good, Mama. I sure did miss your cooking this week."

"Well, I'll send some good food back with you this time," she answered. "Now go on and go to bed."

Charlie drifted into a satisfying sleep that night, comforted by the familiar feel of home, the chorus of an army of crickets competing with the metallic ringing in his ears.

6

As Bertie stepped out onto the porch, Annie Jeffries called after her, "How come you don't never go to church with us, Bertie?"

Bertie turned to face her. "I do, sometimes," she answered. "I just don't feel like going today. I'm going to go for a long walk instead."

Annie nodded, skeptically, as Bertie turned and walked away. When she was out of earshot Annie said, "What do y'all make of Bertie wandering off like that all the time? Reckon she's got a beau she ain't told us about?"

Lucy Lou, brushing her hair on the other side of the room, laughed loudly. "Ha! That's a hoot. That girl is scared to death of boys. Ain't no way she's got one."

"So how come she goes off by herself instead of coming to church on Sunday?" Annie asked.

"She probably don't want to come to church because there's boys in it," Lucy Lou answered confidently, continuing to brush her hair. "Which is what I like about it," she added with a mischievous grin.

"You are a mess, girl," Annie said with a smile, shaking her head.

"All right, come on and hurry up y'all," Lucy Lou said, tying a ribbon in her hair. "Let's go so we can get a good seat."

By the time her housemates left for church, Bertie was at the riverbank. After tossing a rock into the water then watching the ripples float away from the splash, she turned, glanced around, and, seeing that there was no one watching her, ducked onto the path that led to her secret place.

Hours later, after a peaceful nap on the sand and a long talk with Susannah, Bertie crawled through the tunnel, blocked it, and made her way out of the thicket and back toward home.

Bertie loved Sunday afternoons in the mill village nearly as much as she loved Sunday mornings at her secret place. On Sunday afternoons, the streets that would be empty and quiet during the workweek were crowded with children playing and grownups out for walks. It seemed to her that only on Sunday afternoons were the people free from machines and unnatural demands. For a few hours a week, it seemed people were free to relax. But Bertie also knew that out back of many of the mill houses women were washing clothes, Sunday afternoons being the only time they had to do it. And she knew that many of those who weren't washing clothes, were sewing or cleaning or cooking for the week. On Sunday afternoons there was *some* rest for the weary, but not much.

Thinking of the chores awaiting her began to cloud her walk home. But before getting to them she decided to stop and visit Rose, who she knew to be struggling lately. Seeing that the door was open she walked up the steps to the porch, leaned in the doorway and called out, "Anybody home?"

Across the room Bertie saw Rose spin around, turning her back to the door. "Come on in, Bertie," she said, while wiping her eyes with her apron.

Bertie stepped cautiously toward her. "Rose. Are you all right, honey?"

Rose turned back toward her, dabbing her eyes. "Yes, yes. Sorry but you caught me feeling kind of blue."

"I just stopped in to see if I can help you with anything. What's the matter?" Bertie asked.

"Oh, Bertie," Rose said, as she plopped down in one of the two chairs at the table in the room. "I feel so worn down sometimes."

Bertie had seen Rose carrying the burden of trying to keep her family fed and housed for the past month after her husband's injury—almost impossible on a spinner's wage. Samuel had tried to return to work every week since his injury, but each time had been sent back home. Bertie had seen the emotional toll he was paying as well.

"Where is everybody?" Bertie asked.

"Purl is napping, and Gem is out back tending to his little garden. He has a green thumb," Rose said, ending with a shaky smile.

"Samuel?" Bertie asked.

Instantly she regretted the question, seeing Rose's eyes filling with tears.

"He went with those two new boys, Tick and Tom, down to see if they can get an odd job at a warehouse." Rose paused, wringing her hands. "Oh Bertie, I'm so scared he's going to hurt his arm again. He ain't supposed to be doing no heavy work till it heals but he just won't listen to nobody. The doctor told him that if he ain't careful with it, it might not ever heal."

"It's his pride," Bertie said quietly.

"I know that. He can't stand that I'm working and he ain't. But I'm so scared he's gonna make it worse," Rose said, a tear sliding down her face.

"I don't know what to say, Rose. He's a tough man. He'll be all right," Bertie said, at a loss for words that might comfort her friend.

Rose just nodded, looking down and continuing to wring her hands.

"I know you been taking in washing and mending from other girls, and I come over to help you with it. Don't say no, 'cause I ain't leaving till you let me," Bertie said.

"Oh, honey, bless your heart," Rose said, looking up and smiling. "That's kind of you, but I done finished already. There won't much to do today and I got it done first thing this morning."

Suddenly Gem burst into the room, his face streaked with dirt. "Bertie!" the boy exclaimed, rushing over and wrapping her in a hug. "Come and look at my garden, Bertie," he said with excitement. "You come too, Mama. It's gonna be a fine garden!" he said, beaming.

Bertie stood up and Gem took her by the hand. "What you growing, Gem?"

"Tomatoes and string beans!" he answered quickly. "I can't wait!"

"Me neither," his mother answered, as the boy led them out behind the house.

"See here," he said, leading Bertie to a little patch of dirt, marked off by sticks. The little plants were hilled and green, the soil around them moist from being watered, and completely free of any grass and weeds.

"It looks real good, Gem," Bertie said. "Did you do

all this yourself?"

Gem nodded, smiling. "Yep!" He paused then added, "Well, Mama and Daddy do help some."

"Not much," Rose said. "Gem is doing just about all of this by himself. I sure am proud of him."

"And I am too," Bertie said. "Looks like you've got the knack for growing things."

"Maybe next year Mama and Daddy will let me grow some corn too," the boy said, looking up at his mother.

"That will be fine by me," Rose said with a laugh.

"I'm gonna go get some more water for them," Gem said, snatching up a bucket and dashing away.

"Well, if you ain't got nothing I can help you with, I reckon I'll get on back home and get my washing done," Bertie said.

"Much obliged, Bertie. You're a good friend," Rose answered.

Bertie hugged her. "See you in the morning," she said, before walking away, toward home.

Lucy Lou was sitting on the porch when Bertie arrived. She had pulled her dress up over her knees and had her legs stretched out to catch the sun.

"Don't you reckon it would be better to do that in the back yard?" Bertie asked as she climbed up the steps.

"Sun is better here," Lucy Lou answered with a smile.

Both girls looked toward the street when they heard a voice cry out. "Howdy, ladies," Jimmy Key said from the street, lifting his hat. "Ain't it a fine afternoon?"

"Tolerable," Lucy Lou answered lazily.

"I was just wondering…" Jimmy began, before being suddenly interrupted as the tall gangly boy he'd seen Lucy Lou with before came hurrying over from across the street.

"What's your business here?" the boy demanded.

"Just passing the time of day," Jimmy said.

"Well pass it somewhere else," he said, issuing a challenge with his glare.

Jimmy nodded, first toward the boy, then toward the girls. "Afternoon," he said, strolling away.

"Ackley, quit being such a ninny. I can talk to whoever I want to," Lucy Lou shouted at the boy as he turned and walked back across the road, waving a hand at her dismissively.

"Who was that boy, Lucy Lou?" Bertie asked. "He looks familiar."

Lucy Lou shook her head. "Somebody told me his name, but I don't remember it. He was with that new boy, Charlie. Don't you remember?" Lucy Lou said. Smiling, she added, "Now that's the boy I want to come over. Just wait. I betcha he does."

Bertie blushed and turned away.

By the time the rooster crowed, Charlie and the rest of the household were already up. His mother sent John to the well to fetch a bucket of water, which she heated on the stove. When the water was hot enough, she carried it out behind the house and poured it into a washtub, which she commanded Charlie to enter. "Don't stop scrubbing until you're clean, Charlie. And if I don't think you're clean enough, I'll wash you myself!" she said sternly.

Charlie laughed, but he obeyed. Just as he thought he was completely shed of the dust and lint and grime, his mother appeared with another bucket and ordered him to lower his head. She then slowly emptied the water over Charlie's lint-filled head, as he rubbed his scalp with lye soap. After she was satisfied, she had John bring up a third bucket, which he left by the tub for Charlie to rinse with.

By the time Charlie had finished bathing, his older sisters had milked the cows and left the milk in the springhouse to cool, while his younger sisters were helping their mother cook breakfast. Charlie had taken these morning routines for granted his whole life. A week in the cotton mill had shown him how precious they were.

On any other summer day, after breakfast, once the sky had lightened enough to see, the whole family would go to the fields to work. But Sunday was different. Beyond what was absolutely necessary, Betsy allowed no work on the Lord's Day. Anything that needed doing in the tobacco fields would have to wait until Monday. Sunday was for church.

Every member of the family had one set of "Sunday clothes," reserved for wearing to church. Although not fancy or stylish, their Sunday clothes were their best and newest. Everything else was called "everyday clothes." Betsy's children all knew without having to be told that as soon as they were done with breakfast and morning chores, they were to put on their Sunday clothes and get ready to leave for church. Some days they would hitch the mule to the wagon and ride there. But on fair days, like this one, they walked.

It was a five-mile ride to Lockett's Field Primitive Baptist Church by wagon. By foot, on the path that cut through woods and across pastures, it was only half that far.

As the sun continued rising into the clear summer sky, they all set off single file along the path, carrying their shoes. In the summer, the family wore shoes only on Sunday, and only at church. On the walk there and back they carried their shoes, so as not to dirty them on the way, and because of frugality (with every wearing, their mother reminded them, the shoes were closer to being worn out). Like most of the other families who walked to the church, they would stop at the creek that ran alongside the churchyard, and there they would wash their feet before putting on their shoes.

After the service, the congregants were all milling around outside chatting when Charlie saw James approaching his mother. "Come on Betsy and I'll give you a ride home in the buggy," he said.

"Much obliged, James, but I reckon I'll walk back with the young'uns," she answered.

James nodded, then looked over at Charlie. "I heard you went to Danville to work at the mill," he said. "Looks like that didn't last long."

"I just come home for today," Charlie replied. "I'm going back tonight."

James just grunted and nodded his head. After a few seconds he crooked his neck to indicate he wanted Charlie to follow him, as he walked a few steps away. Charlie hesitated a moment, but then walked over to him, out of earshot of his mother and the others.

"Charlie," James said, "I wish you'd talk some sense into your mama. I know y'all are barely scraping by out there and I done offered her a real fair price to buy the place. She could sell it to me, get out from under the burden of it, and your whole family could move to town and do public work. The mill would hire every one of y'all in a flash."

It was the first time James had ever spoken to him as if he was not a child. Charlie looked James in the eyes but didn't answer him.

"That farm is wearing her out, Charlie, and you know as well as me that y'all can't hang on to it much longer. And even if you did, it ain't big enough to split and there's two of y'all boys. Better to take the money now and go on and start a life in town," James said.

"Daddy left the farm to Mama," Charlie answered.

"Supposedly," James replied contemptuously. "I know full well he wanted me to have our home place.

116

Ain't no way he wouldn't have left it to his oldest son."

"He left it to Mama," Charlie repeated.

"Well, somebody got him to sign a will saying that. Or else somebody signed his name to it. Either way, that don't make it right," James answered.

Charlie reddened at the accusation. "Daddy told us all the same thing he told you. With you and Ben having the Talbert place, he felt like y'all had plenty. He wanted us to have the Lawton place." It was the first time he'd ever said Ben's name without "Uncle Brother" before it.

James stepped closer and opened his mouth, but before his harsh words could escape, he caught them and swallowed them back. His face relaxed and he continued. "I don't see it that way, Charlie. It's foolish of y'all to try to hold onto that farm. You're the man of the house now. You think about what I said. Think about how every one of y'all could be drawing pay every single week instead of your mama worrying and working herself to an early grave. I know you're trying to help your family make it. Just think about how much better it would be for them in a house in town."

Charlie stared back at James but didn't answer him.

After a moment James smiled, a smile that Charlie recognized as patronizing and arrogant, not friendly.

James reached up and patted his hand on Charlie's shoulder. "Come over and see us sometimes, boy," he said, before turning and walking away.

Charlie was burning with anger when his mother walked up to him. "What did he want?" she asked.

Charlie beat back his rage, then answered, "Same as always. Nothing but our farm."

"Seems like he don't want to take 'no' for an answer," she said.

Charlie shook his head. "Why does he want our place so bad? He's already got more than he knows what to do with."

Betsy shrugged and let out a little snort. "Why does anybody want more than they need?" she asked. "I reckon it's just the way some folks are."

The Sunday dinner that the family set down to after church was much like every other Sunday dinner in Charlie's life. But after a week of dietary privation, it seemed to him a magnificent feast. He ate ravenously, to his mother's delight.

Charlie was heaping a second pile of mashed potatoes onto his plate when his brother asked him about girls. "So, Charlie," John said, "are there any pretty girls at the mill?"

Charlie saw his mother fire a stern glance at John while his younger sisters giggled.

"Some," Charlie answered.

"Some?" John responded, pressing the subject jokingly. "Some a few, or some a lot?"

"Just some," Charlie said, continuing to focus on his food.

"Well," Betsy said, pushing her plate away. Charlie braced himself for what he knew was coming next.

"You best be on your guard against them mill girls, son. Don't let them fool you. They'll come around acting all friendly and nice and 'fore you know you it one of them will have done tricked you into having to marry her," Betsy said, with authority.

"How do they trick 'em into getting married, Mama?" eleven-year-old Jillianne asked innocently, triggering giggles from her sisters.

"They got their ways!" Betsy said, her voice rising.

"How do you know that Mama?" Charlie asked,

immediately regretting it.

"I've heard plenty, believe you me!" she answered, in a shout, her face flushed. "And mamas just know these kinds of things." She lifted her hand and pointed a thin finger at Charlie. "You best be careful, Charles Nathaniel Lawton! Them girls that you think is pretty are like snakes in the grass aiming to bite you on the ankle. Don't be alone with none of them. Never, never, never!"

When their mother's tirade ended, the children were all staring down at their plates, avoiding her glare. An awkward silence descended over the room, broken a few seconds later when Betsy added, "And don't never let a drop of liquor pass your lips!"

Charlie nodded and he and his siblings cautiously resumed their meals.

As the day went on, Charlie felt a sadness settling over him. He knew he had to be on the 4 o'clock train back to Danville, and he didn't want to go. He felt time rushing by, even as he was wishing for it to slow down. His mother was carrying dishes to the dish pan when Charlie came up from behind, hugged her and kissed the top of her head.

"I've got to be on the Number Eleven, Mama," he said.

Betsy nodded and turned to face him. "Seems like you just got here, son. I'm going to pray that the week goes by as fast as your time home did." She took Charlie's face between her hands and kissed him on the forehead. "You be careful, son. And be good."

"Yes, ma'am," he answered with a smile.

"Now here," his mother said, taking up a cloth satchel from behind the stove. "There's some biscuits and some chicken in here. Don't eat it all on the train."

Charlie laughed, took the satchel, and kissed his mother again. "Yes, ma'am," he said.

John stuck his head through the door and said, "I've hitched up the wagon. Come on and I'll give you a ride."

"I don't mind walking," Charlie answered.

"Might as well ride instead," John said. "Come on and let's go."

Charlie stepped out onto the porch, where his other siblings were waiting for him. After giving them all hugs, he climbed up into the wagon. John shook the reins and the mule stepped off.

After riding silently for a while John said, "So what about the girls, Charlie? Are there lots of pretty ones there or not?"

"I've seen some pretty ones," Charlie answered. "Funny thing about the girls there—well, the men too—is that they all look like they ain't never been outside. And it seems like the workers is always covered in lint. Reckon that's why folks call them lintheads."

"What you mean 'them.' You're one too now," John said with a chuckle.

"Yeah, I reckon I am," Charlie said.

"But there ain't no girls where I work and there ain't no time for courting. The folks that work there are all friendly and nice, though. I was glad about that. When somebody needs help, they step up and help him," Charlie said. "That reminds me. You ain't got a dollar, do you?"

John laughed. "A dollar? What's that?"

"Yeah," Charlie said, laughing with him. "I figured that. I meant to ask Mama, but she probably ain't got one neither. A fella at work loaned me the money for my train fare and I wanted to pay him back. Reckon I'll have to wait till I'm paid."

After another long stretch of silence, John spoke again. "Are we going to make it, Charlie?"

Charlie knew what he meant. It was a question that gnawed at him continually.

"It's all riding on this year's crop," he said.

"Tobacco is going sky high because of the war," John said quickly. "We ought to make enough this year to pay off Mr. Lockett and cover next year's guano too."

"A lot can happen between now and sale time," Charlie replied.

"Everything is looking good," John said, sounding cheerful. "A good crop this year can get us out of the hole for good."

"And a poor crop will sink us for good," Charlie answered.

John fell silent, affirming the truth of Charlie's comment. After a few minutes, he spoke, "So all we need is a summer with no hail, no floods, no drought, no tobacco worms, no mosaic, no barn fires, and for us and the mule to stay healthy. Then it will all be fine. Oh, and for Mr. Lockett to keep giving us credit at the store."

"Fear not, my brother," Charlie said. "I'm steadily working at the mill and once they've got a free month out of me then I'll have close to a dollar a day coming in. We'll be living like Rockefellers then."

They laughed as the mule pulled them along indifferently.

"We got the best news this morning, Bertie," Rose said with a smile as she and Bertie walked into the spinning room, to begin another work week.

"Let me tell her! Let me tell her, Mama. Please!" Gem said, hopping with energy.

Rose smiled broadly at her son. "All right, Gem. You can tell her. But tell her quick, 'cause you need to go start setting up the spindles."

Gem turned to Bertie, his face beaming. "They called Daddy back to work! Starting next Monday!"

Bertie threw her hand to her mouth and let out a little squeal. She impulsively grabbed Rose and hugged her tightly. "Oh, Rose, I am so happy to hear that. Wonderful! I'll bet Samuel is just as happy as can be."

"Oh, he is!" Rose said. She turned to Gem and said, "Now go on and start getting the machines set up." The boy hurried away. Like the young children of many of the spinners, Gem helped his mother tend her spindles.

Turning back to Bertie, Rose continued, "He went to the gate this morning like he's been doing every Monday since he got hurt. This time Mr. Webb told him to come back next Monday and he'll put him back on. Oh Bertie, it is such a blessing. I just feel like everything is going to start going our way now."

With tears in her eyes, Bertie hugged Rose again. "Y'all have been through so much, Rose. This is just the very best news I've heard in a long time."

As the machines began to hum back to life, Rose exclaimed, "Oh goodness, honey. We best get ready!"

The women hurriedly stuffed cotton balls in their ears. Both reached into their dress pockets and pulled out cans of snuff, along with the little crushed twigs they called toothbrushes. They quickly coated their bottom gums with tobacco, then rushed over to their row of machines.

The spinning room was stiflingly hot in the summer, and the summer was young enough that the spinners hadn't yet fully acclimated to it. So, by the time their ten-hour workday was done, Bertie and Rose were exhausted and drained, lint and cotton dust clinging to their sweat-drenched faces and clothes. Crowding through the mill gate with dozens of other girls, they coughed lint and dust into their handkerchiefs. When they stepped through the door, the stagnant humid air outside felt cool and refreshing by comparison to what they'd been breathing all day.

"Thank goodness this long day is finally over," Bertie said, after spitting out the lint in her mouth. "I'm going to go straight to the pump and get a bucket of water to pour over my poor nasty head."

"That sounds like a good idea to me," Rose said as she brushed lint off her shoulders. "But I think I'm going to go down the store and use up some mill money to make us a good supper tonight, to celebrate Fuller getting his job back."

Bertie smiled. Every now and then Rose called her

husband "Fuller." She had always considered it an odd pet name, but she never had the courage to ask Rose about it.

In her excitement, it seemed Rose couldn't stop chattering about how she expected their lives to improve now that Samuel had his job back.

"As soon as we can, before the cold weather for sure, I'm going to buy new shoes for the young'us. And I'm going to have milk for them every morning now. And butter too! And oh, Bertie, I'm just so happy for Samuel. He's been so blue. You know how much he hates being out of work. I just know he's going to be his old self again now."

His mother's enthusiasm was infectious, and Gem, trailing them and leading his sister by the hand, was bouncing with joy, both at the thought of his father's happiness and at the prospect of better fare on the table.

When they reached Rose's house Bertie declined her polite invitation to join them for supper and continued on toward home. When she drew close, she saw Lucy Lou standing in the road out front, talking to a boy. Coming closer she saw who it was. Charlie Lawton. The new boy.

Impulsively, Bertie stamped her foot. "Don't she have enough boyfriends already?" she muttered.

Then suddenly she noticed Ackley coming up quickly from behind her, with an angry scowl on his face. He tossed away his cigarette and charged at Charlie like a mad bull, rushing up to him and shoving him angrily with both hands. Bertie gasped, her eyes widened.

9

While filing out through the mill gate Charlie heard someone mention that one of the carders had been badly hurt on the job that day. Worried that it might have been Ricky Gresham, instead of going straight home from work, as he normally did, he decided to first go check on Ricky, who lived on the other end of Floyd Street. As he was walking down the road, he heard a girl's voice call out.

"Why if it ain't Charlie Lawton! What you looking for, Charlie?"

Charlie turned toward the voice, to see a smiling tall girl approaching him. After a moment he recognized her as the big-dimpled girl he and Jimmy had seen a week earlier.

"My name is Lucy Lou," the girl said buoyantly as she drew closer. "And you're that new boy Charlie from the country, ain't you?"

Charlie stopped walking. "Yes. My name is Charlie," he said.

"Well hey, Charlie," Lucy Lou said flirtatiously. "It's about time you came around to visit your neighbors."

"Umm," Charlie stammered. "I'm just on my way down the road to see about a friend of mine."

"Well there ain't no need to rush off," Lucy Lou said. "Come on up and sit on the porch awhile," she added as she reached out and took Charlie by the arm.

At that moment Charlie suddenly felt himself reeling, nearly knocked off his feet. He stumbled backwards, barely catching his balance. Glancing up quickly to see what had happened, he found himself staring into a young man's enraged face.

"That's my girl you're messing with!" Ackley shouted.

Charlie straightened himself. "What? I ain't messing with nobody. Who are you and why did you push me like that?"

"You're fixing to get a lot worse than a push," Ackley said, raising a balled fist. "How about I give you a knuckle sandwich?"

Charlie felt his temper rising. "How about you go jump in a lake instead?"

When Ackley drew back his right arm, preparing to throw a punch, Charlie dropped his head and plowed his shoulder into Ackley's chest, driving him to the ground. Ackley crashed into the hard dirt road with a thud and a groan, Charlie's full weight coming down on top of him and pushing the air from his lungs. Charlie stood up, leaving Ackley sprawled on the road, gasping for air while Lucy Lou looked on, her eyes wide with delight.

After a few seconds Charlie stepped toward the boy on the ground. "Are you all right?" he asked.

Ackley, who seemed to have caught his breath, nodded. Charlie reached down his hand, to help the other boy up. As he did, Ackley drew back his leg and launched a savage kick into Charlie's groin, sending him staggering. Ackley then sprung up, stepped toward

Charlie and swung at his face. Charlie dodged the punch enough to avoid its full force, but not enough to prevent it from grazing his cheek and opening a cut.

Charlie had been wrangling calves, mules, hogs, and plows since he was old enough to walk, and he was a seasoned veteran of innumerable after-church wrestling and boxing matches. This boy wasn't throwing anything at him he hadn't seen before. As Ackley's fist slid off his cheek, Charlie stepped forward and delivered a right uppercut that crashed into Ackley's chin, snapping back his neck, and sending him reeling. A split-second later Charlie's left fist slammed into Ackley's ear, sending him crashing down like falling timber.

Charlie stared down at the fallen boy for a moment, as a murmur passed through the crowd of onlookers who had surrounded them. Once Charlie was certain that the fight was over, he turned away in disgust, muttered "Excuse me, y'all" and begin pushing his way through. Feeling something trickling down his face he reached up and touched his cheek, drawing back his hand to see the blood. At that moment, a hand reached out with a handkerchief. "Obliged," Charlie said, taking the handkerchief and pressing it to his cheek. Looking up to see who had handed it to him, to his surprise he saw a bashful face looking back at him. It was the little dark-eyed girl.

10

For Bertie, the whole fight had raced by in a blur. She had seen Ackley rushing at Charlie, then felt herself being jostled as people on the road crowded forward to see. By the time she'd found a clear line of sight, it was over. Ackley was sprawled out on the ground and Charlie was walking away with blood dripping down his cheek. Impulsively she had reached into her pocket for a handkerchief, pushing it toward Charlie as he walked by. "Obliged," he said absently as he took it, without seeming to notice her. Then he stopped suddenly, turned his head and looked her in the eyes. She saw his face flash recognition, then embarrassment.

"Here," he said, handing back the handkerchief. "I don't want to ruin it."

Bertie blushed. "It's just a mill discard. You can't hurt it and there's plenty more."

"No shortage of cotton around here, I reckon," he answered, pressing the cloth against his cheek.

With the road still crowded with people arriving to see the fight and with onlookers pressing forward to get a look at Charlie, Bertie hadn't been able to hear what he said.

"Sorry, but I didn't hear you," she said, raising her voice.

Charlie nodded and motioned with his head for her to follow him. They moved quickly down the road, separating themselves from the crowd. Once they were clear, Charlie stepped off the road into the yard of one of the mill houses and Bertie followed him.

"I said thank you and I'll get you another handkerchief," he said.

"That's all right. You don't need to bother," Bertie answered, carefully avoiding making eye contact.

"I'm sorry about that back there," he said, tossing his head in the direction of the fight. "I don't know who that was or why he came after me like that."

"Oh, his name is Ackley Waller. He's Lucy Lou's boyfriend, I reckon, and he's powerful jealous," Bertie said, eyes downcast.

"Who's Lucy Lou?" Charlie asked, still holding the handkerchief to his cheek.

"That girl you were talking to," Bertie answered.

"I don't know her neither," Charlie said. "I reckon he must have thought I was someone else."

"He's a hothead," Bertie answered. "And I think Lucy Lou likes to egg him on." She instantly regretted adding that.

"Well, hopefully it won't get neither one of us fired," Charlie said.

Bertie shook her head. "The mill don't care about that. Long as y'all are at work on time."

Charlie smiled and reached out his left hand. "I'm Charlie," he said.

Bertie took his hand, shook it quickly and cautiously, then released it. "I'm Bertie," she said. "Bertie Bovry."

"Nice to meet you, Bertie," Charlie answered. "Thanks for being nice to me," he added with a chuckle. "Busted cheek and all."

Bertie looked down at her feet, blushing. "Well, I reckon I best be getting home," she said.

"I'm going that way. Can I walk with you?" Charlie asked. The words had sprung from him seemingly involuntarily. A few moments of awkward silence followed, before Charlie spoke again. "Oh, wait," he said. "Maybe that ain't such a good idea. Have you got a crazy boyfriend too?"

Bertie looked up quickly and defensively, intending to tell him no. But when she saw the twinkle in Charlie's eyes, she saw that had been joking. She giggled, which caused Charlie to laugh out loud. In moments they were both laughing heartily.

To Bertie the short walk back to her house seemed like one of the most thrilling moments of her life. Painfully shy, she couldn't bring herself to look at Charlie while they walked, and she was unable to take up any of his attempts to start a conversation. When they reached her house, Bertie finally found the courage to look up briefly. "Thank you for walking me home, Charlie," she said with a fleeting and timid smile, before dashing into the house.

Hidden behind a window, Bertie watched as Charlie strolled away, whistling. Once he was safely out of sight, she rushed back outside and toward her secret place. She was dying to tell Susannah what had happened.

11

The next day after work Charlie stopped at his house, washed his face, dusted off his clothes, then rushed over to Bertie's. As he approached, he saw Lucy Lou sitting on the front porch.

"I figured you'd be back today," she said with a smile.

Charlie took another couple of steps, then stopped and was about to answer her when Lucy Lou continued.

"Poor old Ackley. He done run off and joined the army. He's been saying he was going to do that, but I think you might have made up his mind for him," she said, still smiling.

Charlie shuffled his feet nervously, then awkwardly pulled his hat from his head. "What I come over to ask was…"

Lucy Lou interrupted him. "You can come on up here and sit on the porch awhile if you want to."

While Charlie was stammering for words, Bertie was watching from inside the house, behind a window, bathed in disappointment (at Charlie) and anger (at Lucy Lou). She stuck out her tongue at Lucy Lou and stamped her foot. As she turned to walk away, she heard Charlie speak, and her heart jumped.

"I come to see if Bertie is home," he said.

"Bertie?" Lucy Lou said with surprise. Then a sly look spread across her face. "Well, yes, I'm sure she is. Let me get her for you," Lucy Lou said as she stood and walked to the door, confident that Charlie had been too shy to reveal his true reason for the visit.

"Bertie!" she shouted after opening the door. "We have company!"

Suddenly Bertie became uncomfortably aware of her appearance. Still grimy and lint-covered from a long day in the spinning room, she hesitated. Then the thought of leaving Lucy Lou alone with Charlie supplied her with a jolt of boldness and she walked out onto the porch.

"Look, Bertie. Charlie has done come to see us," Lucy Lou said teasingly. "Now that he's done run off poor Ackley," she added, smiling impishly.

Charlie ignored her, keeping his eyes on Bertie, who glanced up, then dropped her gaze after their eyes met briefly.

"Hey, Bertie," Charlie said.

"Hey," she answered quietly.

"Umm, I was wondering if you might want to go for a walk. Maybe just up to the church and back," Charlie said.

Bertie's head was swimming, her bashfulness and low self-esteem conflicting with her powerful desire to rush out and take Charlie by the hand. "Well, I, umm…" she stammered, looking down at her feet.

Lucy Lou stepped toward Charlie. "I'll go walking with you, since Bertie don't want to," she said with a smile.

"I *do* want to," Bertie said defiantly, shooting a

glance at Lucy Lou and feeling a surge of courage. Turning to Charlie, she said, "All right, Charlie. I'll go walking with you."

Charlie smiled as Bertie descended the porch steps.

"I'll come too," Lucy Lou said, following her.

Bertie felt a flash of anger, but before she could speak, Charlie looked at Lucy Lou and said, "I'd rather just walk with Bertie. There's something I need to talk to her about."

Dumbfounded, Lucy Lou froze in her tracks. Watching as Bertie and Charlie strolled away, she struggled to make sense of what happened. After a few moments she smiled knowingly. I know why he did that, she thought. He's just trying to make me jealous. Reassured and with her ego assuaged, Lucy Lou returned confidently to her chair on the porch, and resumed judging the people who passed by on the street.

"What do you need to talk to me about?" Bertie asked, once they were out of earshot.

"Huh?" Charlie replied. Then, a moment later, he laughed. "Oh, nothing particular. I just didn't want your friend coming along. Is that all right? Do you mind?"

Bertie shook her head quickly. "Oh, no. I didn't want her coming neither," she said, then blushing deeply as she realized how that sounded.

"But I did want to thank you again for being nice to me when my cheek was bleeding. I ain't got a new handkerchief for you yet, but I *am* going to get you one," Charlie said.

Bertie, still blushing and looking down, didn't answer.

"Did that other boy really join the army?" Charlie

asked.

"I don't know," Bertie said. "But that's what I heard."

"I reckon the army might get all of us before the war's over," Charlie said. "I ain't planning to go though, unless they make me. I don't see how it's our fight."

"They say don't no millworkers have to go in the army on account of us making blankets and uniforms and such," Bertie answered.

"That's what they're saying now. I 'spect they'll be singing a different tune once they start running low on soldiers," Charlie said. "I ain't old enough to be drafted yet. But I'll be 21 in January, so my time is probably coming."

"So, you're 20?" Bertie asked.

"Yep. I'm a 20-year-old bale buster," he said with a laugh. "How 'bout you, Bertie? How old are you?"

"Seventeen," she answered. "I'm a 17-year-old spinner," she added with a sigh.

"Do you like working in the spinning room?" Charlie asked.

"Compared to what?" Bertie answered. "I ain't never done nothing else. I been working there since I was nine."

"Goodness. I didn't know spinners started that young," Charlie said.

"You're supposed to be ten, but they ain't got no way of knowing," she said.

"This ain't but my second week. I reckon I'm an old man next to a lot of the boys here," Charlie said.

Reaching the end of the street, they crossed over and began walking back.

"How'd you learn to read and write if you been here

so long?" Charlie asked.

Bertie looked up at him, inquisitively. "Who told you I can read and write?" she asked.

"Oh, a fellow hears things," Charlie answered with a smile.

"I can read and write a little," Bertie said. "My daddy taught me."

"Is your daddy a teacher?" Charlie asked.

Bertie fell silent and Charlie sensed her discomfort. He regretted his question.

"No. My daddy passed when I won't but five," Bertie said. "My mama passed before that. I ain't got no family left."

Charlie stopped walking. Resisting the temptation to take her hand, he paused until Bertie looked him in the face. "I'm real sorry, Bertie. I didn't know."

She turned away and continued walking. Charlie followed and caught up.

"That's all right," she said. "I've got good friends here."

They walked silently until, a few moments later, they had reached Bertie's house. She stopped, turned to Charlie with a timorous smile and said, "I liked walking with you, Charlie. I'll see you later."

"All right," he answered. "Thanks, Bertie," he said as they both turned and walked away from each other.

Lucy Lou's eyes were shining in anticipation as Bertie climbed the steps to the porch. "Well, what did he say about me?" she asked eagerly.

Bertie just rolled her eyes and walked through the door.

12

Bertie went walking with Charlie every evening that week. At first, whenever Charlie came by Lucy Lou flirted with him, then peppered Bertie with questions when she returned. But after a few days she lost interest, having directed her attention to a new boy who had just started working in the weave room.

With each walk, Bertie's shyness diminished, and she became more comfortable and open. But her low self-esteem remained. Bertie had come to believe that there was nothing about her that a boy would find attractive or desirable, and even Charlie's seemingly sincere attentions weren't enough to rid her of that belief. She could accept that Charlie was kind and that he was lonely, but not that his interest was or ever would be romantic, even as her heart swelled at the thought of him, and even as she began to think of little else.

They chatted when they walked. Charlie did most of the talking and the subjects were light—the events of the workday, the weather, community news and gossip. Charlie didn't ask Bertie anything else about her life or family, and she was too shy and nervous to inquire about his, even though she ached to know more about him.

On Friday evening Charlie came by as usual. As they were walking, Bertie was having trouble concentrating on what Charlie was saying. She had been screwing up her courage all day to ask him something, but now that she had the opportunity, she couldn't bring herself to do it—held back by bashfulness and fear of rejection. As she was struggling to find the strength to speak, she realized Charlie was asking her a question.

"Well, can I, Bertie?" he said, smiling sweetly at her.

"I'm sorry. What?" she answered, confused.

"I said, can I hold your hand? Would that be all right?"

Bertie flushed, her heart pounding against her chest. She wrung her hands together and looked away. "Umm, well…," she stammered.

"It's all right," Charlie said, turning away and trying to conceal his hurt. "I understand. Anyway, like I was saying," he continued, "I told them that I reckoned I ought to be able to do something else than just break bales and that I figured I could…"

Bertie interrupted him suddenly. "Do you want to come to church with me on Sunday?" she blurted out.

"Do what?" Charlie said, having been caught by surprise in mid-sentence.

As soon as her words had escaped her mouth Bertie had regretted them. "Nothing. I'm sorry," she said, her eyes filling with tears.

"Did you ask me to go to church with you?" Charlie said, trying in vain to make eye contact.

Bertie nodded, then said, "Never mind, Charlie. I don't know what made me think you might want to do that. I just thought maybe you didn't have nowhere to go on Sunday…"

Charlie interrupted her. "I would love to go with you, Bertie, and it makes me happy that you asked, but I go back home on Saturday nights and don't come back until Sunday night. I go to church with my family back in Raye."

"Oh, all right," Bertie said, trying to clear her eyes.

"I catch the Number Eight on the R&D. I don't get home till late, but I like seeing my mama and my brother and sisters every Sunday. And I like being back on the farm too," he said.

"What is your farm like?" Bertie asked cautiously.

"Well," Charlie laughed, "I never thought much of it until I started working in the mill. Now I see how pretty it is."

"Do y'all raise tobacco?" Bertie asked.

"Yep. And corn, of course," Charlie answered.

Her heart racing, Bertie turned toward him. "Do you have a garden? And a milk cow?"

"Sure do. And hogs and chickens," Charlie said with a laugh.

"How many brothers and sisters do you have?" Bertie asked.

"Five sisters and one brother," Charlie said. "I'm the oldest boy."

"Why did you come to the mill?" Bertie asked.

"To earn money, of course," Charlie said. He laughed, but then added somberly, "We need some extra money, and my brother is able to do most of the men's work now, so I come here to help them out."

"So, nobody made you come?" Bertie asked.

"Made me? Naw. I'd rather be back on the farm, but this is where my family needs me to be. So, I reckon I'm here 'cause I want to be," Charlie said.

Bertie sighed, looking off into the distance, her

mind wandering through the dark caverns of her past. After they had walked silently for a while, she reached over and took Charlie's hand.

13

As Charlie was boarding the train that would take him home, Bertie was sitting cross-legged on the sand, in her secret place, facing Susannah.

"He lives on a great big farm Susannah, with a big family and they all love each other very much. His mama is sweet and kind and so are his brother and sisters. They got a milk cow and a big flock of chickens in the yard. It just sounds like heaven to me, don't it to you?"

Tears were streaming down Bertie's face as she continued.

"And guess what, Susannah? Charlie don't think I'm ugly! Or if he does, then he don't mind. He treats me just as nice as he does Lucy Lou. Even nicer! You know what, Susannah? You ain't gonna believe it. Yesterday... Yesterday he asked me if he could hold my hand!"

Bertie stared quietly at Susannah for a few moments.

"Yes, I sure did. But let me tell you, I was just about scared to death. And you ought to have seen the look on Lucy Lou's face when I come walking up to the house holding Charlie's hand. Girl, she liked to died!"

Bertie laughed and wiped her eyes. She sat silently for a few minutes, gazing out across the river, before turning back to Susannah.

"What am I supposed to do now?"

A long silence followed, and another tear slid down Bertie's cheek and dropped onto the sand.

"You know what I'm most scared of? I'm scared that I like Charlie a lot more than he likes me. See, I can't help thinking about him all day long. I cry myself to sleep at night thinking about him. Susannah, I even dream about him. And there ain't no way he thinks about me that much. I know he's been coming to see me every day, but he's probably just passing the time till he can get home to his family and his farm. I bet he don't think about me for one solitary second once he's gone."

14

Staring out the window as the train rolled across the countryside, all Charlie could think about was Bertie. Just two weeks earlier he had dreaded the thought of having to return to Danville on Sunday. Now it seemed he couldn't wait to be back to Bertie again. He chuckled quietly as he stared out the window, thinking about how his mother would scold him if she knew he was seeing a girl. But what's the harm in it, he wondered. I enjoy her company. And it's not like we're getting married or anything.

The train rolled to a stop at the Raye station and Charlie stepped out into the night. "See you tomorrow," he said to Ricky as his friend started off toward home.

Glancing around, Charlie saw that John wasn't there. Dropping down on a bench to wait, he closed his eyes and drew in deep lung-filling breaths of the cool clean country air. He felt himself drifting off to sleep when he suddenly stood up and shook his head vigorously, shaking away the sleep. Maybe John isn't coming, he thought. He looked around one last time, then started the long walk home.

After walking about a mile, Charlie saw John in the

distance, riding up on the mule. "Hey, Charlie!" he shouted, and Charlie raised his hand in response. As John drew nearer, he shouted, "Did you think I forgot you?"

"Figured you must have been too busy," Charlie answered as John pulled him up onto the mule's back.

"Well you figured right, brother," John answered. "It's been a hard week, let me tell you."

"Everything all right?" Charlie asked.

"Same as usual, I reckon. Stuff broke down. Cow sick. Can't keep the weeds out of the tobacco. No rain. You know how it goes. Can't hardly keep up this time of year," John said, as he kicked the mule in the side and shook the reins.

"Well if you get too busy, just let me walk home. Won't hurt me none," Charlie said.

"Might have to do that sometime, but I'll come get you when I can," John answered.

They rode the rest of the way home in silence. Once again, as they neared the house his mother stepped out onto the porch holding a candle. And once again, she fed him and berated him for being so dirty.

The next day after church Charlie was relaxing on the front porch when Ely Lockett pulled up in his buggy.

"Howdy, Charlie," he said.

"Howdy, Mr. Lockett," Charlie answered.

"Want to go for a little ride?" Lockett asked.

"Thanks, but I reckon I'll just rest here on the porch. I got to get to the station soon," Charlie answered, puzzled.

Lockett glanced around then nodded, signaling that he wanted Charlie to approach. Understanding him, Charlie got up and walked over to the buggy.

"Get in and ride with me a minute, Charlie," Lockett said quietly. "There's something I need to talk to you about."

Charlie nodded and climbed into the buggy. Lockett made a clicking sound and his mare pulled them away.

After they'd gone about a hundred yards, Lockett spoke. "Y'all have a pretty big balance on your account now."

Charlie felt his stomach drop. The family had had to carry over a balance at Lockett's store the past two years and the interest was causing it to mushroom.

"We'll get it paid up in full after we sell this year's crop, Mr. Lockett," Charlie said.

"I hope so, son. That would be good," Lockett said, looking off into the distance.

They rode quietly for a while longer then Lockett spoke again. "James came to see me about buying y'all's note."

Charlie didn't understand. "Buying our note? What do you mean?"

"I mean he asked me about paying off y'all's account and taking the note," Lockett answered.

Charlie shook his head. "James wants to pay off our account? That don't sound like him."

"He wants the note, Charlie," Lockett replied.

"The note?" Charlie answered, confused.

"He wants to own the debt. That's why he wants to pay me off," Lockett said.

Charlie still didn't understand the meaning of it. "Why?" he asked innocently.

Lockett stopped the buggy and turned to face Charlie.

"James is a good customer. I don't want none of this to get back to him," Lockett said sternly.

"Yes, sir," Charlie replied.

"Don't you see what I'm saying, Charlie? James wants to own the note so he can enforce it. He can call it due and if you don't pay it, he can take your farm," Lockett said.

Charlie's head swam as he took it in.

"Now James didn't tell me that, mind you. But I've known him all my life and I know durn well he don't want to pay your account out of Christian kindness," Lockett said.

"He's been pushing Mama to sell him the farm," Charlie said vacantly. "He thinks it ought to belong to him."

"That's what I figured," Lockett said, with a scowl.

"Mr. Lockett, we aim to pay you off in full this year. We've got a good crop coming and if we can just…"

Lockett interrupted him. "I told James I didn't want to sell the note just yet. I let on that maybe I wanted to foreclose it myself. I told him I'd think more about it."

"If we could just have till this year's crop is sold…" Charlie began, pleading.

Lockett held up his hand, stopping him. "I ain't going to sell your note to James. Not now, at least. I just wanted you to know about it."

Charlie nodded. "We're much obliged, Mr. Lockett."

"But look here Charlie, y'all *have* to pay it off this year. I know you've gone and took a job at the mill, but if you want my opinion your first priority needs to be getting this crop in."

"We're going to get it in, Mr. Lockett," Charlie answered, his stomach twisted in knots. "You ain't got to worry about that."

Lockett laughed. "Oh yes I do." A serious look

swept over his face. "I've been working with y'all a long time, Charlie. Me and your daddy go way back. But I've got bills to pay too. I'm going to be brutally honest with you now. If you don't make a good crop this year, y'all are going to lose your farm."

Charlie nodded, staring at his feet.

Lockett clicked to start the mare, turning her around in a cut out beside the road. As they rolled back toward the house Lockett said, "I'm asking you to keep this talk between ourselves."

"Yes, sir," Charlie answered.

15

"Oh Bertie, I am just so worried about Samuel," Rose said, with moist eyes, as she and her friend sat on the porch, watching children playing in the street. "The good Lord knows we can't make it without him working, but I am so scared that he's going to get hurt again that I can't hardly even think straight."

Bertie reached over and took her hand. "He's a strong man, Rose. It's going to be all right."

Rose sniffled, then turned to Bertie and spoke quietly. "It ain't just his arm I'm worried about." After a pause she continued. "Have you noticed his cough?"

Bertie had noticed, even as she had pretended not to. "I've seen him coughing once or twice. Figured he must have a little cold."

"Oh Bertie, I hope and pray that's all it is. But what if it's…" She hesitated, her voice cracking and her eyes filling with tears. "What if it's consumption?"

The word sent a chill through Bertie. Consumption, what she would later know to call tuberculosis, was a mill worker scourge. Bertie had seen it take the lives of many of them over the years.

"Don't seem like a consumption cough to me, Rose," Bertie offered, although unconvinced.

Rose quickly wiped away a tear. "Pray for us, Bertie. We'll starve if Samuel don't go back to work and we'll starve if work kills him. I won't be able to make it without him."

Bertie wrapped her friend in a hug and said, "Now Rose, ain't nobody gonna starve. Y'all are all going to be fine. I ain't never met a better man than your Samuel and I just know that he'll be as healthy as a horse and the top producing weaver in the mill again in no time."

As Bertie released Rose from the hug, they both gazed back into the street. Three young men were sitting on the porch directly across the road from them, playing a fiddle, a banjo, and a guitar. A swarm of children were in the street, dancing and laughing. And right in the middle of all of them stood Samuel, with Purl perched on his shoulders. He was laughing and flatfooting, while holding onto his daughter, who was squealing with delight. Little Gem stood beside them, clapping his hands, beaming, and looking up at his father with joyous admiration.

Rose straightened up, cleared her throat, wiped her eyes and said, "I know I ought not worry so much. I just have to keep my trust in the Lord to look after us." She paused then added, "Please don't let on to Samuel that I said anything about his cough. He's right touchy about it."

Bertie took Rose's hand, squeezed it, and nodded.

16

Charlie joined the mob of men pushing toward the door, feeling relieved to have finished another work week, when he heard his supervisor call out, "Hold on, Charlie. I need to talk to you." He stopped, turned toward the voice, and saw his supervisor approaching with another man, whose tie identified him as another boss man.

"Decided to pay me for this week's work, Mr. Elrod?" Charlie asked, frustration in his voice. Elrod ignored the question.

"Charlie, this here is Mr. Webb. He needs a hard worker to put in the weave room and I recommended you," Elrod said.

Charlie nodded. "All right," he said.

"I need a man to start in the weave room on Monday morning. You want the job?" Webb asked.

It was just the opportunity Charlie had been hoping for. Had this happened at the beginning of the week he would have responded differently. But it was Saturday, he was eager to get home, and he'd just put in a long hard week for which he would be paid nothing—a fact that had been eating at him all day.

"Will I have to put in four weeks of training time?"

he asked, betraying no emotion.

"Yes. But once you're done with training, you'll make a lot more than you're making now," Webb answered.

Charlie wiped the sweat off his forehead and looked directly at Webb. "But I ain't making *nothing* now. I just finished my third week here, and I ain't been paid a dime yet."

"Them's the rules, boy," Elrod said. "You knew 'em when you took the job."

Charlie ignored him, keeping his gaze locked on Webb.

"Mr. Elrod says you're a good worker, and I need somebody right now," Webb said. "Are you a quick learner?"

Charlie nodded. "Yes, sir," he said.

"Well," Webb continued, "considering the circumstances, I'll cut the weave-room training time in half. You can start drawing your pay after you finish two weeks."

Charlie decided to gamble. "Cut my bale breaking training time in half too, and it's a deal," he said.

"What?!" Elrod interjected. "Sorry about this, Webb. I got another man you can take instead."

Still looking directly at Webb, Charlie said, "I've put in three solid weeks here, without pay, and I had to borrow the money for train fare home. I'll work as hard as any weaver in this mill, Mr. Webb, and you won't be sorry you hired me. But it ain't right to work a man for a full month for nothing. Let me draw pay for this week of busting, so I can pay back what I owe and take a little bit home to my family. Then you can start me weaving Monday morning and I'll be glad to put in my two weeks training time there."

"Look here, you ungrateful hick," Elrod said, angry at being embarrassed before another supervisor. "Don't bother showing up here Monday morning. I don't need your kind of attitude…"

Webb, who had never broken eye contact with Charlie, interrupted Elrod. "It's five dollars a week for breaking bales, right?"

"Yes, sir," Charlie answered.

"All right," Webb said. Turning to Elrod he said, "Pay this man five dollars today. I'll get bookkeeping to debit our department for it."

Elrod began to protest, but Webb just stuck out his hand toward Charlie, who shook it firmly. "I'll see you first thing Monday morning, Charlie." With a faint smile he added, "And I'll make sure I get that five dollars' worth out of you too."

Charlie nodded, then released Webb's hand, walked over, and took a place in the pay line. As he shuffled toward the front of the line, he could hear Webb complaining to Elrod about injured workers, War Department contracts, and labor shortages.

When the man in front of him drew his pay and walked away, Charlie stepped up to the pay table.

"Lawton, I done told you before that…" the man with the ledger began, stopping as Elrod bent down and whispered something in his ear. The man looked up at Elrod, seemingly confused, and Elrod responded with a stern stare, pointing his finger at the ledger.

"All right, Lawton," the man said, making a notation in the ledger. He turned to the man with the cash box. "Five dollars," he said. He looked back up at Charlie and said, "Move on."

Charlie stepped to the side as the other man counted out five dollars and handed it to him, feeling a little thrill as he took the money. It was the most money he had ever held in his hand at one time.

As he stepped away from the table, Charlie noticed Press Dinwiddie in the crowd of men pushing toward the door.

"Hey, Press! Hold on!" he hollered, holding a dollar up above his head as he hurried toward him.

17

Seeing Bertie passing by in the street, Rose called out to her from the porch. "Hey Bertie! You just gonna stroll right by without stopping to visit?"

Bertie turned and faced her. "What's that Rose? Sorry but I didn't hear you good."

Rose smiled. She had noticed how distracted Bertie had seemed lately and she had heard rumors of why.

With a laugh, she replied, "I *said* how come you don't stop and say hey to your friends no more?"

A look of concern flashed over Bertie's face and she hurried over to the porch. "Oh, I'm sorry, Rose. I didn't mean nothing by it. I reckon my mind was just somewheres else."

"Yes'm, seems like it was. Looks to me like your mind has been somewheres else all this week," Rose answered with a friendly smile.

Bertie sat down on the porch step next to Rose, tucking a few stray strands of hair back under her bonnet as she did.

"Didn't see you in church this morning neither," Rose said teasingly.

Bertie looked down at her feet, wiggling her toes. "Shame on me for that, I reckon. I went for a walk this morning and looks like I sorta lost track of time," Bertie replied.

"Now Bertie," Rose said, taking her hand, "you and me has been good friends a mighty long time, ain't we?"

Bertie looked into Rose's face, puzzled. "Well, yes. Of course, we have."

"Looks like to me if as a good a friend as you went and got herself a beau, she woulda done told me about it by now," Rose said, her eyes twinkling with laughter.

Bertie blushed and looked away. "Well, I don't know about that."

Rose squeezed her friend's hand and answered quickly, "Now Bertie, you ain't gonna sit right there and make like you ain't got no beau, are you?"

Bertie, eyes still downcast, spoke quietly. "I don't know if I got one or not." After a pause she added, "I'm confused. And I'm scared."

Rose threw her arm across Bertie's shoulders. "Now, honey! What in the world are you scared about?"

"I don't know, Rose," Bertie said, still looking down and speaking barely above a whisper. "I just don't know nothing about having a beau."

"There ain't nothing to know, sweetie," Rose said cheerfully. "If you got one, you just do."

"There is a nice boy who comes by and goes for walks with me," Bertie said quietly. "And sometimes he holds my hand."

"There!" Rose squealed girlishly. "So, you do have one!"

"But I don't know if he figures he's my beau or not," Bertie replied. "He's real nice to me, though."

Rose squeezed her friend's shoulders. "Ain't that

just the sweetest thing," she said cheerfully.

"But Rose," Bertie said bashfully, "I don't know what I'm supposed to *do*."

Rose answered, after a pause. "Well, honey, the good Lord knows I can't claim to be no expert on it, but it seems to me like there ain't nothing you're supposed to do, other than just what you're doing. Things just go on naturally from there."

Bertie turned and looked expectantly into Rose's face. "Is that how it was with you and Samuel?" she asked. "Did he go walking with you, and sometimes hold your hand?"

Rose looked quickly away, and a little sigh escaped involuntarily. "It mighta been sorta like that," she said quietly. "Me and Samuel didn't have what you might call no old-fashioned courting."

Bertie sensed that it wasn't something Rose wanted to discuss, so she changed the subject.

"I'll bet Samuel is feeling great about being back at work," she said.

"He sure was proud to draw his pay this week," Rose answered, brightening. "But mercy, this week just about liked to plumb wear him out. He's in yonder now taking a nap."

"Well, he's been out so long I 'spect it's gonna take a little while for him to get back up to full speed," Bertie replied.

Rose nodded, looking off into the distance. "Keep praying for us, Bertie," she said. "His arm is mighty sore and I'm afraid it ain't all the way healed yet. And sometimes now when he starts coughing it seems like he can't hardly stop."

Bertie took Rose's hand and squeezed it. "I just know he's going to be fine." Releasing her friend's hand, she stood up and stretched out her arms, looking up into the sky. "Good things are happening, Rose. I can just feel it. Don't it feel to you like something real good is fixing to happen?"

18

Bertie was walking to work with Rose and her family as the sky brightened. Even after over eight years of working in the spinning room, Monday mornings still weighed on her. Her one free day of the week always seemed to rush by, while the six long workdays dragged along slowly and tediously. She sighed deeply as they fell in with the crowd filing through the mill gate.

Samuel was leading the way, carrying Purl on his shoulders. They all stopped suddenly when they heard a voice crying out.

"Samuel! Samuel! Hold on a second!"

Turning to face the voice, they saw Mr. Webb hurrying toward them. Following him was a young man wearing a cloth cap, faded overalls, and a pair of tattered brogans. He looked much like all the other men crowding toward the mill gate. But when Bertie saw him, her heart began to race. It was Charlie.

When Webb and Charlie reached the group, Bertie and Charlie exchanged quick bashful smiles, then Bertie dropped her head, blushing.

"Samuel, this is Charlie Lawton," Webb said, causing Samuel and Charlie to nod at each other. He's been breaking bales, but I want you to train him to weave."

Samuel smiled broadly, answering cheerfully, "Well then, you sure brought him to the right man!" He lifted his daughter off his shoulders, sat her down, then reached out his right hand and said, "Pleased to meet you, Charlie."

Charlie took Samuel's hand and shook it firmly. Bertie noticed that the handshake caused Samuel to flinch and grimace slightly, a reaction that Samuel quickly tried to conceal. She also saw Rose turn away with a pained look. She had seen it too.

"Likewise, Samuel," Charlie answered, as the men shook hands. Peering over Samuel's head at the blushing girl behind him, he added, "Good morning, Bertie."

With a slight smile, she answered quietly, "Hey, Charlie."

"You work with Samuel, Charlie," Webb said. Turning to Samuel he continued, "Samuel, teach him the entire operation." He turned to leave but stopped after a few quick steps, turned back around and added, "But don't let your production drop. This man should speed you up, not slow you down."

As Webb turned and walked away, Samuel saluted him comically. He gave Rose a quick kiss, rubbed Gem on top of his head, then turned back to Charlie with a smile. "Well, come on into my world, Charlie. I'll start by teaching you how to set up the machines."

As Samuel marched off toward the gate, Charlie followed, then stopped and turned back to Bertie. "Bye, Bertie," he said shyly, before turning back around and hurrying to catch up with Samuel.

Bertie answered with a quick wave and another blush.

As the men filed through the gate, Rose spoke hurriedly to her son. "Gem, take your sister to the nursery. Then go ahead and start setting up the spindles. I'll be there directly."

"Yes, ma'am," the boy answered, taking Purl by the hand and walking toward the gate.

Once the children were out of earshot Rose turned to Bertie and laughed, her face beaming. "Bertie, honey, you done turned red as a beet!" she exclaimed teasingly. "I believe that boy must be your new beau."

"Aw, Rose," she answered bashfully. "Don't tease me."

"Bless your heart, honey. You didn't tell me how good looking he was," Rose said with a playful grin. As her friend stammered for a response, Rose took her by the hand. "Well, I reckon we better get to work. But I expect you to tell me all about him just as soon as this long day is over. That's gonna give me something good to look forward to."

19

As the two men approached a row of looms, Samuel spoke, while stuffing cotton balls in his ears. "Just watch me for a while. After you get the hang of it, I'll let you help."

Charlie looked at the machines, in awe. "Which one is yours?" he asked.

Samuel looked carefully back at him, to see if he was joking. After a moment he answered with a laugh. "Which one? They're all mine, Charlie!" He swept an arm through the air before the row of machines, "All fifteen of these are *my* looms and I am their doggone master!"

Just as Samuel was speaking the belts overhead began moving and the machines began coming to life. Within moments the cavernous room was echoing the roar of dozens of giant pulsating looms.

"Just watch what I do," Samuel shouted, as he lifted a beam and set it in place on a loom. Keeping focused on his work, he shouted, "You got to keep an eye on the draw-in girls, the creelers, and the warpers. Once the weft is in the shuttle right, then you start fixing the harnesses and the beams. Understand?"

Charlie nodded, although didn't understand a word

of it.

"We're doing sheets now, so this is easy work," Samuel shouted over the din. "You watch me close then after a while I'll let you do some."

Charlie's heart was pounding as he tried to take it all in. The large metal arms of the looms were ramming threaded steel shuttles through wooden frames, twice a second, weaving together the yarn running lengthwise with the yarn running crosswise, as Samuel moved down the row of machines, setting beams and harnesses in place. It was industrial choreography unlike anything Charlie had ever seen before.

"You gotta look for breaks and get 'em fixed quick," Samuel shouted as he worked. "This is piece work. We get paid according to how much cloth we weave. Can't be stopping to fix breaks all the time."

For the first hour Charlie was so confused and intimidated that he was tempted to give up and ask for his old job back. There was no time for slow and careful instruction. He just had to try to figure it out on the run.

But by late morning, the process had begun to make sense to him. He was watching from behind, trying to stay out of the way, as Samuel picked up a beam and moved to set it in place. But as he was lifting it into position, Charlie saw him suddenly grimace and he seemed to be losing his grip with his right hand. As the beam dipped suddenly toward the yarn, Charlie stepped forward quickly and steadied it. Samuel nodded at him, and tried to lift the beam back up, but Charlie could see that he was sputtering and shaking. "Let me set this one," Charlie shouted, taking it from Samuel's hands and lowering it into place. As Samuel nodded his appreciation, he stepped backwards, turned, and began coughing violently. Embarrassed, Charlie pretended not to notice as he swung the harness into place. Wiping his eyes, Samuel stepped up, looked down at the loom, and nodded to Charlie, signaling that he had done it right. Charlie nodded back, with a smile, before noticing Webb in the distance, watching them closely.

At noon the machines all slowed to a stop, for the workers' twenty-minute dinner break. "You're catching on fast," Samuel said cheerfully, as the men stepped over to a corner to pick up the cloth bundles that held their lunches. "I'm obliged to you for catching that beam. I must have got something stuck in my throat. Would've torn up that cloth and had to re-draw the whole frame if you hadn't caught it."

The men sat down in a corner and untied their satchels. Samuel pulled a piece of cornbread out of his and was about to take a bite when he stopped suddenly. "Is that chicken?" He exclaimed. "A drumstick?!"

Charlie paused, a bit embarrassed. "Yeah," he answered quietly.

"Dang, boy. Don't see too many of them around here," Samuel said.

Charlie laughed, and pulled a second one out of the satchel. "Here you go," he said, handing it to Samuel. "Have one."

Samuel shook his head. "No, no, no. I wasn't asking for your dinner. Just ain't used to seeing men eating chicken here, that's all. Most of us are lucky here if we got a little fatback grease to smear on our cornbread."

"My mama packed it for me and gave it to me when I left home last night. She thinks I'm getting skinny and said she wants to make sure I'm getting enough to eat," Charlie said, still holding out the chicken leg, while

Samuel continued to steal longing glances at it.

The change in food was one of the most difficult lifestyle adjustments Charlie had been forced to make. The men in his house rotated cooking responsibilities, though not one of them was a competent cook. When Charlie first arrived and was told he was responsible for cooking once a week, he was taken aback. "Fellas, I don't know how to cook," he had said. He was answered with guffaws. "Well then, you'll just fit right in with the rest of us," one of them replied. On most mornings one of the men would make cornbread, which would be their breakfast. Those who could afford it would buy a biscuit, sometime with a little piece of pork in it, from the children who came into the mill hawking them during dinner break. Those who couldn't would usually have cornbread for dinner (the word they used for the midday meal) as well. As in most of the mill houses, a pot of beans or greens would provide their supper.

The meager and monotonous diet soon gave Charlie a better appreciation for the home-cooked meals he had grown up eating on the farm, and Sunday dinners became feasts for him. Knowing he wasn't eating well, every Sunday evening, when he left for the station to catch the train to Danville, his mother would pack a sack with enough food to last him a week. But every Sunday night before he fell asleep, it was all gone thanks to his ravenous pack of housemates, who waited drooling for his return.

"Go on and take it, Samuel," Charlie said. "I need to get it all eat up. Ever since the boys I stay with figured out I bring food from home on Sundays, they find it and clean me out by Monday. I saved these two legs, but I'll be back to eating nothing but beans tomorrow."

Drooling, Samuel relented. "Obliged, Charlie. Mighty friendly of you," he said, taking the drumstick. "Here," he added, as he tore off a piece of his cornbread and passed it to Charlie, "have some of this. My Rose made it and it's good."

"Thanks," Charlie said, taking it from him.

The men ate silently, save for Samuel's two coughing attacks. "Want me to get you some water?" Charlie asked, during the second one. Samuel shook his head while trying to suppress the coughs. When he finally had his breath back, he smiled awkwardly. "Must be coming down with a cold," he said.

Samuel answered him with a nod.

"So, where you from, Charlie?" Samuel asked.

Charlie answered while chewing, "A farm out in the country. A place called Raye. I'm sure you ain't never heard of it."

Samuel laughed. "Well that explains why you're here at the mill. I used to live on a farm too."

Charlie's eyes brightened. "You did? Where at?"

"Way up in the hills. A place I'm sure you ain't never heard of. Let me tell you, Charlie, I was mighty glad to leave that all behind too. A man can't have a decent life on a farm," Samuel said, before turning his head and coughing.

"I don't know about that," Charlie replied, seemingly reluctantly. "I kinda like living on a farm." After a pause he added, "To tell you the truth, I kinda miss it."

"Miss it!" Samuel exclaimed, slapping his knee with a laugh. "Tell me what you miss most about it. Working sunup to sundown and worrying whether or not your crop is gonna come in? Never knowing if you're gonna be able to sell it, and if you do whether you'll get back what you done already spent? Sun beating down on you all day long while you try to scratch a living out of the clay? Hailstorms? Early frosts? Droughts? Let me tell you Charlie, that life is for the birds."

"Farm life ain't easy. You're right about that," Charlie said. "But I like being outside. I like growing my own food. I like tending to the crops and livestock. I mostly like being my own boss." Charlie paused, then added, "And you ain't got to breathe cotton dust ten hours a day six days a week, with cotton balls stuffed in your ears so your eardrums don't bust."

"Well, you got a point there, Charlie," Samuel said with a laugh and a cough. "But I wouldn't never go back to farming. It's mill life for me! Money in your pocket every week. Your own house to live in. And you know what? I like working those looms. I like seeing that thread turn into cloth. Makes me feel like I'm good at something. And them sheets we're making now are for the U.S. Army. So, you might say we're doing our part to help whip the Kaiser."

Reaching for his satchel, Samuel suddenly grimaced and drew back his arm.

"What's the matter with your arm?" Charlie asked. "I saw that it was hurting you a little while ago."

Still grimacing, Samuel slowly stretched his arm out and pulled it back a couple of times. "I got it caught in the loom a couple of months ago. Tore it up real bad." He stretched out his arm again, this time seemingly without pain. "I was out of work for almost two months. Them was rough times for us." He reached out with the arm and pulled it back again quickly. "It's all healed now, but I get a little hitch in it every now and again."

Charlie was dubious, but he nodded.

The overhead belts began to creak back to life and Samuel popped to his feet. "Time to get back to work, boys," he shouted, with a grin. "Let's weave us some more cotton!"

20

Bertie and Charlie were strolling lazily down the road, flanked by mill houses, holding hands, their hair and clothes still wearing a long-day's deposit of lint and cotton dust. "It's so awful about Eddie Cox," Bertie said. "It's all the girls could talk about today."

Charlie looked down, shaking his head.

"What happened?" Bertie asked.

"I don't know exactly," Charlie answered. "I heard he was pressing down the fly and his hand got drawn in."

Bertie shuddered at the thought. "Is he going to be all right?" she asked.

"As all right as you can be with just one arm," Charlie answered.

Bertie fell silent, pulling closer to Charlie. "Rose is worried half to death about Samuel. He liked to lost his arm when it got caught in his loom last year. I sure hope he's being careful, Charlie. And you too."

The truth was that Charlie was worried about Samuel too, but he didn't say so. "It's carelessness that causes accidents," he said, repeating the supervisors' mantra. "Eddie knew better than to use his hand to press the fly down. He's been carding a long time."

"I heard he always did it that way and ain't nobody ever told him not to," Bertie said.

"Maybe," Charlie said. "But he still ought to have known better."

"I just feel so sorry for him. What will he do now?" she asked.

"I don't know," Charlie answered. "I don't know if he's got any people who can take him in or not."

Bertie shook her head sadly. After a few moments she looked up at Charlie. "Please be careful, Charlie," she said.

Charlie responded with a faint smile. "You too, Bertie. I know girls get hurt in the spinning room all the time."

After that, they both fell quiet, walking silently for a while, before Bertie tried to lighten the mood.

"Have you ever seen a seashell, Charlie?" Bertie asked.

"No," he answered. "Can't say that I have."

"I used to have one," Bertie said. "A long, long time ago. My daddy gave it to me. It was the most beautiful thing I've ever had," she said. Then, remembering Susannah, she quickly corrected herself, "Mi' near, I mean."

"Have you still got it?" Charlie asked.

"No," Bertie answered sadly. She was about to tell Charlie how her Aunt Sue had taken the shell from her, but caught herself, deciding to keep that still-painful memory to herself. "But I sure wish I did. Did you know that when you hold a seashell up to your ear you can hear the ocean?" After a few steps in silence she added, "It's like magic."

In the three weeks since meeting Charlie, desires had awakened within Bertie that she hadn't known she had—desires for intimacy, for possession, for belonging. She would lie awake at night on her little cot, thinking of Charlie, replaying in her mind every word of their conversations, and trying to recall every detail of his face. She imagined his life in the country, and her thoughts kindled dreams—dreams of fulfillment, contentment, harmony; dreams that dragged to the surface and laid bare before her the realities of her life—monotony, deprivation, exhaustion, privation, futility. Whenever she dared to wonder if she might someday have a better, happier life, if she might have a chance to live her haunting dreams in a world as beautiful as she imagined Charlie's to be, her hopes were always quickly swept away by the chastening conviction of unworthiness that had been planted deep into her heart long ago, and she would drift sadly to sleep, with tears on her cheeks.

For the past eight years, Bertie's life had been anchored to the mill. Everyone she knew was, like her, a millworker, and with nearly all her waking hours spent tending spindles, she had been no farther away from the spinning room than the company-owned house, the store, and the church at the end of the road. But in her grey and dreary world there was one bright spot, one peaceful and beautiful oasis—her "secret place." And since Sunday she had felt a powerful desire to share it with Charlie.

But she was also afraid. On one hand, she wanted to bring Charlie into the one beautiful spot she had carved out in her life, but on the other she feared that sharing the place she had enjoyed alone for so long, would be to lose it. That Sunday she and Susannah had argued about it. "Show him! Bring him here!" Susannah had insisted. But Bertie, staring out over the river with teary eyes answered, "I want to, but I can't. I'm scared to." As she walked with him now, the debate within her raged on. I can't see his world, she thought, but maybe I should show him mine, my little spot of happiness.

"Do you want to walk down to the river, Charlie?" Bertie asked, timidly.

"The river? Sure, I reckon," he answered.

Bertie smiled, tugged his hand, and turned them around. She led as they walked east, back toward the mill. After crossing Main Street, they continued down Bridge Street, past the mill gate and toward the spot where the mill race rejoins the river. The sun was sinking rapidly toward the horizon when they reached the river's edge.

"I could be blindfolded, and I'd know I was at the river," Charlie said with a laugh. "There's nothing else on earth that smells like it."

Bertie gazed out across the muddy, dye-streaked water, drifting past, carrying cotton debris floating lazily toward the ocean. Releasing Charlie's hand, she bent down and picked up a rock, then tossed it into the water. She quickly glanced left, then right, her eyes stopping on a narrow opening in the brambles.

"Is this what you wanted to show me? The mighty Dan River in all its stinking glory?" Charlie said with a grin.

Bertie took his hand and looked into his eyes, giving Charlie pause, as there was something written in her face that he had never seen there before.

"Charlie...," she said quietly.

"Yes," he answered with concern.

Bertie hesitated. She turned her gaze downward, then slowly lifted her eyes until they met his.

"There is something I want to show you," she said, her voice cracking and hesitant.

"All right, Bertie," he replied. "What is it?"

The debate, the struggle, the desire, and the doubt, all flashed through Bertie's mind in an instant. She felt herself turning toward the entrance to the hidden path, her heart racing. Then, she heard it. A roaring. She gasped, released Charlie's hand, and threw both her hands over her ears.

She turned suddenly and caught Charlie's puzzled stare.

"Do you hear it, Charlie?" she said excitedly.

"Hear what?" he asked.

"I think I hear…" Then, abruptly, she stopped. As her heartbeat slowed, so did the roar in her ears. And she knew then that she had not heard the ocean.

As she dropped her hands, Charlie took them both, looking with concern into her eyes.

"Bertie," he said softly. "Are you all right?"

Bertie nodded, quickly looking away. Gathering her senses, after a moment she said, "Did I hear a bobwhite? Did you hear one?"

"No," Charlie said. "I don't think so." He lifted his chin and tilted his head, to listen more carefully.

"Oh, silly me," Bertie said with a feigned giggle. "I thought I heard something. Oh, well." Tugging on his hand and turning back to the road she said, "Come on, Charlie. Let's walk back to the house now."

21

Charlie had been deeply affected by the scene at the river. In the days that followed, he could not push it out of his mind. He had sensed a closeness there, a lowering of Bertie's guard, perhaps an invitation to intimacy. But he wasn't sure. He wasn't sure, that is, of how Bertie felt. For himself, what he believed he had seen in Bertie's eyes that evening deepened the slide into what he was afraid to admit. Love. He had felt it growing within him from the time they met, occupying a little more of his heart with each passing day. By now Bertie consumed nearly all his thoughts, and the thought of her caused him to become self-aware in ways he had never been before. He worried about his appearance and the exact words he used when they spoke. He worried that he might displease her. Most of all he felt a powerful desire to possess her, to take her in his arms, to join their worlds together. He woke some morning from dreams that left him embarrassed.

At the same time, he was haunted by his mother's warnings and concern. As much as he desired Bertie, he knew he must be careful not to cause hurt to his mother. When he felt himself in danger of being swept away by desire, of being bold enough to charge in and test Bertie's feelings for him, he remembered his mother—and a terrible price she had once paid because of him. The memory kept him in check.

Charlie slogged through his working days. Although he was supposed to be in training, it had soon become clear to him that Samuel was unable to carry the load assigned to him, so that Charlie was doing more and more of the work. Each day, as the grinding hours dragged by and the cotton dust choked him, he would feel the energy being sapped from him, the incessant roar of the machines pounding in his skull. But then, when he knew the workday was drawing to a close, he would feel his spirits lifting and he would find a second wind. He counted down the minutes until he would be with Bertie again.

But he couldn't shake the concern that by seeing Bertie he was breaching his mother's trust. It was a Friday when the solution to his dilemma dawned on him. Samuel had stepped aside, having a coughing fit, and Charlie was tending the machines alone, when the answer struck him like an epiphany. His mama had warned him not to be alone with a mill girl, because the girl might trick him into having to marry her. So, Charlie reasoned, it was not the "being alone" that concerned her. It was the marrying. Because Bertie was not trying to trick him into marrying her, there was no reason to be concerned about being alone with her. Therefore, Charlie concluded to his satisfaction, he could be alone with Bertie without disobeying his mother. It was curious logic, of course, but Charlie found it convincing. From that moment on, he resolved that he would not feel any guilt about walking with Bertie. Besides, he said to himself confidently, nobody is really alone in this crowded town.

When the turbines finally stopped for the day, and the mill ground to a halt, Charlie pulled the cotton balls from his ears, shouted "See you tomorrow, Samuel," and bolted for the door. An hour later he was strolling along Floyd Street, holding Bertie's hand, feeling like he was walking on air.

When Charlie began to whistle, Bertie cast an amused glance at him. "What has gotten into you today, Charlie?" she asked playfully.

"Well, Miss Bertie, the truth is that I'm feeling mighty fine this evening. Mighty fine," Charlie said with a broad smile.

Bertie giggled, and shook her head.

Charlie began singing the words to the tune he had been whistling. "Well, I wish I was an apple, a'hanging on a tree, and every time my Bertie passed, she'd take a bite of me."

Delighted, Bertie giggled more, and she blushed deeply. "Charlie Lawton, you are being just as crazy as a loon today."

"Well, Bertie," he said mischievously. "Are you gonna?"

"Gonna what?" Bertie answered.

"Are you gonna take a bite of me?" Charlie asked, feeling bold.

"My goodness, Charlie! Have you lost your mind?" Bertie said, her face flushed.

"How about if I take a bite of you instead?" Charlie said playfully, pulling her toward him.

Laughing, they pretended to struggle with each other. When the laughing and wrestling stopped, Charlie had his arms around Bertie. They fell silent and Bertie slowly lifted her chin, until her eyes met his. She was trembling, and her face betrayed her nervousness, but she did not resist as Charlie pulled her closer. She closed her eyes and felt his lips press against hers.

22

The kiss had been brief, and awkward, leaving them both embarrassed and unable to look each other in the eyes during the rest of the stroll. But however imperfect it might have been, it was Bertie's first kiss, and she could not stop thinking about it. The memory of it haunted her. She wanted more.

That Saturday, when the work week came to a merciful end, Bertie emerged from the mill drenched in sweat, dust and lint clinging to the moisture on her skin and clothes. It would be hotter before the summer was over, much hotter, but mid-June was already brutal, turning the mill into a suffocating furnace.

Saturday evenings were hard for her. Charlie left for home immediately after work, meaning she would have to wait until Monday evening to see him again. And without the thrill of being with Charlie to dull it, she felt the draining exhaustion that followed a long hard week in the spinning room. She stopped for a few minutes, allowing the crowd of workers to pass by her. Then she turned and began walking the other way, away from home and toward the river.

At the river's edge, Bertie picked up a stone and tossed it into the murky, swirling water, then glanced around to see if she had been noticed. Seeing that she hadn't been seen, she quickly ducked into the path and made her way to the pile of brush and brambles that blocked the entrance to her little spot of beach. She pulled the barricade away, crawled inside, then re-blocked the entrance. She dropped onto the sand and sighed, feeling a wave of gratitude wash over her. She was in her secret place.

After a few moments, Bertie sat up. Seeing that the sand had stuck to her sweat-soaked dress, she gazed out into the river, imagining how refreshing it would be to cool off it in it—an option not available to her, as she did not know how to swim.

She tucked her legs underneath her and reached into the pocket of her dress, bringing out Susannah and carefully propping the doll up in the sand in front of her.

"You ain't gonna believe it, Susannah! It's the grandest thing that has ever happened to me! You want to guess what it is?"

Bertie, her eyes bright and twinkling, stared at the doll.

"Give up? Charlie kissed me! Yes, he did! Right on the mouth. Oh, my dear Susannah, I plumb liked to died! We was just joking around and then all of a sudden like we was close and looking right at each other and then he just leaned down and kissed me right on the lips! Yep! Cross my heart and hope to die! Now what do you think about that, Susannah?"

Bertie fell silent, looking at the doll for a few seconds.

"No," she said after a pause. "Just the one time."

Another pause. It had been two days since Charlie had kissed her. On neither of the next two evenings did he try to kiss her again, to her great disappointment. Did he regret it, she wondered? Would they ever kiss again?

"I don't know why not," she said. "Maybe he's scared that I don't want him to."

Another pause.

"Oh, for goodness sakes Susannah, I can't do that! I think Charlie is just being a gentleman, that's all."

Bertie stared at the doll for a few seconds, then shook her head.

"Bring him here? Oh, dear Susannah, you keep on telling me that and I do want to, but I'm scared to. Ain't nobody never been here but me and you. This is our place." After a pause she said, "Yes, I know you don't mind, but what if Charlie don't see how special this place is? What if he laughs at it? Oh, honey I just don't know what I'm supposed to do. I'm so mixed up these days. I'm happy and scared both at the same time." After another long pause, Bertie fell backwards so that she was lying on the sand. "And I am just so tired, Susannah. I ain't hardly been sleeping and it's been as hot as fire in the mill every day this week. I think I'll just rest here a minute."

Bertie closed her eyes and was soon overtaken by the deep sleep of a millworker. She was strolling along the river, holding Charlie's hand, when she was awakened by the sound of a train rattling over the bridge, heading north. She sat up and smiled. "Hear that, Susannah? That's the Number Eight, taking Charlie home to his beautiful farm and family. Think about it, Susannah. Ain't it the prettiest thing you've ever thought about?"

23

John was waiting when Charlie arrived at the station. "I appreciate the ride, brother," Charlie said, as he mounted the mule.

"Don't thank me. It's Jack that giving you the ride," John answered.

"Well, I'm obliged to you both," Charlie said.

They rode silently for a while.

"Everything all right on the farm?" Charlie asked.

"Yeah, I 'spect it is," John said. "Some rain would be good," he added.

Nights in the country are loud in June. Even though his ears were still ringing with the roar of machines, Charlie smiled as he heard the songs of a thousand crickets and frogs. After a few minutes, he spoke again.

"Any other news?"

"News?" John replied. "What kind of news you expecting in Raye? You get to spend all week in town. I'm the one ought to be asking you for news."

Charlie chuckled. "My time in town is spent in a cotton mill. Ain't much to talk about."

"Well, I know you ain't in the mill the whole time. I 'spect you got plenty to tell if'n you wanted to."

Charlie wondered if word about him and Bertie had

somehow made it home, then quickly dismissed the thought.

"Sorry to disappoint you, brother. I work all day, don't have nothing decent to eat, sleep a little bit, then do it all over again."

"Uh huh," John said skeptically.

Charlie pondered whether he was being dishonest, as the mule lazily carried them on. He was just about to say something to John about Bertie when John spoke first.

"Mama has taken to making us all pray for you both morning and night," he said.

For a while, Charlie didn't respond. When he did, he said, "Well, I reckon I need all the help I can get."

"She's been making us all pray together for you every night since you first went. But this week she's done added a morning prayer session too. She says she fears the devil is laying temptations in your path," John said.

Charlie grunted. "What kind of temptations?"

"Just the usual stuff, I reckon. Whiskey, cards, unvirtuous women, all manner of sin. You know." After a pause he added, "I wouldn't mind some of them temptations getting laid in *my* path."

Charlie laughed. "Well, little brother. If you're so intent on finding trouble, I 'spect you can find some right here in Raye."

"No time for trouble, I'm sorry to say. Too busy trying to make a crop," John said, seriously.

"Why do you reckon Mama worries about me so much?" Charlie asked. "Seems like she's got plenty of other things to worry about."

John shrugged. "Beats me. But she's bound and determined to keep you from losing your religion in town, and she's done put the whole family on it now. Night and day."

Charlie let it drop and they rode the rest of the way in silence. His mother greeted him at the door, as he always did, with a kiss and a prayer of thanksgiving for his safe return. After having something to eat, he crawled gratefully into his bed and slept away a week's worth of exhaustion.

Awakened by the rooster crowing, Charlie rose the next morning feeling refreshed, and feeling brave enough to mention Bertie to his mother. His plan was to introduce the subject of his courtship gradually over the next few weeks, and he imagined that she would warm to the notion and all would be well. John ruined his plan.

After morning chores and breakfast, just as they were preparing to leave for church, John joked that Charlie would have to go a day with only country girls to look at. "I 'spect you're already missing them town girls, even if Mama keeps making us pray 'em away from you."

His mother flared with anger, pointing her finger at John. "Do not mock the Lord thy God, John Lawton!" she shouted. "There ain't nothing funny about the Jezebels and danger your brother must face in that sinful place and you need to take it serious!" She turned to Charlie, whose stomach had suddenly knotted. "'I find more bitter than death the woman, whose heart is snares and nets. Whoso pleaseth God shall escape from her; but the sinner shall be taken by her.' The word of God, Charlie! Snares and nets! Snares and nets! The sinner shall be taken by her." She finished with a confident nod.

I reckon this isn't the best time for me to mention

Bertie, Charlie thought.

"Yes, ma'am," he answered meekly, casting an angry glance at his brother, who was struggling to suppress a grin.

On the train back to Danville that evening, Charlie fretted. When he had arrived home on Saturday night, he had in his mind a well-rehearsed plan to tell his mother about Bertie. Yet somehow he had allowed all of Sunday to go by without having said a word about her. But as he replayed the day in his mind, he couldn't find that he had missed his opportunity. There simply had not *been* an opportunity. Sure, if he had not wanted to handle his mother's feelings so delicately, he could have told her, but Charlie was determined to introduce the subject of his courtship carefully, in a way that would assuage any of his mother's fears or doubts.

Leaning his head against the window, he closed his eyes and allowed his mind to wander back in time. Charlie shuddered when the memories washed over him—memories that strengthened his resolve to protect his mother from any anxiety. I will tell her, he thought, but only when the time is right.

24

"Let's walk to the river again," Bertie said with a shy smile. She had left Susannah at home, after confiding to her that she was going to try to find the nerve to show Charlie her secret place.

"Sure, Bertie," Charlie answered, taking her hand. He didn't understand her attraction to the river, but he didn't mind. "We'll go wherever you want to go."

When they reached the river's edge, they sat down on the grass, looking out across the swirling brown water. Charlie drew Bertie closer to him, to her delight. They sat quietly for a few minutes, both with racing hearts.

"Bertie," Charlie said, breaking the silence, "I like being with you more than anything I can think of. I think about it all day. So much that I can't hardly keep my mind on my job."

"Oh, Charlie!" she exclaimed, turning to face him. "That's just exactly the way it is for me too!"

Charlie looked for a moment into her deep brown eyes, then felt a surge of desire. As he leaned toward her, Bertie closed her eyes and pursed her lips.

Last week's kiss had been quick and fumbling. This one lingered, neither of them willing to be the first to break it off. They both felt themselves swept over by waves of sensation, unlike anything either of them had ever before known. When they finally pulled apart, to breathe, Bertie dropped her head onto Charlie's shoulder and begin softly sobbing.

"Bertie! What's the matter?" Charlie said, alarmed. Then adding guiltily, "I'm sorry, Bertie. I ought not to have done that. Please forgive me."

Bertie sniffled, wiped her eyes, and looked up at Charlie's worried face. "There ain't nothing wrong, Charlie" she said, her voice cracking. "I don't know what made me start crying. It's just that I'm so happy. Happier than I have ever been. I ain't never felt like this in my whole life. Ain't nobody never wanted me before."

"I want you real bad," Charlie replied, hugging her to him. "But if you knew all about me, you probably wouldn't want nothing to do with me. You probably wouldn't never go walking with me again."

"That's silly," Bertie answered, wiping her eyes again. "I'm the one that ain't fit for you. You got a good family, and a farm. I ain't got nothing and nobody."

"That don't matter one bit," Charlie said. "It's what somebody has done that matters, and I've done something awful."

"I don't believe it," Bertie said, snuggling into this shoulder.

"I mean it, Bertie, you wouldn't want me if you knew all about me."

"And I mean it too, Charlie Lawton. You wouldn't want me if you know all about *me*."

They sat quietly a few minutes, then Charlie said, "And still, here we are. Bertie and Charlie."

"Yep," she said. "Here we are. Bertie and Charlie."

They kissed again, more passionately than before. Charlie could feel Bertie's chest rising and falling with her breath, and it thrilled him. Bertie imagined she could feel his heart beating.

When the kiss ended, Bertie sighed deeply. After a few moments, she stood up, picked up a small rock and tossed it in the river. While Charlie was looking at the ripples spreading from the splash, Bertie quickly glanced around, then said, "Come on. I want to show you my secret place."

At that moment, Charlie was overwhelmed with desire. He understood Bertie's "secret place" to be anatomical. No other possibility even crossed his mind.

As Bertie ducked into a little path through the brambles, pulling Charlie along by the hand. As he followed Bertie along the path, Charlie was completely at the mercy of his hormones; his mind was screaming "No!", but in vain. By the time they scrambled onto the little beach, and Bertie had blocked the entrance, Charlie's heart was pounding so rapidly that he could feel it echoing in his ears. Within moments they were tumbling on the sand, entangled in unchecked passion, each relying on the other to know when to stop, but neither having the will to do so.

Bertie was possessed by an overpowering hunger for Charlie and Charlie had a farm boy's understanding of biology. That was sufficient. Their desire carried them over a waterfall.

Afterwards they lay spent on the sand, Charlie on his back, staring up into the darkening sky, with Bertie curled up next to him, awash in bliss. As he watched the sky begin to dot with stars, Charlie struggled with a confusing jumble of emotions—pleasure, happiness, contentment, satisfaction, and guilt.

"I reckon this means we have to get married," he said softly. All Bertie heard was "married." She was bursting with joy.

When Bertie pulled him closer, it felt to Charlie as if she were purring. Aroused, desire swept over him again like a flood and Bertie eagerly received him.

The Milky Way stretched over them like a celestial blanket.

25

Charlie replayed the scene in his mind dozens of times, and each time he arrived at the inescapable conclusion that he had not been tricked or trapped, not in any way. If there was any blame in what had happened, he knew that blame lay on him more than on Bertie.

He wrestled with two truths that were simultaneously pulling at his heart. One was that he *wanted* to marry Bertie, to have her close to him. Forever. The other was that he had broken his implied promise to his mother. He knew that she would be hurt and disappointed, and that in breaking a promise to her he was breaking a pledge he had made to himself seven years earlier—a pledge to never cause pain or disappointment to his mother, and to obey her with devotion and obedience, a pledge he had made in recognition of a debt that was impossible to repay.

He wanted to revel in the joy of his love for Bertie, but his broken promise and the dread of his mother's broken heart hung over him like a gloomy cloud.

Lying awake on his pallet, an answer to his problem came to him and it settled his mind. The solution was to tell his mother about Bertie, leaving out how far the situation had gone. He need only tell her that he had met a girl and wanted to marry her. Once he had his mother's blessing, he would be able to marry Bertie and live happily ever after. Done with her consent, his mother would not be hurt or betrayed. He never allowed himself to even consider what might happen if his mother refused.

Meanwhile, he and Bertie returned to the secret place every day.

26

It was during one of their visits to the secret place that Charlie and Bertie began to open up with each other about their lives, to exchange their stories. Charlie was astounded to learn that Bertie was only allowed to keep half her pay.

"That ain't right or fair!" he exclaimed.

Bertie just shrugged. "They been taking out half my pay and sending it to Aunt Sue from the day I started working here. I reckon they'll keep on taking it until they think I'm grown."

"But you are grown, Bertie! And that was wrong to do even when you won't. How do you even manage to get by with only half your pay?"

Bertie chuckled. "We make do," she said. "Most all the girls are having some of their pay taken out. Some don't even get half. We just go in together and make ends meet."

She sighed and cuddled closer to Charlie. "It warms my heart to hear about folks like you," she said. "Folks who work here to make money for their families. I know they love you for it. But don't nobody love me for what I do. I work here 'cause Aunt Sue made me. And you know what? I ain't laid eyes on her in years and don't care if I never do."

"Bertie, I'm gonna go down to the mill office tomorrow and speak to them about this. It ain't right what's happening to you," Charlie said, adamantly.

"Don't do that, Charlie," she replied. "I don't want to get in no trouble with the mill. Somebody told me that if you don't have your parents' permission to work, they can fire you. In my case, that must mean Aunt Sue. If she don't get her money, she'll probably tell them to fire me. Then what would I do?"

"I ain't believing that neither," Charlie answered. "You ain't no chap, Bertie! You're grown up!"

Bertie shook her head slightly, then smiled. "There was a man out in the country near Wentworth that folks called 'the money-finder.' He's supposed to be able to come over to your house and find money that you done lost. Well, a few months after Grandma died, Aunt Sue hired him to go look for Grandma's money. I reckon she figured Grandma had it hid somewhere. Aunt Sue took me with her, 'cause she was all the time accusing me of knowing where it was. We met the money-finder man out at Grandma's house. He was a funny-looking man with a scraggly beard, and he didn't have no teeth. When I saw him, I wondered why if he was supposed to be able to find money, he ain't never found none for himself. Anyway, he toted a lantern and went around poking in the ground and in the fireplaces with a sharp stick, while Aunt Sue followed him, keeping her greedy eyes peeled. Well, after a while the man looked at Aunt Sue and said, 'The money ain't here. Her help musta stole it.' Then like a durn fool I just up and said I didn't believe it, and Aunt Sue she spun around and slapped me right across the face and commenced to hollering and saying she bet I knew where that money was and how I won't nothing but an ungrateful and biggety so and so. I remember looking over at the money-finder man and he was just watching Aunt Sue pitching her fit like it was the most peculiar thing he'd done ever seen. After a while she just grabbed me by my arm and yanked it hard as she could, and she drug me off and left that silly looking man standing there."

Charlie, unsure what he should say, responded softly, "I'm sorry she treated you that way."

Bertie shook her head and smiled sadly. "She always treated me like that. Won't nothing different 'bout that day 'cept the money-finder was there to see it. I had to laugh though when I come to find out a long time later that two other folks had done already paid that money-finder man to look for Grandma's money. So, he just took Aunt Sue's money knowing he won't going to find nothing. Served her right I reckon."

Charlie nodded and chuckled.

"But you know what, Charlie? Sometimes I have dreams where Grandma comes to me. She tells me that she loves me and that she is sorry for what happened to me. And then she tells me that she hid a great big pot of money and that she is giving it to me. It's a happy dream right up to that part, but then she don't never tell me where the money is. She always just says, 'Bertie, all that money is yours now and you're rich and you ain't got to work in the mill no more if you don't want to.' And every time I say, 'But Grandma, where is the money at?' and she don't never answer. She just says you're rich now, Bertie, and then she's gone. I reckon I done had that same dream a hundred times."

Bertie snuggled against Charlie's chest. "I know you don't want to hear about the hatefulness in my life. Tell me more about your people, Charlie. It warms my heart to think about your kind and loving family. I don't want to think no more about meanness."

Charlie snorted and shook his head. "Oh, there's meanness in my family too. I got a half-brother that's a whole lot older than me and he is bound and determined to take our farm from us."

Bertie pulled back in surprise and looked into Charlie's face, her eyes widened. "What?" she said incredulously.

"Yep. Ain't that meanness?" Charlie paused before continuing. "But my other half-brother, he was even meaner."

"Oh, no," Bertie said sadly. "Does he live near y'all?"

"Nope. I reckon he's down where he belongs," Charlie answered.

"Down where?" Bertie asked.

"Down *there*," Charlie said, pointing a finger at the ground. "He's dead."

"Oh," Bertie replied. "I'm sorry."

"Well, I ain't," Charlie answered. "I caught him hurting my sister and… Well, I ain't never told nobody this Bertie, but I'm gonna tell you now. You probably won't want to have nothing to do with me no more after I tell you. But he was an evil man and I killed him."

Bertie gasped in shock and drew back. "Charlie!" she exclaimed.

"It's true," he said, with resignation. "When I found out what he was doing to my sister, I snuck over to his house aiming to shoot him. But I chickened out. So, I prayed for God to kill him for me. I ought not to have done that, Bertie. God put it on me to kill him. But I put it back on God because I was scared to. And then Uncle Brother Ben died."

"He just died? You didn't kill him?" Bertie asked.

"I didn't shoot him, but I surely did kill him. And that ain't the worst thing about it," Charlie said, looking down and drawing in the sand with his toe.

"Are you saying you *prayed* him to death?" Bertie asked.

"Something like that," he answered.

"Oh, Charlie! Then you didn't kill nobody! You ain't got nothing to be ashamed of."

"I wanted Ben dead and he needed killing. I ain't ashamed of that part. But believe me, I got plenty to be ashamed about," Charlie said.

"But if you're saying God killed him, then how come you're also saying you killed him? What have you got to be ashamed about?" Bertie asked, confused.

"There's more to it, Bertie. I was supposed to kill Ben and I didn't do it. I tried to put it back on God, but the killing is still on me," Charlie said, glumly.

Bertie shook her head, puzzled. "I don't understand what you're saying, Charlie. It sounds to me like you ain't done nothing wrong. You ain't killed nobody."

"There's more to it," he said softly. "It's just something I have to bear." They sat silently for a few moments. "Still think there ain't no meanness in my family?"

Bertie wrapped Charlie in a hug, pressing her face to his neck. "I reckon there's probably some meanness in every life," she said.

They sat quietly again, listening to the chirping of the crickets.

"I prayed as hard as I could one time," Bertie said. "I prayed and prayed and prayed for God to send a man to take me away from Aunt Sue so I could go to school. I begged him. I finally told him that if he would send that man to our house, I wouldn't never ask for nothing else in my whole life. But you know what? That man never came. All my praying didn't do no good at all." She paused for a while, then continued. "Why do you reckon God wouldn't answer my one little prayer, but he answered yours? Looks like mine was a whole lot easier."

Charlie shook his head. "There ain't no figuring out God, I reckon." After a pause he added, "But if you knew it all, you'd see that he didn't do nothing good for me."

Bertie hugged him tightly again. "I ain't asked God for nothing ever since that time he wouldn't send that man back to my house. But if I was to have prayed for something, there ain't nothing I could have ever prayed for that would be better than this. I love you, Charlie."

"And I love you too, Bertie," Charlie answered, wrapping her in his arms.

27

As the spinners were filing out the door, Rose pulled Bertie aside, speaking quietly so as not be overheard by her son. "Today is Gem's birthday and I'm making him a chocolate pie. Why don't you come over in about an hour and have a piece with us? I know it would make him happy." She smiled when she saw Bertie hesitate. "And please bring your beau Charlie with you," she added, with a playful grin.

Charlie appeared at Bertie's house shortly after work, eager to return to the river. When told that they'd been invited to celebrate a child's birthday instead, he hid his disappointment and went dutifully along.

Gem bounded down the steps and raced up to Bertie when he saw her approaching.

"Bertie!" he squealed with delight, taking her hand. "Guess what Mama's making for supper?"

Bertie laughed and said, "Let's see, I bet she's making a…" She hesitated, pretending to be thinking, then said, "…a chocolate pie!"

"No!," Gem exclaimed, "I mean, yes! She *is* making a chocolate pie. That's my favorite! But she's cooking string beans, Bertie! String beans that *I* grew in my garden."

"That's wonderful, Gem!" Bertie said. She turned to Charlie and added, "His mama says that Gem has a green thumb."

Charlie laughed and nodded. "Yes, I've heard all about it."

"Charlie is a farmer too," Bertie said. "Maybe he can help you with your garden."

"Really?" Gem asked. "Do you grow string beans on your farm? And tomatoes? 'Cause I'm growing some of them too."

"Yes, we do," Charlie answered pleasantly, as Gem led Bertie along by her hand. "But from what I hear you don't need no help from me. Sounds to me like you're a natural born farmer."

As they climbed the steps to the porch, Charlie could hear Samuel coughing inside the house. He had noticed that Samuel's arm became weaker and his cough became worse as the days wore on. Samuel tried to conceal it, but the end of each day, he was coughing with nearly every breath.

Rose met them at the door. "Thank y'all for coming," she said with a smile. "Gem said we couldn't have any of the pie until y'all got here."

"Sounds to me like he's as excited about his string beans as he is about the pie," Bertie said with a laugh.

"Yep," Rose answered. "He sure loves his garden." She rubbed her son on the head and added, "I am so proud of my little man. He is so smart. I can't hardly believe that he's seven years old now." After a moment, her smile disappeared and she said, "Samuel is feeling poorly, so let's just sit out here."

Soon after they had all sat down on the porch, Purl emerged from the house, her face smeared with something like soot.

Rose popped to her feet, hurried over to the little girl, and began wiping her face, "Purl, what have you gotten into now?" Turning to the others she said, "Try as I might, I ain't found no way to keep this young'un clean." As soon as the child's face was clean, she bounded off the porch and raced behind the house.

"That one sure is a handful, Rose," Bertie said sympathetically.

"Oh my goodness, girl. You don't know the half of it," Rose answered.

They sat chatting for a while, letting Gem do most of the talking. A precocious child, he rambled through his thoughts on gardening, chocolate pies, cook stoves, and the war in Europe, to the delight of the grown-ups.

After a few minutes had passed without Samuel joining them, Rose when inside to check on him. When she returned her pale face betrayed her concern and distress. "Fuller says he's too tired and we should just go on and eat without him," she said, using the odd pet name that sometimes slipped into her conversations. "I'll bring out the pie and we can just eat it out here," she said, turning to go back in.

"I'll help you," Bertie said, rising to her feet and following Rose inside.

When they returned with forks and the pie, Rose was trying to force a smile, but it was plain to see that her joy was gone. Only little Purl, who Gem had fetched from out behind the house, seemed unaware of the pall that had fallen over the gathering. She ate with gusto. Gem insisted on taking some of the pie to his father, returning sadly, saying, "Daddy is asleep."

Charlie tried to ease the concern, saying, "We had a hot and hard day today. I'm 'bout ready to fall asleep myself." No one believed him.

After a few minutes of strained conversation, Rose asked Gem to take Purl out to the privy. When the children were gone, she let down her guard.

"I'm just worried sick about Samuel. He keeps on telling me there ain't nothing wrong with him, but it looks to me like he's getting weaker and weaker. I'm scared the mill is killing him. Lord knows we need his pay, but I wish he'd quit until he's better." She turned and looked Charlie in the face. "How is he doing, Charlie?"

Charlie squirmed. He didn't want to be dishonest with Rose, but neither could he bring himself to tell her candidly what he thought. "His arm don't seem to be all the way healed yet and he's got a rough cough, but the other fellows help out and Samuel says he's feeling stronger every day." It was an honest, if evasive, answer, and it was not comforting.

Rose sighed and looked off into the distance. "I'm just plumb wore out every day and Fuller is even worse. I don't know how we're going to make it. If he has to quit working again, I just don't know what we'll do."

Bertie took her friend's hand and squeezed it gently. "He's a strong man, Rose. Charlie says he's getting stronger every day. Everything is going to be good."

That was not what Charlie had said, but he let it go. Rose nodded sadly and they sat quietly, until the children returned.

"Can we try my beans now, Mama?" Gem asked, his face brightened by the prospect. "I want y'all to try them too," he added, looking at Bertie and Charlie. "I planted them from seeds."

"We would love to try some," Bertie answered, Charlie nodding in agreement.

As the sun set over the mill village, they sat on the

front porch, pondering their futures while eating Gem's green beans.

28

"I stepped out the door to go to work and there stood the money-finder. Lord have mercy, Charlie, I like to died. It was like he had been waiting for me right there on the porch.

"He said, 'Bertie, I done found your grandma's money. Turns out she buried it in a pot in the woods, and there's a note in there saying all the money belongs to you.'

"I just looked at him, with my mouth dropped open. I won't able to say a word. And that's when it struck me. I couldn't hardly believe it at first, but the money-finder was the same man who came to see Aunt Sue about me going to school.

"'You're rich now, Bertie,' he told me. 'You ain't got to work in the mill no more.' And I was so happy that I started to squalling just like a baby."

Bertie snuggled up to Charlie, who wrapped his arm across her shoulders. They stared out across the swirling river together, the moon's reflection in the water shimmering as it was broken by cotton debris floating past.

"Oh, Charlie, it was so real. It was the realest dream I done ever had. When I woke up and come to figure out it won't nothing but a dream, it made me blue. I wanted it to be true so bad.

"Do you reckon it means something? Like in the Bible when Pharaoh had dreams and they all meant something? Maybe it means it's going to come true. What do you think, Charlie?"

Charlie answered after a thoughtful pause. "Well, I reckon it's good to have dreams. Maybe yours will come true, but to be honest with you, I wouldn't count on that if I was you."

Bertie laughed, as she snuggled more closely. "I know. But ain't it grand to dream? To hope for good things? What about you, Charlie? What do you dream about?"

He was about to say something Bertie might like to hear—that he dreamed about her, for example, which would be the honest truth. What came out of his mouth instead took him a little by surprise.

"I have a queer dream sometimes. In my dream my daddy is back alive again, and he can still see. And he and Mama are happy and laughing. In the dream they're young, like our age, and Daddy's not a lot older than her, like he was in real life. And my brother and sisters are in the dream too, and they're all young'uns. The funny thing about it, Bertie, is that in the dream I'm older than I am now. I start complaining that the rest of them ain't helping enough on the farm, that there's too much to do for me to have to do it all by myself. Mama and Daddy just laugh and say, 'It's your farm now, Charlie. You have to handle things.' It seems like that ought to make me mad, but in my dream it don't. They're all so happy that it makes me happy too, even though I feel like I've got too much work to do. Ain't that a strange dream? I've had it a bunch of times—always the same."

Charlie didn't mention the thing about the dream that seemed most important to him—Ben and James weren't in it. They didn't exist.

"I wonder what it means," Bertie said. After a long quiet pause, she continued. "Maybe our dreams mean I'm going to come into a big pile of money and you're going to get your family's farm." She sighed deeply. "I like thinking about that."

29

Charlie had screwed up his courage. He was bound and determined to tell his mother about Bertie, no matter the consequences. He would tell her that he'd met a sweet girl, that they had fallen in love, and that he intended to marry her. Of course, he worried that she might be angry or disappointed, but he knew he couldn't put off telling her any longer. He would leave no doubt that Bertie was virtuous—that in no way had she ensnared him, and he convinced himself that his mother would be pleased. It had never occurred to him that he might not have the opportunity.

"Billy come over yesterday to say that Aunt Eliza is sick, and Mama went back with him to help look after her," John told him, as they were riding home from the train station. "She said to tell you she's sorry she won't be here to see you this time, nor to cook you nothing to take back."

"Is Aunt Eliza bad off? What's the matter with her?" Charlie asked.

John shrugged. "I don't know. You know Billy don't talk much. He just said she was sick and would Mama mind coming over to help tend to her."

Charlie nodded, feeling a mixture of disappointment and relief. "You don't reckon she'll be home before I have to go back?"

"I don't 'spect so," John answered. "Maybe Polly or Sally will make some biscuits for you."

"I ain't worried about that," Charlie answered. After a few minutes of silence, he asked, "What happened to Ricky? Why won't he on the train?"

"Oh, I thought you knew," John answered. "He enlisted. Him and some boys from his church. Reckon they want to go see France."

Charlie grunted an acknowledgment.

"I heard the pay is good," John said.

"Maybe, but it's a mighty risky line of work," Charlie replied. After a pause he added, "But so's working in a cotton mill, I reckon."

They rode quietly the rest of the way, Charlie's mind drifting off to thoughts of Bertie. They were nearly home when he thought to ask about the crop.

"It ain't good, Charlie," John answered, surprising him.

"Why not? What's wrong?"

"It still ain't rained," John replied. "We ain't had a drop of rain since we planted. We're gonna lose the whole crop if it don't rain soon."

Charlie shook his head in disbelief. "It don't look like no drought around here to me."

"It ain't no drought," John said. "It's the doggonedest thing. It's been raining all over the county near as I can tell. Just not on our place. Every time a cloud comes up, it just passes right on over us. Seems like ain't nobody in a drought but us."

"That just don't make no sense, John," Charlie said.

"Nope. It sure don't. It's like the Lord has done

shut up heaven, but only over our place."

"Well, that sounds to me like nothing but a little bad luck. Them showers even out over the summer," Charlie said.

"Well, all I'm saying brother is that it best rain on our crop soon or we ain't gonna have no crop," John replied.

At first light the next morning, Charlie was in the field, on his knees looking at the plants, when John walked out and joined him. "The dew has freshened them some, so they don't look so bad right now," John said. "But come look at them again after the sun is up. They'll be drooping within the next hour. Look at the dirt," he said, pointing at the cracked red clay. "Hard as a rock."

"I see what you mean," Charlie said, straightening up and brushing the soil off his hands. "Y'all been doing a rain dance?"

"Very funny," John said sarcastically. "You know what happens if we don't make this crop."

"Yeah, I know," Charlie said grimly. "I know."

After breakfast they all put on their Sunday clothes and walked to church, taking the shortcut path through the woods. It was James' turn to be an usher, and he greeted them as they filed into the building. He shook Charlie's hand firmly and didn't immediately release it. "I'm sorry to hear that your mama's sister has taken sick," he said. "I'll be praying for her."

"Obliged," Charlie answered.

James leaned forward and spoke more softly, locking eyes with Charlie and tightening his grip on his hand. "I hope you've been thinking about what I said, Charlie. I'll be praying for you to find wisdom on the matter."

Without breaking his stare, Charlie squeezed back, soon realizing that he had the stronger grip. Expressing no emotion, he looked at James until he saw a slight facial tic, evidence that the man was desperately trying not to wince. When he had that satisfaction, Charlie relaxed his grip. "Thank you, sir," he said calmly. "I'm much obliged for that too."

James answered with a contemptuous glare as he released Charlie's hand. Charlie knew immediately that his little victory was to James a declaration of war.

Later that afternoon, riding back to the station with John, Charlie pondered how high the stakes were. "We have got to make a good crop this year," he said.

"I know that, brother. It's on my mind every day," John answered. "But I ain't figured out no way yet to make it rain."

They rode quietly for several minutes, Charlie thinking of all the possible reasons for the apparent divine disfavor and finding himself the source of all of them.

"We got to pray hard," he said finally, a statement so obvious that John didn't bother responding to it.

30

Summer days in the weave room were stiflingly hot. Windows could not be opened, and there was no air circulation, as it was believed that fresh air weakened threads and caused them to break. So, in the summer the weavers had to endure the monotony, the deafening noise, and the lint and dust-filled air, all while baking and drenched in sweat.

Samuel arrived every morning, cheerful and high-spirited. Charlie couldn't recall having ever met a more optimistic person. And it amazed him. Day after day he had seen Samuel smiling and eager to begin, and day after day he had seen him coughing and wincing in pain within a few hours of starting work. At first the other weavers had pitched in to help Samuel keep up, but eventually Charlie had learned the job well enough to do it himself. When Samuel fell behind, or missed a break, he would laugh it off and pretend it was part of Charlie's training. Samuel put on an especially strong act whenever Mr. Webb was watching, which was more and more often. "That's the way to do it, Charlie," he shouted one afternoon, pretending he hadn't seen Webb watching them. "You're catching on quick," he said with a laugh. "Soon you'll be almost as good at this job as I am." Charlie grinned and nodded, before noticing Webb turn and walk away.

As they were leaving the building that evening, they heard Webb calling from behind them. "Samuel! Charlie! Hold on a minute." They stopped and waited for him, as the crowd of other workers pushed by them.

"Well, Samuel, how is this new man coming along?" Webb asked.

In his usual cheerful manner, Samuel answered him. "Just fine, Mr. Webb. He's learning fast. I'll be done taught him to be a first-rate weaver by the end of the week." As Samuel finished, his voice cracked. He turned his head and coughed roughly.

"That cough of yours doesn't seem to be getting any better," Webb said.

"Durn summer cold," Samuel answered, trying to suppress another cough. "They're hard to shake sometimes."

Webb gave him a skeptical look. "How's your arm?"

Samuel smiled and answered cheerfully, "Fully healed, sir. Back to a hundred percent." Webb, looking dubious, did not respond. After a pause Samuel changed his tone. "Almost," he said confidently. "Almost there. A hundred percent any day now."

Webb turned to Charlie, "Have you learned the job, Charlie? Ready for looms of your own?"

"Yes, sir," Charlie answered. "Samuel is a good teacher. I believe I'm ready to go."

"All right. We'll see," Webb said, before turning and calling another worker over to him. With a laugh, Samuel saluted him comically as he walked away. Charlie added a nervous, sympathetic laugh.

"Well, look who's here," Samuel said with a laugh,

as he scooped up the little girl who had run to him, wincing as he did.

Charlie saw that Rose, Gem and Bertie were approaching, Rose greeting him with a little wave. "Be easy on your daddy, Purl!" she shouted.

Samuel answered her with a laugh, as Purl tightly hugged his neck. Having spent the day in the nursery, she was the only one in the group who wasn't sweaty and covered in lint and cotton dust.

"We broke a little early today, so we thought we'd just meet y'all here and walk home together," Rose said cheerfully.

Samuel smiled appreciatively, before turning his head to cough. He gently lowered Purl to the ground and received hugs from Gem and from Rose. "That's just fine, Rose. It's been a long hot day and I'm glad it's over," he said.

Charlie turned to Bertie, greeting her with hope in his voice. "Hey, Bertie."

She turned to him and he saw a determined look on her face that he had not seen before.

"You want to walk down to the river?" Charlie asked quietly.

Bertie smiled and began to nod, then she suddenly hesitated and her smile vanished.

Over the past few days Bertie had grown increasingly troubled about her time with Charlie at the secret place—troubled because Charlie had said nothing more about marriage since their first visit. During their dinner break that afternoon she had confided her concerns to Rose.

After Rose had teasingly asked if she was going to see her beau that night, Bertie had answered, apprehensively, "Rose, me and Charlie has been going down to the river at nights." With her face clouded by concern, and after a pause, she added, "I think maybe I ought not go there with him no more until after we're married."

"Married!" Rose had exclaimed.

Bertie continued, bashfully, "Charlie one time said we was going to get married. But he ain't talked none about it lately." After a sad pause she added, "They say won't nobody buy a cow if he can get the milk for free."

Rose smiled sympathetically, reached over and took Bertie's hand. "Getting married is real important, Bertie. If you're going to do it, don't put it off." She released Bertie's hand to quickly wipe away a tear. "If you put it off too long, it might not never happen."

Rose's words and her concerned look flashed through Bertie's mind as Charlie looked expectantly at her.

"I don't think so, Charlie," she said sternly.

"Why not, Bertie?" Charlie asked, confused.

Bertie looked down at her bare feet and shook her head. After a few moments she looked up at Charlie and said firmly, "I don't think I ought to go there no more with you, Charlie. Not until after we're married." She ended her sentence with emphasis.

Samuel and his family were walking just ahead of them. Samuel's head popped up and he turned to them with a delighted look on his face. He had overheard her last word.

"Married?!" he exclaimed, beaming. "Y'all are getting married?!"

Bertie dropped her head, wringing her hands shyly. Charlie seemed momentarily confused. Rose turned to them too, smiling broadly.

"Well…," Charlie said, stammering, "I mean… It's like this…."

Bertie looked at Samuel and answered softly, "Charlie told me we was gonna get married."

Rose suddenly squealed with delight, then ran over and wrapped Bertie in a hug while Samuel grabbed Charlie's hand, shaking it vigorously, before wincing and releasing it. He laughed heartily, then slapped Charlie on the back.

"Well, hot dog!" Samuel shouted. "Don't nothing beat married life, boy, let me tell you! You're a lucky man, Charlie. Bertie is a fine girl!"

"Oh, yes," Charlie said, still confused and stammering. "That's so. But we ain't… I mean…"

Releasing Bertie from the hug, Rose turned excitedly to Charlie. "When are y'all getting married?" she asked.

Charlie hesitated, glancing over at Bertie, who was smiling nervously. Rose and Samuel were staring at him, expectantly. He began to rock back and forth on his feet, then grinned awkwardly and said, "Well, we ain't set no specific time for it yet, have we Bertie?"

Bertie just stared back at him, without answering. Rose and Samuel were still looking at him, too, unsatisfied with his response.

Charlie tried to lighten the mood, laughing nervously, and saying, "Who's got time to get married when we're at work ten hours a day?"

They all continued to look at Charlie, waiting for a serious answer.

"We don't work on Sundays," Rose said.

"Charlie goes home to see his mama on Sundays," Bertie replied, while Charlie continued to squirm.

"Well," Rose answered with a light laugh, "I reckon

he can squeeze a wedding in too."

Samuel began shaking his head, "No, no, no," he said to Rose. "It don't have to be on no Sunday. They can get married anytime they want to. It's easy."

Rose glanced at Samuel, her face betraying a little hurt and the potential for anger. In his usual cheerful manner, Samuel continued, turning to Bertie and Charlie, "The mill's got a preacher! Don't y'all know about the mill preacher?"

"The mill preacher?" Bertie replied, looking at Samuel inquisitively while Charlie continued to fidget.

"Sure!" Samuel exclaimed. "The mill's got everything! You think a mill like this ain't got no preacher?"

Charlie sensed things were careening out of his control, as if he was in a wagon being pulled by a runaway team.

"Samuel…," he said awkwardly. "We ain't… I mean…"

But Samuel was not listening to Charlie. Noticing that Webb had just finished talking to one of the workers and was beginning to walk away, Samuel called out to him. "Hey, Mr. Webb!"

Webb stopped and stepped toward them. "Yes," he said.

"Charlie and Bertie want to get married," Samuel said. "Can the mill preacher marry 'em?"

"Of course," Webb said, matter-of-factly. "No problem." He turned to Charlie and continued, "Just come by my office after work tomorrow and I'll have him there." He paused, then said, "It costs two dollars. We'll take it out of your pay." Turning to Bertie he asked, "Y'all want to split it?"

Bertie nodded with excitement, while Charlie

appeared staggered by it all.

"All right," Webb said. "Be in my office right after the whistle tomorrow." He nodded to the group, then turned and walked briskly away.

Rose and Bertie hugged again, both teary-eyed and squealing with joy. Samuel extended his hand toward Charlie, then pulled it back suddenly. "I reckon you ought to shake my other hand instead," he said with a laugh, extending his left hand, which Charlie took and shook nervously.

Breaking off her hug with Rose, Bertie shyly moved toward Charlie, beaming. Then, abandoning her reserve she suddenly rushed into his arms, hugging him tightly, while Rose and Samuel laughed and hugged, watching them.

Bertie looked into Charlie's face, her eyes filled with tears, "Oh, Charlie," she said, "I am so happy I could just bust wide open!"

Charlie, feeling like he was being swept away in a raging river, offered a nervous and uncertain smile.

With a twinkle in her eyes, Bertie leaned forward and whispered mischievously into his ear, "Let's go down to the river tonight."

31

When she met Rose at the mill gate the next morning, Bertie was wearing the same faded, worn work dress and apron she always wore. Her hair was pulled up and tied atop her head, the way it always was. Like always, she was barefoot. But this morning, unlike any other, she was carrying a sack and in the sack was her only pair of shoes, and in one of the shoes was a little piece of paper on which she had written "18." It was her wedding day.

Seeing Bertie approaching, Rose rushed out to her. "Bertie!" she said, excitedly. "Yonder comes Charlie. Quick! Run inside! It's bad luck for him to see you now!"

Rose began hurrying Bertie away as Charlie was walking past, heading to the weaver's gate, wearing his faded denim overalls and cotton cap. As Rose was pulling her along, Bertie looked back and when she did, she caught Charlie's eye. From a distance, they smiled nervously at each other, then Bertie blushed deeply and rushed inside the building. Charlie was still looking at the gate when Samuel came up from behind him.

"Morning, Charlie!" he said with a friendly slap on the back.

"Hey, Samuel," Charlie answered, walking alongside him, toward the gate.

"Well, today's the big day," Samuel said cheerfully. "Ain't nervous, are you?"

"Naw," Charlie answered. "Well, I mean… Maybe a little bit."

"Ain't nothing to be nervous about, Charlie!" Samuel exclaimed with a laugh. "You're a lucky man!"

Charlie smiled and nodded nervously.

Samuel coughed roughly, then threw his arm across Charlie's shoulders, smiling. "Now look here, Charlie. I know you're gonna have your mind on other things today, but pay attention and be careful with them looms. You don't want to get hurt on your wedding day, do you?"

Charlie shook his head, still smiling nervously.

As they reached the gate, Samuel laughed and said "Well come on and let's get to work, boy. We got a lot of cotton to weave today before you can get yourself hitched!"

For Charlie, the workday was a blur, as the night before had been. Was he really going to get married? In a mill boss's office? With no one from his family there? It seemed unreal to him, out of his control somehow. As he had reflected on his situation the previous night, he had come to what he regarded as two undeniable truths. One was that he was deeply in love with Bertie and wanted to marry her, the sooner the better. The other was that he ought not to be getting married in this way, at this time. Maybe there was a way to reconcile those two truths—to get married, but to do it differently, in church and at home. But he realized that way, if it existed, was not open to him.

Bertie was already in Webb's office when Charlie arrived. Webb was also there, looking impatient. And standing awkwardly in front of the desk was a young man in an ill-fitting suit, holding a Bible, a cow lick defying the Brilliantine that otherwise flattened his hair in place.

The young preacher looked dubiously at Bertie. "How old are you, Miss Bovry?" he asked.

"I beg your pardon?" Bertie said timidly, tilting her head.

Charlie looked at her curiously, never having heard her speak that way before.

"Oh, she's plenty old enough," Webb said. "Get on with it."

The preacher looked down nervously at his notes as if about to proceed, but then looked back up at Bertie. "How old are you?" he repeated.

"Pardon me sir, what did you say?" Bertie asked, innocently.

The young man looked frustrated, and was about to speak, when Webb blurted out, "He just wants to know if you're over eighteen."

"Oh," Bertie said, her face brightening as she looked up at the preacher. "Yes, sir. I sure am. I am over eighteen," she said, wiggling her toes to feel the paper in her shoe.

The preacher nodded, then perfunctorily read the abbreviated ceremony. In due course he pronounced them married, after which Webb offered an insincere congratulations before unceremoniously ushering them out of his office.

Samuel, Rose, and family were waiting for them by the gate. Samuel was standing next to his wife, with his arm thrown across her shoulders. Like Bertie and

Charlie, Samuel and Rose were dusty and lint-covered from the day's work. They were smiling broadly.

When Rose caught sight of the couple, she squealed with joy and rushed to Bertie. They hugged, laughed, and cried.

Samuel walked up to Charlie and extended his hand, unthinkingly, then withdrew it with a laugh and offered his left hand instead. "Well congratulations, old man!" Samuel said. "Welcome to married life!" With a warm smile, Charlie shook his friend's hand.

Rose pushed away from Bertie's hug, looked her in the face and said, "Oh, Bertie, I am so happy for you!"

Wiping her eyes, Bertie said, "It's like a dream. It's real ain't it, Rose?"

Rose drew her in for another hug.

"Sure does look real to me," Samuel said with a laugh. Turning to Charlie he asked, "Are y'all all proper hitched now?"

"There won't nothing to it, Sam," Charlie answered. "They had all the paperwork done already. All we had to do was sign. Their preacher married us right there in Mr. Webb's office, just like he said."

"See there? I told you it was easy," Samuel said, causing Rose's smile to disappear momentarily. "Rose, ain't there something we're supposed to tell these lovebirds?" he asked with a grin.

Brightening again, Rose took Bertie by the hand. "Seeing as how y'all ain't got no place of your own yet, we're gonna go stay with Becky and Richard, so y'all can stay at our house tonight."

Bertie's jaw dropped in surprise, causing Samuel to laugh and slap Charlie on the back, before being overcome by a coughing fit.

"Your house?? Oh Rose, y'all ain't got to do that!"

Bertie exclaimed.

Samuel walked over to his Rose and put his arm around her, both of them beaming.

"We want to, sugar," Rose answered, while Samuel stood beside her, smiling and nodding. "Y'all ought to have a quiet place to yourself tonight and it makes us happy to offer you our house."

Bertie began to cry again. She blushed, dropped her head, covered her eyes, and said softly, "Ain't nobody never been so nice to me."

Rose answered with a laugh, "Oh, now you go on and hush up about that. Ain't no big thing to let our friends borrow our house for a night. You don't get but one wedding night, you know!"

"What about Tick and Tom?" Bertie asked.

"They're staying somewhere else tonight too. Y'all got the whole house to yourselves!" Rose said.

"We're much obliged, Samuel," Charlie said.

Samuel shook his head and waved his hand dismissively, before turning to cough again.

"It's our wedding present," Rose said. "And to make it special, I done baked a pie for y'all. It's sitting on top of the stove and I bet it's still warm."

"This is the best day ever," Bertie said, wiping away her tears. "I ain't never been so happy in my whole life."

"I'll make it up to you, Samuel," Charlie said.

"Ha!" Samuel answered cheerfully. "The last couple days you been doing more of my job than I have." He laughed and added, "Y'all don't owe us a thing."

Rose and Bertie hugged again, then Rose released her with a laugh. "Y'all go on home now," she said. Turning to her children, who were playing nearby, she shouted, "Y'all young'uns come on now! It's time to go!"

Gem and Purl rushed over to their mother, who took them by the hand and began to walk away. Samuel leaned in toward Charlie and said, with a playful chuckle, "Try to get you a little rest, Charlie. The whistle's gonna come mighty early tomorrow."

Charlie blushed an acknowledgement, then Samuel winked teasingly and walked away. Catching up with his family, he rubbed the top of Gem's head playfully, then picked up Purl, wincing as he did, and sat her on his shoulders.

As they walked away, Charlie took Bertie's hands and they looked into each other's faces for a moment, searchingly. They embraced, then kissed. After the kiss they looked into each other's eyes again. After a few seconds Bertie smiled, then giggled. Bertie's giggle made Charlie chuckle, and in a moment they both began laughing. Charlie took Bertie's hand, and they rushed off down the road.

32

Two mornings later, as Rose and family were walking to work, they heard Bertie calling out from behind them.

"Rose! Wait up!" she shouted.

They stopped and waited for Bertie to catch up. She was dressed for work, as usual, but she was carrying a borrowed valise.

"Well good morning, Bertie," Rose said teasingly. "Going somewhere?"

Samuel laughed.

"Oh, y'all stop," Bertie said. "I ain't slept a wink last night. I'm so nervous about meeting Charlie's mama that I'm about to die!"

"Are you fixing to go right now or are you gonna go to work first?" Samuel said jokingly.

"Charlie always leaves right straight after work on Saturday, so I wanted to make sure I'm ready to go just as soon as that whistle blows!" Bertie replied, adding nervously, "Oh law, I surely hope she likes me."

"She's going to just love you to pieces, Bertie," Rose said confidently, drawing a blush from her friend.

As they were talking, Samuel noticed Charlie in the crowd of workers trudging down the road. "Hey,

Charlie," he called out.

Seeing them, Charlie smiled and walked over, all greeting him simultaneously.

"Morning, y'all," Charlie answered, before bending over and kissing Bertie.

"Oh, Charlie. I'm so excited," Bertie said.

"That must have been a heck of a kiss," Samuel said, with a laugh.

Bertie slapped him on the shoulder playfully. "Oh, you hush up," she said. "You know what I meant."

"Well if it ain't me doing it, what *is* exciting you this morning?" Charlie asked jokingly.

"Because it's Saturday, Charlie," Bertie answered.

Charlie looked at her, as if expecting her to say more.

"Saturday!" she said, teasingly. "You know, the day before Sunday…"

With the others all looking at him expectantly, Charlie seemed clueless. After a pause he said, "Yep. It's Saturday all right."

"I'm so excited to meet your mama, Charlie!" Bertie exclaimed, Charlie's smile vanishing as she spoke.

"C'mon, boy" Samuel said, slapping Charlie on the back. "It's time to get to work. Let's go weave us some cotton!"

Bertie rose on her tiptoes and kissed Charlie again. "Bye, Charlie! See you after work!" she said, beaming.

After eight years in the spinning room, it seemed to Bertie that she could do her job without thinking. She kept her spindles going all day, nimbly and skillfully fixing the thread breaks when they occurred ("putting up ends," she would have called it), the roar of the machines pounding in her ears, while she dreamed all day of the beauty and serenity she expected to find on

Charlie's farm. When the whistle blew that evening, the sound sent a chill down her spine.

She retrieved her bag from the corner where she had left it and caught up to Rose and the children as they shuffled through the door and toward the gate. Exiting onto the road, the women brushed lint and cotton dust off their clothes, while Bertie chattered rapidly and nervously.

"I brung my shoes," she said. "You reckon I ought to put them on now, Rose?" Crossing the road and onto a grassy area where they usually waited for the men, Bertie sat down, took her shoes out of the bag, and put them on hurriedly. "I got me a clean bonnet to wear too," she said, taking it out of the bag and opening it. She paused and looked up at Rose with concern. "But, goodness Rose, I'm just as dirty as a hog. I wonder if we'll be able to wash up before we get there. I ain't sure if Charlie does that or not. It'll be late when we get there. But I'm sure she's used to Charlie coming straight from work." A sudden look of alarm swept across her face. "Oh, Rose! Maybe I ought to wash up now! Do you reckon I have time to run down to the river and clean my face at least? What should I do, Rose?"

Rose chuckled and said reassuringly, "What you ought to do is settle down, sugar. Just wait and see what Charlie wants to do."

Bertie nodded nervously, stood up, and began searching for Charlie in the crowd of workers on the road. After a few minutes she exclaimed, "Yonder they are! Here they come!"

Spotting the women, Samuel waved and smiled, cheerful as always, despite looking drained and weak. Walking alongside him, Charlie looked troubled. He began to lag behind as Samuel quickened his pace, walking toward the women. Purl rushed out to him and he lifted her up with a laugh.

Bertie picked up her bag and stepped forward, her face alight. Charlie made eye contact, stepped toward her, then hesitated. He stopped suddenly, looking around strangely, as if confused. Bertie strode toward him, glowing with delight. Then, just as she was nearly within arm's length, Charlie suddenly wheeled around and sprinted away, bumping roughly into another worker, then disappearing into the crowd.

Watching him running, Bertie stood frozen and puzzled. A concerned look swept across Rose's face, causing Samuel to turn around. Seeing what was happening, he let out a laugh.

"Where's Charlie going?" he said, smiling. "He's running like his britches are on fire."

"I don't know," Bertie said, confused and troubled. "He didn't say nothing. He just turned and run off."

"Maybe he's gone back to get something," Rose said.

"Where's he gone to?" Bertie asked, standing up on her tiptoes and searching the crowd. "I can't see him no more."

"Maybe nature was calling," Samuel said with a laugh. "I 'spect he'll be right back."

They stood waiting, chatting nervously, as the crowd of workers on the road dwindled, then vanished. After a while they sat down on the grass. Minutes passed, then an hour. A quiet and tense mood descended over them.

"Y'all go on home," Bertie said, at last, pretending to be less concerned than she was. "Ain't no need in y'all waiting too." Turning to Rose she added, "I know you have to cook supper."

Samuel stood up, no longer cheerful. "Y'all wait here," he said. "I'll go and look for him."

The women waited silently, both knowing that silence was less painful and awkward than filling the time with small talk. After a while Samuel returned, shaking his head. As he approached, Rose looked at him with concern, seeing that he was exhausted and weakened by the day's work, knowing that he needed rest.

"I can't find him nowhere and nobody knows where he went," he said.

Bertie was choking back tears, unable to look her friends in the face, when they heard the whistle of the Number Eight.

"Charlie is on that train," Bertie said softly.

"I don't think so, Bertie. I checked all around the station and didn't see him nowhere," Samuel said.

They watched as, in the distance, the train rolled across the bridge and over the river.

Heartbroken, Bertie said sadly, "He's on that train. He don't want me. He's ashamed of me."

Rose scooted over and put her arm across Bertie's shoulders. "I 'spect he'll be here any minute now," she said, attempting to comfort her friend. After a pause she added firmly, "And when he gets here, he can explain why he run off like that—without saying nothing!"

The awkward and tense silence returned, broken when Purl walked up. "I'm hungry, Mama," the little girl said. Standing behind her, Gem nodded.

Bertie reached out and took Purl's hand. "Oh, bless your heart, child," she said. "Rose, you go on home and feed these children. I'll wait here for Charlie, and if he comes back, I'll tell you all about it on Monday morning."

Samuel turned to his wife. "Y'all go on home and I'll wait here with Bertie. I 'spect I'll be there directly."

"You go on home too, Samuel. I thank you kindly, but y'all ain't got to wait with me," Bertie said.

Samuel looked at Rose and saw the pleading look in her eyes. She nodded.

"All right, Bertie," he said reluctantly. "And when that boy gets back, knock him upside the head one time for me."

Rose hugged Bertie again, she and Samuel said their goodbyes, and then they walked away, toward home. Bertie maintained her composure until they were out of sight, then she buried her face in her hands and began to sob—heartbroken by the soul-crushing loss of her dreams.

When, after a while, the tears stopped coming, Bertie lay back on the grass and stared up at the sky. She retreated mentally back to her life before Charlie, to the familiar assurance of her lack of worth, to the absence of any dignity, value, or self-esteem. Charlie was right to leave her behind, she concluded. She realized she had been a fool to ever expect otherwise.

It was dark when Rose returned, finding Bertie lying on her back, looking up at the stars. She sat down on the grass, next to her friend, putting her hand gently on Bertie's shoulder.

"It's late, Bertie," she said, trying to mask her own heartbreak. "Come on and stay with us tonight."

"Charlie don't want me, Rose. I ain't nothing but an ugly, stupid girl. He's done got all he wanted from me," Bertie said softly.

Rose wiped away a tear. "Come on, Bertie," she

said, fighting back the urge to cry. "Time to go home."

Bertie sat up, slowly, her face streaked by tears. She took off her shoes and put them in her bag, then stood up and wiped her eyes. Gathering her strength, she looked into her friend's concerned face. "Thank you, Rose. You have always been so kind to me. But I'm going back to my room now. I'll see you Monday morning."

Rose reached for her, but Bertie raised her hand, gave her a hint of a smile, then turned and walked slowly away. Watching her leave, Rose began to cry.

33

Charlie banged his head against the train window so many times that the passenger sitting nearest him got up and moved, no doubt assuming he must be either dangerously drunk, or a lunatic.

He had panicked, and it left him deeply ashamed of himself. He had intended to tell Bertie that he needed to go home alone first, to tell his mother about the marriage, and that he would return the next morning to get her. But when he saw Bertie standing there with Rose, holding her bag, wearing her shoes, and looking so happy and expectant, he had completely lost both his tongue and his nerve. He had felt physically ill and needed to get away to collect himself. He hid behind a pile of coal near the depot and tried to settle his nerves. But no matter how hard he tried, he couldn't calm himself, and no matter how many times he tried to make his little practiced speech, he couldn't find the words. Then it was too late. He heard the call to board, debated what to do, then finally rushed out and jumped up onto the running board even as the train had begun to pull away.

He hated himself for having left Bertie behind, with no warning or explanation. It was impossible for him to justify what had happened. On the one hand, he was certain that he could not just show up at home with a bride no one expected. On the other hand, staying another night in Danville wasn't an option. His family would assume the worst, be worried sick, and would probably come looking for him. Charlie felt helpless, as if he was just being dragged along by events that he was unable to control.

I can fix this, he told himself. I *must* fix this.

The solution, the only one that made sense to him, was to go straight home, tell his mother about the wedding, hope the news didn't kill her on the spot, then immediately return to fetch Bertie. He would go back that very night, even if he had to walk. When he explained what had happened, Bertie would surely forgive him. He didn't dare consider that she might not.

John was waiting for him at the Raye depot, as usual. Catching sight of him as he was exiting the train, Charlie knew immediately something was wrong. John looked as if he was just as distressed as Charlie.

"Something ain't right, brother. What is it?" Charlie asked as he walked with John to the waiting mule.

"It's over for us," John said gloomily. "We ain't had a drop of rain all week. This crop is lost. And you know what that means."

It was a punch in the gut that Charlie hadn't expected.

"Are the plants dead?" Charlie asked, incredulous.

"Probably," John replied. "If they ain't, they surely will be after they get another day of cooking tomorrow."

Charlie felt as if his head was spinning. He pushed the thought of the lost crop out of his mind for a moment, returning to his immediate emergency.

"John, I have got to get back to Danville tonight. I may need to take Jack. Else I'll walk. It can't wait till tomorrow," Charlie said.

"Tonight?" John said, puzzled. "What for?"

"I'll explain it to you after I tell Mama," he answered, as they mounted the mule. "But I'm in an awful hurry, so see if you can make Jack go a little quicker tonight."

"Brother, you know there ain't no way to hurry this mule," John said, shaking the reins and giving the animal a little kick in the side. "Try to rush Jack and he'll just stop altogether."

"Well, do the best you can," Charlie said, frustrated.

The mule plodded along at his usual leisurely pace, indifferent to all efforts to speed him up, adding to Charlie's anxiety. John seemed sunk into a deep funk, so they rode without speaking, leaving Charlie time to wallow in his guilt. When they finally neared the house, Charlie spoke. "Take me to the field first. I want to see the plants," he said. John grunted and turned the mule in that direction.

Charlie examined the plants by moonlight. Withered and drooping, he agreed with this brother's assessment of them. If the plants were still alive, they were barely so. His heart sank even further. This is the crop they had counted on. Without it, the farm was lost.

On his knees, Charlie dug his hands deep into the furrow. The red clay was as dry as a bone.

Why, he thought. This isn't fair. Why us? Why now? But he knew the answers. "This is punishment," he said out loud, speaking to no one. "This is *my* punishment."

"What?" his brother asked, standing off in the distance.

Charlie turned to face him. "I said..." he began. Then something caught his eye. He looked up just in time to see a shooting star blazing across the sky, the largest one he'd ever seen. And in a flash, it was gone.

"What did you say, Charlie?" his brother asked, walking toward him.

Charlie stood staring into the sky, where the meteor had been.

"Are you all right, Charlie?" John asked. "What are you looking at?"

Charlie lowered his eyes until he was looking John in the face. "Have y'all been praying for rain?" he asked.

John nodded. "Been praying like there ain't no tomorrow."

"And it ain't rained?"

"Not a drop," John answered.

Charlie looked down at the plants, then put his hand over his eyes, as if deep in thought. After a few moments he looked back at John again. "Maybe this is something God wants us to do for ourselves."

"Do for ourselves? What?"

"We have got to water these plants," Charlie said, firmly.

"Water them?" John said, shaking his head in disbelief. "How are we going to water all this tobacco?"

"One plant at a time, I reckon," Charlie answered.

After a pause he began speaking rapidly, "We'll need more water than we can take from the well, so first thing in the morning we'll hitch Jack to the wagon, load up the empty flour barrels, then go down to the creek and fill them up with water. We'll take the well bucket. Oh, and the milk pails too. That's what we'll use to dip out the creek water. Then we'll haul the water to the field and pour it on the plants with dippers and Mason jars and whatever else we got."

"That's just about the craziest dang thing I've ever heard in my life," John said. "You can't water this field with dippers of creek water."

"We can and we will," Charlie answered. "Come on. Let's go home right now and start getting ready."

Charlie turned and stepped toward the mule.

"Charlie," John said. "Tomorrow is Sunday."

"I know that," Charlie said.

"It's the Sabbath," John said.

"The ox is in the ditch," Charlie answered, as he began untying the mule. "Now come on if you want to ride."

Bewildered by it all, John shook his head and hurried over to the mule, Charlie having already mounted and taken the reins. After his brother pulled him up onto the animal's back, John said, "I thought you had to go back to Danville tonight."

Charlie felt a quick stabbing pain in his heart at the thought of Bertie abandoned. Then he shook his head. "I can't go back tonight, John. We've got to try to save this crop."

34

Bertie went home, but only long enough to get Susannah. She slipped the doll into her pocket and walked sadly toward her secret place. Dazed, she did not take her usual precautions.

Jimmy Key was shooting dice in an alley, splitting a jug with a couple of Craghead Street regulars, when one of them said, "Well, lookie yonder fellas. Looks to me like that sweet young thing could use some company."

Jimmy looked up from the game to see a moonlit girl in the distance, standing alone by the river. The girl bent down, picked up a stone, and tossed it in the water. After a moment, he recognized her.

"Let her be, Barnie," Jimmy said. "That's Charlie's girl."

"Who the hell is Charlie?" Barnie answered as he stood up.

"Whoever he is, it don't look like she's his girl right now," the other man said, as he too rose to his feet. "Looks to me like there's gonna be plenty for all of us," he added with a lewd sneer.

Jimmy staggered as he stood, unsteadied by alcohol. "Come on, boys," he said. "Leave her alone and let's finish the game."

"We'll finish later," Barnie said, stepping in Bertie's direction. "I got me some business to tend to first."

The other man laughed and said, "You and me both," stepping away also.

Jimmy sighed, knowing what he had to do and what the consequences would be. He lunged forward, driving his shoulder into Barnie's back, knocking him to the ground. The other man, briefly startled, turned around just as Jimmy's fist landed on the bridge of his nose.

It took less than a minute for the two men to beat Jimmy senseless, but when they turned their attention back to the girl, she was gone. The last thing Jimmy saw before losing consciousness, was Bertie in the distance, ducking out of sight.

Bertie had been oblivious to it all. She snaked along the narrow, overhung path until she reached the concealed entrance to her secret place. She pulled back the brambles and crawled inside, onto the little strip of beach. Once inside, for the first time ever, she did not bother to block the entrance.

Bertie took the doll out of her pocket and stuck it into the sand, facing her. Then she laid back, staring up into the sky.

For over an hour, she lay there silently, mourning the loss of her hopes for happiness and belonging. When at last she felt like she had no more tears to shed, she sat up. Looking at the doll, she smiled sadly.

"We've had us some nice times here, ain't we Susannah?"

Bertie reached out for the doll, then pulled it to her breast. "I love you, Susannah," she said, the tears coming again. "You ain't never been nothing but nice to me. Thank you for everything."

After sobbing for a few minutes, Bertie opened her eyes and looked out over the water, then up into the sky. "Look, Susannah," she said, turning the doll to face the sky. "There's the Lady of the Chair. See her? My daddy told me all about her. How she was a queen and she bragged that she was the most beautiful woman in the world, so the old-timey gods tied her to a chair and stuck her up in the sky like that, to spin around the North Star till the end of time. Ain't that a sad story?"

Bertie sighed, then kissed the doll and stuck it back into the sand. She stared at it for a few moments, then said, "No, my dear. That is sweet of you. But you stay here. Don't forget me, and I won't never forget you. Goodbye, my precious friend."

Bertie stood up, stepped over the doll, and walked to the edge of the river. Resisting a powerful urge to look back at her friend one last time, she lifted her right foot and stepped out into the water, finding it to be surprisingly warm. Bertie closed her eyes and took another step, then another, and another. When the water had reached her neck, she shuddered and swallowed hard. She opened her eyes and looked up. "Goodbye, Lady," she said, as a tear slid down her cheek. "I'm sorry about what happened to you." She lowered her eyes and lifted her foot to take a final step when something caught her attention. She glanced back up in time to see a flash, a fiery meteor blazing across the constellation.

Bertie gasped. Instinctively she closed her eyes and made a wish. Opening them again, she stood staring at the stars for a few moments, then suddenly turned and hurried back, stumbling, splashing, and struggling toward the shore. By the time she reached the beach, she was nearly out of breath.

Bertie fell to her knees before the doll, "Did you see it, Susannah? Did you see the shooting star? Right across the Lady of the Chair!" She plucked the doll out of the sand and squeezed it to her breast. "Oh, Susannah, it must be a sign! I just know it. A sign from the Lady!" She pulled the doll out to arms' length, looked in its face and exclaimed, "You know what it means, Susannah? It means something good is going to happen to me! Something good! I just know it!"

35

By the time the sun rose the next morning, the whole family was already headed to the creek, John driving the wagon, his mother sitting beside him, and the rest of them—Charlie and his five sisters—walking alongside. Charlie had expected his mother to put up more of a fight. She had protested violating the Sabbath, as he knew she would, but had relented in the face of his justifications, both theological and practical. Charlie's ultimate argument was simple and compelling— "Mama, if we don't get water on the crop, we're going to lose this farm." She had fallen silent for a few moments, her head bowed, before looking up and agreeing. "The ox is in the ditch," she said.

John got the wagon as close to the creek as he could, but that still left a distance of over a hundred yards that the water would have to be carried, much of that up a steep bank. Charlie had them stretch out into a bucket line. He would dip out the water, then pass the bucket to Polly, who would carry it to Sally, who would carry it to John, and so on, ending at the wagon, where it would be passed up to their mother who would dump the water into the barrel, then send the bucket back down the line. It was far from ideal, but it was the best they could do.

Only having three buckets to work with, the well bucket and the two milk pails, and having to stretch five people over a hundred yards, the work went slowly. It was especially hard on Jillianne, so that their mother soon required that she only carry every other bucketful. As the July sun rose in the cloudless sky, it began to wither them as it had withered the tobacco. It took the better part of the morning to fill the two barrels, and they were all exhausted as they trudged toward the field, following the wagon.

They were almost there when one of the wagon wheels slipped into a rut, the jolt toppling one of the barrels and pouring their morning's work out into the road. Sally wailed. John muttered and kicked the footboard. Charlie fought to keep his composure. "Next time we won't fill them so high," he said, pretending to be calm. "They'll ride better if they ain't all the way full."

John drove the wagon the rest of the way, stopping at the edge of the field. Once there, Charlie gave the instructions. "We'll do three rows at a time," he said. "Me and John and Polly will carry the buckets. Everybody else will dip the water and pour it onto the plants. Put it right where the plant goes into the ground and be careful not to waste none."

Standing on the wagon, their mother dipped the buckets into the barrel, then handed them down, and they marched to the field. They had just begun pouring on the water when James arrived.

The congregation had been restless throughout the service that morning, passing whispers of concern for the absent Lawtons, who had never before missed a service. Charlie had insisted that his mother go without them, but she had refused. It was the first Sunday in her life that she hadn't gone to church. The elder tried to carry on as normal, but he too was worrying about the family, and when James Lawton suddenly stood up and left the building, the elder abbreviated the service and dismissed his flock after a quick final prayer.

James had gone directly from the church to the Lawton farm, and he was astonished at what he discovered there. "What in the Sam Hill are y'all doing?" he shouted from the seat of his buggy.

"Morning, James," Betsy said calmly, as she passed down a bucket of water to John.

"Don't you know that this is the Lord's day?" James replied accusingly.

"I do," she answered. "God be praised."

From the field, Charlie heard the exchange. He felt a flash of anger but beat it back. "Here," he said, handing his bucket to Sally. "Keep pouring. I'll be right back." He hurried over until he was standing between his mother and James.

"Morning, James," he said, again dropping the once obligatory "Uncle Brother."

"This is a disgrace, Charlie. Is this your doing?" James demanded.

"Yes, it is. We're going to lose this crop if we don't get water on these plants right now," Charlie answered.

"Boy, if God wants water on that crop, he'll water it," James said.

"Maybe that's what he's doing," Charlie replied, bringing a smile to his mother as she went on filling buckets.

At the sound of a horse approaching, they turned to see the elder—Joseph Watkins—riding hurriedly toward them on a bay mare. James smiled triumphantly when he saw the preacher coming.

Watkins pulled up the reins, stopping his horse beside James' buggy.

"Do you see what they're doing?" James said, gesturing toward the field.

Watkins took his time, surveying the scene before answering. "I do." After a pause he continued, "It looks to me like they're trying to save their crop."

"On the Lord's day!" James exclaimed.

Ignoring the comment, Watkins turned to Charlie. "Still ain't got no rain here, Charlie?" he asked.

"No, sir. Not a drop," Charlie replied. "We're hauling water up from creek. I couldn't think of nothing else to do."

Watkins nodded, then looked around pensively.

"I told them that if the Lord wanted it to rain here, it would've rained already," James said. "This is how people behave when they ain't got no faith."

After a few moments Watkins spoke to Charlie, making no indication that he had heard James. "I'm going home to get my boys," he said. "We'll be back shortly to help you."

"Much obliged, sir," Charlie answered.

Watkins turned to face James. "Which of you shall have an ass or an ox fallen into a pit and will not straightway pull him out on the sabbath day?" he said. "I believe this is all right."

James's face reddened. "They ain't doing nothing that can't wait till tomorrow! The word of God is clear that…"

Watkins interrupted him. "Excuse me Brother James, but I'm in a hurry. I'll be pleased to discuss it with you later," he said, turning his horse and trotting away.

Charlie couldn't resist. "I'm in a hurry too, James." He touched his cap. "Good day to you," he said.

James shouted from his buggy as Charlie turned and walked away. "You think you're smart, don't you boy? Well let me tell you, there ain't no way in hell you can haul enough water up here to get this tobacco watered. No way!"

Charlie kept walking, hearing James rolling away behind him after ordering his horse to gitty-up. As much as he enjoyed his little victory, Charlie's stomach was twisted nevertheless. He knew James was right.

John was waiting for him when Charlie got back to the field. "This ain't going to work, Charlie," he said.

Charlie had realized that just before James pulled up. The dirt was so baked and parched that when water was poured on it, it just rolled off the bed. And the entire barrel was empty in minutes, before they had finished even a quarter of the three rows.

"It's going to take us at least an hour to fill the barrels again, probably more," John said, shaking his head. "And the water ain't going to the roots no how."

"It don't look good, but we got to keep trying," Charlie answered. "We'll use well water this time—that will be a lot quicker. And I think that if we take a stick and poke a hole in the ground next to the plant, we can pour the water in the hole and maybe that will get it to the roots."

"You're the boss," John replied, making no effort to conceal his skepticism.

They drove the wagon to the well. Using both the re-tied well bucket and the hand pump, they soon had the barrels filled, being careful not to fill them to the top and make them unsteady.

Back at the field, Charlie had his two youngest sisters go down the rows with sticks, poking watering holes next to the plants. When they poured water into the holes, the parched soil sucked it down greedily.

"Charlie," John said, resignedly, "there ain't near enough water in the well to water this field, and we'd run the well dry trying."

Charlie nodded in agreement. "You're right," he said. "There ain't no point in this."

By the time they had emptied the second load, Elder Watkins and his sons had arrived, pulling a wagon with an empty barrel in it. "You want us to fill this from the creek?" Watkins asked.

Not having the heart to admit defeat, Charlie nodded. "Thank you, sir. We're much obliged."

By then the word had spread throughout Raye. Mr. Lockett was the next to arrive. "I brought some extra pickle barrels for y'all to use," he said, stepping down off the wagon and gesturing toward the barrels. Looking down at the plants, flopped and browning, he asked, "Y'all reckon this is going to work?"

Charlie sighed before answering, "No, sir. I don't 'spect so. It was worth a try, but it ain't working."

"Well, let me give you a hand anyway," Lockett answered.

Moved to see his family's principal creditor come to their assistance, Charlie nodded and answered, "Thank you, sir. We're much obliged."

Over the next hour or so, more neighbors arrived with buckets, dippers, and barrels, keeping a steady procession of wagons going to and from the creek and field.

It was past noon when Betsy pulled Charlie aside and said, "I can't cook enough to feed all these folks, but I'm going to make as much cornbread as I can."

Charlie couldn't help but laugh. "Too little cornbread to go along with too little water." When he saw that his mother didn't see the humor in it, he answered more seriously, "All right, Mama."

By the time Betsy brought out the cornbread, more neighbors had arrived, and the atmosphere was nearly festive. Seasoned farmers all, everybody saw quickly that Charlie's plan couldn't succeed, but they kept on, cheerfully working and pretending they were doing some good for the Lawtons' crop. To Betsy's surprise, there was enough cornbread to go around. All the workers seemed to get their fill and when she gathered up the pans, there was still a little left over.

Sometime mid-afternoon John came over to Charlie and said, "You best leave now or you ain't gonna make the Number Eleven."

Charlie put down his bucket, pulled a handkerchief from his back pocket, and wiped the sweat off his face. "I'll take the Number Thirteen," he replied.

John nodded. "Better not risk it, Charlie. You don't want to lose that job. I 'spect we're all going to be there with you 'fore too much longer."

Charlie sighed, picked up his bucket of water and marched back to the field. When he returned to the wagon, he handed the empty bucket up to his mother. Taking it from him, she said gently, "Son, we ought to thank these folks and send them home."

Charlie fought the urge to protest, then the urge to cry. Instead, he just bit his bottom lip and nodded knowingly.

As Charlie walked toward the field, Mr. Lockett came up and met him. "That watering hole is about dry now, Charlie. There ain't enough water."

Charlie nodded. "We've very much obliged, Mr. Lockett," he said. "It's time to call it quits."

Charlie went to each group of neighbors, thanking them again for their kindness, and promising to return the favor whenever they were able. "We've all got evening chores to do, so I reckon we all ought to call it a day," he said. Putting on a good face he added, "It was worth a try."

Little by little, their neighbors and friends left for home, promising to pray for them. When the last of them had left, John told Charlie, "I'll put the wagon up and I'll pick you up at the house directly." Charlie nodded and walked toward the house, feeling defeated.

When he arrived, he found his mother sitting on the porch step, waiting for him. "Sit down, Charlie," she said, patting the step beside her.

Charlie plopped down on the step, sweaty and exhausted.

"I'm sorry for all that, Mama. I thought it would work. I should have thought it through better," he said.

"I want to tell you something, Charlie," she said, putting her arm tenderly across his shoulders. "I'm proud of you, son. I'm proud of all you do for us. I'm proud of how hard you work. You're a good man."

Charlie's heart ached as he thought of the disappointment he was about to bring her.

"Here," she said, handing him a little cloth satchel. "I put the last of the cornbread in here for you. Sorry I didn't have time to make nothing else."

Charlie took the satchel from her, then swallowed hard, screwing up his courage. "Mama," he said. "There's something I have to tell you."

At that moment Jillianne came rushing out of the door behind them, laughing merrily. "Look at that!"

she exclaimed, pointing out into the yard.

Out in the yard, a mother hen, her chicks trailing behind her, was puffed up menacingly, charging their bewildered and suddenly frightened dog. "Did y'all see that?" the girl asked, giggling. "Lucy is the scarediest hen in the flock but look at her running Bandit off!"

Betsy looked up, then said softly, "When a mama knows her babies are in danger, she can find strength she never knew she had. There's nothing she won't do to protect them."

Charlie felt a lump rise in his throat. He tried to speak but found himself unable. As he was struggling to regain his composure, John rode up on the mule. "Best come on, Charlie. We're running late."

Charlie swallowed hard, feeling angered at his weakness. He turned to face his mother. "Mama…," he began. But looking into her gentle, expectant face, he just couldn't do it. He couldn't make the words come out.

"Come on, Charlie. Time to go," John shouted.

Charlie dropped his head and squeezed his eyes shut. After a few moments, he stood up, then leaned over and hugged his mother. "Bye, Mama. I love you," he said, his voice cracking a little.

John pulled him up onto the mule's back, then clicked the command to go.

They arrived at the station five minutes after the Number Eleven passed through on the way to Danville. Charlie insisted that John go on home. He spent the next few hours alone on a bench in the depot, thinking of all the ways he had failed over the past few days. And thinking about Bertie.

It was nearly midnight when the Number Thirteen pulled into the Danville station. Charlie stepped out into the quietness of night and set off gloomily down the deserted road toward his house on Floyd Street.

36

As he was shuffling down the road in a crowd of workers headed to the mill gate the next morning, Charlie heard someone calling out to him from behind. "Hey Charlie, hold up."

When he turned toward the voice, Charlie saw that it was Jimmy, his left eye swollen and blackened, and his lip cut and bruised. "What happened to you?" Charlie asked reflexively.

Jimmy laughed. "You ought to see the other boys," he said.

Charlie shook his head and turned back toward the gate. "Down on Craghead Street, I reckon," he said. "I told you something like this was going to happen."

"Ha!" Jimmy said. "You better be glad I was there."

"Why?" Charlie asked.

"Let's just say you owe me a few knots on the head," Jimmy answered. He seemed about to explain, then he gestured toward a group of workers at the spinners' entrance. Charlie looked in that direction, then stopped in his tracks. "I'll tell you about it at dinner break," Jimmy said, before hurrying on.

Charlie took a deep breath and walked toward the spinners' gate, toward Bertie and Rose.

A minute earlier, Samuel had just given Rose and the children kisses and headed off toward the weave room entrance, when Rose saw Bertie approaching, downcast, her eyes swollen and red. Rose stepped toward her and took her hand.

"How are you, sweetie?" she asked.

Bertie gazed at her feet and shook her head sadly.

"If you ain't feeling like working today," Rose said kindly, "me and the other girls will take care of your spindles."

Bertie sniffled, wiped her eyes and said, "Thank you Rose, but I'll be all right. It's been so long since anybody wanted me, I ought to be used to it by now."

"Oh, Bertie, sugar," Rose answered. "You are loved! The Lord has plans for you. I just know that everything is going to be all right."

Bertie looked up into her friend's caring eyes. "I've been wondering, Rose. Is a mill preacher a real preacher?"

"Well, sure he is a real preacher," Rose answered, somewhat startled. "Why in the world would you ask something like that?"

Bertie shook her head sadly. "It seems like to me that maybe he won't no real preacher. Maybe me and Charlie ain't really married, Rose. Maybe it won't real."

"Stop being silly, Bertie," Rose replied, trying to be cheerful. "Of course it was real and of course y'all are married."

"If Charlie don't want me no more, maybe it'd be better if it won't real," Bertie answered quietly. "Maybe I don't want it to be real neither."

Rose drew her friend into a hug, trying not cry. "Oh, Bertie," she said. "Bless you heart! Bless your precious heart!"

Bertie was wrapped in Rose's hug when she noticed Charlie approaching sheepishly, hat in hand. Her gasp caused Rose to release her, and they both turned to face Charlie.

Bertie stood trembling for a moment, then burst into tears, turned, and rushed through the gate. Rose, burning with anger, put her hands on her hips, threw back her head, turned indignantly away from Charlie and walked away. Watching her, little Purl imitated her mother exactly, putting her hands on her hips, throwing back her head and marching off behind Rose. Gem, confused, and unsure of what to do, offered Charlie a concerned smile, then ran off to catch up to them.

Charlie, distraught, put on his hat and walked sadly away, back toward the weave room entrance. Seeing him coming, Samuel slowed down to let him catch up.

"Sure is hot today," Samuel said, walking alongside Charlie.

Charlie nodded and grunted but didn't look up.

"Been hot all week," Samuel said.

Again, Charlie just nodded and grunted.

"Probably gonna be hot tomorrow, too," Samuel said.

This time Charlie made no response.

Samuel opened his mouth as if about to speak, then stopped. After a few moments, he again began to say something, then again stopped, seemingly unsure of what to say or how to say it. Finally, he said, reluctantly, "Now, look here, Charlie. I know it might not be none of my business but…'

Charlie suddenly stopped walking, turned to face Samuel, and began speaking rapidly. "I got scared, Samuel! When it come time for us to leave, I chickened out and couldn't do it!'"

"Couldn't do what?" Samuel asked, confused. "Scared of what?"

"Scared of taking Bertie home with me! My mama don't know about us being married. What was I supposed to do? Just walk up in the house and say 'Hey, Mama. I got married and here's my new wife'?

"Sure," Samuel answered, sincerely. "Why not? What's wrong with that?"

Charlie shook his head and began to walk again. "It just ain't that easy, Samuel," he said.

"I don't get it, Charlie," Samuel said, walking alongside him. "Why not?"

Charlie abruptly stopped walking. He looked up in the air, then buried his face in his hands. After a few moments he lifted his head and looked Samuel in the eyes. "I know it might make me sound like a mama's boy, Samuel, but I'm afraid of hurting her. She depends on me." Charlie paused before continuing.

He paused again, composing himself. "I been looking after Mama for a long time now, Samuel. She trusts me. It's liable to break her heart if she finds out I done got married without even telling her. It might even kill her. What kind of man would get married without telling his mama first? I just couldn't do it to her, Samuel. I was scared to. I've let her down before in ways she don't even know about and I don't want to do it again. It just couldn't risk hurting her like that."

"Didn't you tell her yesterday when you was home?" Samuel asked.

Charlie looked down at the ground and shook his head.

"Why the devil not, Charlie? You got to tell her sometime!"

"I don't think Bertie even wants me no more," Charlie answered, dejectedly. "Maybe we ought to see if the preacher can undo it."

"There ain't no such thing as 'undoing' getting married," Samuel exclaimed. "Ain't you promised 'till death do you part'?"

"I don't know what to do," Charlie said.

"Ain't but one thing to do," Samuel said, "and that's tell Bertie you're sorry and take her home to meet your mama!"

Charlie resumed walking. "Do you reckon she'll forgive me?" he asked.

"I reckon they both will," Samuel said, as they walked. "But first you got to step up and be a man. In this case that means being a good son, but it means being a good husband too."

"You're right, Samuel," Charlie said sadly. "I ain't been neither one so far, have I?"

"Well, I 'spect you can make it all work out," Samuel answered. "And anyway, you're too old now to get a whipping for it."

"Don't be so sure about that," Charlie said, causing Samuel to laugh heartily. But the laugh morphed immediately into a rough coughing fit forcing Samuel to stop walking and leaving him bent over at the waist, wheezing.

Concerned, Charlie asked, "You all right, Samuel?"

Samuel nodded, still coughing. After a few moments he recovered enough to speak. "Still ain't got over this durn cold yet," he said, wiping his eyes. Straightening up fully, he forced a smile and said, "Come on, Charlie. Time for us to get to work."

37

When the looms powered down at the end of the day, Samuel pulled the cotton balls from his ears and put a hand on Charlie's shoulder. "Come with me," he said.

It had been a brutal day for Samuel. By mid-afternoon he had lost the strength in his right arm, and he was overcome by several severe coughing attacks. Worried that he might collapse, Charlie had begged him to go outside and rest a while in the shade. But Samuel had stubbornly refused, staying at his looms, and insisting that he would be better any minute.

While he still looked beaten and drained, Charlie saw that when they stepped outside, Samuel seemed to improve a little, somewhat invigorated by the sunshine and the relatively fresh air. He led Charlie to the place where he always met Rose and the children after work. As they approached, Charlie saw that Bertie was there, with her back to them, talking to Rose.

When close enough to be heard, Charlie said softly, "Bertie."

Bertie spun around, a confused mixture of emotions displayed on her face, still wet with sweat and streaked by cotton dust.

She stammered, then said, "I ain't sure I want to talk

to you right now."

Rose reached out, taking Bertie by the hand.

They were interrupted by a shouting voice.

"Samuel! Charlie! Wait up! I need to talk to y'all."

They all turned to face Webb, who was hurrying toward them, pushing his way through the crowd of workers. As Webb drew close to the men, Rose pulled Bertie away, putting her arm across her friend's shoulders and whispering in her ear to comfort her.

When Webb caught up to the men, he stood facing them awkwardly for a moment.

"Yes, sir," Samuel said.

Webb sighed. "I'm sorry to tell you this Samuel, but you're being dismissed."

A look of shock, and fear, swept suddenly over Samuel's face. "That ain't right, Mr. Webb," he stammered. "You know I'm one of the best workers in this mill."

"You have been, Samuel, but you're not now," Webb said. "You know as well as me that you're not able to do this job anymore."

Samuel pulled off his hat, wringing it in his hands. "Mr. Webb, the truth is that we can't make it without me working," he said, swallowing his pride. "I'll do better. But I just can't lose my job right now."

"I'll keep you on till the end of the week Samuel, but that's it," Webb said. He paused, his concern obvious. "I'm sorry about it," he added.

Webb turned to face Charlie, who was stunned. "Charlie, you're taking over Samuel's looms."

Charlie reeled. "But sir… I mean… I ain't trained yet. I can't do Samuel's job."

"Yes, you can," Webb replied. "I've been watching you. You've been doing it just fine." He hesitated before adding, "But if you don't want the job, we can always give it to someone else."

"Mr. Webb…," Samuel began, pleading.

"Samuel, I'm sorry," Webb said, interrupting him. "I really am. But the decision has been made." He turned and walked away.

Charlie looked at his friend. "Samuel, I…"

Samuel shook his head and interrupted. "It's all right, Charlie," he said gloomily. "There ain't nothing you can do."

Samuel looked sadly in the direction of Rose, who was still talking with Bertie. "I can't hardly bear the thought of telling Lillie Mae," he said, distantly. "This is all my fault."

Charlie stood back, as Samuel turned and walked slowly toward the women. Looking up and seeing the distressed look which had replaced his normal cheerfulness, Rose immediately recognized that something was terribly wrong.

"What's the matter?" she asked, alarmed.

Samuel dropped his head, saying nothing. Rose rushed over to him, leaving Bertie. Charlie cautiously approached her.

Bertie and Charlie watched as Rose and Samuel spoke. Unable to hear what was said, they saw Rose gasp, then suddenly put her hand over her mouth, as she began to cry, Samuel's head still hanging down in dejection. After a moment, Rose hugged her husband and they walked slowly away, trailed by their children.

"What happened?" Bertie asked with concern.

"Samuel got fired," Charlie answered.

"Fired?!" Bertie exclaimed. "That ain't right! It ain't fair!" A pained look came on her face and she put her hand over her heart, looking off at them walking in the distance. "Oh, Lord have mercy. Poor Rose. What will they do now?"

"Bertie, I'm sorry," Charlie said.

Bertie turned to face him.

"I'm sorry I run off like that," he said remorsefully. "I just got scared. I needed to tell you something, but I couldn't."

Bertie looked down at her feet. "Are you ashamed of me, Charlie?"

"No! No, Bertie!" Charlie exclaimed. He reached out and took her hand. "I ain't ashamed of you. I'm ashamed of *me*."

"Are you sorry we got married, Charlie?" she asked softly.

"No, Bertie. I ain't sorry. I'm glad." He paused before continuing. "But I am sorry that I didn't tell my mama first. I can't hardly stand the thought of hurting her."

Bertie began to cry, still looking down at her feet.

"I need to explain something to you, Bertie. Please? Will you listen to me?" Charlie asked pleadingly.

Bertie nodded, still not looking at him.

Charlie took her by the hand and led her off the road, to a quiet spot under a tree, as Bertie continued crying softly.

"I have to be 'specially careful with Mama's feelings, Bertie," he said. "I brought terrible sin into her life."

Charlie paused, put his palm on his forehead and squeezed his eyes shut for a few moments.

"Remember I told you I killed a man?" he asked.

Bertie looked up at him. Sniffling, she wiped her eyes. "You told me God killed that man."

"No," Charlie corrected her. "I said I *prayed* for God to kill him. There's something else I didn't tell you.

Something I ain't ever told nobody. It's the reason I can't bear to hurt my mama."

That's when I told her, Flora. I told her what happened when I was underneath Ben's porch that day. Didn't neither one of us ever speak of it since then. What I told her was this.

I heard Mama's voice. It was her and Aunt Shirley June and they walked on over to the edge of the porch till they was standing just right over me, without them knowing I was down there.

Aunt Shirley June, she said Mr. Ben was mighty pleased that you brought him over that piece of pie, Miz Betsy. He said it had done been a long time since you had ever brought him anything like that. Then she said, seems like he took to feeling poorly right after he ate that piece of pie. Then Mama she said real calm like, you must have heard that wrong. Said, it was a couple of weeks ago that I brought over that piece of pie. No ma'am, Aunt Shirley June said, I spect I'm sure it was yesterday. Right before he took sick.

Let me tell you, Flora, my skin was crawling, and I had done broke out in a cold sweat.

Was a long silent pause with neither one of them saying nothing then Aunt Shirley June she said that man was full of meanness. I'm sorry to say it, but ain't nobody gonna miss him. I ain't said nothin to nobody bout that pie, Miz Betsy. Come to think of it, you must be right. I recollect that 'twas some time ago that he said you brung it to him.

And there I sat under that porch, realizing what God had done to me.

I done told you once, but I can't say it enough. Your grandma, my mama, she was a saint. A saint. I never knew her to do a sinful thing in her whole life. She might have been the godliest, the kindest, and the sweetest woman that ever lived. And look what I had done to that saintly woman. Me and God.

You can say that all you want, Flora, but I know what happened and I know why it happened. I asked God to kill Ben so I wouldn't have to. I have to live with how that prayer was answered. I have to live with how I brought sin into the life of that saintly woman.

"That's why I say *I* killed him, Bertie. I don't mind that part too much. Ben needed killing. But it tears me up to think of how it happened. Because of me. So, I say it was me that done it. Me. Nobody else. Me."

Bertie stood staring at Charlie, open-mouthed in amazement.

"I was a coward, Bertie. And I was a coward again when I ran off and left you here. I should have told Mama before marrying you, but two wrongs don't make a right. And now I feel like she's being punished again because of me. My whole family is." Charlie shook his head, anguish on his face.

"But I been thinking long and hard on this, Bertie," Charlie continued. "If you want me to, I can just go home, you won't never see me again, and we can just pretend we ain't never been married. But Bertie," he said, reaching out and taking her hand, "I do love you with all my heart. And if you'll still have me, then I promise to be a good husband to you from now on." Charlie paused, looking into Bertie's eyes, and forcing back the lump that had risen in his throat. "I want you to come home with me, Bertie."

Bertie suddenly brightened. "Do you mean it, Charlie?"

Charlie nodded, keeping his eyes locked on hers. "I do," he said. "With all my heart."

Bertie dropped her face into her hands, weeping. "Oh, Charlie," she said through her tears. "That will make me so happy!" She looked up into his face and said, "I can't hardly wait for Saturday to be here."

Charlie shook his head and chuckled. "I ain't talking

about Saturday, Bertie. I'm talking about right now. Tonight."

"Tonight?" Bertie replied, puzzled. "But we can't get out there and back tonight, can we? Ain't no way we could be back in time for work."

"I ain't coming back," Charlie answered.

"I don't understand. What do you mean?" she asked, confused.

"I mean I'm quitting, Bertie. Quitting. For good." Charlie began speaking rapidly. "Let's both quit right now and just go on home to Raye. I don't want to work here no more. Once we're all used up and wore out, they're just gonna throw us away someday, like pieces of trash. You saw what they just done to Samuel. I ain't gonna wait for my turn."

"But what will we do?" Bertie asked.

"I don't know yet," Charlie said. "We'll figure something out."

"Do you mean it, Charlie?" Bertie pinched herself on the arm. "Is it real?"

"It is if you will have me," Charlie said.

Bertie threw her arms around his neck, crying with joy and feeling as if her heart might burst in her chest. "Forever and ever, Charlie. Forever and ever!"

38

There was no one waiting for them at the Raye station, of course. They were not expected. So, Bertie and Charlie walked the five miles from the depot to the farm, through the muggy summer night, saying little.

Bertie shivered when at last they came within sight of the house. As they drew closer, a dog began to bark and from inside the house a light appeared, a candle being lit. Charlie reached over and took his wife's hand. "Charlie, I'm scared," she said, her voice trembling.

As they stood there in the dark, looking toward the house, it began to rain.

Charlie

It come to me right there what we should do. I said, Bertie, if any lies get told, I'll be the one to tell em. I asked her did she trust me and she said she did.

Mama like to had a fit when she saw us. I told her I'd done quit and this here is Bertie. I said, she ain't got no people, we are in love, and we want to be married, which was the honest truth. Mama might have looked for reasons not to like Bertie, but if she did, she couldn't find none. Bertie went and stayed at Aunt Eliza's house until we got married—two weeks later. And didn't nobody in Raye ever know the difference.

Flora, you remember how much them two loved each other? Yep. My mama came to love Bertie as if she was her own child.

It rained soft and steady for two solid days and we raised the prettiest crop of tobacco that year that I ever grew. Like I told you before, there ain't no figuring out God.

Bertie

When Charlie went to town to sell the crop six months later, I went with him. That evening we went down to Floyd Street to see my dear friends Rose and Samuel. But they was gone. Folks said Samuel passed not long after the mill fired him, and poor sweet Rose, she come down with the consumption too and she died right after Christmas. Nobody knew what had happened to little Gem and Purl, and that breaks my heart to this day. Me and Charlie would have taken in those precious little ones. I just cried my eyes out.

Somebody said he heard that a man came and got them children that morning right after Rose passed. I sure hope and pray things turned out all right for them.

The End

ACKNOWLEDGMENTS

This is the place where it is customary for an author to thank all the people who read and helped edit his manuscript, while reserving to himself the blame for any remaining flaws. In the case of this book, I don't need to do that. While I have benefitted immensely from friends who have taken to the time to read and critique previous manuscripts, I didn't show this one to anyone before publishing it. Honestly, I didn't want to take the risk that some thoughtful reader might cause me to lose faith in the story. So, in this case, without any doubt, I am entirely to blame for all the errors and shortcomings of this novel.

Having said that, I do want to thank a few people for their contributions. Thanks to my wonderful wife Cherie, who has encouraged this project and has provided invaluable proofreading help. Thanks to the Library of Congress for the use of the Lewis Hine photographs that were adapted into cover art by the immensely talented Jason Fowler of Wisely Woven. Thanks to the all the people who read *Jim Wrenn*, and especially to those who said enough good things about it to give me the confidence (whether justified or not) to take a stab at writing another novel. Thanks to Jesse and Alease, who got married while working at the mill, but didn't tell their families. The values they imparted on me have been great blessings in my life. And thanks to Gustave Flaubert for Berthe.

ABOUT THE AUTHOR

Bill Guerrant and his wife live on a farm in southern
Virginia. He is the author of *Jim Wrenn*.

Made in the USA
Middletown, DE
19 March 2022